THE SEVEN WONDERS

The
SEVEN
WONDERS

A NOVEL OF THE ANCIENT WORLD

STEVEN SAYLOR

MINOTAUR BOOKS

NEW YORK

THE SEVEN WONDERS. Copyright © 2012 by Steven Saylor. All rights reserved. Printed in the United States of America. For information, address St. Martin's Press, 175 Fifth Avenue, New York, N.Y. 10010.

www.minotaurbooks.com

Some chapters of this novel, in slightly different form, were first published as short stories in the following magazines and anthologies (listed by publication date): "The Witch's Curse" (as "The Witch of Corinth") in *The Magazine of Fantasy & Science Fiction*, July/August 2011; "The Monumental Gaul" in *Ellery Queen Mystery Magazine*, August 2011; "Something to Do with Diana" in *The Mammoth Book of Historical Crime Fiction*, edited by Mike Ashley (London: Constable & Robinson, August 2011; Philadelphia: Running Press, September 2011); "Styx and Stones" in *Down These Strange Streets*, edited by George R. R. Martin and Gardner Dozois (New York: Penguin, November 2011); "The Widows of Halicarnassus" in *Ellery Queen Mystery Magazine*, March/April 2012; "O Tempora! O Mores! Olympiad!" in *Ellery Queen Mystery Magazine*, May 2012; "The Return of the Mummy" in *Ellery Queen Mystery Magazine*, June 2012.

The Library of Congress has cataloged the hardcover edition as follows:

Saylor, Steven, 1956–
     The seven wonders : a novel of the ancient world / Steven Saylor.—1st ed.
     p. cm.
     ISBN 978-0-312-35984-3 (hardcover)
     ISBN 978-1-4668-0196-7 (e-book)
     1. Gordianus the Finder (Fictitious character)—Fiction.
     2. Rome—History—Republic, 265–30 B.C.—Fiction. I. Title.
     PS3569.A96S48 2012
     813'.54—dc23

                                                            2012005475

ISBN 978-1-250-02160-1 (trade paperback)

Minotaur books may be purchased for educational, business, or promotional use. For information on bulk purchases, please contact Macmillan Corporate and Premium Sales Department at 1-800-221-7945 extension 5442 or write specialmarkets@macmillan.com.

First Minotaur Books Paperback Edition: April 2013

10 9 8 7 6 5 4 3 2 1

CONTENTS

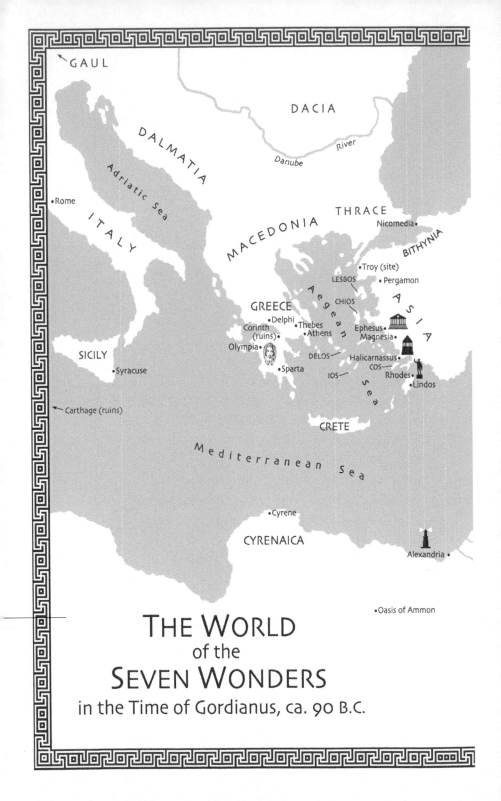

GAUL

DACIA

DALMATIA

River

Danube

Adriatic Sea

•Rome

ITALY

MACEDONIA

THRACE

Nicomedia•

BITHYNIA

•Troy (site)

LESBOS

•Pergamon

Aegean

CHIOS

GREECE

•Delphi

Corinth   •Thebes

(ruins)•   •Athens

Olympia•

Ephesus•

Magnesia•

DELOS

Halicarnassus•

COS

SICILY

•Syracuse

•Sparta

IOS

Rhodes•

•Lindos

Sea

Carthage (ruins)

CRETE

Mediterranean   Sea

•Cyrene

CYRENAICA

Alexandria •

•Oasis of Ammon

THE WORLD
of the
SEVEN WONDERS
in the Time of Gordianus, ca. 90 B.C.

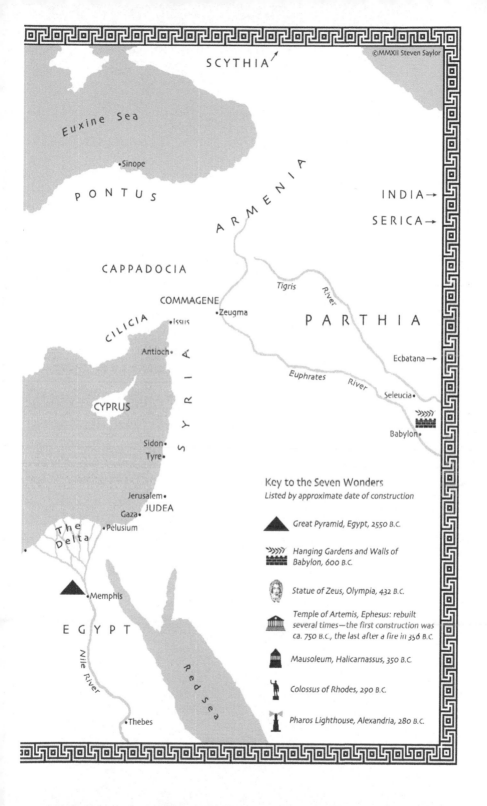

SCYTHIA

©MMXII Steven Saylor

Euxine Sea

•Sinope

PONTUS

ARMENIA

INDIA→

SERICA→

CAPPADOCIA

Tigris River

COMMAGENE

•Zeugma

PARTHIA

CILICIA

•Issus

Antioch•

SYRIA

Ecbatana→

Euphrates River

Seleucia•

CYPRUS

Babylon•

Sidon•

Tyre•

Jerusalem•

JUDEA

Gaza•

•Pelusium

The Delta

•

Key to the Seven Wonders
Listed by approximate date of construction

EGYPT

Great Pyramid, Egypt, 2550 B.C.

•Memphis

Hanging Gardens and Walls of
Babylon, 600 B.C.

Nile River

Statue of Zeus, Olympia, 432 B.C.

Red Sea

Temple of Artemis, Ephesus: rebuilt
several times—the first construction was
ca. 750 B.C., the last after a fire in 356 B.C.

Mausoleum, Halicarnassus, 350 B.C.

Colossus of Rhodes, 290 B.C.

•Thebes

Pharos Lighthouse, Alexandria, 280 B.C.

With a favorable wind, Apollonius and his disciple Damis arrived in Rhodes. As they approached the Colossus, Damis exclaimed, "Teacher, could anything be greater than that?" To which Apollonius replied, "Yes, a man who loves wisdom in a sound and innocent spirit."

—PHILOSTRATUS
THE LIFE OF APOLLONIUS OF TYANA, 5:21

THE SEVEN WONDERS

I

Prelude in Rome:

THE DEAD MAN WHO WASN'T

"Now that you're dead, Antipater, what do you plan to do with yourself?"

My father laughed at his own joke. He knew perfectly well what Antipater was planning to do, but he couldn't resist a paradoxical turn of phrase. Puzzles were my father's passion—and solving them his profession. He called himself Finder, because men hired him to find the truth.

Not surprisingly, old Antipater answered with a poem made up on the spot; for yes, the Antipater of whom I speak was *the* Antipater of Sidon—one of the most celebrated poets in the world, famed not only for the elegance of his verses but for the almost magical way he could produce them impromptu, as if drawn from the aether. His poem was in Greek, of course:

"I died on my birthday, so I must leave Rome.
Now your son has his birthday—is it time to leave home?"

Antipater's question, like my father's, was merely rhetorical. For days the old poet and I had been making preparations to leave Rome together on this day. He gave me a smile. "It does seem unfair, my boy, that your birthday should be overshadowed by my funeral."

I resisted the urge to correct him. Despite his lingering habit of addressing me as a boy, I was in fact a man, and had been so for exactly a year, since I put on my manly toga when I turned seventeen. "What better way to celebrate my birthday, Teacher, than to set out on a journey such as most people can only dream of?"

"Well put!" Antipater squeezed my shoulder. "It's not every young man who can look forward to seeing with his own eyes the greatest monuments ever built by mankind, and in the company of mankind's greatest poet." Antipater had never been modest. Now that he was dead, I suppose he had no reason to be.

"And it's not every man who has the privilege of gazing upon his own funeral stele," my father said, indicating with a wave of his hand the object of which he spoke.

The three of us stood in the garden of my father's house on the Esquiline Hill. The sky was cloudless and the air was warm for the month of Martius. In front of us—delivered only moments before from the sculptor's workshop—stood a riddle in marble. It was a funeral stele for a man who was not dead. The rectangular tablet was elegantly carved and brightly painted, and only about a foot tall. Later it would be placed atop the sepulcher intended for the dead man's ashes, but for now it was propped atop the crate in which it had been delivered.

Antipater nodded thoughtfully. "And not every man has the opportunity to design his own monument, as I have. You don't think it's *too* irreverent, do you, Finder? I mean, we don't want anyone to look at this stele and realize it's a hoax. If anyone should surmise that I've faked my own death—"

"Stop worrying, old friend. Everything is going as we planned. Five days ago I entered your death in the register at the Temple of Libitina. Thanks to the rich matrons who send a slave to check the lists several times a day, word of your demise spread across Rome in a matter of hours. People assumed that your old friend and patron Quintus Lutatius

Catulus must be in possession of your remains and in charge of the funeral arrangements. There was disbelief when it was discovered that a citizen as humble as myself had been named executor in your will, and that your remains were to be displayed in the vestibule of my house. But so it was. I summoned the undertakers to wash and perfume the body, purchased flowers, cypress sprigs, incense, and a very elegant bier—your will provided for all necessary expenses—and then I put your corpse on display in the vestibule. And what a turnout you've received! All the poets and half the politicians in Rome have come to pay their respects."

Antipater flashed a wry smile. "My demise has allowed you to make the acquaintance of the best people in Rome, Finder—just the sort who are always getting dragged into court for murdering each other. I daresay this could prove a windfall for you—meeting so many potential new clients!"

My father nodded. "Everyone has come to have a look, it seems—except Catulus. Do you imagine your patron is sulking, because the will didn't name him as executor?"

"More likely he's been holding off, waiting until today to pay his respects—the day of the funeral—so that his visit will be as conspicuous as possible. Catulus may have the soul of a poet, but he has the instincts of a politician—"

Antipater fell silent at the sound of a knock at the front door.

"Another caller. I shall disappear at once." Antipater hurried to the concealed door that gave access to a narrow chamber next to the vestibule, where a tiny crack in the wall served as a peephole and allowed him to observe all that transpired.

A moment later, my father's doorkeeper—the only slave he owned at that time—appeared in the garden.

"You have a visitor, Master," Damon wheezed. The constant flood of callers was running the poor old fellow ragged. He cleared his throat and I saw him concentrate, determined to get the name right. "Lintus Quitatius Catulus, former consul of the Republic, has come to pay his respects to the deceased."

"Quintus Lutatius Catulus, I think you mean," said my father indulgently. "Come, son, let us greet the consul."

The man in the vestibule was perhaps sixty years old. Like my father and me, he was dressed in a black toga, but his was embroidered with a purple band that marked his status as a senator. Ten years ago Catulus had served as consul and commander of the legions; it was his army that annihilated the Cimbri at the battle of the Raudine Plain. But Catulus was also a man of culture and learning, and was said to have a sensitive nature. He stood stiffly upright before the funeral bier with his hands crossed before him.

My father introduced himself, and me as well, but Catulus hardly seemed to notice. "Your distinguished presence graces my home, Consul, though I regret the sadness of the occasion. Did you come alone?"

Catulus raised an eyebrow. "Of course not. I left my retinue outside, so that I could spend a moment alone with my old friend—face-to-face, so to speak. But alas, his face is covered." Catulus gestured to the mask, made of wax, which concealed the face of the corpse. "Is it true that his features were damaged by the fall?"

"I'm afraid so," said my father. "The undertakers did what they could to make him presentable, but the damage was such that I decided it was preferable to conceal the injuries. Normally, a death mask is made from the direct impression of the face in repose. But in this case, I hired a sculptor to create the likeness. The mask will be used in the funeral procession, as usual, but until then I've placed it over his face. I think the sculptor did a very good job, don't you? It really does look like Antipater, lying there with his eyes shut, as if he slept. Still, if you wish to gaze upon his face. . . ."

Catulus nodded grimly. "I'm a military man, Finder. I've seen the most terrible things that can be done to human flesh. Show me."

My father stepped to the bier and lifted the death mask.

The staid consul's abrupt, girlish shriek, stifled by a fist to his mouth, was so incongruous that I almost laughed out loud. Behind the wall, I heard a noise like loose plaster falling, and imagined Antipater shaking with mirth.

Catulus glanced at the wall. My father shrugged and looked embarrassed, as if to apologize for the presence of rats.

"But how could a mere fall have resulted in such terrible disfigurement?" Catulus kept his fist pressed to his mouth. He looked a bit green.

"It was a long fall," explained my father, "from the top floor of an apartment in the Subura, five stories up. He landed on his head. As I say, the undertakers did what they could—"

"Yes, I understand. Replace the mask, please."

"Of course, Consul."

Not for the first time, I wondered about the true identity of the corpse upon the bier. My father had declined to tell me, following his long-standing practice of keeping to himself any aspect of his work that he deemed unnecessary for me to know. When I turned seventeen, I had thought my father might see fit to share all his secrets with me, but if anything, he had become more guarded than ever during the last year. I knew that something very dangerous must be afoot in Rome, for Antipater to fake his own death, and for my father to assist him in such a wild scheme, but regarding the details, I had been kept in the dark.

The elderly body on the bier was apparently an excellent match for Antipater; not one of the many visitors had expressed the least doubt. Of course, the only parts of the corpse that were visible were the long white hair and beard and the wrinkled, age-spotted hands crossed over the chest, the rest being covered by one of Antipater's favorite garments and by the mask. The man truly had died from a fall in the Subura, just as my father described, cracking his skull and shattering his face. Had he been a slave, discreetly acquired from his owner? Or some lowlife criminal whom no one cared to claim? Or simply some ancient citizen of the Subura without family or friends to mourn him? Whoever he was, he had died at the right time and in such a manner that he could be passed off as Antipater. In a way, my father had done the poor fellow a favor; the dead man had been mourned by the best people in Rome and was about to receive funeral rites far above his station.

"How sad," said Catulus, "that Antipater should have died on his birthday—the one day of the year that he allowed himself to get completely, blindingly drunk. 'My annual birthday fever,' he called it—as if such a malady actually existed!—and would have none of his friends around him, pretending to be confined to his bed all day by illness. I presume his drunkenness led to his death?"

"It appears that Antipater was indeed quite drunk," said my father. "The body still exudes an odor of wine. If you put your nose to the flesh—"

"That will not be necessary," snapped Catulus, who still looked a bit green. "Is it true that he was visiting a prostitute?"

"It seems likely. The room from which he fell is known to be used for such assignations."

"At his age!" Catulus shook his head but smiled faintly. "But there was no indication of foul play?"

"None that I could find," said my father.

"And finding foul things is your profession, I understand. Male or female?"

"I beg your pardon, Consul?"

"The prostitute Antipater was visiting—male or female?"

No one else had asked this particular question, and I could see that my father was having to make up an answer on the spot. Catulus, I recalled, was known to favor young men, and had even composed poems in Greek to flatter his lovers—something rather daring for a Roman aristocrat of the older generation.

My father pursed his lips. "Antipater's companion apparently fled after the fatal accident, leaving nothing behind, but I believe a patron in the tavern downstairs saw a handsome young man in Antipater's company earlier that evening." My father could lie shamelessly, a skill he was never able to satisfactorily pass on to me. Inside the wall, I heard more plaster falling. Did Antipater shake with laughter, or had he kicked the wall in indignation?

"Ah!" Catulus nodded knowingly. "Antipater was discreet about his love life—so quiet about such matters, in fact, that I presumed the old fellow was past all that, freed from the chains of Eros like boy-crazy Sophocles in his dotage. But I always suspected he had it in him to appreciate a beautiful youth. How else could he have composed that lovely epitaph for Anacreon?"

The consul put a hand over his heart and declaimed:

"Here lies Anacreon—poet, singer, player of the lyre.
Hear now his song about love's unquenchable fire—
The mad, unfettered love of Anacreon for Bathyllus the dancer,
To whom he posed this question, desperately seeking an answer. . . ."

Catulus sighed and wiped a tear from his eye. Up to this point, he had scarcely acknowledged my presence, but now his gaze fell on me. "So this boy is your namesake, eh, Finder? The young Gordianus."

"Yes. But as you can see by his manly toga, my son is no longer a boy. Today is his eighteenth birthday, in fact."

"Is it, indeed?" Catulus raised a quizzical eyebrow. "Well, I must counsel you *not* to follow Antipater's example when it comes to celebrating your birthday, but in all other things you would do well to emulate him. You were his pupil, were you not?"

"I was proud to call him Teacher," I said.

"So you should be. He was very selective about whom he would take on as a pupil. He must have seen something very special in you, young man," said Catulus.

I shrugged, a bit unnerved by the consul's steady gaze. In fact, it was a bit presumptuous of me to present myself as a pupil of the great Antipater of Sidon; my father could never have afforded to hire such a distinguished poet to be my tutor. Our relationship as teacher and student had always been informal; nonetheless, on his regular visits to my father's house over the years, Antipater never left without drilling into my head a few lines of Greek poetry, or the names of Alexander's generals, or some other bit of knowledge. From my father I had learned to pick any lock, ten ways to tell if a woman is lying, and how to follow someone without being seen; but whatever I knew of literature, history, mathematics, and especially the language of the Greeks, Antipater had taught me.

"Perhaps you'd like to see the funeral stele?" offered my father.

"It's already been carved?" said Catulus.

"It was delivered not an hour ago. Since Antipater was so very proud of his Greek heritage, I thought it would be appropriate to follow Greek customs. According to the ancient rule set down by Solon of Athens, no monument should be so extravagant that it cannot be carved by a workshop of ten men in three days. The marble tablet was delivered this morning; the paint is barely dry. Follow me, Consul."

My father led the way to the sunlit garden. I heard a faint rustle from the wall where Antipater was hiding; he would have to stay there, unable to observe whatever transpired in the garden.

"As you can see, Consul, the monument is in the style so fashionable nowadays among the learned Greeks. The tablet is of modest size, meant to be set atop the plain stone sepulcher that will receive his ashes. The design is what in Latin we call a rebus; the images tell a story, but only to those who can decipher their meaning."

"Ah, yes," said Catulus, "Antipater himself wrote a number of poems about such tombstones. How appropriate that his own should be rendered in this cryptic style. Let me see if I can puzzle it out."

An elaborately decorated pediment with columns on either side— this part of the tablet was readymade—served as a frame for the images that had been carved in shallow relief to memorialize Antipater. Catulus furrowed his brow as he studied the picture-puzzle.

"A rooster!" he exclaimed. "Why a rooster? To be sure, the cock is finely rendered. The eyes are quite fierce, the beak is opened wide to crow, and the outspread wings are painted a vivid shade of red. Now, what are these items he clutches in his talons? A scepter in one claw—a symbol of royalty—and in the other, a palm branch, a token of victory such as might be awarded to an athlete." Catulus hummed thoughtfully. "And what's this, balanced on the very edge of the base, as if it might fall off? A knucklebone of the sort our ancestors used for dice. When such a die is thrown, one of four sides comes up. I'm not a gaming man, but even I know that this particular throw is a loser. What do the Greeks call it? Ah yes, the Chian throw, named for the island of Chios."

THE DEAD MAN WHO WASN'T

Catulus stepped back and assumed a pensive posture, with his right hand to his mouth and his left hand clasping his right elbow.

"A scepter—yet Antipater was not of royal blood. A palm branch—yet Antipater was never famed for athletic prowess, even as a youth. Why a cock? And why a losing throw of the die?"

He pondered a while longer, then smiled. "The palm is a victory token, yes, but it's also a symbol of the city of Tyre—and despite the fact that Antipater claimed Sidon as his native city, he was actually born in Tyre, a few miles down the Syrian coast. Antipater revealed that fact to very few people; I see that you were among them, Finder. How clever of you to include this detail, since only those closest to Antipater will be able to figure it out."

My father gave an unassuming shrug—or did the opposite, I suppose, since by this gesture he accepted credit for the design that had been created by Antipater.

"The crowing cock—that suggests a man who made himself heard far and wide, as did Antipater with his verses. And as the king of poets, the scepter is rightfully his. But the knucklebone, and the Chian throw . . ."

Catulus puzzled a while longer, then clapped his hands. "By Hercules, that's the cleverest stroke of all! You've managed to symbolize not just the beginning of Antipater's life—his birth in Tyre—but also his end, and the exact manner of his death. 'Chian' is a bad way for the die to fall, but the island of Chios is also famous for fine wine. By drinking too much wine, Antipater took a terrible tumble—befallen by a veritable Chian throw. You've created a pun in stone, Finder. It's not merely clever; it's downright brilliant!"

My father actually blushed, and lowered his eyes, as if he were too modest to accept such a compliment.

Catulus drew himself stiffly upright and gathered the folds of his toga. "Finder, I owe you an apology. When I heard that the affairs of my dear friend Antipater had been entrusted to—well, to a person not of *our* circle—I thought that Antipater must have lost his wits prior to making his will. But I now see how very close the two of you must have

been, and the special attention he gave to your son, and most of all, your
extreme cleverness, which only a man of Antipater's intellect could fully
appreciate. You've done the old fellow proud with this tombstone.
I couldn't have created a better one myself."

And with that, the consul burst into tears and cried like a woman.

"Antipater, this is madness!" My father shook his head. "You can't
change our plans at the last moment. You cannot take part in your
own funeral!"

After composing himself, the consul Catulus had rejoined his retinue in the street outside our house, where the funeral procession had
begun to gather. I could hear the musicians warming up, playing shrill
notes on their pipes and rattling their tambourines. The professional
mourners were loosening their throats, making loud, ululating sobs. In
a matter of moments, bearers would arrive to carry the bier out of our
vestibule and into the street, and the procession would begin.

Antipater studied his reflection in a polished silver mirror, stroking
his newly shaven chin. For as long as I had known him, he had worn a
long white beard. But for his exit from Rome, he had allowed Damon
to cut his beard and shave his cheeks. It was not exactly a disguise, but
he did look quite different, and considerably younger.

The plan was this: once the funeral procession disappeared down
the street, Antipater and I would slip out the front door; there could be
no better time to leave unobserved, since anyone likely to recognize Antipater would be attending his funeral. We would steal across the city to
the docks along the Tiber and board a boat headed downriver to Ostia. Such boats departed throughout the day and even during the
night, so we would have no problem finding one.

But now, at the very last moment, just as we should have been making ready to set out, Antipater had proposed a change of plan. Yes, he
and I would leave for Ostia, and then for Ephesus—but not until after
the funeral. He wanted to see the cremation and hear the speeches,
and he had thought of a way to do it.

"When the archmime arrives, Finder, you'll tell him you don't need his services after all and send him home. And I shall take his place!"

It was the duty of the archmime—a trained professional—to walk in front of the bier, wearing the death mask of the deceased. Some archmimes made quite an art of their impersonation, duplicating the exact gait and gestures of the dead man, performing mute, impromptu skits to remind anyone who knew the deceased of some familiar behavior.

"But I hired the best archmime in Rome," my father complained, "just as your will instructed. He's the most expensive player in the whole procession."

"Never mind," said Antipater. "Who better to play me, than me? I'm already suitably dressed; you wanted me to wear black today, so that if anyone should glimpse me I'd not look out of place. And young Gordianus is still wearing his black toga. He, too, will be able to take part in the funeral." Antipater raised the wax mask, which was affixed to a pole, and held it before his face.

"Madness!" My father declared again, and then fell silent, for the consul Catulus, coming from the direction of the vestibule, suddenly joined us in the garden.

"Finder, it's time to begin," said Catulus, with the tone of a man used to taking charge. "The bearers have arrived—I took the liberty of escorting them into the vestibule. And look, here's the archmime!" He stared at Antipater. "How did you enter the house, and I failed to see you?"

Hiding his face behind the mask, Antipater performed an elaborate shrug and gracefully extended one arm, making a flourish with his fingers.

Catulus frowned. "That's nothing at all like Antipater! But the mask is a good likeness, so I suppose he'll do. Finder, shall we begin?"

My father sighed and followed Catulus to the vestibule, where the bearers had gathered around the bier. In lieu of the death mask, a sprig of cypress had been laid over the ruined face of the deceased. I gave a start when I saw the archmime, a redhead with a weak jaw, standing in the front doorway; apparently he had just arrived. I tugged at my father's toga and pointed. He quickly moved to whisk the actor back into the street. Catulus was never aware of his presence.

The bearers lifted the bier. Antipater, keeping his mask raised, strode before them as they carried the body over the threshold and into the street. At the sight of the deceased, the hired mourners broke into a lament.

I looked up the street, and was startled by the size of the crowd that had gathered for Antipater's funeral. I suppose I shouldn't have been surprised; he was one of the most famous poets in the world, after all.

The musicians commenced a plaintive dirge. The procession slowly wended its way up the narrow streets of the Esquiline Hill until we passed through a gate in the city wall and arrived in the necropolis, the city of the dead. The bier was placed upon a pile of wood. Many speeches were made, extolling the virtues of the dead man, including a memorable one by Catulus. Antipater's poems were recited at great length. Then, at last, the bonfire was lit.

The remains were reduced to ashes, and the ashes were gathered in an urn. The urn was placed in a simple stone tomb, and atop the tomb was placed the marble tablet with its image of a cock clutching a palm branch and a scepter, with a knucklebone precariously balanced at the edge of the base.

Throughout the proceedings, watching all, and watched by all, the archmime wore the death mask and performed an uncanny imitation of the way that Antipater had been known to walk or stand or tilt his head just so.

As the old Etruscan adage goes, every man attends his own funeral— but Antipater was the first man I knew to walk away from his.

"Did you hear what Catulus called me? 'The greatest poet of his genera-tion'!" Antipater grinned. "But he misquoted my epitaph for Homer. 'Herald of heroes, spokesman of gods, glory of the Muses,' he said, but what I actually wrote was '*light* of the Muses.' Still, it was flattering to hear my own humble efforts compared to those of Homer—"

"I hardly heard a word," said my father. "The whole time I was waiting for someone to realize your deception and expose the hoax. I'd have been ruined. No longer the Finder they'd call me, but the Fraudster!"

"But no one suspected a thing. It went off brilliantly! Though I must say it's a bit unnerving to see yourself consumed by flames, then scooped up like so much dust and gravel and poured into an urn." Antipater took a long sip of wine. Night had fallen, and we had returned to the house on the Esquiline to share a hastily gathered dinner of scraps from the pantry. There was not much food in the house; my father had expected us to be gone by now.

"To be candid, Antipater, this makes me doubt your judgment," he said. "I'm having second thoughts about entrusting my son to your care on such a long journey. Who knows what mad risks you're likely to take, if today is any example?"

"If it's danger you fear, will the boy be any safer if he stays here with you? One of the reasons for him to accompany me was to get him out of Rome while—"

"I'm not a boy," I felt obliged to point out. I would have done better to keep my mouth shut and listen to the rest of what Antipater had to say. How young I was, and how blissfully unaware of all that was going on in the world around me! I looked to my father to deal with all that; he was my shield against the winds of war and upheaval. The law might call me a man, but truly I was still what Antipater had just called me, a boy.

Why was Antipater leaving Rome, and in such a secretive way? I was vaguely aware that toleration for Greek intellectuals like Antipater was at a low ebb in the city. Some among the Roman elite, like Catulus, admired all things Greek—Greek art, Greek literature and learning, even Greek philosophies of how to live and love. But others remained suspicious of the Greeks, considering them nothing more than a conquered people whose inferior, foreign ways were likely to corrupt Roman youth. That Rome was the master of Greece, no one disputed; all Greek resistance had ended a generation before I was born when the Roman general Lucius Mummius annihilated the city of Corinth, a terrifying example that cowed all the other Greek cities into submission. But as the wily Greeks had stolen into Troy by the ruse of a giant horse, so there were those in Rome who thought that Greek poets and teachers were a sort of Trojan horse, insidiously undermining the Roman way of life. Antipater had fervent supporters in the city, like Catulus, but he had enemies as well, and at the moment they were ascendant.

Other changes were afoot. The long-simmering discontent of Rome's subjects in Italy—conquered territories whose people had been granted only a portion of our own rights and privileges—was rapidly coming to a boil. If open revolt broke out, there could be violence on a scale that had not been seen in the Italian peninsula in a very long time. More trouble was brewing abroad, where Rome's imperial ambitions were about to collide with those of King Mithridates of Pontus, who fancied that he, not the Romans, should dominate the wealthy city-states, provinces, and petty kingdoms of the East.

All these concerns seemed very distant to me. I had only a nebulous sense that something dangerous loomed over Antipater and my father, and by extension myself. Any worries about this were relegated to the background of my mind. In the foreground was the immediate distress I felt at my father's threat to keep me from going with Antipater.

"I'm not a boy," I repeated. "I'm a man now. It should be my decision whether I go with Antipater or not."

My father sighed. "I won't stop you. I only feel a need to express my displeasure with the irresponsible way he behaved today. I hope it won't happen again, in some circumstance that may cause you both to lose your heads!"

"Finder, you worry too much," said Antipater. "Young Gordianus and I will be among friends in many of the cities we visit, and when we venture to new places, we shall make new friends."

My father shook his head, then gave a shrug of resignation. "Have you finally settled on a name to use while traveling incognito?"

"I have," said Antipater. "It came to me in a flash of inspiration while I was watching myself burn on the funeral pyre. Allow me to introduce myself." He cleared his throat, gave a flourish, and bowed deeply, which cause his joints to creak. "I am Zoticus of Zeugma, the humble tutor and traveling companion of young Gordianus, citizen of Rome."

My father laughed. I summoned up my spotty Greek, and caught the joke.

"Zoticus," I said, "Greek for 'full of life.' "

"What better name for a man supposedly dead?" said Antipater with a smile.

"Actually, I was laughing at the choice of Zeugma," said my father. "A rich man might come from Alexandria, a wise man from Athens, but no one comes from Zeugma—which makes it an ideal choice, I suppose."

"Actually, we may travel through Zeugma on our way to Babylon, depending on which route we take," said Antipater. "We may have a chance to visit Issus as well, which isn't that far from Zeugma.

"On the promontory of Issus by the wild Cilician shore,
Lie the bones of many Persians, slain in days of yore.
The deed was Alexander's. So states the poet's lore."

My father continued to fret. "But are you not *too* famous, Antipater, to travel incognito? You saw how many people attended your funeral today. The name of Antipater of Sidon is familiar to anyone who knows even a smattering of Greek—"

"The *name* is known—exactly so," said Antipater. "And a few of my more famous verses are known as well, I should like to think. But my face is not known, nor the sound of my voice. People read Antipater; people have heard of Antipater; but they have no idea what he looks like. Once the news of my death spreads, no one will be expecting to

see me in some city far from Rome. With my face clean-shaven, even
the rare acquaintance who might recognize me won't give me a second
look. No one will connect the late, lamented Antipater of Sidon with
the humble tutor, *Zzzzoticus of Zzzzeugma*."

Antipater seemed to take great pleasure in drawing out the buzzing
sound of the initial letters. Later I would realize another reason that
"Zoticus of Zeugma" pleased him so much: no name could be more
Greek, or less Roman, since neither word could even be properly rendered in Latin, the letter *Z* having been eradicated from our alphabet
two centuries ago by Appius Claudius Caecus, who complained that
it produced an abhorrent sound, and the physical act of pronouncing
it made a man look like a grinning skull. This tidbit of knowledge I
had learned from Antipater, of course.

That night, at an hour when all the reputable citizens who might
recognize Antipater were presumably indoors, we stole across the city—
a young Roman suitably dressed for a journey, his father, his white-
haired traveling companion, and the old slave who tended to our baggage cart. Poor Damon! Once Antipater and I were finally gone, he
could look forward to getting some rest.

At the dock, my father assumed the role of Roman paterfamilias—
which is to say, he did his best to show no emotion, even though an
old friend was setting out on a journey from which, at Antipater's age,
it was unlikely he might ever return, and even though the son who had
been at his side from birth was about to be parted from him, for the
first time and for a duration neither of us could foresee.

What did I feel, as I embraced my father and gazed into his eyes?
I think I was too excited at the prospect of finally setting out to realize
the gravity of the moment. I was only eighteen, after all, and knew
very little of the world.

"You have her eyes," he whispered, and I knew he meant my
mother, who had died so long ago I barely remembered her. He almost never spoke of her. That he should do so now caused me to blush
and lower my eyes.

Damon embraced me as well, and I was taken aback when he burst into tears. I thought he must be exhausted from working so hard. I did not understand that a slave who moved in the background of my world could form attachments and experience the pangs of parting as acutely as anyone else.

As it turned out, Antipater and I were the only passengers on the little boat. As we glided down the Tiber under starlight, nestled amid our baggage, I was too excited to sleep. Antipater, too, seemed wakeful. I decided to ask him about something that had been puzzling me.

"Teacher, the Tiber will take us overnight to Ostia, correct?"

"Yes."

"And at Ostia, we'll book passage on a ship to take us to our first destination: the city of Ephesus, on the coast of Asia."

"That is the plan."

"Ephesus, because there you have a trusted friend with whom we can stay—but also because Ephesus is home to the great Temple of Artemis, one of the Seven Wonders of the World."

"That is correct."

"Because it is your intention that on our journey we shall visit all seven of the Wonders."

"Yes!" Even by starlight, I could see that he smiled and that his eyes sparkled.

"Teacher, I've been thinking about something I overheard you say to my father, earlier today. You said to him: 'People are always saying, "Before I die, I want to see the Seven Wonders." Well, now that I'm dead, I shall finally have time to see them all!'"

"And what of it?"

I cleared my throat. "Teacher, did you not compose these verses?

"I have seen the walls of Babylon, so lofty and so wide,
And the Gardens of that city, which flower in the skies.
I have seen the ivory Zeus, great Olympia's pride,
And the towering Mausoleum where Artemisia's husband lies.

I have seen the huge Colossus, which lifts its head to heaven,
And taller still, the Pyramids, whose secrets none can tell.
But the house of Artemis at Ephesus, of all the Wonders Seven,
Must surely be the grandest, where a god may rightly dwell."

I paused for a moment. The Tiber, reflecting starlight, glided past us. Frogs croaked along the riverbank. "So, in the poem, you declare the Temple of Artemis to be the greatest. But if you haven't actually seen all the Wonders, with your own eyes, then how could you—"

"First of all, my name is Zoticus, and I never wrote that poem; a famous fellow named Antipater did." Antipater spoke in a low voice, and even by starlight I could see that he scowled. "Second, your accent is atrocious. I pity that Antipater fellow, that anyone should declaim his verses in such a manner. You murder its music! We must drill you on the finer points of Greek pronunciation daily between now and our arrival in Ephesus, or else you shall cause laughter every time you open your mouth."

"Teacher—Zoticus—please forgive me. I only wondered—"

"Third, a young Roman does not ask his Greek tutor for forgiveness, at least not where anyone might overhear. And finally, have you never heard of poetic license?" Antipater sighed. "As a well-traveled Greek, I've seen *most* of the Wonders, of course—at least the ones in the Greek part of the world."

"But if you've never been to Babylon and Egypt—"

"Well, now I shall rectify that omission, and you shall come with me, and together we will see all seven of the Wonders, and you may judge for yourself which is the greatest."

I nodded. "And what if I find the Great Pyramid to be more impressive than the Temple of Artemis?"

"Then you can write your own poem, young man—if you think you have the Greek for it!"

And that was the end of that discussion. For an hour longer, perhaps, I listened to the croaking of frogs passing by, but eventually I must have slept, for when I opened my eyes, the world was light again. I smelled the salt of the sea. We were in Ostia.

Among the ships preparing to set out, we looked for one that would take us to Ephesus. Antipater—now Zoticus—haggled over the price, pretending to do so on my behalf, and before noon we had settled on a ship that was taking a load of premium-quality garum from Rome to Ephesus.

As the ship cast off, Antipater and I stood at the stern and gazed back at the docks of Ostia, where a number of women—some possibly wives, some certainly whores—stood and waved farewell to the departing sailors.

Antipater breathed deeply of the sea air, spread his arms wide, and loudly recited one of his verses.

> "'Tis the season, men, to travel forth, thrusting through the spume.
> No longer does Poseidon froth and Boreas blow his gale.
> Swallows build their cozy nests; dancing maidens leave the loom.
> Sailors—weigh anchor, coil hawsers, hoist sail!
> So bids Priapus, god of the harbor."

As Antipater lowered his arms, the captain, who was Greek, sidled up alongside him. "Antipater of Sidon, is it not?" he said.

Antipater gave a start, and then realized the captain had identified the poem, not the poet. "So it is," he said.

"A pity the old fellow's dead. I heard the news only yesterday."

Antipater nodded. "A pity indeed. Yet the best parts of him live on, I like to think."

"Ah yes, his verses." The captain smiled "That one in particular I've always liked, being a sailing man. It's a bit suggestive, don't you think? All that talk of thrusting, and cozy nests, and dancing maidens. And Priapus is the god of rut, not harbors. The occasion may be the return of the sailing season in the spring, but I think perhaps the poet was also speaking of the randiness of sailors in springtime, when they leave their winter lovers to go plowing through the waves, looking to drop anchor in unfamiliar harbors."

Antipater looked dumbfounded for a moment, so pleased was he by the captain's insight, then he caught himself and managed to look merely impressed. "Captain, you are a man of considerable discernment."

"Merely a Greek, and what Greek is not stirred by the beauty of his mother tongue?" He gave Antipater a friendly slap on the back. "You'll have to recite more poems, old fellow, to keep us entertained during the voyage. Do you know any others by Antipater?"

"I daresay I can recite the whole body of his work," said my traveling companion Zoticus, with a smile.

II

SOMETHING TO DO WITH DIANA

(The Temple of Artemis at Ephesus)

"Ah, Ephesus!" cried Antipater. "Most cosmopolitan of all Greek cities—pride of Asia, jewel of the East!" He stood at the prow of the ship and gazed with glittering eyes at the city before us.

As soon as the ship left the open sea and entered the mouth of the Cayster River, Antipater had used his sharp elbows to force his way to the head of the little group of passengers, with me following in his wake. Our first glimpse of Ephesus came as we rounded a bend and saw an indistinct mass of buildings clustered against a low mountain. Moment by moment we drew nearer, until the city loomed before us.

The harbor was pierced by a long pier that projected far into the water. So many ships had moored alongside that it seemed impossible we should find a spot, especially because other ships were arriving ahead of us, with their sails aloft and colorful pennants fluttering in the breeze. By the Roman calendar this was Aprilis, but in Ephesus this was the holy month of Artemision, marked by one festival after another in honor of the city's patron goddess, Artemis. Antipater had told me that the celebrations drew tens of thousands of visitors from all over the Greek-speaking world, and it appeared he had not been exaggerating.

A harbor master in a small boat sailed out to inform the captain that there was no room for our ship to dock at the pier. We would have to pitch anchor and await a ferryboat to take the passengers ashore. The ferrymen would have to be paid, of course, and Antipater grumbled at the extra expense, but I was glad for the chance to remain for a while in the harbor and take in the view.

Beyond the crowded wharves rose the famous five-mile walls of Ephesus. Where the pier met the shore these walls were pierced by an ornamental gate flanked by towers. The tall doors of the gate stood wide open, welcoming all the world into the city of Artemis—for a price, Antipater explained, for he anticipated that we would have to pay a special fee to enter the city during the festival. Beyond the walls I saw the rooftops of temples and tall apartment buildings. Farther away, clustered on the slope of Mount Pion, were a great many houses. Some were like palaces, with ornate terraces and hillside gardens.

The most prominent building to be seen was the enormous theater built into the hillside. The semicircular tiers of seats that faced the harbor were filled with thousands of spectators, apparently watching a comedy; every now and then I heard a burst of distant laughter. Scores of towering, brightly painted statues lined the uppermost rim of the theater; these images of gods and heroes appeared to be gazing not at the stage below them but across the rooftops of the city, straight at me.

"I see the famous theater," I said, shading my eyes against the late-morning sun above Mount Pion, "but where is the great Temple of Artemis?"

Antipater snorted. "Gordianus! Have you forgotten the geography I taught you? Your head is like a sieve."

I smiled as the lesson came back to me. "I remember now. The Temple of Artemis was built outside the city, about a mile inland, on low, marshy ground. It must be . . . somewhere over there." I pointed to a spot beyond the steep northern slope of Mount Pion.

Antipater raised a bushy eyebrow. "Very good. And why did the builders choose that site for the temple?"

"Because they decided that building on marshy soil would soften the effect of earthquakes on such a massive structure."

"Correct. To further stabilize the ground, before the cornerstone was laid, they spread a deep layer of crushed charcoal. And then what?"

"Atop the charcoal they put down many layers of fleece, taken from sheep sacrificed in honor of the goddess."

"You are an apt pupil after all," said Antipater.

The sun was directly above our heads by the time a ferryboat arrived. Antipater again elbowed his way to the front, with me following, so that we were among the first to be ferried ashore. As soon as we alighted on the pier, a group of boys swarmed around us. Antipater chose the two who looked most honest to him and tossed each of them a coin. They gathered our bags and followed us.

We strolled up the pier, which seemed like a small city itself; the crowded ships were like dwellings along a broad thoroughfare. I saw people everywhere, heard babies crying, and noticed that many of the masts were strung with laundry. A great many of the visitors to Ephesus, unable to find accommodations in the city, were apparently residing aboard ship.

"Where will we stay in Ephesus?" I asked.

"Years ago, when I lived here for a while, I had a pupil named Eutropius," said Antipater. "I haven't seen him since, but we've corresponded over the years. Eutropius is grown now, a widower with a child of his own. He inherited his father's house, about halfway up the hill, not far from the theater. Eutropius has done rather well for himself, so I'm sure our accommodations will be quite comfortable."

We reached the end of the pier and arrived at the open gate, where people stood in long queues to be admitted to the city. I was unsure which queue we should get into, until one of the gatekeepers shouted, in Latin, "Roman citizens and their parties in this line! Roman citizens, queue here!"

As we stepped into the line, I noticed that some in the crowd gave us dirty looks. The line was shorter than the others, and moved more quickly. Soon we stood before a man in a ridiculously tall hat a bit like a quail's plume—only a bureaucrat would wear such a thing—who glanced at my iron citizen's ring as I handed him the traveling papers my father had secured for me before I left Rome.

Speaking Latin, the official read aloud: "'Gordianus, citizen of Rome, born in the consulship of Spurius Postumius Albinus and Marcus Minucius Rufus—that makes you what, eighteen years old?—'of average height with dark hair and regular features, no distinguishing marks, speaks Latin and some Greek'—and with an atrocious accent, I'll wager." The man eyed me with barely concealed contempt.

"His Greek accent is actually rather good," said Antipater. "Certainly better than your Latin accent."

"And who are you?"

"I am the young man's traveling companion, formerly his tutor— Zoticus of Zeugma. And you would not be speaking to us this way if my friend were older and wearing his toga and followed by a retinue of slaves. But Gordianus is no less a citizen than any other Roman, and you will treat him with respect—or else I shall report you to the provincial governor."

The official took a long look at Antipater, made a sour face, then handed my documents back to me and waved us on.

"You certainly put that fellow in his place!" I said with a laugh.

"Yes, well, I fear you may encounter more than a little of that sort of thing here in Ephesus, Gordianus."

"What do you mean?"

"Anti-Roman sentiment runs deep throughout the province of Asia—through all the Greek-speaking provinces for that matter—but especially here in Ephesus."

"But why?"

"The Roman governor based at Pergamon taxes the people mercilessly. And there are a great many Romans in the city—thousands of them, all claiming special privileges, taking the best seats at the theater, rewarding each other with places of honor at the festivals, sucking up the profits from the import and export trade, even sticking their fingers into the treasury at the Temple of Artemis, which is the great bank for all of Asia and the lifeblood of Ephesus. In the forty years since the Romans established their authority here, a great deal of resentment has been stirred up. If even a petty document-checker at the gate feels he can speak to you that way, I fear to imagine how others will behave. I think it might be best if we speak no more Latin while we're here in Ephesus, Gordianus, even among ourselves. Others may overhear and make assumptions."

Somewhere in the middle of this discourse, he had switched from Latin to Greek, and it took my mind a moment to catch up.

"That may be . . . a challenge," I finally said, pausing to think of the Greek word.

Antipater sighed. "Your words may be Greek, but your accent is decidedly Roman."

"You told the document-checker I had a good accent!"

"Yes, well . . . perhaps you should simply speak as little as possible."

We followed the crowd and found ourselves in a marketplace thronged with pilgrims and tourists, where vendors sold all sorts of foodstuffs and a great variety of talismans. There were miniature replicas of Artemis's temple as well as images of the goddess herself. These images came in many sizes and were fashioned from various materials, from crudely made terra-cotta or wooden trinkets to statuettes that displayed the highest standards of craftsmanship, some advertised as being cast of solid gold.

I paused to admire a statuette of the goddess in her Ephesian guise, which seems so exotic to Roman eyes. Our Artemis—we call her Diana—is a virgin huntress; she carries a bow and wears a short, simple tunic suitable for the chase. But this manifestation of the goddess— presumably more ancient—stood stiffly upright with her bent elbows against her body, her forearms extended and her hands open. She wore a mural crown, and outlining her head was a nimbus decorated with winged bulls. More bulls, along with other animals, adorned the stiff garment that covered her lower body, almost like a mummy casing. From her neck hung a necklace of acorns, and below this I saw the most striking feature of Artemis of Ephesus, a mass of pendulous, gourd-shaped protrusions that hung in a cluster from her upper body. I might have taken these for multiple breasts, had Antipater not explained to me that these protrusions were bulls' testicles. Many bulls would be sacrificed to the virgin goddess during the festival.

I picked up the image to look at it more closely. The gold was quite heavy.

"Don't touch unless you intend to buy!" snapped the vendor, a gaunt man with a long beard. He snatched the little statue from my hand.

"Sorry," I said, lapsing into Latin. The vendor gave me a nasty look.

We moved on. "Do you think that image was really made of solid gold?" I asked Antipater.

"Yes, and therefore far beyond your means."

"Do people really buy such expensive items for keepsakes?"

"Not for keepsakes, but to make offerings. Pilgrims purchase whichever of the images they can afford, then donate them to the Temple of Artemis to honor the goddess."

"But the priests must collect thousands of talismans."

"Megabyzoi—the priests are called Megabyzoi," he explained. "And yes, they collect many talismans during the festivals."

"What do the Megabyzoi do with all those images?"

"The offerings are added to the wealth of the temple treasury, of course."

I looked at the vast number of people around us. The open-air market seemed to stretch on forever. "So the vendors make a nice profit selling the images, and the temple receives a hefty income from all those offerings."

Antipater smiled. "Don't forget what the pilgrims receive— participation in one of the most beloved religious festivals in the world, an open-air feast, and the favor of the goddess, including her protection on their journey home. But the donation of these trinkets is only a tiny part of the temple's income. Rich men from many cities and even foreign kings store their fortunes in the temple's vaults and pay a handsome fee for the service. That vast reservoir of wealth allows the Megabyzoi to

SOMETHING TO DO WITH DIANA 27

make loans, charging handsome interest. Artemis of Ephesus owns vineyards and quarries, pastures and salt-beds, fisheries and sacred herds of deer. The Temple of Artemis is one of the world's great storehouses of wealth—and every Roman governor spends his tenure trying to find some way to get his hands on it."

We bought some goat's cheese on a skewer from a vendor and slowly made our way through the crowd. The crush lessened as we ascended a winding street that took us halfway up Mount Pion, where we at last arrived at the house of Eutropius.

"It's larger than I remember it," said Antipater, gazing at the immaculately maintained facade. "I do believe he's added a story since I was here."

The slave who answered the door dismissed our baggage carriers and instructed some underlings to take our things to the guest quarters. We were shown to a garden at the center of the house where our host reclined on a couch, apparently just waking from a nap. Eutropius was perhaps forty, with a robust physique and the first touch of frost in his golden hair. He wore a beautifully tailored robe spun from coarse silk dyed a rich saffron hue.

He sprang up and approached Antipater with open arms. "Teacher!" he exclaimed. "You haven't aged a bit."

"Nonsense!" Antipater gestured to his white hair, but smiled, pleased by the compliment. He introduced me to our host.

I heard a muffled roar as the air above our heads resounded with the sound of a great many people laughing.

"From the theater," explained Eutropius.

"But why are you not there?" asked Antipater.

"Bah! Plays bore me—all those actors making terrible puns and behaving like idiots. You taught me to love poetry, Teacher, but I'm afraid you were never able to imbue me with a love of comedy."

"Artemis herself enjoys the performances," said Antipater.

"So they say—even when the actors are as wooden as she is," said Eutropius. Antipater cackled, but I missed the joke.

Antipater drew a sharp breath. "But who is this?"

"Anthea!" Eutropius strode to embrace the girl who had just entered the garden. She was a few years younger than I, and golden-haired like her father. She wore a knee-length purple tunic cinched with a silver chain tied below breasts just beginning to bud. The garment hung loosely over her shoulders, baring her arms, which were surprisingly tawny. (A Roman girl of the same social standing would have creamy white limbs, and would never display them to a stranger.) She wore a necklace of gilded acorns and a fawn-skin cape. Strapped across her shoulder was a quiver filled with brightly painted, miniature arrows. In one hand she carried a dainty little bow—clearly a ceremonial weapon—and in the other an equally dainty javelin.

"Is it Artemis herself I see?" whispered Antipater in a dreamy voice. I was thinking the same thing. The exotic Ephesian Artemis of the talismans was alien to me, but this was the Diana I knew, virgin goddess of the hunt.

Eutropius gazed proudly at his daughter. "Anthea turned fourteen just last month. This is her first year to take part in the procession."

"No one in the crowd will look at anyone else," declared Antipater, at which the girl lowered her eyes and blushed.

As lovely as Anthea was, my attention was suddenly claimed by the slave girl who followed her into the garden. She was older than her mistress, perhaps my age, with lustrous black hair, dark eyes, and a long, straight nose. She wore a dark blue tunic with sleeves that came to her elbows, cinched with a thin leather belt. Her figure was more womanly than Anthea's and her demeanor less girlish. She smiled, apparently pleased at the fuss we were making over her mistress, and when she saw me looking at her, she stared back at me and raised an eyebrow. My cheeks turned hot and I looked away.

"Look at you, blushing back at Anthea!" whispered Antipater, mistaking the cause of my reaction.

Another burst of laughter resounded above us, followed by long, sustained applause.

"I do believe that means the play is over," said Eutropius. "Teacher, if you and Gordianus want to wash up a bit and change your clothes before the procession begins, you'd better do it quickly."

I looked up at the sky, which was beginning to fade as twilight approached. "A procession? But it'll be dark soon."

"Exactly," said Antipater. "The procession of Artemis takes place after sundown."

"Roman festivals happen in daylight," I muttered, lapsing into my native tongue.

"Well, you are not in Rome anymore," said Antipater. "So stop speaking Latin!"

"I'll call for the porter to show you to your quarters," said Eutropius. But before he could clap his hands, the slave girl stepped forward.

"I'll do it, Master," she said. She stood directly in front of me and trained her gaze on me. I realized, with some discomfort, that to meet her eyes I had to look up a bit. She was slightly taller than I.

"Very well, Amestris," said Eutropius, with a vague wave.

We followed Amestris down a short hallway and up a flight of stairs. Her shapely hips swayed as she ascended the steps ahead of us.

She showed Antipater to his room, then led me to the one next to it. It was small but opulently appointed. A balcony offered a view of the harbor. On a little table I saw a basin of water and a sponge.

"Will you require help to bathe yourself?" said Amestris, standing in the doorway.

I stared at her for a long moment. "No," I finally managed to say, in Latin—for at that moment, even the simplest Greek deserted me. Amestris made an elegant bow that caused her breasts to dangle voluptuously for a moment, then backed away.

"Amestris—that's a Persian name, isn't it?" I blurted, finally thinking of something to say.

For an answer, she merely nodded, then withdrew. I could have sworn I heard her laughing quietly.

After we had refreshed ourselves and changed into our most colorful tunics, Antipater and I returned to the garden. Eutropius had been joined by another man about his own age and of his own class, to judge by the newcomer's expensive-looking garments. Anthea had also been joined by a friend, a girl attired exactly as she was, in the guise of Artemis the huntress, but with flowing red hair and plainer features.

"This is my friend and business partner, Mnason," said Eutropius, "and this is his daughter, Chloe, who will also be taking part in the procession for the first time." Under his breath he added, to Antipater, "The two of us are both widowers, sadly, so quite often we take part in festivals and civic celebrations together with our daughters."

The six of us set out. Amestris came along as well, to make sure that all was perfect for Anthea's and Chloe's appearance in the procession. I tried to keep my eyes off her, determined to take in the sights and sounds of the festive city.

A short walk brought us to the main entrance of the theater. There were a great many people in the square, and the crowd was still letting out. Everyone looked quite cheerful, and for those who needed more cheering up, vendors were selling wine. Some in the crowd had brought their own cups, but the vendors were also selling ornamental cups made of copper, or silver, or even gold set with stones. Like the talismans for sale in the market, these precious objects were destined to be offered to Artemis at the end of the procession.

As darkness fell, lamps were lit all around the square, casting a flickering orange glow across the sea of smiling faces. The crowd suddenly grew hushed. A way was cleared in front of the theater entrance. I assumed some dignitary, perhaps the Roman governor, was about to make his exit. Instead, a statue of Artemis emerged, carried aloft by a small group of priests wearing bright yellow robes and tall yellow headdresses.

Antipater spoke in my ear. "Those are the Megabyzoi, and that statue is *the* Artemis of Ephesus, the model for all the replicas we saw in the marketplace."

The statue was made not of stone or bronze, but of wood, probably ebony to judge by the few areas that were not adorned with bright paint. Her face and hands were gilded. An elaborately embroidered robe with broad sleeves had been fitted over her body, and a veil covered her face. A wagon festooned with wreaths and strings of beads approached, drawn by bulls decorated with ribbons and garlands. The Megabyzoi gently placed the statue upright in the wagon.

Suddenly I understood Eutropius's pun about the wooden statue watching a wooden performance. Artemis herself, brought from her temple and specially dressed for the occasion, had been the guest of honor at the play.

The wagon rolled forward. With Artemis leading the way, others took their place in the procession. Musicians with flutes, horns, lyres, and tambourines appeared. Eutropius gave his daughter a kiss on the forehead, and Mnason did likewise, then Anthea and Chloe ran to join a group of similarly dressed girls who gathered behind the musicians. The girls performed a curious dance, leaping in the air and then crouching down, looking this way and that, mimicking the movements of birds. Then the hunted became hunters, as in unison the girls raised their little bows, notched miniature arrows, and shot them in the air. Women in the crowd laughed and rushed forward, trying to catch the harmless arrows as they fell.

"The arrows are tokens of childbirth," Antipater explained. "The women who catch them hope to enjoy a quick conception and an easy delivery."

"But how is it that a virgin goddess is also a fertility goddess?" I asked.

Antipater's sigh made me feel quite the ignorant Roman. "So it has always been. Because she herself does not conceive, Artemis is able to act as helpmate to those who do."

The dancers put their bows over their shoulders, pulled the little javelins from their belts, and began a new dance, forming a circle and rhythmically tapping their javelins against the ground inside the circle and then outside. Even among so many young and lovely girls, Anthea stood out. From others in the crowd I overheard many comments about her beauty, and more than one observer echoed Antipater's observation that she appeared to personify the goddess herself.

The wagon bearing Artemis rolled out of sight around a corner. The musicians and dancing girls followed. Close behind the girls came a large contingent of boys and youths wearing colorful finery; these were athletes who would be taking part in various competitions in the days to come. Cattle, sheep, goats, and oxen destined for sacrifice were herded into the procession by the representatives of various trade guilds and other organizations who carried aloft their symbols and implements. Antipater explained to me how all these diverse groups figured into the long and fabled history of the city, but most of what he said went in one ear and out the other. I was distracted by the presence of Amestris, who followed our party, keeping a discreet distance. Every so often our eyes met. Invariably, it was I who looked away first.

At the very end of the official procession came the Megabyzoi, a great many of them, all wearing bright yellow robes and headdresses. Some carried sacred objects, including knives and axes for sacrifice, while others waved burning bundles of incense. The smoke wafted over the vast crowd of Ephesians and pilgrims that moved forward to follow the procession.

"Aren't the Megabyzoi eunuchs?" I said, recalling something I'd once heard and trying to get a better look at the priests over the heads of the crowd.

Eutropius and Mnason both laughed, and Antipater gave me an indulgent smile. "Once upon a time, that was indeed the case," he said. "But your information is a few centuries out of date, Gordianus. The ritual castration of the priests of Artemis ended many generations ago. Even so, the goddess still demands that those in her service, both male and female, be sexually pure. Though his manhood remains intact, each Megabyzus takes a vow to remain unmarried and celibate for as long as he serves in the priesthood of Artemis."

"That seems practical," I said.

"What do you mean?"

"With all the wealth that flows into the temple coffers, it's probably a good thing that the priests aren't married men. Otherwise, they might be tempted to put the interests of their children ahead of their sacred service."

"Gordianus is wise for his years," said Eutropius. "What father doesn't do all he can for his child? The chastity of the Megabyzoi should, in theory, make them less greedy. But sometimes I think it only makes them grumpier. And it certainly doesn't keep them from meddling in politics."

Mnason raised an eyebrow, glanced at me, then gestured to his friend to be quiet. Did he feel the need to be discreet because I was Roman?

Antipater ignored them. "How can I explain this to you, Gordianus? Think of the Roman goddess Vesta, and how vital it is for the well-being of Rome that the Vestals maintain their virginity. So it is with Ephesian Artemis. Chastity is absolutely essential for those who serve her, and not just her priests, or the women who work in the temple, called hierodules. All the girls who dance in the procession today must be virgins. Indeed, no freeborn female who is not a virgin may so much as step foot inside the Temple of Artemis, upon pain of death."

We followed the procession out of the square and down a broad, paved street called the Sacred Way, lit all along its length with torches. After we passed though a broad gate in the city's northern wall, these torches were set farther apart and in the intervening patches of deep shadow I could see the starry sky above our heads.

The Sacred Way took us gradually downhill. In the valley ahead, at the end of the winding line of torches, I saw our destination—the great Temple of Artemis. A huge crowd of pilgrims, many carrying torches, had already gathered at the temple to welcome the procession. The structure had the unearthly appearance of a vast, rectangular forest of glowing columns afloat in a pool of light. Though it was still almost a mile away, the temple already looked enormous. Antipater had told me it was the largest temple ever built by the Greeks, four times the size of the famous Parthenon atop the Acropolis in Athens.

The temple loomed larger with each step I took. I was astonished by the perfect beauty of the place. Gleaming marble steps led up to the broad porch. The massive walls of the sanctuary were surrounded by a double row of columns at least sixty feet high. White marble predominated, but many of the sculptural details had been highlighted with red, blue, or yellow paint, as well as touches of gleaming gold.

Even to my untrained and untraveled eye, the elegance of the columns was breathtaking. The bases were decorated with elaborate carvings, and each of the capitals ended in a graceful spiral curve to either side.

"It was here that the order of columns called Ionic originated," said Antipater, following my gaze. "The architects deliberately imbued the columns with feminine attributes. Thus you see that the stacked marble drums ascend not to a plain, unadorned capital, but to those elegant whorls on either side, which mimic a woman's curls. The whole length of each column is fluted with shallow channels, in imitation of the pleats of a woman's gown. The proportion of the height to the circumference and the way each column gently tapers is also meant to give them a feminine delicacy."

My eyes followed the columns to the pediment high above the porch, where I saw something I was not used to seeing in a temple—a tall, open window with an elaborate frame around it. I assumed it was there to admit light in the daytime, but as I was about to discover, this window had a far more important purpose.

In front of the temple, some distance from the steps, a low wall enclosed an elegantly carved altar for sacrificing animals. As the procession arrived before the temple, some of the yellow-robed Megabyzoi broke away from the larger contingent and took up places at this altar, producing ceremonial daggers, ropes for holding down the animals, butchering knives and axes, and other implements for the sacrifices. Other Megabyzoi stoked the pyres upon which the carved and spitted meat would be roasted. Others unloaded the statue of Artemis from the cart, carried her up the steps and into the temple. Yet another group of priests unyoked the garlanded bulls that had pulled the cart and led them toward the altar. A great many other animals, including sheep, goats, and oxen, were already being held in pens in the enclosure. They were to be sacrificed and roasted in the course of the evening, to satiate the appetite of the vast crowd.

The first of the bulls was led up a short ramp onto the altar, pushed to its side, and securely trussed. Megabyzoi intoned prayers to Artemis and walked among the crowd, carrying bowls of smoking incense. One of the priests, apparently the foremost among them to judge by the special embroidery on his robe and the height of his headdress, mounted a platform beside the altar where everyone in the crowd could see him. He raised his arms aloft.

"That's Theotimus," whispered Eutropius to Antipater, "head priest of the Megabyzoi." There was an edge in his voice, and he scowled as he gazed at the priest. So did Mnason.

The musicians ceased their playing. The girls stopped dancing. The crowd fell silent.

"People of Ephesus," cried Theotimus, "welcomed visitors, all who have gathered here for the love and adoration of the goddess—the sacrifices are ready to begin. If our rituals in your honor are pleasing to you, great Artemis—protector of virgins, supreme huntress, patron of wild places, benefactor since its beginning of the grateful city of Ephesus—we beg you, Artemis, to step forth and witness our propitiations to you."

The expectant crowd turned its gaze from the priest to the window set high in the temple. From within came a flicker of light, and then the goddess appeared at the window, her outstretched hands open in a gesture of acceptance. The apparition was so uncanny that it took me a moment to realize that I was seeing the statue that had been paraded in the cart. Unless Artemis had propelled herself, the priests had somehow managed to get the image all the way up to the window. Her veil had been removed and her gilded face shone brightly, reflecting the light of the torches and the roasting pyres around the altar.

As the crowd erupted in cheers, Theotimus strode to the altar, raised a dagger, and slashed the bull's throat. The bound creature kicked and thrashed, then fell limp. With a single, deft movement, the Megabyzus sliced off the bull's testicles and held them aloft. The crowd again erupted in cheers.

"For Artemis!" shouted Theotimus, and others took up the cry: "For Artemis!"

Eutropius saw the dumbfounded expression on my face. I was used to seeing animal sacrifices, but I had never witnessed a postmortem castration. "The sacred testes are reserved for the virgin goddess; the rest will be for us," said my host matter-of-factly. "I'm rather partial to the meat of the flank, especially if it's nicely grilled."

One beast after another was slain, with Artemis looking on from her high window, and the process of carving and cooking the meat began. The crowd gradually broke into groups, moving forward to receive their portion according to rules of rank and seniority determined by the Megabyzoi, who moved among the crowd to keep order, especially among those who had imbibed a great deal of wine. Clouds of smoke enveloped the crowd, and the smell of roasting meat mingled with the sweet fragrance of incense.

"Unless the two of you are terribly hungry, Teacher, this would be a good time for your young Roman friend to have a look inside the temple," suggested Eutropius. "Anthea and Chloe and the other virgins will be performing more dances."

Antipater declared this a splendid idea, and together we followed our host and Mnason up the broad marble steps and onto the porch.

Amestris came with us. Did that mean she was a virgin? Then I recalled Antipater's precise words—that no *freeborn* female could enter the temple unless she was a virgin. If this rule did not extend to slaves . . .

I shook my head and put aside this train of thought. What business was it of mine whether Amestris was a virgin or not?

Striding between the towering columns, we entered the grandest space I had ever seen. The sanctuary was lit by many lamps and decorated with many statues, but was so vast that no part of it seemed cluttered. The floor was of shimmering marble in a dizzying array of patterns and colors. High above our heads was a ceiling of massive cedar beams, alternately painted red, yellow, and blue, outlined with gold and decorated with gold ornaments. Adorning the marble walls were paintings of breathtaking beauty. Surely every tale ever told of Artemis was illustrated somewhere upon these vast walls, along with the images of many other gods and heroes.

Antipater drew my attention to the most famous painting in the temple, the gigantic portrait of Alexander the Great by Apelles. By some trick of coloring and perspective, the conqueror's hand and the thunderbolt he held appeared to come out of the wall and hover in space above our heads. The effect was astounding.

The acoustics of the space were also extraordinary, amplifying and somehow enhancing the tune being played by the musicians who had taken part in the procession. They stood to one side. In the center of the vast space, with a crowd looking on, the virgins performed another dance.

"They're enacting the story of Actaeon," whispered Eutropius, leading us closer. I saw that one of the girls had put on a Phrygian cap and wrapped a cloak around herself to play the part of the young hunter; from her red hair, I realized it was Chloe. Other girls, with dog pelts over their heads and shoulders, played the part of Actaeon's hounds. Others, holding bits of foliage, acted as trees. Actaeon, thirsty and eager to reach a pool hidden by the trees, pushed aside the leafy branches—at his touch the dancers yielded and twirled away—until, suddenly, the goddess Artemis was revealed, bathing in the imaginary pool.

Beside me, Antipater drew a sharp breath. I stifled a gasp and glanced at Eutropius, who smiled proudly. It was Anthea who played the startled goddess, and there was nothing imaginary about her nakedness. The milky white perfection of her small breasts and pale nipples seemed to glow in the soft light, radiating an almost supernatural beauty.

The music rose to a shrill crescendo. The hunter looked startled. So did the goddess. Artemis reached for her tunic to cover herself, and Actaeon moved to avert his eyes, but too late. Anthea threw her tunic into the air and raised her arms; the garment seemed to float down and cover her nakedness of its own volition. She whirled about, waving her arms wildly and mimicking a furious expression. Suddenly her whirling stopped and she froze in an attitude of accusation, pointing at Actaeon, who drew back in terror.

As Chloe darted this way and that, the forest closed around her, concealing her. The music abruptly stopped, then resumed with a new, menacing theme. The dancers playing trees drew back, revealing Actaeon transformed into a stag. Chloe now wore a deerskin. Completely covering her head was a mask of a young stag with small antlers.

The dancers playing the forest dispersed. The dancers playing hounds converged. To a cacophony of yelping pipes and agitated rattles, the hounds pursued the leaping stag until they surrounded it. Around and around they whirled, tormenting the stag who had once been their master. Chloe was completely hidden from sight, except for the stag's-head mask with antlers, which whirled around and around with the hounds.

The frenzied music changed. The hounds drew back. The stag's head fell to the floor, not far from where I stood, trailing bloodred streamers. Of Actaeon—torn to pieces in the story—nothing more remained to be seen.

Amid the whirling crush of the dancing hounds, Chloe must have removed the stag's head, pulled a dog's hide over her costume, and disappeared among the hounds. It was a simple trick, but the effect was uncanny. It seemed as if the hounds had literally devoured their prey.

Nearby, Anthea looked on with a suitably stern expression. Artemis had exacted a terrible vengeance on the mortal who had dared, however inadvertently, to gaze upon her nakedness.

Suddenly, one of the dancers screamed. Other girls cried out. The company began to scatter.

The music trailed off and fell silent. In the middle of the temple, one of the dancers lay crumpled on the floor. By her red hair, I knew it was Chloe.

Mnason rushed to his daughter. Eutropius hurried after him. I began to follow, but Antipater held me back.

"Let's not get in the way, Gordianus. Probably the poor girl merely fainted—from excitement, perhaps. . . ." His words lacked conviction. Antipater could see as clearly as could I that there was something unnatural in the way Chloe was lying, with her limbs twisted and her head thrown back. Mnason reached her and crouched over the motionless body for a moment, then threw back his head and let out a cry of anguish.

"She's dead!" someone shouted. "Chloe is dead!"

There were cries of dismay, followed by murmurs and whispers.

"Dead, did someone say?"

"Surely not!"

"But see how her father weeps?"

"What happened? Did anyone see anything?"

"Look—someone must have alerted the Megabyzoi, for here comes Theotimus."

Striding into the sanctuary, the head Megabyzus passed directly by me. He reeked of the smell of burning flesh and his yellow robes were spattered with blood.

"What's going on here?" His booming voice reverberated through the temple, silencing the crowd, which parted before him. Even Mnason drew back. The Megabyzus strode to the girl's body and knelt beside it.

Amid the hubbub and confusion, I noticed that the stag's-head mask was still lying on the floor. Chloe was the focus of all attention; no one seemed interested in the mask. I walked over to it, knelt down, and picked it up. What instinct led me to do so? Antipater would later say it was the hand of Artemis that guided me, but I think I was acting on something my father had taught me: *When everyone else is looking at a certain thing, turn your attention to the thing at which they are not looking. You may see what no one else sees.*

The mask was a thing of beauty, superbly crafted from the pelt of a deer and real antlers. The eyes were of some flashing green stone; the shiny black nose was made of obsidian. The mask showed signs of wear; probably it had been handed down and used year after year in the same dance, worn by many virgins at many festivals. I examined it inside and out—and noticed a curious thing. . . .

"Put that down!" shouted the Megabyzus.

I dropped the mask at once.

Theotimus turned from his examination of Chloe, rose to his feet, and strode toward me. The look on his face sent a shiver up my spine. There is a reason men like Theotimus rise to become the head of whatever calling they follow. Everything about the man was intimidating—his tall stature and commanding demeanor, his broad shoulders and his booming voice, and most of all his flashing eyes, which seemed to bore directly into mine.

"Who are you, to touch an object sacred to the worship of Artemis?"

I opened my mouth, but nothing came out. Latin and Greek alike deserted me.

Antipater came to my rescue. "The boy is a visitor, Megabyzus. He made an innocent mistake."

"A visitor?"

"From Rome," I managed to blurt out.

"Rome?" Theotimus raised an eyebrow.

Antipater groaned—had he not warned me to be discreet about my origins?—but after giving me a last, hard look, the Megabyzus snatched up the stag mask and seemed to lose interest in me. He turned to the crowd that had gathered around the corpse.

"The girl is dead," he announced. There were cries and groans from the spectators.

"But Megabyzus, what happened to her?" shouted someone.

"There are no marks upon the girl's body. She seems to have died suddenly and without warning. Because her death occurred here in the temple, we must assume that Artemis herself played a role in it."

"No!" cried Mnason. "Chloe was as devoted to Artemis as all the other virgins."

"I am not accusing your daughter of impurity, Mnason. But if Artemis struck her down, we must conclude that the goddess was sorely displeased with some aspect of the sacred ritual." He glanced at

the mask in his hands. "I take it the dance of Actaeon was being performed. Who was dancing the part of Artemis?"

The dancers had drawn to one side, where they huddled together,
clutching and comforting each other. From their midst, Anthea stepped
forward.

The Megabyzus approached her. Eutropius moved to join his daughter, but the priest raised a hand to order him back.

Theotimus towered over the girl, staring down at her. Anthea quailed
under his gaze, trembled, and bit her lip. She began to weep.

The Megabyzus turned to address the spectators. "The girl is im-
pure," he announced.

"No!" shouted Eutropius. "That's a lie!"

There were gasps from the crowd.

"You dare to accuse the head of the Megabyzoi of lying?" said
Theotimus. "Here in the sanctuary of Artemis?"

Eutropius was flummoxed. He clenched his fists. His face turned
bright red. "No, Megabyzus, of course not," he finally muttered. "But
my daughter is innocent, I tell you. She is a virgin. There must be a
test—"

"Of course there will be a test," said Theotimus, "just as Artemis
decrees in such a terrible circumstance as this. My fellow Megabyzoi,
remove this girl from the temple at once, before her presence can pol-
lute it further."

Priests moved forward to seize Anthea, who shivered and cried out
for her father. Eutropius followed after them, ashen-faced. More Megabyzoi picked up the body of Chloe and bore it away, followed by her
distraught father. The dancers dispersed, looking for their families.
The musicians stared at one another, dumbfounded.

I turned to Antipater, and saw tears in his eyes. He shook his head.
"How I looked forward to this day, when I might stand once again in
the Temple of Artemis. And how I looked forward to showing it to you,
Gordianus. But not like this. What a terrible day! What a disaster!"

I felt someone's eyes on me, and turned to see, some distance away,
amid the dwindling, dazed crowd that remained in the sanctuary, the

slave girl, Amestris. Her gaze was so intense, it seemed to me that she must have something she wanted to tell me, or to ask. But for the first time that day, it was she who looked away first, as she turned and hurriedly left the temple.

The atmosphere was gloomy in the house of Eutropius that night. I imagine the mood was little better in all the other households of Ephesus, for the death in the temple and the accusation against Anthea had put an end to the feasting and celebration. The Megabyzoi had instructed the people to return to their homes and to pray for the guidance of Artemis.

In the garden, Amestris served a frugal meal to Eutropius, Mnason, Antipater, and me—though I was the only one who seemed to have any appetite.

"A youth of your age will eat, no matter what the circumstances," said Antipater with a sigh. He passed his untouched bowl of millet and lentils to me.

"No one will ever convince me that it was the will of Artemis that Chloe should die," muttered Mnason, staring into space with a blank expression. "Our enemies are behind this, Eutropius. You know whom I mean."

Eutropius looked not at his friend, but at me. I felt like an intruder.

"If the rest of you don't mind, I'll finish this in my room," I said, picking up my bowl.

"I'll go with you," said Antipater.

"No, Teacher—stay. We could use your advice," said Eutropius. He issued no such request to me, and avoided meeting my eyes. I took my leave.

Alone in my room, once the bowl was empty, I found it impossible to simply sit on the bed. I paced for a while, then took off my shoes and walked quietly down the hallway to the top of the stairs. The conversation from the garden carried quite well to that spot. I stood and listened.

"Everyone knows that Theotimus is completely in the grip of the Roman governor," Mnason was saying. "He's determined to bring down all who oppose him—those of us who believe that Ephesus should be free of the Romans."

"But surely you're not saying the Megabyzus had something to do with Chloe's death," said Antipater.

"That's exactly what I'm saying!" cried Mnason with a sob in his voice.

After a long silence, Eutropius spoke. "It does seem to me that his accusation against Anthea was too well-timed to have been spontaneous. As unthinkable as it sounds, I have to wonder if Theotimus played some part in your daughter's death, and then used it as an excuse to make his foul accusation against Anthea—an accusation that will destroy me as well, if the test goes against her."

"This test—I've heard of it, but I've never witnessed it," said Antipater.

"It's seldom used, Teacher. I can count on the fingers of one hand the occasions it's been performed in my lifetime."

"I seem to recall it involves a cave in the sacred grove of Ortygia," said Antipater.

"Yes. Until the test takes place, the accused girl is kept by the hierodules, the female acolytes who serve under the Megabyzoi. On the day of the test, they escort the girl to the ancient grove, which is full of sacred sites, including a cave near the stream where Leto gave birth to Artemis and her twin brother, Apollo. In that cave, hanging by a chain from the ceiling, are some Pan pipes; there's a story that explains how they came to be there, but I won't recount it now. Long ago, an iron door was put in place across the opening of the cave, and only the Megabyzoi have the key. This is the test: if a maiden is accused of having lost her virginity, the truth of the matter can be determined by shutting her up in the cave, alone. If she is truly a virgin, the Pan pipes play a melody—whether Pan himself performs on the pipes, or a divine wind blows through them, no one knows—and the door opens of its own accord, allowing the virgin to emerge with her reputation for purity intact."

"And if the girl is not a virgin?"

"Then the pipes are silent—and the girl is never seen again."

"She dies in the cave?" said Antipater with a gasp.

"The door is opened the next day, and the Megabyzoi enter, but no body is ever found. As I said, the girl is simply . . . never seen again." Eutropius spoke with a quaver in his voice.

"So the sacred cave is exclusively in the keeping of the Megabyzoi?" said Antipater.

"Of course, as are all the sacred places of Artemis."

"But if you suspect Theotimus to be capable of murder—indeed, of profaning the very Temple of Artemis with such a crime—then might he not contrive to somehow falsify the virgin test, as well? You must protest, Eutropius. You must come forward with your suspicions."

"Without proof? With no evidence at all, except for Theotimus's animus toward Mnason and myself, because we hate the Romans? The Roman governor certainly won't help us, and if we dare to impugn the validity of the virgin test, the people will turn against us as well. We'll be accused of sacrilege and put on trial ourselves."

"And subjected to some other supernatural test equally under the control of Theotimus, no doubt." Antipater sighed. "You find yourselves in a terrible situation."

"It's the Romans who've turned the priests against their own people," muttered Mnason. "The Megabyzoi should be the champions of the people, not their enemy."

"To be fair," said Eutropius, "there are divisions within the Megabyzoi. Most are as loyal to Ephesus and to our way of life as you and I, Mnason. Theotimus is the exception, but he also happens to be the head priest. He always takes the side of the Romans, and he does all he can to silence those of us who oppose them. That sorry state of affairs will all change when Mithridates comes."

Mithridates! No wonder they dared not speak openly in front of me, a Roman. For years, the King of Pontus had been positioning himself as the rival of Rome. Everyone in Rome said that an all-out war with Mithridates was inevitable. It was clear which side Eutropius and

Mnason would take. From the way they talked, perhaps they were even agents of the king.

"Mithridates may indeed drive the Romans out of Ephesus some-day," said Antipater quietly, "but that is of no use to us here and now. What can we do to save Anthea?"

"We must pray that Artemis is more powerful than the corrupt priest who speaks in her name," said Eutropius quietly. "We must pray that the virgin test will give a true answer, and that Anthea will be vindicated."

There followed a long silence from the garden. I suddenly felt that I was being watched, and turned to see Amestris behind me.

"Did you need something, Roman?" she said.

"How long have you been standing there?"

"About as long as you have." She flashed a crooked smile.

I swallowed hard. "Then you heard everything that I heard."

"Yes."

"This grove called Ortygia—where is it?"

"Not far from the city. You take the Sacred Way, but you go in the opposite direction from the Temple of Artemis, to the south. Outside the city walls, the road turns west and goes up a steep hill, where a cliff overlooks the harbor. Go a little farther, and you arrive at the sacred grove."

"And this cave they spoke of?"

"The Sacred Way leads directly to it."

"I see."

"Why do you ask, Roman?"

I shrugged. "My tutor says I should learn the geography of all the places we visit."

"You'll see where the cave is, soon enough. The whole city will march out there tomorrow, to see the test performed." There was a catch in her voice. She lowered her eyes. "Poor Anthea!"

"Do you not believe that she's a virgin?"

"I know she is. My mistress and I have no secrets from each other. But I fear the test, even so."

"Yes, so do I," I said quietly. There was more talk from the garden, too low to make out, and the rustle of men rising from their chairs. "I should go back to my room now."

"And I should see if my master requires anything else."

I watched her walk down the stairs, then returned to my room. A little later I heard Antipater enter the room next to mine. The old fellow must have been completely exhausted, for only moments later I heard the sound of his snoring through the wall.

I rose from my bed, slipped into my shoes, and pulled a light cloak over my tunic. The front door would be barred, with a slave sleeping beside it. Might it be possible to jump from the balcony off my bedroom? By the bright moonlight, I saw a good spot to land. I had no idea if I could climb back up again, but I decided not to worry about that.

The jump and the landing were easier than I had hoped. I found my way to the front of the house, and from there retraced the route we had taken to the theater, where I had no trouble locating the Sacred Way. The torches that had lit the street earlier had all gone out. According to Amestris, my goal lay in the direction away from temple, so I turned and headed south.

Bathed by moonlight, the unfamiliar precinct seemed at once beautiful and eerie. I passed the elegant facades of grand houses, gymnasia, temples, and shopping porticoes, but saw not a single person. The goddess had been gravely offended on her feast day, and the people of Ephesus were keeping to their houses.

I feared that I might encounter a locked gate in the city wall, but the high doors stood wide open, and a group of officials, including some Megabyzoi—the first people I had seen—were conversing in a huddle to one side of the Sacred Way, discussing preparations for the trial that would take place the next day, when thousands of people would pass through this gate.

I stole through the opening and kept to the shadows, following the Sacred Way through a region of gravesites and then up a hill, where the road became more winding and narrow, and the paving more uneven. Now and again, beyond the rocks and trees to my right, I caught glimpses of the harbor. The woods became thicker; cypresses towered above me, and the smell of cedars scented the cool night air. I heard the splashing of a stream nearby, and gasped to think that I might be standing at the very place where Artemis and Apollo were born.

I came at last to an opening in the woods. Across a meadow bright with moonlight, in the center of a rocky outcrop, I saw the iron door of the cave, glinting in the moonlight.

I skirted the meadow, keeping in shadow, until I reached the door. From my tunic I took out a small bag my father had given me before I left on my travels. In it were some tools he had taught me to use. Some were veritable antiques; others he had fashioned himself. While other fathers were teaching their sons to barter in the market, or build a wall, or speak in the Forum, my father had taught me everything he knew about picking locks.

I was happily surprised to discover that no guard of any sort had been set on the door; the meadow and the grove all around appeared to be deserted. Perhaps the place was considered too sacred for any mortal to inhabit except on ritual occasions.

Still, I dared not strike a flame, and so I had to work by moonlight. The lock was of a sort I had never encountered before. I tried one tool, then another. At last I found an implement that seemed to fit the keyhole, and yet I could not make the lock yield, no matter how I twisted or turned the tool—until suddenly I heard a bolt drop, and the door gave way.

The fact that I might be committing a crime against the goddess gave me pause. I was poised to enter the cave—but would I ever step foot outside it? I took heart from something my father had told me: *The threat of divine punishment is often invoked by mortals for the sake of their own self-interest. You should always evaluate such claims using your own judgment. I myself have made a lifelong habit of violating so-called divine laws, and yet here I stand before you, alive and well, and at peace with the gods.*

I stepped inside the cave, leaving the door open behind me as my eyes adjusted to the greater darkness. The cave was not completely black;

here and there, from narrow fissures above my head, shafts of moonlight pierced the darkness. I began to perceive the general shape of the chamber around me, and saw that it opened onto a larger one beyond. That chamber was illuminated by even brighter shafts of moonlight. Dangling from a rocky roof three or four times the height of a man, suspended from a silver chain, I saw the Pan pipes. They were in the very center of the chamber and I could see no way to reach them.

A third chamber lay beyond. It was the smallest and the darkest. Only by feeling my way around the walls did I discover a small door, barely big enough to admit a stooping man. I attempted to pick the lock, but I dropped my tools, and in the darkness despaired of retrieving them. As I groped about, my hands chanced upon several objects, including a knife and an ax of the sort the Megabyzoi used to sacrifice animals, and a sack of some strong material, large enough to accommodate a small body.

Then I touched something bony and pointed, like a horn, which seemed to be attached to an animal's hide.

I gave a cry and started back, hitting my head on an outcrop of stone. By the dim light, I saw the glinting eyes of some beast, very close to the ground, staring up at me. My heart pounded. What was this creature? Why did it make no noise? Was this the guardian of the cave, some horned monster set here by Artemis to gore to death an impious intruder like myself?

Gradually, I perceived the true shape of the thing that seemed to gaze up at me. It was the stag's-head mask that had been worn by Chloe in the dance of Actaeon.

I picked it up and carried it into the larger chamber, where I could examine it by a better light.

Suddenly I realized that I had never shut the door by which I had entered. I returned to the antechamber, pulled the door shut, and heard the bolt drop into place.

Taking my time, I retrieved the tools I had dropped and eventually managed to open the door in the third chamber. Fresh air blew against my face. I ventured a few paces outside and found myself in a rocky defile overgrown by thickets. Clearly, this was a secret rear entrance to the cave.

I stepped back inside the cave and locked the small door behind me. I returned to the large chamber and tried to find a comfortable spot. I had no worries that I would fall asleep; I kept imagining that the stag's-head mask was staring at me. Also, from time to time I imagined I heard someone else in the cave, breathing softly and making slight noises. I remembered another of my father's lessons—*His own imagination is a man's most fearsome enemy*—and assured myself that I was completely alone.

Eventually I must have dozed off, for suddenly I awoke to the muffled sound of women lamenting, and the discordant music of rattles and tambourines from beyond the iron door.

A ceremony was taking place outside the cave. The words were too indistinct for me to make them out, but I recognized the stern voice of Theotimus, the head Megabyzus.

At length, I heard the iron door open, and then slam shut.

The music outside ceased. The crowd grew silent.

The sound of a girl sobbing echoed through the cave. The sobbing eventually quieted, then drew nearer, then ended in a gasp as Anthea, dressed in a simple white tunic, stepped into the large chamber and perceived me standing there.

In the dim light, she failed to recognize me, and started back in fear.

"Anthea!" I whispered. "You know me. We met yesterday in your father's house. I'm Gordianus."

Her panic was replaced by confusion. "What are you doing here? How did you come to be here?"

"Never mind that," I said. "The question is: how can we get those pipes to play?" I gestured to the Pan pipes dangling above our heads.

"They really exist," muttered Anthea. "When the hierodules explained the test to me, I didn't know what to think—pipes that would play a tune by themselves if I were truly a virgin. But there they are! And I *am* a virgin—that's a fact, as the goddess herself surely knows. These pipes will play, then. They must!"

Together we gazed up at the pipes. No divine wind blew through the cave—there was no wind of any sort. The pipes hung motionless, and produced no music.

"Perhaps *you're* the problem," said Anthea, staring at me accusingly.

"What do you mean?"

"They say the pipes refuse to play in the presence of one who is not a virgin."

"So?"

"Are *you* a virgin, Gordianus of Rome?"

My face grew hot. "I'm not even sure the term 'virgin' can be applied to a male," I said evasively.

"Nonsense! Are you sexually pure, or not? Have you known a woman?"

"That's beside the point," I said. "I'm here to save you, if I can."

"And how will you do that, Roman?"

"By playing those pipes."

"Do you even know how to play them?"

"Well . . ."

"And how on earth do you propose to reach them?"

"Perhaps you could play them, Anthea. If you were to stand on my shoulders—"

"I'm a dancer. I have no skill at music—and even if I did, standing on your shoulders wouldn't raise me high enough to reach those pipes."

"We could try."

We did. Anthea had a fine sense of balance, not surprising in a dancer, and stood steadily on my shoulders.

"Try to grab the pipes and pull them free," I said, grunting under her weight. She was heavier than she looked.

She groaned with frustration. "Impossible! I can't reach them. Even if I could, the chain holding them looks very strong."

From out of the dim shadows came a voice: "Perhaps *I* could reach them."

Recognizing the voice, Anthea cried out with joy and jumped from my shoulders. Amestris stepped from the shadows to embrace her mistress, and both wept with emotion.

I realized Amestris must have followed me to the cave, slipped inside while the door was still open, then concealed herself in the shadows. It was her breathing I had heard in the quiet darkness.

Amestris drew back. "Mistress, if you were to stand on the Roman's shoulders, and I were to stand on yours—"

"I'm not sure I can hold both of you," I said.

"Of course you can, you brawny Roman," said Amestris. Her words made me blush, but they also gave me confidence. "And *I* can play the pipes," she added. "You've said yourself, mistress, that I play like a songbird."

From outside, after a long silence, the sound of lamenting had gradually resumed. Women wailed and shrieked. Hearing no music from the cave, the crowd assumed the worst.

Anthea put her hands on her hips and gazed up at the pipes, as if giving them one last chance to play by themselves. "I suppose it's worth a try," she finally said.

She climbed onto my shoulders. While I held fast to her ankles, she extended her arms to steady herself against the rock wall. Amestris climbed up after her. I thought my shoulders would surely collapse, but I gritted my teeth and said nothing. I rolled up my eyes, but I couldn't lift my head enough to see what was going on above me.

Suddenly I heard a long, low note from the Pan pipes, followed by a higher note. There was a pause, and then, filling the cave, echoing from the walls, came one of the most haunting melodies I had ever heard.

The wailing from outside ceased, replaced by cries of wonderment— and did I hear the voice of Theotimus, uttering a howl of confusion and disbelief?

The strange, beautiful tune came to an end—and just in time, for I could not have supported them a moment longer. Amestris climbed down, and Anthea leaped to the ground. I staggered against the wall and rubbed my aching shoulders.

"What now?" whispered Anthea.

"Supposedly, the door should open of its own accord," I said.

"If it doesn't, the Megabyzoi have the key," said Amestris. "Perhaps they'll unlock it."

I shook my head. "I wouldn't hold my breath waiting for that to happen. But I wouldn't be surprised if Theotimus joins us soon."

"What do you mean, Gordianus?" said Anthea.

I hurriedly explained that there was a secret entrance in the chamber beyond—and told them what I wanted them to do.

Only moments later, there was a sound from the rear entrance, and a flash of light as it was opened and then shut. I heard a stifled curse and an exclamation—"By Hades—the ax, the knife, the mask—where are they?"—and then Theotimus stepped into the main chamber. In one hand he held his priest's headdress, which he must have removed in order to duck through the small doorway. He stopped short at the sight of Anthea and Amestris standing side by side, then gazed up at the dangling Pan pipes.

"How did the slave girl get in here?" he said in a snarling whisper. "And how in Hades did you manage to play those pipes?"

He was unaware of my presence. I stood behind him, my back pressed against the wall, hidden in a patch of shadow. At my feet were the knife and the ax—the deadly implements with which he had intended to kill Anthea.

I had moved the weapons deliberately, so that he could not pick them up when he entered—and also so that I could use them myself, if the need arose. Theotimus was a large, strong man—he had a butcher's build, after all—and if we were to come to blows, I would need all the advantages I could muster. But before resorting to the weapons, first I wanted to try another means of dealing with him. In my hands I held the stag's-head mask.

While the sight of the two girls continued to distract the Megabyzus, I stole up behind him, reached high, and placed the mask over his head. His head was larger than Chloe's, and it was a tight fit. I shoved downward with all my might, and through the palms of my hands, I could feel the impact of the short, needle-sharp spike fixed inside the top of the mask as it penetrated his scalp.

I had glimpsed the spike the day before, in the temple, when I looked inside the mask. If my guess was correct, the spike had been covered with a poison that had caused the death of Chloe; her motions of panic and dismay had not been acting or dancing, but death throes, as the poison entered her skull and worked its evil on her. After the mask was removed, the puncture mark and any traces of blood amid her lustrous red hair would not have been visible to anyone unless they closely examined her scalp, and there had been neither time nor reason to do so before Theotimus arrived and took control of the situation. No wonder the Megabyzus had expressed alarm and moved so quickly to snatch the mask from me after I picked it up, and afterward had brought it to this hiding place, along with the implements with which he intended to put an end to Anthea and a sack for the disposal of her corpse.

No doubt it had been his intention to wait until the grieving crowd dispersed, and then, at his leisure, to return to the cave, come in by the secret entrance, and deal with Anthea. Before killing her, what other atrocities had he planned to commit on her virgin body? A man who would commit murder against one of Artemis's virgins in the goddess's temple certainly would not stop at committing some terrible sacrilege in the sacred cave of Ortygia.

Theotimus was a monster. It seemed fitting that his own murder weapon should be used against him.

But did enough poison remain on the spike to work its evil on Theotimus? The puncture certainly caused him pain; he gave a cry and reached up frantically. Clutching the antlers, trying desperately to remove the mask, he lurched this way and that, looking like a dancer playing the role of Actaeon. He ran blindly against one wall, butting it with the antlers, and then against another. Convulsing, he fell to the ground, kicked out his legs—and then was utterly still.

The three of us stared down at his lifeless body for a long moment. I was hardly able to believe what had just happened. Never before had I caused a man's death. I had done so deliberately, and without compunction—or so I thought. Nonetheless, I was gripped by a succession of confusing emotions. I became even more confused when Anthea grabbed my shoulders and kissed me full on the mouth.

"My hero!" she cried. "My champion!"

Beyond her, I saw Amestris gazing at me. Strangely, her smile meant even more to me than Anthea's kiss.

"Come, Anthea," I said, stepping back from her embrace, "there's no reason for you to remain a moment longer in this terrible place. I can open the iron door from the inside, using the same tool I used to get in. The door will open, you will step into the daylight, and the door will shut behind you. The trial shall end just as it should."

"What about you and Amestris? What about—him?" She looked at the corpse of Theotimus.

"Amestris and I will leave by the back way. And later, after we've talked with your father, we'll figure out what to do about Theotimus."

So it happened. Staying out of sight, I opened the iron door for Anthea and then shut it behind her. Through the door, I heard a loud cry of joy from Eutropius, and the cheering of the crowd.

Amestris and I headed toward the back of the cave. Under the pipes of Pan, she grabbed me and pressed her mouth to mine. Her kiss was very different from the one Anthea had given me.

It was she who broke the kiss, with a laugh. "Gordianus, you look as if you've never been kissed that way before."

"Well, I . . ."

She gazed up at the pipes and frowned. "What do you think? Would the pipes have played if I hadn't come along?"

"What do you mean?"

"Did the presence of one who was not a virgin prevent the pipes from playing? I worried about that when I decided to follow you inside. But a voice in my head said, 'Do it!' And so I did. And surely it was the right thing to do, for only with the three of us working together were we able to save my mistress."

"I'm sure we both did the right thing, Amestris. But are you saying that you're not . . ."

She cocked her head, then smiled. "Certainly not! No more than you are, I'm sure." She laughed, then saw my face. Her smile faded. "Gordianus, don't tell me that *you* have never . . ."

I lowered my eyes. "I don't know how these things are done in Ephesus, but it is not uncommon for a Roman citizen to wait until a year or so after he puts on his manly toga before he . . . experiences the pleasures of Venus."

"Venus? Ah, yes, that's the name you Romans give to Aphrodite. And when did you put on your manly toga?"

"A year ago, when I turned seventeen."

"I see. Then I suppose you must be due to experience the pleasures of Venus any day now."

I didn't know what to say. Was she making fun of me?

Feeling suddenly awkward, I led her to the rear door and we made our exit from the cave unseen.

That night, after the initial joy of his daughter's salvation had subsided a bit, Eutropius conferred with Antipater and Mnason and myself. The others were at first shocked at my impious behavior in breaching the entrance of the cave of Ortygia—"Crazy Roman!" muttered Mnason under his breath—but Antipater suggested that perhaps Artemis herself, driven to extreme measures to rid her temple of such a wicked priest, had led both Amestris and me to the cave, and to Anthea's rescue.

"The gods often achieve their ends by means that appear mysterious and even contradictory to us mortals," said Antipater. "Yes, in this matter I see the guiding hand of Artemis. Who else but Gordianus—a 'crazy Roman,' as you call him, Mnason—would have even thought of breaking into the cave, and entering ahead of Anthea? Theotimus was counting on our very piety to doom the girl, knowing we would do nothing to stop or affect the trial. Yes, I believe that Gordianus and the slave girl were nothing more or less than the agents of Artemis," he declared, and that seemed to settle the matter.

As for the body of Theotimus, Antipater said that we should do nothing and simply leave it where it was. Perhaps it would not be found for a very long time—unless some of the Megabyzoi were in league with Theotimus, in which case they might or might not realize the cause of his death, and either way would be unable to implicate Anthea or anyone else, and would almost certainly conceal the fact of his death. It would seem that the head of the Megabyzoi, after making a foul and false accusation against Anthea, had vanished from the face of the earth. The people of Ephesus would draw their own conclusions.

"Everyone knows Theotimus was a puppet of the Romans," said Mnason. "People will see his downfall and disappearance as a divine punishment, and a sign that the rule of the Romans and the traitors who support them is coming to an end. Perhaps—perhaps the death of my dear Chloe will serve a greater purpose after all, if it brings her beloved city closer to freedom."

Antipater laid a comforting hand on the man's shoulder. "I think you speak wisely, Mnason. Your daughter was a faithful servant of Artemis, and she will not have died in vain." He turned to Eutropius. "I had hoped to stay longer in Ephesus, old friend, but the situation here makes me uneasy. With all that's happened, I fear that anti-Roman sentiments are likely to turn violent. The faction that favors Mithridates will be emboldened, the Roman governor will feel obliged to react—and who knows what may happen? For the sake of my young Roman companion, I think we should move on, and sooner rather than later."

Eutropius nodded. "I, too, had hoped for a longer visit. Tomorrow, let us all go to the Temple of Artemis to make a special sacrifice of thanksgiving, and another sacrifice to ask the goddess to bless your travels, and then I shall see about booking passage for you and Gordianus to sail to your next destination."

We all retired to our separate rooms for the night.

I was unable to sleep. The room was too bright. I drew the heavy drapes to shut out the moonlight and went back to bed. I tossed and turned. I stared at the ceiling. I buried my face in my pillow and tried to think of anything except Amestris.

I heard the door open quietly, then click shut. Soft footsteps crossed the room.

I looked up from the pillow. All was dark until she drew back the drapes and I saw her naked silhouette framed by moonlight. Before I could say her name, she was beside me in the bed.

I ran my hands over her naked body and held her close. "Blessed Artemis!" I whispered.

"Artemis has nothing to do with this," said Amestris, with a soft laugh and a touch that sent a quiver of anticipation through me. "Tonight, we worship Venus."

And so, in the city most famously devoted to the virgin goddess of the hunt, I killed my first man, and I knew my first woman.

After our visit to the temple the next morning, Antipater and I set sail. Amestris stood with the others on the wharf. We waved farewell. Gazing at her beauty, remembering her touch, I felt a stab of longing and wondered if I would ever see her again.

As I watched the city recede, I made a silent vow. Never in my travels would I pass a temple of Artemis without going inside to light a bit of incense and utter a prayer, asking the goddess to bestow her blessings upon Amestris.

"Gordianus—what is that strange tune you're humming?" said Antipater.

"Don't you recognize it? It's the melody Amestris played on the Pan pipes."

It haunts me still.

III

THE WIDOWS OF
HALICARNASSUS

(The Mausoleum)

The rugged coast of Asia is a jumble of promontories and inlets and
scattered islands. Some of the islands are mere fingers of stone, barely
rising above the waves; others are like mountains erupting from the sea.
More mountains loom along the inland horizon, green and gold under
the noonday sun, hazy and purple at twilight. In the month of Aprilis,
the color of the water changes from moment to moment, depending
on the sunlight, from a harsh lapis blue to the iridescent green of a but-
terfly's wing. Sometimes, at dawn or dusk, the calm sea takes on a me-
tallic luster, like a sheet of bronze beaten perfectly flat.

Amid this profusion of natural splendors, tucked away behind concealing islands and peninsulas, lies the city of Halicarnassus. The south-
facing harbor is protected both from storms and from sight. Traveling
aboard ship, one might never know the city was there, until the ship
sails past a rocky cliff, and suddenly one sees in the distance, set in a
semicircular bowl of land that tilts gently to the sea, a walled city
with a harbor full of ships. Rising impossibly high above the skyline of
Halicarnassus, so madly out of scale that it seems unreal, is the great
Mausoleum.

I had never seen a building so tall. Until that moment, I had not imagined a building could *be* so tall. How could something made of stone rise so high into the air without crumbling under its own weight? How could mere mortals construct such a thing? The Mausoleum was universally acclaimed as one of the Seven Wonders of the World, and now I saw why.

Imagine a solid rectangular podium made of dazzling white marble, rising higher than the pediment of most temples and decorated all around its upper edge with huge statues, like a vast crowd of giants standing in a continuous row along all four sides. Atop that base, slightly stepped back, rises another podium of stone, topped by more statues, and then yet another layer, as tall as the other two combined, with a decorative frieze running around the top, vividly colored in shades of vermillion, yellow, and blue. Atop these three massive layers, envision a temple as wide as the Parthenon with a colonnade all around and colossal statues placed between the columns. Atop that templelike structure, for a roof, place a stepped pyramid of almost equal height, where gigantic lions appear to prowl back and forth—an illusion, since these lions are made of marble. And finally, atop the stepped pyramid, place a colossal four-horsed chariot covered in gold, so high in the air and so blazingly bright that one might mistake it for the chariot of Helios himself, shedding light on the world below instead of merely reflecting it.

Of course, at first sight, the mind takes in the immensity and the complexity of the Mausoleum far more quickly than the monument can be described. The impression is instantaneous: this is a building of the gods set in a city of men, a piece of Olympus come down to earth. As if conscious of its special nature, the building keeps its distance from the lesser structures of the city; surrounding it on all sides is a vast courtyard, a sacred precinct decorated with altars, fountains, and gardens. The monument completely dominates the city, yet at the same time seems alien to it and set apart, an intrusion from a divine realm. This was no doubt the intention of the grieving queen who built it as a tomb for her husband 260 years ago.

I glanced at the wrinkled face of Antipater and saw that my tutor and traveling companion was nearly as awestruck as I was.

"You *have* seen the Mausoleum before, Teacher, have you not?" I said.

My words seemed to shake Antipater from a trance. He snapped shut his gaping jaw. "Of course I have, Gordianus. As I told you, I have family here. We shall be staying with cousin Bitto. Why do you ask?"

I only smiled and fixed my eyes on the shoreline, watching in amazement as the Mausoleum loomed ever larger before us.

As the ship maneuvered around the breakwaters and drew into the harbor, Antipater pointed out other features of the city. Surrounding it were formidable walls set with watchtowers and patrolled by armed soldiers. While much of Asia had been gobbled up by Rome, Halicarnassus, though closely allied with Rome, remained independent. Much of what I could see, including the walls, had been built by the great King Mausolus, whose remains gave the Mausoleum its name. It was Mausolus who made Halicarnassus the capital of the kingdom of Caria and subsequently spared no expense to make it one of the world's most opulent cities. Built into the hillside beyond the Mausoleum was a beautiful theater. Crowning the hill that was the city's highest point was the Temple of Ares, which according to Antipater housed a colossal statue, the finest image of the god anywhere in the world. To our extreme right, spread across another hillside, was the rambling palace built by Mausolus. To our extreme left was another impressive temple, which Antipater explained was dedicated jointly to Aphrodite and Hermes.

"To both deities?" I said.

"Yes. Next to that temple, just inside the city wall, is the grotto and sacred spring of Salmacis. Do you know the story of the nymph Salmacis, and her love for the son of Aphrodite and Hermes?" When I gave a shrug, Antipater sighed and shook his head. "Ah, you Romans! Intent on conquering a world of which you know so little!"

"You know I'm eager to learn, Teacher."

"Then we must be sure to visit the spring while we're here, and I can tell you the story of Salmacis. You can even bathe in her pool—if you dare!" He laughed at some secret joke.

I might have asked for an explanation, but the captain, having spotted a berth, abruptly turned the ship about so that the Mausoleum again loomed directly before us, larger than ever. I could now make out the details of the painted frieze along the top of the upper podium, which depicted a fierce battle between Amazons and Greek warriors. Higher up, I could see the faces of the colossal statues situated between the soaring columns.

"Do you see those two statues in the center, of a bearded king and his queen?" said Antipater. "They depict King Mausolus and Queen Artemisia, forever side by side, forever gazing out to the sea, greeting every visitor who arrives in the harbor of Halicarnassus."

"Extraordinary!" I whispered.

"When we have a chance to inspect the Mausoleum more closely, and circle the building at our leisure, you'll see that the four sides are all slightly different. Artemisia hired the four greatest sculptors of her day and assigned each to design and sculpt the decorations for one of the four faces of the monument. She made it a contest. She also sponsored competitions between playwrights and poets and athletes, and awarded generous prizes, all to honor her dead husband."

"She must have been very devoted to him," I said.

"So devoted that in the end she could not stand to be parted from him. When the time came to inter his remains in the sepulcher of the Mausoleum, Artemisia insisted on keeping some of the ashes for herself. She mixed them with wine and drank them, hoping to quell the pain of her grief. But her grief only grew sharper. Artemisia died before the Mausoleum was completed."

"Of a broken heart?" I said.

"So goes the legend. Her own ashes were placed beside those of Mausolus in the sepulcher, and then a huge stone was used to plug the entrance at the base of the Mausoleum, sealing their tomb forever."

"To die for love!" I said. "But surely that's madness."

"Love is always a kind of madness, sometimes mild, sometimes severe. Even when not deadly, its consequences can be drastic. Consider the story we were just talking about, of Salmacis the nymph, and her passion for—"

But again, as if an impish spirit wished to prevent him from speaking of Salmacis, Antipater was interrupted by the captain, who shouted at us to get out of the way while his men attended to the ropes and sails.

"Bitto is the youngest daughter of my late cousin Theo," Antipater explained as we traversed the city on the back of a mule-drawn cart he had hired on the waterfront to carry our baggage. Normally I would have preferred to walk, but the wide, well-paved streets of Halicarnassus allowed us to ride on the cart without being jostled. We passed through the public square and the markets and then through a succession of residential districts, each finer than the last, as we began to go uphill in the direction of the royal palace. Sitting on the back of the cart, I watched the Mausoleum steadily grow more distant, yet its vastness never ceased to dominate the view.

"I haven't seen Bitto in years," Antipater continued. "Her two daughters are grown and married now, and her husband died a couple of years ago. She must be forty now—a hard age to be a widow. 'Too young to die and too old to marry,' as the saying goes. Unless of course the widow inherits a fortune, but that was not the case with Bitto. Her husband was a successful merchant, but he had a run of bad luck toward the end. At least she's managed to hold on to the house. When I wrote and asked if she could accommodate us, Bitto replied at once and said we'd be very welcome." He craned his neck and looked ahead. "Ah, but there's the house. At least I think that's it. It's a brighter yellow than I remember. Can it be freshly painted? And the front door, with all those bronze fittings and decorations—I don't recall it being so ornate. Can it be new?"

While the carter unloaded our baggage, Antipater strode to the doorstep and reached for the bronze knocker beside the door—then drew back his hand when he realized that the knocker was in the shape of a phallus. He raised an eyebrow, then gingerly took hold of the knocker and let it drop. The heavy metal struck the wood with a resounding noise.

A few moments later, a handsome young slave opened the door. He was just about to speak when a hand adorned with many rings landed on his shoulder and pushed him aside. Taking the slave's place was his mistress, a tall woman dressed in a long red gown belted in several places to accentuate the ample curves of her breasts and hips. Multiple necklaces matched the rings on her fingers, showing off stones of lapis and carnelian in settings of silver and gold. Her dark hair had a crimson luster, as if washed with henna; a complicated arrangement of curls and tresses was held in place by ebony combs and silver pins. Her features might have been those of a woman of middle age, but my first impression of Bitto was of sparkling green eyes, henna-red lips, and a dazzling smile.

"Cousin!" she cried, stepping forward with her arms wide open. Antipater seemed taken aback by her enthusiasm, but submitted to the hug and eventually reciprocated. "Notice, cousin," she said quietly, "that I refrain from shouting your name for the whole street to hear. I read your letter, and I comply. But you'll have to remind me of your new name. Something rather silly, as I recall—oh, yes, I remember." She raised her voice. "Welcome to my house, Zoticus of Zeugma!"

Bitto stepped back and gave me an appraising look. "And this must be the young Roman. Well, Gordianus, what do you think of Halicarnassus so far?"

"I . . . it's . . ."

"Tongue-tied?" She nodded knowingly and rested one hand atop her capacious bosom. "A bit overwhelming, isn't it?" She laughed. "The Mausoleum, I mean. One sails into the harbor and there it is, right in your face, so to speak. One gets used to it, of course, rather like the sun coming up—a miracle every morning, but eventually one takes it for granted. Even so, every now and again I'll be crossing the city and suddenly it's as if I'm seeing the blessed thing for the first time, and truly, it takes my breath away—the way you sometimes notice a sunrise, and think, now *that's* amazing! But listen to me prattle on. Come inside!"

She took us each by the arm and led us through the vestibule, across a beautifully appointed room with vivid images painted on the walls, and finally to the garden at the center of the house where a statue of Aphrodite presided over a splashing fountain. The half-nude Aphrodite stood in a classic pose with one hand resting on her bare breasts, and I suddenly imagined it was a statue of Bitto before me; the voluptuous proportions were the same. I think I must have blushed, for my hostess gave me a look of concern.

"Are you overheated from the journey, Gordianus? I'll have a slave bring cool water and wine, and something to eat. For you, as well, cousin," she added. I saw that Antipater, too, appeared flushed.

We sat in the garden and conversed. Antipater seemed uncharacteristically stiff and ill at ease. If Bitto noticed, she gave no sign. I said little, and tried not to stare at my hostess. I had never met a woman like her. She seemed at once sophisticated and down to earth, mature and yet vivacious.

At length Bitto excused herself, saying she would soon return.

The moment she was out of earshot, Antipater grunted with disapproval. "A hetaera!" he said.

I gave him a questioning look.

"A hetaera!" he repeated. "Cousin Bitto has made herself into a woman of pleasure, and turned this house into a—well, what else can I call it? A brothel!"

"Surely not," I said. I had some knowledge, if not experience, of brothels in the Subura in Rome, and the women who worked in them were nothing like Bitto. They were poor, uneducated women struggling to survive, not the mistresses of their own homes in the better part of town. I frowned. "What exactly do you mean by 'hetaera'?" I said, pronouncing the Greek word with some difficulty.

"There is no equivalent in Rome," said Antipater, ever willing to play the pedagogue, "but hetaerae have existed in Greek society for centuries; Plato and Demosthenes speak of them. They are courtesans of a very high caliber, educated in poetry and art, often talented as singers and dancers. A hetaera may even be invited to a symposium of philosophers, and allowed to express her ideas, and some hetaerae entertain in their own homes, where even the most respectable men are not embarrassed to be seen coming and going. But in the end, of course, their work is to pleasure their clients, like any other prostitute. And cousin Bitto is a hetaera!"

"I'm sure you're mistaken," I said.

"Am I? Did you not see that knocker on the door? A clear indication of the kind of house this has become."

"Perhaps it's there to avert the Evil Eye. I see phallic talismans everywhere in Rome, and they don't always mean—"

"And this statue of Aphrodite looming over us—the goddess of love!"

"Anyone might have such a statue. Who doesn't worship Aphrodite?"

"And those paintings on the walls of the room we passed through—did you not observe the subject matter? Apollo and Daphne, Paris and Helen, Leda and the swan—all stories of lust and seduction."

"I did notice that the paintings were rather . . . suggestive."

"Suggestive? Prurient, I would say! And there's the simple fact that Bitto obviously has money. When her husband died, he left her in dire straits; I know that for a fact, because she wrote to me asking for a loan, and I sent it to her. But look at this house—freshly refurbished and beautifully decorated. And the delicacies we were served, and the wine—that was no cheap vintage. How else could a woman possibly earn so much money? Not by weaving or making baskets or any other respectable occupation, I can assure you of that! And her appearance—it's downright scandalous. She's a widow and should be in black."

"But you said it's been a couple of years since her husband died—"

"In black, I say, until she either remarries or dies. Instead she's wearing a red gown that looks as if she were poured into it, and her hair is all pinned and piled atop her head, when it should be in a snood!"

I considered the implications. "What if Bitto *is* a hetaera? Is that such a terrible thing? If her clients are respectable men, and if she's able to make a good living—"

"But Gordianus—at her age? It's outrageous."

"Is she really that old? I think she's rather . . ." I left the thought unspoken. It would hardly be proper for me to express to Antipater the thoughts I was having about his kinswoman.

"Thank you, Gordianus," said Bitto, for suddenly she had rejoined us in the garden. "I'm not sure what you were about to say, but I'll presume it was a compliment. As for your concerns, cousin Antipater—"

"How much did you hear?" he sputtered.

"Quite enough. I suppose it was improper of me to eavesdrop, but then, it's not exactly proper to speak ill of a woman in her own house."

"Cousin Bitto, I have only your best interests at heart."

"Do you? Then I should think you would be glad to find me prospering. And by the way, before you leave Halicarnassus I intend to pay back to you every drachma of that loan you so generously provided in my time of need."

"Bitto, the loan means nothing—"

"It meant a great deal to me. And the fact that I am now able to repay it also means a great deal to me. Whatever you may think of me, Antipater, I have my pride."

"And yet—"

"And yet I see fit to become a hetaera? I'm proud of that, as well."

"Bitto!"

"Perhaps you forget where you are, cousin. Halicarnassus has a somewhat different heritage from that of other Greek-speaking cities. This was the capital of Caria, and Caria has a long history of strong, independent women—like Queen Artemisia."

"But when Artemisia became a widow, her chief concern was to honor the memory of her husband. If you were to follow her example—"

"I would die of grief, and follow my late husband to Hades! That aspect of Artemisia's legacy I do *not* intend to emulate. I prefer to live, cousin, and to live I must have money, and to have money, a widow of limited means has only two options—and I have no interest in weaving. On the day I entered this profession, I broke my loom into pieces and burned it on Aphrodite's altar. What I do, I do in her honor. I don't take my profession lightly, cousin."

"Even so . . ." Antipater averted his eyes and shook his head.

"Is it that you still think of me as cousin Theo's little girl, and it makes you uncomfortable to imagine me as a woman, capable of pleasing men?"

Antipater frowned. "If anything, my objection is quite the opposite. It's so unseemly, for a woman of forty—"

Bitto laughed. "Cousin Antipater, as long as Aphrodite gives me the strength, and as long as there are men who enjoy my company, what does it matter how old I am? What do you think, Gordianus?"

Unprepared for the sudden question, I opened my mouth to speak, but nothing came out.

Bitto returned her gaze to Antipater. "Cousin, you are more than welcome to stay here, for as long as you like. But I do intend to go about my business. I host small gatherings a few times a month. Other women—some of them widows, like myself—join me in entertaining a very select group of invited guests. The women sing and dance. The men drink wine and talk politics and philosophy, and occasionally, when they say something really silly, I feel obliged to join in the conversation. Later in the evening, some of the guests retire to private quarters off the dining chamber, and in the morning, everyone returns to their workaday life, refreshed and rejuvenated. What could be more pleasing to Aphrodite?"

"And what am I to do during these parties?" said Antipater.

"Participate, of course. The food and wine are excellent. The girls are beautiful and talented. The conversation is seldom dull; some of the richest and most highly educated men in Halicarnassus regularly dine under this roof."

"Rich, I'm sure," said Antipater, "but educated?"

"Oh, what a snob you are, cousin! I daresay you'll find the wealthy men of Halicarnassus to be as refined as those of Ephesus or Rhodes or even Athens. They know your poetry."

"Do they?" Antipater pricked up his ears.

"Indeed, they do, and it's a great disappointment to me that I won't be able to introduce you as my dear cousin Antipater of Sidon, since you're supposed to be dead. When word of your 'death' reached Halicarnassus, you were the talk of all my gatherings."

"Was I?" Antipater could not suppress a smile of pleasure.

"Everyone agreed that the world had lost its greatest poet."

"Well, perhaps not *the* greatest," said Antipater, trying to sound humble.

"In your honor, the girls and I took turns quoting your epigrams about Myron's cow, and we debated which was cleverest. Have you ever actually *seen* that statue in Athens? And can any statue really be so life-like?" She quoted:

> *"Had Myron not fixed my hooves to this stone,*
> *I would have gone to pasture and left you alone."*

Antipater tittered with delight and matched her with another of his epigrams:

> *"Calf, why nuzzle my flank and suckle my udder?*
> *I am the cow of Myron, not your mother."*

I rolled my eyes and cleared my throat. Greeks and their epigrams! Given all the poems Antipater had written about that cow, such an exchange could go on indefinitely.

Bitto sighed. "Alas, I shall have to introduce you as Zoticus of Zeugma, and no one will be at all impressed. But you're so good at making verses on the spot, I'm sure you'll win them over. Well, I'm glad that's all settled."

Antipater blinked, suddenly realizing he had been outflanked. "Bitto, I never agreed that I would attend these parties of yours."

She shrugged. "If you prefer, you can sequester yourself in the library while they're going on. You'll be glad to see that I managed to keep every scroll my husband collected. For a while I thought I'd have to sell them, before my parties proved successful. There's a complete set of *The*

Histories by Herodotus in there. He was born in Halicarnassus, you know."

Antipater's eyes lit up. "I suppose, on those evenings when you play hostess, Gordianus and I can use the time to better acquaint ourselves with Herodotus."

Speak for yourself! I wanted to say, but bit my tongue. Bitto saw the look on my face and laughed. "We shall see," she said. "But look—we've lost the sunlight here in the garden. You can almost see Aphrodite shiver. Shall we move to the balcony?"

She led us to a terrace on the downhill, west-facing side of the house. The view was spectacular. To the left I could see the glittering harbor, to the right the hilltop crowned by the Temple of Ares, and looming directly before us, my mind still hardly able to accept its reality, was the vast Mausoleum. The lowering sun was directly behind the golden chariot atop the monument, framing it in silhouette like a flaming halo.

For a long moment we stood in silence at the balustrade and took in the view. Gradually, I realized I could hear someone talking. Some distance below us and to one side, I looked down on the balcony of a neighboring house, where two women dressed in black sat side by side, the older one reading quietly aloud to the younger. That the reader was older I could tell by flashes of silver amid her blond hair, most of which was contained in a netlike snood. The younger woman's head was uncovered, and her unpinned hair seemed to float like a golden cloud about her face, catching the last rays of the sunlight. Her black gown covered her arms and legs, but she appeared to have a long, slender body. She listened to the older woman read with her head tilted back and her eyes closed, her expression as serene as if she slept. Her features were lovely. I judged her to be not much older than myself.

Bitto followed my gaze. "My neighbors," she said, lowering her voice, "Tryphosa and her young daughter-in-law, Corinna."

"Are they in mourning?" I asked.

"They wear black because of a death in the household, yes. Whether they mourn is another question. I'd advise you to keep your distance from those two." She looked sidelong at Antipater. "And if you wish to fix your disapproval on a misbehaving widow, cousin, turn your attention from me and consider Corinna."

"That harmless young creature?" said Antipater. "She's lovely."

"Quite," agreed Bitto. "And possibly deadly."

"What!"

Tryphosa must have heard his exclamation, for she stopped reading and looked up at us. Corinna opened her eyes at the interruption, glanced at her mother-in-law, then also looked in our direction. At once she reached for a black veil pinned to her gown and pulled it over the bottom half of her face. Her eyes, I saw, were a bright blue. Something in her gaze unsettled me—or was I only imagining it, because of what Bitto had just said about her?

"Greetings, Bitto," the older woman called out.

"Greetings, Tryphosa."

"Are you having a party?" Was there a note of sarcasm in the woman's voice?

"These men are houseguests," explained Bitto. "This young one is Gordianus, who's come all the way from Rome, and this is his tutor and traveling companion, Zoticus of Zeugma. Zeugma—that's in the part of the world you come from, isn't it, Corinna?"

Above her veil, the younger woman's blue eyes widened a bit. "Yes, Zeugma is in Commagene," she said, in a voice almost too low to be heard. "But I'm sure your guest and I have never met."

"I never suggested you had," said Bitto, flashing a brittle smile that perhaps looked more genuine at a distance.

"We've lost the sunlight," noted Tryphosa, and indeed, the sun had just vanished behind the Mausoleum. "Corinna and I shall go inside now. Come, daughter-in-law."

Without another word the two women withdrew from their balcony and into their house.

That evening, while we reclined on plump couches and dined on delicacies from the sea, Bitto told us the story of the two women who lived next door.

"Tryphosa is about my age, but she was widowed long ago—not long after the birth of her son, in fact. Her husband left her very well provided for. By law, the baby boy was his heir, of course, but Tryphosa was able to take control of the estate. That's seldom the case. Usually the husband's male relatives take over and the widow is elbowed rather brusquely aside. But because of a dearth of adult male relatives on both sides of the family, Tryphosa was able to establish herself as head of her own household, in control of the inheritance and free to raise her little son as she saw fit—an unusual circumstance for a woman."

"How is it that you control your own finances, Bitto?" I asked.

"Technically, I don't. My affairs have to be overseen by my late husband's younger brother. Fortunately, he's very amenable."

"You mean you have the fellow eating from the palm of your hand," said Antipater wryly.

Bitto cleared her throat. "To continue the story: Tryphosa managed to become an independent woman, and from early on, there was talk about the way she raised little Timon—that was the boy's name. I suppose he received an education from tutors who came to the house, but most boys of good family are also sent to the gymnasium, to meet one another and receive athletic training. Tryphosa kept him at home. He never made close friends among boys his own age, or took part in competitions."

"Having lost her husband, perhaps the mother was overly protective of the boy," said Antipater.

"Perhaps," said Bitto, "but there was always something odd about that household. Was Tryphosa cautious, as you suggest, or uncaring and neglectful? One hardly ever saw little Timon; it was almost as if she kept him imprisoned in that house. And when he reached the age to marry, a few years ago, instead of meeting with local families who had an eligible daughter, Tryphosa took the young man off to Commagene to seek a bride there. Apparently that's where her own family comes from, and she was able to marry Timon to a girl with a very handsome dowry—young Corinna, whom you saw on the balcony today.

"The three of them returned to Halicarnassus and settled down in that house. There was no party to introduce the new bride to the neighbors. Every now and again I'd see Timon and his mother out and about, but the bride from Commagene hardly ever stirred from the house. Of course, that's not unusual; often a young bride is kept secluded until she's given birth to her first child. I'm probably one of the few people ever to see her, because of my view overlooking their balcony. She likes to bask in the sun for bit in the afternoons. Occasionally I try to engage her in conversation, but it's awkward, having to raise one's voice, and the girl is about as talkative as a stone. It's all I can do to pry a 'yes' or 'no' out of her before she scampers back into the house."

"I imagine she's just shy," said Antipater charitably. "The poor girl comes from far away, and from what you say, she doesn't know anyone outside her mother-in-law's household. A big city like Halicarnassus must seem quite overwhelming to a girl from Commagene, and I imagine she's rather intimidated by a woman of your . . . sophistication."

Bitto smirked. "You mean Tryphosa has told her that I'm a wanton creature and warned her to avoid speaking to me. 'Sophisticated' I may be—but no one has ever whispered that I'm a murderer."

"What are you saying, cousin?"

"Hardly a year after he brought his bride home to Halicarnassus, Timon died quite suddenly—supposedly of a fever, and not yet twenty years old. He had just come into his majority and gained control of his inheritance. Think about it. The boy's father also died at a young age. Tryphosa became a widow shortly after becoming a mother. Corinna didn't even have a child before she lost her young husband. The two of them are *both* widows now."

"Two victims of tragedy!" declared Antipater. "Women of different generations sharing a house, each robbed of her husband, together maintaining a widow's decorum, dressing in black. The older reading aloud to the younger on that balcony—what a touching scene! Do you know, I think there could be a rather good poem in all this." Antipater drew a breath and extemporized:

"Two widows of Halicarnassus lived under the same roof,
One beautiful, young, and shy, the other stern and aloof—"

"You haven't heard the whole story," said Bitto, cutting him off. She was peeved, I think, by his comment about maintaining a widow's decorum. "No one really knows how Timon died, you see. It happened quite suddenly, and the funeral ceremony took place with hardly any notice. By the time most people heard about his misfortune, the poor young man's ashes were already interred in the family sepulcher beside those of his father. Everyone agreed the funeral was arranged with undue haste. Supposedly Timon died of a fever—"

"It happens," said Antipater.

"But when people began asking questions, no one could find a physician who had been called to attend the young man. Nor could we find anyone who'd attended the funeral. It seems to have been strictly a family affair, with only his wife and mother and the household slaves in attendance. Once a body is burned, there's no way of knowing the cause of death—any evidence of poison or injury is gone forever. And then people began to recall the death of Timon's father, which in retrospect began to seem equally suspicious. He, too, died suddenly. And in both cases, due to a dearth of male relatives, it was the widows who came into the estate, despite all the provisions in the law that hamper a woman from owning property outright. And so, what we end up with are two men, both dead, and two women, very much alive, who have managed to inherit everything."

Antipater was aghast. "Are you suggesting that the lovely young creature we saw on that balcony murdered her young husband to acquire his property—and did so with the connivance of the young man's own mother? And now the two of them are happily living together, a pair of cold-blooded killers, enjoying the spoils of an unspeakable crime? Where is your evidence for such a terrible accusation? The whole idea seems absurdly far-fetched."

"To you, perhaps," said Bitto. "I think I may be a better judge of the lengths to which a woman might go to live the life she chooses."

"But for a mother to participate in the murder of her own son, in preference to a daughter-in-law? That makes no sense."

"Again, cousin, I think you underestimate the complexities of the emotions and desires that may drive a woman. You consider mother-love to be the beginning and end of female existence, but not every woman fits the mold of dutiful wife and doting mother. The ways of the world may be more complicated than you imagine." Bitto lowered her voice. "People are even beginning to wonder if Tryphosa and her daughter-in-law might actually be lovers."

"Enough, cousin! When you say 'people,' I presume you mean the men and women who frequent this house on the nights you play host-ess." Antipater scowled. "Well, if this is an example of the sort of wild gossip they propagate, I do believe I would prefer to spend those evenings in the far more rational company of Herodotus."

"As you wish, cousin," said Bitto evenly. Like a good hostess, seeing that the conversation had become overheated, she deftly changed the subject, and we talked of more pleasant matters.

The meal that night must have been too rich for Antipater's constitution, for the next day he complained of indigestion and kept to his room. Bitto could see that I was eager to explore the city, and offered to be my guide.

"Just the two of us?" I said.

She smiled. "Of course not. I'll bring along a slave to attend to our needs. Oh, and a bodyguard to carry my money; eventually we'll want to hire a litter for two, when we tire of walking."

"No, I mean—"

"I know what you mean. Is it really proper for a woman like myself to go about the city accompanied by a handsome fellow half her age, who is not a kinsman? Well, Gordianus, you're a grown man and a citizen of Rome, and you must decide for yourself whether you'll be seen with me in public."

"Will you take me to see the Mausoleum?"

"You won't find a more knowledgeable guide. I know the origin and significance of every piece of sculpture on the monument. If the right guards are on duty, I can even arrange for us to ascend to the uppermost tier. Not everyone is allowed to do that."

"What are we waiting for?" I said.

She was indeed a splendid guide. We began by having a look at the nearby royal palace built by Mausolus. Its design and the methods used to build it, so Bitto informed me, were unique; the ornaments were made of marble, but the massive walls were made of brick covered by a sort of plaster, so highly polished that they glittered like glass under the sun.

A litter took us all the way to the top of the hill where the Temple of Ares stood. Having come from Ephesus, where Antipater and I had seen the Temple of Artemis, I could not be easily impressed by another temple, but it was certainly grand, and the colossal statue of the god inside was truly awe-inspiring.

We descended by way of the theater, so that I could have a look at it, then crossed a lively district of shops and taverns where we stopped for a bite to eat, and then at last arrived at the Mausoleum. First, we circled the monument on foot, so that I could appreciate the decorations on all four sides. Bitto was not sure how many statues adorned the monument, but estimated there were at least 250—the population of a substantial town, I thought. She pointed out the various architectural influences to be seen in the monument, indicative of Caria's location at the confluence of the world's greatest cultures—the lower tiers suggested an impregnable Persian citadel, the upper level with its columns was clearly Greek, and the roof suggested Egypt and another of the Seven Wonders, the Great Pyramid. All these influences had merged in magnificent harmony to create the Mausoleum.

True to her promise, Bitto was able to sweet-talk one of the guards into letting us enter the monument. To my surprise, there was no grand space within, only a narrow, winding staircase that ascended to a promenade that circled the upper level with columns. I had assumed there were rooms within the lower tiers, and that the upper level was an actual temple with a sacred chamber, but according to Bitto, except for the sealed sepulcher at ground level, the entire structure was solid. A hollow space, like the cella of a temple, would have been an engineering impossibility; only a core of solid stone could support the incredibly heavy stepped-pyramid roof with the colossal chariot atop it.

Leaving her slave and bodyguard behind, the two of us ascended the narrow spiral staircase all the way to the promenade. I was panting for breath by the time I took the final step. The size of the columns, seen so close, was truly astonishing, and with the gigantic statues of Mausolus and Artemisia and their ancestors towering above us, I felt rather as a canine must feel standing in a human's shadow.

But when I saw the view, I felt godlike. Beyond the harbor, filled with tiny ships, I gazed over islands and craggy promontories all the way to the open sea. Ships in the far distance appeared as mere points of white, their sails catching the sunlight. I had never been so high up, not even when I stood atop the Capitoline Hill in Rome. To think that I had attained such a height by ascending a man-made structure was almost beyond belief.

"Truly, this is a wonder!" I whispered.

Bitto smiled and placed her hand on my arm. I felt a quiver of pleasure at her touch. The height made me giddy. We were alone on the promenade. Impulsively, I kissed her on the mouth.

She did not draw back. After a couple of heartbeats, she separated her lips from mine, and smiled.

"I think cousin Antipater would disapprove of your behavior, young man."

"Antipater isn't here. He would never have made it up those stairs!"

We both laughed. She began to stroll. I followed her. We slowly circled the monument. Each of the four sides offered a new, breathtaking view.

"Bitto, may I ask you a personal question?"

"You may."

"What you do—is it just for the money?"

She laughed. "That is indeed a personal question! But because you ask so politely, I'll answer. No, it's not only for the money. The life of a hetaera is something I'd always been curious about. I never dreamed I'd have the chance to experience it for myself."

"Then . . . you *like* what you do?"

She laughed again. "Believe it or not, Gordianus, a woman—even a woman of my years—is capable of experiencing carnal pleasure."

"I know that, of course. I didn't mean—"

"Why did Artemisia drink the ashes of her dead husband? As part of some magical spell, because she thought she could bring him back to life? No. She did it because she yearned for him physically, so acutely that she mingled his substance with hers in the only way that remained possible. After my husband died, I found that I had yearnings, too—but I saw no reason to settle for ashes when warm, living flesh was available. For Artemisia, desire was stronger than death. For me, desire is stronger than age." She strolled ahead of me, gazing at the view. "But what about you, Gordianus? Have you known many partners?"

My face grew hot. "I'm not a virgin," I said, recalling my last night in Ephesus.

She looked back at me and nodded. "But there are experiences you've not yet had. That's not a bad thing, Gordianus. It means you have much to look forward to. My cousin is taking you to see the so-called Seven Wonders, but you'll find the world holds many other wonders, made not of stone and bronze, but of flesh and blood."

I think you're a wonder, Bitto! I wanted to blurt out, but I feared I would sound like a fool. "Do you always charge for your company?"

"What an interesting question, Gordianus. No, not always, and not for everyone." She turned about and faced me squarely. "But whether I sell my favors or give them away, I remain a free woman. It's important that you understand me, Gordianus. Men may pay me, but they do not purchase me. No man owns me, and no man ever will. Please remember that, if you should ever feel an urge to kiss me again. Do you understand?"

"Yes."

"I doubt it. You're young, Gordianus. Your heart will go where it wants. But I mean to be clear with you from the start, no matter what should happen between us."

We came to the west-facing side of the monument, and watched the sun sink behind the distant hills. I learned that the only sight in Halicarnassus more spectacular than watching the sun set behind the Mausoleum was watching a sunset from the Mausoleum itself, and to do so standing beside Bitto.

Even though Bitto proclaimed it her favorite temple, since she was an avid worshipper of the goddess of love, we had no time that day to see the Temple of Aphrodite and Hermes, or the spring of Salmacis, which Antipater had mentioned. Bitto said there was to be an annual ritual at the spring later that month, and we would go then.

Antipater's indigestion lingered for several days, but he gradually recuperated. He was at last feeling fit again on the day when Bitto was to hold one of her parties.

"Have you had a change of heart, cousin?" she asked, in between ordering her slaves to get this and that ready for her guests. "Will Zoticus of Zeugma be attending as an honored guest?"

"Alas, Bitto, your food does not agree with me, and I fear that your guests and their conversation would give me indigestion as well. I shall spend the evening with Herodotus, if you don't mind."

"And what about you, Gordianus?"

Both of them looked at me, and both raised an eyebrow.

"I think I *will* attend the party, if I may."

Antipater pursed his lips but said nothing. Bitto looked pleased.

The first guests to arrive that evening were the other hetaerae. There were five of them. As each arrived, Bitto introduced me. Three were of foreign birth, with exotic accents. The other two were widows. They were all younger than Bitto but there was not a tittering girl among them; these were women of the world, poised and self-assured. Physically, each filled a particular niche; one was a voluptuous blond, another a slender redhead, and so on. Their gowns were tucked and belted to accentuate their assets, but were not unduly revealing. Bitto's garment was the most daring; this was the first time I had ever seen the sheer fabric called the silk of Cos. Its green matched her eyes; its translucent shimmer gave the illusion that she was clothed in nothing but a rippling sheet of water that somehow clung to her flesh.

As the hetaerae settled themselves and the serving slaves made final preparations, Bitto drew me aside. "The men will be arriving soon," she said. "Before they get here, perhaps you'd like to choose your partner for the evening."

"My partner?"

"For later."

"Ah," I said softly.

"Is there one you like more than the others? Have another look."

I didn't even glance at the others, but gazed steadily into Bitto's green eyes. "I think you know my choice," I said.

She smiled and gave me a kiss so delicate I hardly felt it, like a warm breeze brushing my lips.

The five men whom Bitto entertained that night were impeccably groomed and well-dressed, wearing colorful Roman-style tunics and expensive-looking shoes. They were all well spoken, and there were a couple whom even Antipater would have considered witty. The conversation ranged from politics (cautious observations on the looming conflict between Rome and King Mithridates of Pontus), to business (the effect such a war would have on trade), to art (the revival of Euripides' *Phaëton* at a recent festival, which all agreed had been a triumph). The food was excellent. The wine flowed steadily but was mixed with water, so that no one became too quickly inebriated.

After the meal, there was entertainment. One of the girls played the lyre while another sang. Both were accomplished performers. Then, while the other women shook rattles and tambourines, Bitto danced.

Watching her, I thought of one of Antipater's poems, about a famous courtesan of Corinth who moved to Rome to ply her trade:

Melting eyes cast glances softer than sleep.
Arms undulate like water from the deep.
Her body when she dances seems boneless,
As soft and pliant as cream cheese.
Now she crosses to Italy, where the Romans she will tease
To lay down arms, their warlike ways to cease.

Bitto was certainly capable of making *this* Roman lay down his arms, I thought, unable to take my eyes off her.

When the dance was over, Bitto joined me on my dining couch. She was flushed from the exertion; I felt the radiant warmth of her body next to mine. Errant thoughts distracted me, and only gradually did I realize the conversation had drifted to the subject of Bitto's neighbors.

"We saw them just a few days ago, out on their balcony," Bitto was saying. "Tryphosa was reading aloud to her daughter-in-law—"

"This scandal has gone on long enough!" declared one of the men, who was younger and more hotheaded than the others.

"But what can be done?" said another, whose few remaining strands of hair were carefully arranged and plastered down on his bald crown. "We all know what must have happened in that house—the poor young man was strangled in his sleep, or more likely poisoned—but we have no evidence."

"Even so, something should be done," declared the hothead. "Indeed, I make a pledge here and now that I *shall* do something about it."

"But what?" said Bitto.

"Surely a male relative can be found somewhere—if not in Halicarnassus, then abroad—to lay claim to the estate and put these dangerous women in their place. And if not, then the city magistrates need to take action. If an accusation is officially registered, the magistrates can seize and interrogate the household slaves. Slaves always know the dirt."

The bald man shook his head. "But slaves can be very loyal—"

"Not when questioned under torture. Give me an hour with those slaves and I'll get at least one of them to confess what he knows about the crimes of his mistresses. And once one slave confesses, the others will follow suit, and then we can bring down the wrath of the law on these deadly widows!"

Alarmed by the man's vitriol, I glanced at Bitto, who flashed an indulgent smile and deftly redirected the conversation to a less volatile subject. Probably the fellow was all hot air and no flame, I thought, but the idea of slaves being tortured and the young widow from Commagene becoming the target of so much hostility made me uneasy. I found myself wishing that Antipater were present; Antipater would have put the hothead in his place. But if Antipater had been in the room, I would not have had the courage to press my thigh alongside that of Bitto, who gently pressed back.

I drank more wine, and soon had difficulty remembering what had made me uneasy, especially when Bitto whispered in my ear that the time had come for the two of us to retire to a private room.

Life at Bitto's house was rather like a dream. The spring weather could not have been more perfect. Antipater seemed quite content to immerse himself day and night in the volumes of the library. As for Bitto and myself, we, too, found ways to amuse ourselves. Indeed, I was surprised that so many ways existed, and that Bitto seemed to know them all.

One evening, as night fell, the three of us—Antipater, Bitto, and I—made ready to head out across the city to have a look at the Temple of Aphrodite and Hermes, and to attend the annual ritual at the spring of Salmacis.

Just before we left, I stepped onto the balcony, and for only the second time since our arrival, I caught a glimpse of the young widow from Commagene. Veiled and dressed in black, Corinna sat on her balcony and gazed at the sunset. She must have felt my eyes on her, for suddenly she looked up at me. Again I saw her bright blue eyes, and again I wondered if I detected something strange in them, or if that idea had been planted in my mind by Bitto's suspicions.

A team of bearers carried us in a single large litter across the city. While Antipater gazed at the Mausoleum, which was in shadow on one side and ablaze with the glow of sunset on the other, I turned to Bitto.

"Do you think that fellow at your party was serious about making an official accusation against your neighbors?"

"What fellow?"

"The hothead."

"Ah, Straton! He often blusters like that. But he's not afraid to take legal action. He's always dragging others into court. A very litigious fellow! I wouldn't be at all surprised if he makes good on his promise, if only to impress me."

"And would you be impressed, if he succeeds in punishing the widows?"

Bitto frowned. "I'm not sure. If only we knew the truth about those two, and what happened to Timon."

Antipater, who had not been listening, suddenly spoke up. "The spring of Salmacis! I haven't been there since my first visit to Halicarnassus, many years ago—you were only a child then, Bitto. But one never forgets the story of the nymph Salmacis. Do you know it, Gordianus?"

"No. Tell me, please."

"Ah, what a poem it would make! Once upon a time, long before there was a city here, the nymph Salmacis dwelled in the grotto that contains the sacred spring that bears her name. One day, a beautiful youth happened by. Since it was a hot day, he stripped off his clothing and made ready to take a dip in the spring. Salmacis, gazing up at him from the bottom of the pool, was overcome with desire—for the youth was no mere mortal, but the child of two gods, Hermes and Aphrodite. His name combined those of his parents: Hermaphroditus.

"Salmacis suddenly emerged from the water, giving the boy a start. She at once began speaking words of love, and reached out to caress him. But Hermaphroditus was only fifteen, and not ready for love, and he found the frantic, wet kisses of the nymph repellent. He dove into the water to escape her, not realizing that in the spring lay her power. She dove in after him. Making herself as supple as seaweed, she wrapped herself around him, entangling his limbs with hers. Try as he might, there was no escape."

"She drowned him?" I said.

"If only she had!" said Antipater. "Since he would not yield to her, and since she could not stand to be parted from him, she cried out to the gods to join his body with hers, to graft them together as two branches may be grafted, merging two living things into one. The gods answered her prayer. When the son of Hermes and Aphrodite emerged from the pool of Salmacis he was no longer a young man, but a creature of both sexes. And from that day forward, the pool of Salmacis has this special property: any man who drinks from it or swims in it becomes partly female."

"If that's true, surely no man goes near the spring!" I said, laughing a bit nervously at the very thought.

"You might be surprised," said Bitto. "There are some who would like to change their sex. They come to the spring of Salmacis seeking such a favor from the gods. Do you disbelieve the story, Gordianus?"

"Well . . ."

"Wait until you've seen the ritual."

Night had fallen by the time we joined a gathering of a hundred or so people in the Temple of Aphrodite and Hermes. Incense was burned on altars. Prayers were chanted to the god and goddess and also to their son. Then the worshippers, most of them women, filed out of the temple.

We followed a winding path through a grove of ancient trees and entered a cavernous recess. Water seeped from the mossy walls that encircled a pool perhaps twenty feet wide and twice that long. The shadowy space was dimly lit by lamps hung from hooks driven into the grotto walls. Points of flame danced on the water. The only sounds were the hushed murmur of the crowd and the quiet splash of water dripping into the pool.

The priests stepped to the edge of the pool. With them was a boy with shoulder-length black hair who wore only a loose robe. While the priests chanted, the boy shrugged the robe from his shoulders and slowly turned about, so that everyone could see him naked. He was still a child and did not yet have a man's hair on his body.

The boy stepped into the pool. The chanting grew louder as the priests called upon Salmacis to show her power. As the boy strode forward, his back to us, the water rose to his knees, then to his hips, then to his chest. He never broke stride, but kept walking until the water closed over his head. For a long moment there was no sign of him, not even bubbles on the surface of the water, and then he suddenly re-emerged, continuing to stride away from us. First we saw his black hair, shimmering and wet, then his shoulders and back, then his buttocks and legs. He emerged from the pool at the far side, and slowly turned to face the crowd.

Some gasped. Other cried out with joy. By the flickering light of the lamps, we saw the power of Salmacis made manifest. The naked boy who entered the pool had emerged from it as a girl.

"Impossible!" I whispered, but beside me Bitto joined the others in singing what I took to be a traditional song performed every year at the ritual, praising the awesome power of the gods to change the unchangeable.

I looked over my shoulder at the crowd. Lamplight flickered across their joyous faces. For a moment, I thought I saw the young widow from Commagene, but the light was uncertain, and the ritual had left me afraid to trust my own eyes.

The priests announced that any who wished to drink from the spring or enter the pool should remain, but that all others must leave. I was not sorry to leave that dark, dank, mysterious place.

"Twins!" I said to Antipater, as we sat on the balcony the next day. "They do it using twins!"

Antipater frowned. "Are you still going on about the ritual? What we witnessed was a divine transformation, Gordianus, not a mime show. It's a wonder to be marveled at, not a puzzle to be figured out."

I rose from my chair and began to pace. "The grotto has all sorts of recesses and fissures; there must be a chamber under the water, large enough to contain the girl, with enough air for her to breath. One twin enters the pool, takes the place of his sister in the underwater cave, and the other twin emerges."

"Gordianus, do you really imagine there's such an abundance of twins that the priests can come up with a new pair every year, never before seen by the worshippers? Besides, boy and girl twins are never identical."

I frowned. "I suppose they don't have to be twins. They merely have to look alike—the same size, the same hair. It's awfully dim in that cave, and the firelight plays tricks with your eyes, and the far side of the pool isn't that close—"

"Do be quiet, Gordianus. I'm trying to compose a poem." Antipater closed his eyes and lifted his face to the sun.

"What makes the females of Halicarnassus so possessive?
To drink a husband's ashes is surely obsessive.
To emasculate a god, as did Salmacis,
Joining her sex with his . . . joining her sex . . . with his . . ."

Antipater's voice trailed off. He mumbled for a bit, then began to snore.

"How my cousin loves his naps," said Bitto, joining me on the balcony. "It's so warm today—such a lazy afternoon. Perhaps we should take a nap, too."

"In the middle of the day? I'm not sleepy."

"You will be."

"I will?"

"After I've tired you out." She raised an eyebrow, then turned and headed toward her room.

I followed.

An hour or so later, I woke in a cold sweat, though the room was stifling hot.

I had been dreaming. In my nightmare, armed men broke down

the doors of the house next door—the house where the widow Try-phosa and her daughter-in-law lived. Their slaves were rounded up and dragged screaming into the street, then loaded into a wagon that was to take them to a place of torture. Tryphosa, resisting arrest, ran to her balcony and threatened to jump. Corinna was driven into a corner, where the mocking soldiers cruelly laughed and tore away her black veil, then ripped the black garments from her body. . . .

I got out of bed without waking Bitto and quickly dressed. Out on the balcony, Antipater was still snoring, with his head thrown back and his mouth wide open.

I slipped out the front door and headed down the winding street to the residence of the two widows. I knocked on the door.

I explained to the gruff doorkeeper that I was a houseguest next door, and that I needed to see his mistress. He told me, in surprisingly crude language, to move on. I insisted that I had something of the utmost importance to discuss with Tryphosa. He slammed the door in my face.

I returned to Bitto's house and stepped onto the balcony. Antipater continued to sleep soundly, though his snoring had ceased. I paced for a while, then leaned over the balustrade and looked down at the neighbors' empty balcony. It occurred to me that, by traversing a couple of narrow ledges and taking a short leap at the end, it might be possible for a surefooted young man to climb from Bitto's balcony to that of the neighbors—or else fall and break his neck.

There are things a man will do at the age of eighteen that he will balk at doing later in life, when he has more sense. This was one of those things.

More than once, poised on my toes, slowly shifting sideways and clinging to small declivities in the wall with my fingertips, I came very near to losing my balance and tumbling backward into empty space. At last I took the final leap and landed safely on the neighbors' balcony.

The brush with danger only served to exhilarate me, so that I felt emboldened to take the next and potentially more dangerous step, to enter a house where I had no right to be. So far as I knew, Halicarnassian law would permit the occupants to kill a trespasser on the spot. But I was learning to follow my nature—to willingly take small risks when greater consequences were at stake. If what I suspected was true, the widows might be guilty of fraud, but not of murder, and I had no intention of allowing the hothead at Bitto's party to destroy the lives of two women simply to impress a third.

Insofar as I had a plan, it was to encounter one or both of the widows, very quickly reassure them of my peaceful intentions (so as to forestall them from having me bludgeoned or hurled from the balcony), then inform them of the danger facing them, and only then to let them know that I suspected the truth. But I was learning that plans, however carefully or carelessly made, have a way of playing out in unexpected ways. Thus it was that the thing I thought would happen last happened first.

From the balcony I passed through a small but beautifully appointed dining room. Finding that room empty, I moved on to a short hallway, where I stepped into the first room I came to, which happened to be the dressing chamber of young Corinna. Because she happened to be naked when I entered—about to step into her undergarments, assisted by her mother—I knew at once that my suspicions were correct. Corinna was no one's widow and no one's daughter-in-law.

I never said a word to Antipater about what I had done, but I saw no way to avoid telling Bitto everything, since it was upon Bitto that I staked my hopes, and the hopes of her neighbors, to stop the hothead from taking action.

After dinner that night, Antipater retired to the library. Bitto could see I was bursting to share something with her. First I made her vow, before the statue of Aphrodite in her garden, to reveal to no one what I was about to tell her, then we withdrew to the balcony and sat under the stars.

First I told her what I had surmised—she raised her eyebrows but did not say a word—and then I explained how I had confirmed it, by trespassing.

"But how is it that you're still alive?" said Bitto, when I told her of my encounter in Corinna's dressing room. "The punishment Actaeon received when he saw Artemis naked is nothing compared to what *I* should do if a stranger suddenly appeared in my room while I was undressed!"

"The two of them were not pleased to see me," I said, vastly understating the uproar of their initial reaction. "So I had to talk very fast—while dodging vases and other things they threw at me—to convince them that I was there to help them. It was actually a good thing that I came upon Corinna naked. If I had encountered her in her black mourning garb, and stated what I believed about her, she and her mother would almost certainly have denied it, and might have continued to deny it, no matter what I said. But since I had seen the truth with my own eyes, there was no use trying to convince me I was wrong. And when I made them see the threat posed by your hotheaded friend, and told them I wanted to stop him, they realized that I was their friend, not their enemy. They've built such a wall of secrecy around themselves, they're not used to trusting anyone other than their slaves and each other. When Tryphosa finally decided to tell me everything, she wept with relief. I think she's wanted desperately to share the truth with someone for a long time. So—can you do it, Bitto?"

"Do what?"

"What I promised them: throw your hotheaded friend off the scent, make him back off his pledge to lodge an accusation against them."

Bitto dismissed the question with a wave of her hand. "It will be no problem. I'll tell Straton that we've all been mistaken about the two widows, that I had a long talk with them to clear the air, and I now see that all those rumors of murder are completely unfounded."

"And will Straton simply take your word for that?"

Bitto narrowed her eyes. "Do you doubt my powers of persuasion, Gordianus?"

I nodded thoughtfully. "I've heard of such people—born in the image of the god Hermaphroditus, having parts of both sexes—but I've never encountered such a person before."

"I have," said Bitto, "but only in certain temples on certain sacred occasions. Many believe that such individuals possess magical powers, and their peculiarity is a mark of divine favor that especially suits them to serve in certain sacred capacities—as the mouthpiece for an oracle, for example. When Tryphosa gave birth and saw the child's dual sex, she might have proclaimed the truth instead of hiding it."

I shook my head. "I suggested something like that to her myself. 'And have my child be raised as a holy freak?'—those were her exact words. Apparently, when the child was born, there was some indication of dual gender, but the male aspect appeared to predominate, and the midwife told them that the female cavity might eventually close up altogether, so Tryphosa and her husband decided to name the child Timon and raise it as a boy. Then her husband died, and Tryphosa had sole responsibility for the boy's upbringing. But beginning with puberty, the 'boy' increasingly took on feminine characteristics—not just physically, as when her breasts began to bud, but in her personality, as well. The child began to think of herself as a girl, and wanted to dress and behave as one. Mother and child experienced a great deal of confusion and indecision, but ultimately, together, they concocted a scheme to go off on a journey and return with a bride—the bride being Timon himself, or herself, now renamed Corinna."

"So bride and groom were one and the same!" said Bitto. "Did no one ever see the two of them together at the same time?"

"From what Tryphosa told me, there were a handful of occasions, as when they first returned to Halicarnassus, when the bride and groom were seen in public together—but the bride was played by one of their slaves, who wore a veil so that no one could see her face."

"And the 'death' of Timon—how was that managed?"

"They waited until they could acquire a recently deceased body, reasonably similar in age and appearance to Timon, then hastily held a private funeral ceremony and burned the corpse. I suspect they had to pay a few bribes along the way, but 'Timon' was dead and his body reduced to ashes before any outsiders had a chance to pose awkward questions. From that time on, the child lived exclusively as Corinna, the widow of her former self."

"But how can Corinna hope to maintain this pretense? If she ever tries to marry—or 'remarry,' I suppose—her husband will see her for what she is on their wedding night."

I shrugged. I was learning that the world was not a simple place, and the people in it were full of surprises. "However Corinna plans to deal with her future, she's determined to do so as a woman. That is her choice, and her mother has done everything possible to help her realize her transition from boy to girl. That's why they attended the ritual at the spring of Salmacis the other night."

"I didn't see Corinna there."

"I thought I did, but I wasn't sure, so I didn't mention it at the time. After everyone else left, a few people, under priestly supervision, were allowed to enter the pool. Corinna drank from the pool and stayed in the water a long time, hoping to eradicate the vestiges of her masculinity. Alas! Having seen her naked, I must conclude that the gods did not see fit to grant her wish."

"Poor girl!"

I nodded. "So you can see, Bitto, why it would be such an injustice for those two to be persecuted by Straton or by anyone else. In a way, they did 'murder' Timon, but his disappearance harmed no one. I believe mother and child should be left alone, each free to pursue her destiny as she chooses, don't you? You might even consider befriending them, Bitto. They are your neighbors, after all."

She pursed her lips. "I suppose I could invite them over to dinner sometime."

"Corinna is shy, but she's a lovely girl. As for her mother—what is it about Halicarnassus that breeds such strong widows? Tryphosa struck me as a very forceful woman, intelligent and resourceful and fiercely independent. She reminded me of you, in fact."

Bitto smiled at this compliment. There on her balcony, beneath a sky full of stars, she rewarded me with a tender kiss.

Spring turned to summer. The month of Sextilis arrived, and if Antipater and I were to attend the Games at Olympia—and see the Temple of Zeus with its colossal statue of the god—it was time to board a ship and set sail.

Bitto had warned me that no man could possess her, including myself. When she saw us off at the wharf, she waved until she dwindled from sight, but I saw no tears in her eyes. It was I who felt a pang of loss at our parting. I blinked and bowed my head.

"What's the matter, Gordianus?" asked Antipater.

"Just a bit of sea spray. It stings a little," I said, wiping my eyes.

The last I saw of Halicarnassus was the Mausoleum, its massive tiers rising to a templelike facade of huge columns and gigantic statues, and the step-pyramid roof with its quadriga of glittering gold surmounting all—the widow Artemisia's everlasting mark on the landscape. But it was another widow of Halicarnassus who left an everlasting mark upon my life.

IV

O TEMPORA! O MORES! OLYMPIAD!

(The Statue of Zeus at Olympia)

"Have you ever seen anything like it?" said Antipater. "Have you ever imagined such a spectacle?"

I had not. Romans love a festival; a play or two put on in a makeshift theater, an open-air feast, chariot races in the Circus Maximus—all these things I had seen many times in my eighteen years. But no celebration in Rome could compare with the free-spirited chaos, or the sheer magnitude, of the Olympiad.

Greeks love an athletic competition. One could almost say they live for these events, where naked young men show off their manly prowess in fierce competitions. Several cities in Greece host such contests, but the Games at Olympia, held every four years, are the grandest and most well attended. They are also the oldest. Antipater and I had arrived for the 172nd Olympiad. Multiplying that number by four, I realized that the Games at Olympia had been going on for nearly seven hundred years. When the first Olympiad was held, Romulus and Remus were mere infants suckling at the she-wolf's teats, and Rome did not yet exist.

This would be the third Olympiad Antipater had attended in the span of his long life. It was to be my first.

Simply to reach Olympia proved to be an ordeal. From Elis, the city that administered the Games, the journey took two days. The road was jammed with wagons and pedestrians. Antipater and I rode in a hired mule-cart along with several other travelers, proceeding on the crowded road at a pace that bored even the lazy mules. Food and wine, sold at roadside stands or from moving carts, were plentiful but expensive. Water was harder to come by. After a long, hot summer, the river that ran alongside the road was nearly dry. Local landowners with access to a spring charged exorbitant fees for drinking water. Bathing was out of the question.

On the first night out we slept on the ground, for the rooms at every inn were already taken, with some guests sleeping on the rooftops. Many travelers brought their own tents. Some of the richer visitors, accompanied by entourages and slaves, brought entire pavilions. Competition for flat, smooth patches of ground amid the rocky terrain was fierce.

"Where will we sleep when we reach Olympia?" I asked.

"About that, Gordianus, you need not worry," said Antipater, and I did not ask again. On our journey to see the Seven Wonders, I was learning to trust my old tutor about our travel arrangements and not to question him too closely.

On the second day, as we drew near Olympia, the road became so congested that the cart came to a standstill.

"Let's walk the rest of the way," said Antipater, climbing cautiously from the cart. He stepped behind a boulder and I followed him, thinking he meant to relieve himself and ready to do so myself. But as soon as we were out of sight, Antipater produced an eye patch and affixed a putty nose to his face.

I laughed. "What's this, Teacher? Do you intend to put on mime shows when we finally reach Olympia?" The query was half in earnest. Antipater loved to entertain an audience.

"I am disguising myself because I do not wish to be recognized in Olympia," he whispered.

"But that hasn't been a problem in our travels so far."

"True, Gordianus, but as you can see, the whole of the Greek world is arriving in Olympia. There's no telling whom we might encounter. So while we are here, I shall sport a false nose as well as a false name."

"You're likely to run into something, wearing that eye patch."

"I'll take the risk."

I laughed. "How peculiar you sound! It must be the putty, pinching your nose."

"Good. My voice shall be disguised as well."

Instead of returning to the crowded road, Antipater insisted that we follow a winding footpath up a hillside, saying it would be worth our while to see the lay of the land. When we reached the crest of the hill, I saw below us the valley of the river Alpheus, with Olympia laid out like a city in miniature.

Properly speaking, Olympia is not a city, but a religious center. Its only purpose is to host the Games, which are dedicated to Zeus. I had expected to see a racetrack or two, some public squares for the wrestling and boxing competitions, crowds of spectators here and there, and of course the Temple of Zeus, which contained the famous statue by Phidias, the Wonder of the World we had come to see. But everything about Olympia was of a magnitude far exceeding my expectations.

I took in the awesome natural beauty of the setting, an alluvial plain dotted with poplars, oaks, and olive trees, with pine-covered hills in the distance. Looming just behind Olympia was Mount Kronos, not a particularly high peak but imposing because it stood alone, and famous because of its history; on its summit Zeus wrestled his father, the king of the Titans, for control of the universe. In the valley below, Apollo once took on Ares in a boxing match, and emerged victorious. Off to the east, where the stadium now stood, Apollo defeated Hermes in a footrace. Hercules himself paced out the running track for them—and there it was, freshly groomed and ready to be used by this year's contestants, covered with raked white sand that sparkled under the bright sun.

At the heart of the complex was the famed Altis, the Sacred Grove of Zeus. Enclosed by a wall, the Altis still contained a number of trees—including the fabled olive tree planted by Hercules, from which the winners' wreaths would be harvested—but where once a wild forest grew, there now stood a host of temples, shrines, civic monuments, and colonnades, erected over the centuries. The Altis also contained thousands of statues, some of gods, but many more depicting nude athletes, for every winner of an Olympic event was entitled to be immortalized in bronze. Dominating all else was the massive Temple of Zeus with its soaring columns and a roof made of marble tiles. The frieze that ran all the way around the temple, below the roof and above the columns, was decorated with gilded shields that glittered under the afternoon sun.

Outside the Altis were a great many buildings of practical purpose, including assembly halls, barracks for athletes, and an opulent lodge where only the most important visitors to the Games would be housed.

Thronging the entire site, filling the valley and spilling onto the hillsides, were tens of thousands of visitors. I had never seen so many people in one place.

We descended into the valley and were swallowed by the festive crowd. My eyes and ears were given no rest. Here was a juggler, and there a poet with a lyre reciting verses. A hawker announced the upcoming program of recitations, musical performances, and philosophical debates. A herald called for family members of contestants to register for a limited number of reserved places in the stadium. A buxom fortune-teller at a makeshift stall loudly proclaimed to a doddering graybeard that he would live to be one hundred, then took the fellow's money, pushed him aside, and called for the next customer.

Men rushed this way and that, or stood in groups, talking, eating, and laughing. A religious procession passed by, headed by a priestess in a trailing white gown followed by little boys carrying trays of burning incense. The sweet smoke mingled with the scent of freshly baked flatbread from a nearby food vendor, and then with a confusion of perfumes as a party of visiting dignitaries—Egyptians, to judge by their *nemes* headdresses—passed in the opposite direction, carried on gilded litters.

We found ourselves in a vast marketplace where vendors hawked an amazing variety of charms, amulets, and souvenirs. There were tiny images of athletes—runners, wrestlers, boxers, javelin throwers, charioteers—as well as miniature replicas of Phidias's statue of Zeus, executed in painted wood, metal, and even glass.

While Antipater examined a small statue of the famous Discus Thrower by Myron, I was distracted by a pair of beautiful women who sauntered by, laughing and whispering to each other. One was blond and the other brunette and both were as tall as Amazons. Their chitons were so flimsy it seemed the merest breeze might blow them away. Married women were not allowed in Olympia, but other sorts of women were. The blond saw me looking at her and nudged her companion. They both gave me sultry smiles, making it clear their company was for sale—and far beyond my means.

It seemed that the entire world had contracted to a single, swirling vortex, and I stood in the very center of it.

That was when Antipater saw the look on my face and asked if I had ever seen or even imagined such a spectacle—the crowded, chaotic festivity of Olympia on the eve of the Games—and I could only shake my head in wonder, admitting by my silence that I had not.

Continuing to make our way through the throng, we came to a group of spectators who stood in a compact circle. From their bursts of laughter I assumed quite a funny mime show was being performed—or perhaps not, for the laughter had a derisive edge to it and was peppered with catcalls and scoffing noises. Some of the spectators turned away and stalked off, shaking their heads and making faces. Antipater and I slipped into their spots to see what the fuss was about.

The tall man who was holding the crowd's attention was barefoot and dressed in beggar's rags, with long, scraggly hair and a beard that might have concealed a bird's nest or two. His naked limbs were long and spindly. His skin, dark and leathery from long exposure to the sun, made his blue eyes all the more startling, especially since he maintained a wide-eyed stare that showed circles of white all around.

"Fools!" he shouted, shaking a gnarled walking stick in his equally gnarled fist. "You say you come here to honor Zeus, but all you honor is your own appetites. Those you truly worship are not the gods, but the athletes who compete for your amusement—the stupidest and most worthless among you!"

"If the Games are so stupid, what are you doing here, you old fool?" someone shouted back at him.

"Just as a good doctor rushes to help in places full of the sick or wounded, so the wise man must go where idiots gather," declared the beggar.

"Ugh!" exclaimed Antipater. "The man is a Cynic, here to spoil everyone's enjoyment."

"Ah! So that's what a Cynic looks like." I had heard of these itinerant philosophers, who cared nothing for personal comfort (or hygiene) and went about loudly disparaging all the things that gave their fellow mortals pleasure. According to Antipater, Cynics were common in the Greek-speaking world, but I had never seen one in Rome, where it was hard to imagine that such antisocial gadflies would ever be tolerated.

A man in a green chiton spoke up. "How dare you come here, to the most sacred of all the Games, and speak against the athletes? What gives more pleasure to the gods than beauty, and what could be more beautiful than the sight of young men running in competition? I put it to you that running is the most noble of mortal pursuits."

"What you're really saying is that you get a thrill from watching all those naked, straining backsides," said the Cynic. The crowd laughed and the object of his derision blushed bright red. "What's so noble about running, anyway? The rabbit and the antelope are the fastest of creatures—and the most timid! Do you think Zeus gives a whit which coward can flee the fastest?"

This elicited more jeering. In Rome, the crowd would have pelted the fellow with bits of food, or even with stones. But though they sneered and shook their heads, no one raised a hand against the Cynic or made any effort to silence him. Just as the Greeks worship athletes, they also respect the free speech of philosophers—even Cynics.

I turned to Antipater and lowered my voice. "The fellow does have a point."

"What do you mean?"

"Well, what is all this fuss about who can run the fastest, or throw a stick the farthest, or keep on throwing punches after his head's a bloody pulp? The idea that all these tens of thousands of people should travel hundreds of miles just to watch some athletic competitions—it's all a bit silly, isn't it?"

Antipater looked at me as if I had uttered a shocking blasphemy. "I suggest you keep those thoughts to yourself, Gordianus. A Cynic can get away with saying such things, but a visitor from Rome is expected to show more respect."

"But surely you're not like these others, Teacher? You're a poet. What have you to do with running and jumping and throwing?"

Antipater simply stared at me. I had forgotten how very Greek he was—and how passionately all Greeks love athletics. Cynics are the only exceptions.

"You can take the boy out of Rome . . . ," Antipater muttered, shaking his head. Then he stiffened as the Cynic suddenly rushed up to him.

"You! One-eye!" shouted the Cynic. "Don't I know you?" He twisted his head this way and that, crouching low and peering up at Antipater, as if trying to see under the eye patch.

"I think not." Antipater drew back, looking flustered. All eyes were on him now. "Who are you, Cynic?"

"I am Simmius of Sidon. And *who* are *you*? And how did you lose that eye?"

"That is none of your business. But if you must know, I am Zoticus of Zeugma."

"And who's this young fellow?" The Cynic turned to me. The odor of his unwashed body was overpowering. "Is this one of the athletes who'll be competing tomorrow? He has a boxer's nose—a wrestler's arms—a discus thrower's chest. A candidate for the pankration, perhaps?"

As Antipater had informed me, the pankration was the most brutal of Greek combat sports, invented by Hercules and Theseus. It was a combination of boxing and wrestling with no holds barred; broken bones and even fatalities could result.

"My name is Gordianus," I declared, straightening my back. *Of*

Rome, I was about to add, but there was no need, since the Cynic spotted my accent at once.

"What's this? A Roman, taking part in the Games?"

I shook my head. "I've come to see the statue of Zeus—"

Ignoring my answer, the Cynic turned to the crowd and launched into a fresh rant. "From the beginning, and for hundreds of years, only those of Greek descent could compete in the Olympiad. Now, to please our Roman overlords, there's talk of allowing anyone who can simply speak Greek to take part in the Games—even Romans! What's next? Shall we open the Olympiad to competitors from all over the world, so foreigners can boast and spit on the ground and erect statues of themselves in the Sacred Grove of Zeus?"

Simmius abruptly wheeled around, ran back to Antipater, and resumed his scrutiny. "But I could swear I know you. What's this thing?" He reached out with two fingers, and I realized he was about to pinch Antipater's putty nose, which had lost some of its shape under the fierce sun and was looking a bit peculiar.

"Come away, Teacher!" I grabbed Antipater's arm and pulled him out of the Cynic's reach. "I've had enough of this fellow's rancid odor."

The Cynic peered after us for a while, then turned back to his audience and resumed his diatribe.

"Simmius of Sidon, the fellow calls himself. That's your hometown, Teacher. *Does* he know you?"

Antipater shrugged. "A man meets many people over the course of a long lifetime. One can't remember them all."

"He might look very different if he were to take a bath and trim his beard. But surely you wouldn't forget those blue eyes. They're quite striking."

Antipater shook his head. "Who can remember anything, in this stifling heat? Come, let's find our quarters for the night."

"And where would that be?"

"We must look for the tent that's been pitched by a man named Exagentus."

We asked around, and soon enough were directed to an area not far from the stadium. I had been expecting a modest accommodation where we might stow our things and later bed down with others in cramped quarters, but the tent of Exagentus turned out to be one of the grander pavilions, a veritable palace of many rooms made of brightly colored canvas held up by ornately carved poles. Exagentus was not about, but a slave who had been told to expect Zoticus of Zeugma greeted us and allowed us to enter, asking us first to remove our shoes. The ground inside the tent was strewn with rugs that felt delightfully soft under my tired feet. The slave showed us to a small side chamber and informed us we would have it all to ourselves. The space contained two narrow cots for sleeping. Between them was a small table with a silver pitcher filled with water and two silver cups. Next to one of the cots a flap opened to the outside, so that we could come and go as we pleased.

I filled a cup and drank thirstily. The water was sweeter than any wine. "How did you merit this bit of luxury?" I asked, falling back on one of the cots, which was surprisingly comfortable.

Antipater shrugged. "One knows people. One calls in a favor now and then." He pushed the eye patch up to his forehead and rubbed the skin around his eye.

"But who is our mysterious host?"

"A friend of a friend."

"But surely you know something about him."

"Exagentus is a wealthy man from Pontus, if you must know," said Antipater curtly. The long day of traveling had made him testy.

"Pontus? The kingdom of Mithridates?" It seemed that Mithridates came up everywhere we went. "Pontus is awfully far from Olympia, isn't it?"

Antipater nodded. "Pontus is at the farthest edge of the Greek-speaking world, to be sure, but King Mithridates himself is part Greek, and a great many of his subjects are Greek speakers of Greek ancestry. No doubt there will be athletes from Pontus competing in the Games, and our host wishes to cheer them on."

"Whoever he is, he must be wealthy indeed, to afford such a—"

A braying of trumpets interrupted me. The steady murmur of the crowd outside the tent rose to a cheer.

Antipater smiled. "They've arrived!"

"Who?"

"Come and see, Gordianus!" He put on his shoes and hurriedly replaced the eye patch. "Is my nose on straight?"

I followed him out the flap and into the crowd, which was moving in a rush to greet the arrival of the athletes. The procession was headed by men in purple robes wearing olive wreaths and clutching wooden rods forked like a serpent's tongue at one end. These were the Olympic judges, who would oversee each event; their forked rods were not mere symbols of authority, but weapons to be used on any athletes who dared to cheat or flout a rule. Behind the judges were several hundred youths, some dressed in loose chitons but most wearing only loincloths, all tanned to a golden brown after a month of outdoor training and elimination rounds in Elis. Some had the long legs and slender build of runners, while others were brawny with muscle. Most were my age or only slightly older. Only a handful looked to be in their late twenties, and even fewer in their thirties—longtime veterans of the Games who, against the odds, were still viable competitors.

The procession drew nearer, passing between us and the wall that enclosed the Altis. The crowd went wild with excitement. Men waved their arms and shouted the names of the most famous athletes, who smiled and waved back. Some of the competitors looked cocky and aloof, but most of the young men in the procession appeared to be as giddy with excitement as the spectators. For many, this was their first journey away from home.

"Behold the best that Greece can offer!" cried Antipater. "It brings a tear to one's eye." I grunted and shrugged, then realized he meant this literally, for I saw him reach up and dab a bit of moisture from each cheek. I looked around and realized that Antipater was not the only spectator shedding a tear at the sight of the athletes entering Olympia. How sentimental these Greeks were, especially the older ones, always looking back to the golden days of their youth spent in a gymnasium!

From the corner of my eye I saw a figure in rags scramble atop the Altis wall. Simmius of Sidon stood upright and loomed above the parade of athletes, waving his scrawny arms and howling like a dog to catch everyone's attention.

"Are these your heroes?" he shouted. "These vain young cocks, all puffed up with pride and self-love? What good is an athlete, I ask you? What do they do but run around in circles, punch each other in the face, and roll in the dirt like animals, grunting and grabbing each other by the crotch? And for such nonsense you all cheer and roll your eyes to heaven! Shame on you all! Instead of fawning over these brutes, you should line them up and slay them for sacrifice, like oxen—that way you'd all at least get a good meal out of them. Oh, you find my words offensive, do you? I say that a young man who exalts his body and neglects his mind has no more soul than an ox, and should be treated with no more consideration, yet you make idols of these creatures. What truly makes a man noble? Not playing games, but confronting the hardships of everyday life. Not wrestling for an olive wreath, but wrestling day and night to sort truth from falsehood. Not lusting after fame and prizes, but seeking truth, and living an honest life."

"The athletes are here to honor Zeus!" shouted someone.

"Are they? I'll tell you why most of these greedy fellows come here—they're hoping to strike it rich. Oh, an olive wreath is all they'll get from the judges, but every city rewards its winners with a fortune in gold and silver, as we all know. Not only do you bow down to these men and throw your sons and daughters at them, you make them rich as Croesus. Then you watch them grow fat and bloated and turn into the very opposite of what they once were. Your beloved Olympiad is a farce!"

Some in the crowd jeered at the Cynic, while others tried to ignore him. The athletes passing before the wall looked up at him and laughed. Some made obscene gestures at him. Suddenly, one of them bolted from the procession and bounded up the wall. He was tall and broad, with massive limbs and a deep chest, and wore only a loincloth. His pale, close-cropped hair and eyebrows, bleached by the sun, were almost as white as his dazzling grin.

"Isn't that Protophanes of Magnesia?" said someone in the crowd.

"He's favored to win the pankration," said another. "What a splendid specimen!"

The young athlete certainly presented a striking contrast to the shaggy, bony Cynic. Protophanes might have been satisfied to show off his own physical perfection next to Simmius's unsightliness, but with his fellow competitors cheering him on, the brawny athlete stripped off his loincloth, grabbed hold of the Cynic—who flailed his arms in a show of feeble resistance—and stuffed the garment in Simmius's mouth, tying it in place. The humiliated Cynic turned his back on the crowd and struggled to remove the gag. Next to him, Protophanes stood naked atop the wall, stuck out his chin, and raised his arms in a victor's pose, pumping the air with his fists.

The crowd roared with laughter. Athletes jumped up and down, grinning and slapping each other on the shoulder. In a spontaneous act of homage, some of them followed Protophanes' example and stripped off their loincloths, then waved them above their heads. The action spread like wildfire through the procession. In a matter of moments, every one of the hundreds of athletes was naked and had his arms in the air. The onlookers were delighted.

I looked back at the wall and saw that Simmius had vanished; the Cynic must have climbed down the far side, into the Altis enclosure. Protophanes remained atop the wall for a moment longer, soaking up the adoration of the crowd, then jumped down to rejoin his fellow athletes, who cheered and swarmed around him, playfully pelting him with their discarded loincloths.

I glanced at Antipater, half-expecting to see another sentimental tear run down his cheek, but his expression was grave.

"Are you not amused, Teacher? Much as I might tend to agree with your fellow Sidonian, I wasn't sad to see someone shut him up. What a grating voice he has!"

Antipater shook his head. "I fear it's the judges who are not amused. Look at them."

The purple-robed elders at the head of the procession had come to a halt and were staring, stone-faced, back toward the commotion. They whispered among themselves, then at last turned around and strode on. The grinning athletes fell back into ranks and resumed the procession. Protophanes strutted past us, smiling and waving to acknowledge the accolades of the crowd, unaware of the judges' dour reaction.

As the last of the athletes passed by, the crowd gave a final cheer and then quieted down. Gradually, people resumed the business of shopping, eating, and otherwise amusing themselves. The day's excitement was over. The swearing of oaths by the athletes and the first of the competitions would begin the next morning.

"There's still an hour or two of daylight left. What shall we do now?" I asked Antipater. I feared he might suggest that we attend a philosophical debate or poetry recitation, but instead he pointed toward the Altis enclosure. Above the wall I could see the marble roof of the Temple of Zeus, and some of the golden shields that decorated the frieze above the columns.

"We came here to see a Wonder of the World, did we not? I should hate for us to miss a single one of the competitions in the next few days, so why not see it now?"

To this proposal I enthusiastically agreed.

There was a queue to enter the Temple of Zeus. A donation was demanded of each visitor, and admission was by guided tour only. Our group of fifteen gathered at the bottom of the steps. There we were met by a young guide who informed us that he was a descendant of Phidias, the Athenian sculptor who had created the fabled statue of Zeus.

"As you may know," the guide said, "the statue is of a type invented by Phidias which is called 'chryselephantine'—the god's flesh is made of ivory, while his hair, sandals, and drapery are plated with gold. The statue of Athena by Phidias that stands in the Parthenon in Athens is of this same sort. The gold is incorruptible, but the ivory must be regularly oiled and polished to prevent it from cracking. Here in Olympia, this sacred duty was bequeathed to the descendants of Phidias. It is our hereditary honor to anoint the statue of Zeus. Thus we serve the god, and also the memory of our ancestor, who was the greatest of all the sculptors who ever lived."

This seemed a rather extravagant claim, and a bit suspect, coming from a descendant. But I decided to reserve judgment until I saw the statue for myself.

"Before we enter the temple, allow me to give you some history, and to point out some architectural details," the guide continued. "The Temple of Zeus was completed in time for the eighty-first Olympiad; that was three hundred sixty-four years ago. The statue of Zeus was not installed until some twenty-four years later, in time for the eighty-seventh Olympiad. Thus, the statue you are about to see is three hundred forty years old. When you see it, you will understand why it is commonly said that nature created the elephant so that Phidias might harvest the tusks to make his statue."

I rolled my eyes. "He certainly fawns over his ancestor," I whispered to Antipater, who shushed me.

"The temple itself is a marvel. It is two hundred thirty feet long and ninety-five feet wide, and stands sixty-eight feet high. The apex of the pediment is surmounted by a thirty-foot statue of Nike, goddess of victory; appropriately, she gazes down on the ancient stadium to the east, from which the runners can look up to her for inspiration.

"Any questions? No? In a moment, then, we shall enter the antechamber of the temple. There you will see a statue of King Iphitos of Elis, who established the games here at Olympia. He did so at the behest of the Oracle at Delphi, who declared that all Greeks must cease fighting and lay down their arms in the months preceding the Games. Thus did the Olympiad bring to the Greeks the boon of peace and put an end to constant warfare."

"It's the Romans who enforce the peace between us now," mumbled a man behind me. Others in the group grunted to acknowledge this comment. Though they had no way of knowing that I was Roman, I suddenly felt self-conscious.

"In the antechamber," the guide continued, "you will also see the heavy bronze shields that are carried in the footrace of the armored hoplites on the last day of the Games. And around the top of the chamber's walls you will see a frieze that depicts the labors of Hercules, an inspiration to the athletes who come here and a reminder that, like Hercules, they must constantly prove themselves. Now, if you will follow me—"

I raised my hand. "Actually, I have a question."

The man behind me, who had mumbled the anti-Roman comment, made a grunt. I felt painfully aware of my Roman accent, but pressed on. "You mentioned the shields carried by the hoplites in their race. But I've been wondering about the gilded shields that decorate the frieze that runs all the way around the temple. What do they signify?"

"An excellent question! There are twenty-one gilded shields in all. They were donated some fifty-four years ago by the Roman general Lucius Mummius when he visited Olympia after he put down the revolt of the Achaean League."

"After he stamped out the last flicker of Greek resistance!" hissed the man behind me. Antipater looked back at the man and shushed him.

The guide continued. "It was feared that Mummius would do to Olympia what he had done to Corinth—loot the temples and shrines, perhaps raze the entire site—but instead Mummius saw fit to honor the Altis with new statues of Zeus, and to donate the golden shields that you see adorning the frieze of the temple."

"Paid for by booty from defeated Greeks!" growled the man behind me.

"In gratitude," the guide went on, "the city of Elis, which administers the sanctuary of Olympia, erected an equestrian statue of Mummius, which stands in a place of honor among the statues of gods and athletes here in the Altis."

"And should be pulled down!" declared the man behind me, no longer lowering his voice.

"You there!" said the guide. "I remind you that we are about to enter the house of Zeus. You will not raise your voice again—indeed, you will not speak at all once we enter the temple—or I shall have you ejected. Do you understand?"

I turned around to take a good look at the grumbler. He was a brawny fellow with blond hair and a neatly trimmed beard—perhaps a former athlete himself. He stared back at me for a moment, then at Antipater, who was also looking at him. The man looked elsewhere and mumbled a begrudging acknowledgment to the guide.

We followed the guide up the steps to the entrance, where the huge bronze doors stood open. I paused for a moment to gaze up at the massive marble columns of the portico, then followed the group into the temple.

Perhaps the statue of Iphitos and the hoplites' shields were impressive, but I could not say, for upon entering the antechamber I had my first glimpse of the statue that occupied the farthest recess of the temple, and from that moment my senses could register nothing else.

I forgot my discomfort at the anti-Roman sentiment I had just encountered. I gaped, and would have walked straight on, directly to the statue, had not Antipater taken hold of my arm. The guide droned on—recounting each of Hercules' labors, I imagine—but I did not hear. I stared in awe at Zeus seated upon his throne.

There are rare moments in life when the mind refuses to accept what the eye beholds, because the thing beheld simply cannot exist in the world as we know it; it has no place in nature, is thus unnatural and therefore *cannot* be. Almost always the mind is correct and the eye is mistaken, duped by an optical illusion; but until this tug-of-war between mind and eye is resolved, a kind of stupor grips the beholder. So it was when I beheld Zeus—for surely this was not a mere statue, but the god himself.

At last the guide ceased chattering and stepped past me, inviting the group to follow. With Antipater still holding my arm—a good thing, for I needed his touch to steady me—I moved forward. Each step brought me closer to the god. Larger and larger he loomed, until I felt almost suffocated by his presence. As vast as it was, the temple could hardly contain him. Indeed, were he to rise from his throne, the temple would have been unroofed and the columns scattered.

The dim lighting contributed to the eerie effect. The doorway faced east, to catch the rays of the rising sun, and to allow Zeus to gaze out at the stadium in the distance; by late afternoon, the daylight that penetrated the temple was soft and uncertain, supplemented by braziers on tripods and by torches set in sconces along the high galleries on either side. A long pool directly before the throne of Zeus reflected his image, along with flickering points of light from the flames. The pool added yet another element of unreality, for there was something very strange about the surface. It seemed somehow denser than water, shimmering with a reflectivity more akin to polished black marble. When we reached the edge of the pool and stared down at it, I realized that it was not filled with water at all, but with olive oil. This was the reservoir used by the descendants of Phidias who daily anointed the statue.

The voice of the guide gradually penetrated my consciousness. "The throne of the god is itself a remarkable creation, larger and more opulent than the grandest monument to be found in many a city. Fierce-looking sphinxes form the arms of the chair; their wings curve up to support the god's elbows. The massive struts and sides of the throne are covered with exquisite paintings and sculptures depicting tales of gods and heroes. Not even the smallest portion of the throne is without ornament; every surface is decorated with elaborately carved marble, or plated with precious metals, or encrusted with sparkling jewels. If Phidias had created nothing more than the Throne of Zeus, we would still say he was the greatest of all artists.

"But behold Zeus himself! The awesome serenity of his visage beneath the golden wreath upon his brow, the majesty of his broad chest and powerful arms, the elegance of the golden drapery that falls from one shoulder and covers his loins. In his left hand he holds a scepter surmounted by a golden eagle. In his right palm he displays to us winged Nike, goddess of victory. Some say that Phidias took his inspiration from the *Iliad;* when Zeus merely nodded his head, says Homer, 'All Olympus to the center shook!' Others think that Phidias must have beheld Zeus with his own eyes."

"I can believe it!" I whispered.

"Now, if you will follow me back toward the antechamber, we shall ascend to the gallery, and you will be privileged to behold the statute at even closer quarters."

As we made our way up a narrow spiral staircase in single file, my attention was briefly drawn from the statue. In a daze I took in the sumptuous architectural details of the temple interior. This was a smaller structure than the great Temple of Artemis in Ephesus, but impressive nonetheless. What amazing wealth these Greeks had accumulated in previous centuries, and what remarkable artists and engineers had lived among them!

When we reached the gallery I paused to lean over the parapet and look down at the long reflecting pool, which seen from above was utterly black. Another group of tourists had just entered and were gazing in awe at the statue.

Antipater hissed at me, and I hastened to join the rest of our group at the western end of the gallery. Our guide was silent, which seemed appropriate, for no words could adequately capture the sensation of standing so near the god. Pressed against the balustrade, I stood as close as any mortal could to the face of Zeus Almighty. Had the god turned his head, we would have been eye to eye. Even seen this close, the details of his golden beard, ivory flesh, and lapis eyes were uncanny. Had he blinked, or raised his mighty chest with a sigh, or shaken his head to unloose the golden curls upon his shoulders, I would not have been surprised, for in that moment I had no doubt that the vessel created by Phidias did in fact contain the god.

I flinched, for by the flickering light I perceived a tremor of intent.

Zeus was about to turn his face to mine! I braced myself, for were the god to speak, his voice would surely be more deafening than a thunderclap.

Then I blinked, and realized the movement I perceived had been an illusion, for no one around me had reacted to it, and the statue remained just as it was. *Fool!* I said to myself. *Everyone knows the gods in temples never speak aloud. They express themselves through oracles, or dreams, or flights of birds that only augurs can decipher.*

Still, as the tour reached its end and the guide led us back to the entrance, I kept looking over my shoulder, feeling the gaze of Zeus upon me.

As we exited the temple and reemerged into daylight, I blinked and shook my head, as if awakening from a dream. The guide seemed unfazed. After all, he gave this tour many times each day, and was privileged to actually touch the statue to anoint the ivory. He handed each of us a small wooden disk. "Use it today, and this token will allow you to visit the workshop of Phidias for half the usual donation requested. The workshop still contains the actual tools and molds used by the master sculptor and his assistants."

"Shall we press on to see the workshop, Gordianus?" said Antipater.

I sighed, feeling suddenly exhausted. "I think I should lie down for a while. It must be the heat." I felt a bit chagrined, because it was usually Antipater who grew tired first.

"Very well, let's return to our host's pavilion. The crowd will be up and milling about until long past sundown, but there's no reason we shouldn't go to bed early."

"Should we buy a bit of food from one of the vendors, so as to have something to eat later?"

"Oh, I suspect there will be plenty to eat and drink in the pavilion, anytime we need it. Our host can afford to be generous."

The sun was low on the horizon as we crossed the Altis. The statues all around cast long shadows. One of the longest was that of a warrior atop a horse. His Roman armor made him conspicuous among the naked bronze athletes. I paused to read the Greek inscription on the pedestal:

TO THE HONOR OF LUCIUS MUMMIUS
COMMANDER-IN-CHIEF OF THE ROMANS
THE CITY OF ELIS ERECTS THIS STATUE
IN RECOGNITION OF HIS VIRTUE
AND THE KINDNESS HE HAS SHOWN
TO ELIS AND TO THE REST OF THE GREEKS

I gazed up at the figure of Mummius. His bland face showed no emotion. One hand held the reins of his horse. The other was raised in a gesture of peace.

"So here it is, the statue the guide mentioned. What do you think of it, Teacher?" I turned my head, only to see that Antipater was striding quickly on. I hurried to catch up.

Back at our quarters, I fell onto my cot and was asleep at once.

In the middle of the night I woke, prompted by a need to pass water. I stumbled out the flap, still half-asleep, and made my way to a nearby trench that had been dug for the purpose. The moon was nearly full, filling the valley with a dull white light and casting stark black shadows. Not everyone was dozing; above the general quiet I heard echoes of drinking songs and bits of distant conversation, and here and there I saw the glow of a few campfires that were still burning.

I returned to the tent, lifted the flap to our quarters, and was about to duck back inside when I heard a voice coming from elsewhere within the pavilion.

"Something will have to be done about him, and soon!" The speaker seemed to have raised his voice in a sudden burst of emotion. He sounded oddly familiar. Someone answered him, but in a much lower tone that was barely audible.

The first man spoke again. "Harmless? It's all an act! The fellow's dangerous, I tell you. Deadly dangerous! I think he's a spy for the Romans."

This prompted another hushed reply, and then the first man spoke again. His voice was naggingly familiar. "Whether he's a spy or not, he's still liable to expose us as agents of Mithridates. The Sidonian must die!"

At this, I was wide awake. Not only had Antipater been recognized, but someone was talking about killing him—someone in the very pavilion where we were sleeping!

I ducked under the flap. The little room was so dark that I could barely make out the shape of Antipater on his cot, apparently sound asleep. But when I reached out to shake him awake, what I took to be his shoulder turned out to be only a pillow and some folds of a blanket.

"Teacher?" I whispered.

Antipater was gone.

I stood stock-still in the silence and listened. I no longer heard the others elsewhere in the pavilion. Had they heard me whisper? I considered trying to find my way through the maze of flaps and dividers to confront them—whoever they were—but decided that would be madness. If they thought Antipater was a Roman spy, they would know that I was his traveling companion, and would surely wish me harm as well. What had Antipater been thinking, to arrange for us to lodge in a pavilion full of agents for the King of Pontus?

And where *was* Antipater?

I could not possibly stay in the tent. Nor did it make sense to go about shouting for Antipater, waking others and calling attention to myself. I left our sleeping quarters and under the bright moonlight I threaded my way past smaller tents nearby as well as a number of men sleeping in the open on blankets. By a lucky chance I found an unclaimed spot under an olive tree. Sitting with my back against the trunk, hidden amid deep moon-shadows, I had a clear view of the flap to our quarters. I settled in to watch for Antipater, thinking he would surely return soon. Perhaps, like me, he had gone out to relieve himself, or, unable to sleep, had taken a nocturnal stroll. I would watch for his return, and stop him before he entered the tent where someone—perhaps even our host?—was plotting to kill him.

I underestimated the power of Somnus—or Hypnos, as the Greeks call the god of sleep. Though I fought to keep my eyes open, a power stronger than myself kept shutting them, and the next thing I knew, someone was shaking me awake. I opened my eyes and was startled to see, crouching beside me, a stranger with an eye patch and a lumpy nose—then realized it was Antipater.

"Teacher! Are you all right?"

"Of course I am. And you, Gordianus? Could you not sleep inside the tent?"

By the soft light of dawn, people all around were waking and stirring. In starts and stops, for I was not yet fully awake, I tried to explain to him what I had overheard during the night.

Antipater was silent for a long moment, then shook his head. "It was a dream, Gordianus. What you heard were voices from a dream."

I shook my head. "No, Teacher, I was wide awake—as awake as I am right now."

He raised an eyebrow. "Which is still half-asleep, I think. Perhaps you heard something, yes, but I'm sure you misunderstood."

"No, Teacher, I'm absolutely certain. . . ."

But was I? The day before, I had been certain that Zeus was about to speak to me, and that had been an illusion. Suddenly the events of the night seemed murky and unreal. "But where were you last night, Teacher? Where did you go?"

He smiled. "It was too hot and stuffy inside the tent for me to sleep. Like you, I found a spot outdoors and slept like a stone. Now wake up, sleepyhead! Let's have a bite to eat in our host's pavilion."

"Are you mad? They may poison you!"

"Gordianus, your fears are groundless, I assure you. But if you wish, we can purchase our breakfast from a vendor on our way to the Bouleuterion."

"The what?"

"The building in which the athletes will take their solemn oath. They must all promise, before a statue of Zeus clutching thunderbolts, to compete fairly, obey the judges, accept no bribes, and foreswear the use of magic. They do so in small groups, then come out to be greeted by the crowd. It's a wonderful chance to see all the athletes at close quarters."

"Didn't we already see them all yesterday, in the procession?"

Antipater rolled his eyes, then without another word he stood up and headed off. I followed, stumbling a bit, for my limbs were still heavy with sleep.

Outside the Bouleuterion, a crowd had already gathered, but something was amiss. No sooner had we arrived than a complete stranger turned to Antipater and asked, "Is it true, what people are saying?"

"What is that?"

"That Protophanes of Magnesia won't be allowed to take the oath this morning—which means he won't be able to compete in the pankration!"

"But why not?"

"Because he laid hands on that Cynic yesterday. Had Protophanes not touched the old fool, there'd be no problem. But because he manhandled the fellow, and because it happened on the Altis enclosure wall, the judges think Protophanes may have broken some sacred law or other."

"It's ridiculous!" said another man. "Protophanes only did what we all wanted to do."

"But he shouldn't have touched the philosopher," said another, piously wagging his forefinger.

"They say it may all be up to Simmius the Cynic," said another.

"How's that?" said Antipater.

"It seems that none of the judges actually saw what happened—they were too far ahead and didn't look back in time. So they've called on Simmius to testify. If he shows up this morning and declares that Protophanes laid hands on him atop the Altis wall, then it's all over for Protophanes. Four years of training and his chance for fame and glory—gone like a puff of smoke! And all because of a technicality."

"And if the Cynic doesn't show up?" said Antipater.

"Then perhaps Protophanes can take the oath after all. I doubt that any of the other athletes will testify against him, and nor will any of the spectators."

There was a sudden commotion. The crowd parted for Protophanes, who was coming through, dressed in a modest chiton. Men cheered and clapped. Some rushed forward to give him a supportive slap on the shoulder. The young man, who had been so exuberant the previous day, showed a very different face this morning. Looking grim but determined, Protophanes mounted the steps to the Bouleuterion, but two of the purple-robed judges stepped forward and used their forked rods to block his way.

"You know the charge against you, Protophanes," said one.

The athlete opened his mouth to speak, then thought better of it. Showing disrespect to the judges would disqualify him from competition as surely as an act of impiety. He swallowed hard and spoke in a low growl. "When will it be decided?"

"Soon enough, I think," said the judge. "Here comes the Cynic now."

People stepped back to make way for Simmius, who had just appeared at the edge of the crowd. As usual, the Cynic was making a spectacle of himself, staggering as if he were drunk, clutching at his throat with one hand and making a beseeching gesture with the other.

"What's he playing at now?" said one of the onlookers in disgust.

"He's making fun of Protophanes—holding up his right hand, the way fighters in the pankration do when they admit defeat! What nerve the Cynic has, to make fun of a young man even as he's about to ruin his life!"

Simmius staggered directly toward Antipater and me, coming so close I jumped back. As he veered away, I heard him cry out in a thin, croaking voice, "Thirsty! So thirsty!"

"He's not acting," I said to Antipater. "Something's really wrong with him."

On the steps of the Bouleuterion, directly in front of Protophanes and the judges, Simmius collapsed. He thrashed his bony arms and legs and rolled his head. "Thirsty! By the gods, so thirsty!"

After a final, hideous convulsion, Simmius rolled over, facedown, with his limbs splayed—and did not move again. The Cynic was dead. His right arm was extended above his head, so that his gnarled forefinger appeared to be pointing directly at Protophanes.

The event was so unexpected and so bizarre that for a long moment no one moved or spoke. Then someone cried out: "Protophanes has killed him!"

There was a great commotion as people pressed forward, drawing as close to the dead Cynic as they dared. The judges took charge, fending off the crowd with their forked rods. Protophanes stayed where he was, looking dumbstruck.

Pushed forward by those behind me, I found myself at the front of the crowd, very close to the corpse. More judges appeared from inside the Bouleuterion. One of them poked his rod at me and told me to back away. I pushed back against the crowd, which pushed forward. Fearing I might step on the corpse, I found myself staring down at the dead Cynic. The forefinger that pointed toward Protophanes was smeared with blood. Looking closely at the finger, I saw two puncture wounds.

"Poisoned! The Cynic must have been poisoned!" cried someone.

"For shame, Protophanes! Why did you do it?" cried another.

"We all know why," said someone else. "But murder, Protophanes? No man can commit such a shameless crime and expect to compete in the Games of Zeus."

It appeared that Protophanes was to be tried then and there, if not by the Olympic judges, then by the court of public opinion. People immediately assumed he must be guilty of the Cynic's death.

"For shame!" said a man behind me. I felt a shiver of recognition. It was the same voice that had muttered words of disdain about Mummius and the Romans behind me at the Temple of Zeus. I frowned, for his voice was familiar for another reason. . . .

I turned around and spotted the speaker in the crowd, recognizing him by his brawny shoulders and blond beard. In one hand he held a sack made of thick leather, tightly cinched with rope at the top.

"But how did Protophanes manage it?" asked someone.

"Must have tricked the old fool into eating something," answered another.

"Or more likely *drinking* something!"

"The Cynic wasn't poisoned," I said.

"What's that?" The judge who had poked me now peered at me and wrinkled his brow. "Speak up, young man!"

I cleared my throat. "Simmius wasn't poisoned. Not properly speaking—not by anything he ate or drank, anyway."

"Then what killed him?" said the judge.

"A snake."

This caused a new commotion in the crowd. Was a deadly snake loose among us?

"Look there," I said, "at his finger. A snake bit him. I can see the marks from here."

Some of the judges stooped down to examine the puncture wounds in Simmius's forefinger.

"He complained of a terrible thirst," I said. "My father—" I was about to explain to them that my father back in Rome had taught me everything there was to know about snake venoms and their effects, the handling of snakes, the extraction of their venom—but what did they care about that? "It was probably a dipsas that bit him. The venom of the dipsas causes terrible thirst, then convulsions, and then death, all in a matter of moments."

"I think this young man may be right," said one of the judges who had been examining the wounds. "But I'm not sure this absolves Protophanes. It's awfully convenient that the Cynic should have died just now. How did he come to be bitten by a dipsas just when he was about to testify before the judges? Where is this snake, and how did it come to be here? If Protophanes didn't do the deed himself, perhaps he arranged for someone else—"

"The snake was brought to Olympia not by any friend of Protophanes," I said, "but by an agent working for a foreign king—the sort of person who's used to carrying poisons and other weapons for killing people. This man was plotting to kill Simmius of Sidon at least as early as last night; I know, because I overheard him. He's standing right there." I pointed at the man with the blond beard. "How he tricked Simmius into reaching into that sack he carries is anyone's guess."

The crowd stepped back from the man, who gave me a venomous look.

"You, there!" cried one of the judges. "What do you carry in that sack?"

The man smiled crookedly. "That's what the Cynic said, when I told him it contained a gift for him. See for yourself!" he shouted, untying the rope and flinging the sack before him. A serpent as long as my fore-arm flew through the air and landed on the steps, not far from the body of Simmius. Hissing and writhing furiously, the creature darted first in one direction, then in another.

The crowd panicked. Men shouted and tripped over one another in a mad rush to flee.

I grabbed a rod from the nearest judge, who cried out in protest. Ig-noring him, I stepped toward the snake and used the forked end of the rod to scoop it up. I grasped the close-set prongs so that the creature was trapped just below the head and could not escape, no matter how furi-ously it twisted and writhed.

I held the snake aloft. "Someone, cut the creature in two!" I shouted.

Men looked at each other in helpless confusion. No one carried weapons in Olympia.

Protophanes bounded down the steps. He seized the snake with both hands and tore the creature in two, then threw the wriggling re-mains on the ground and stamped them into oblivion.

The gaping crowd was silent for a long moment. Then a great cheer went up—for Protophanes, not for me.

In all the excitement, the killer had escaped.

After swearing the oath, the athletes went to the Altis to make offerings at the altars of various gods in preparation for their events. The crowd drifted toward a lavishly decorated marble structure called the Colon-nade of Echoes, where the heralds and trumpeters of the Games com-peted in their own contests, seeing who could hold a note the longest or send the most echoes up and down the colonnade. This tradition had been going on for hundreds of years, and was more engaging than I expected.

The contest had just ended when I saw a familiar figure striding toward us. It was Protophanes. His broad, handsome face was lit with a grin.

"You're the one who caught the snake, right?"

"I am. Thank you for noticing." For my quick thinking that morning, I had expected some sort of acknowledgment—perhaps even a reward—but all I got was a begrudging grunt from one of the judges when I returned his forked rod.

"You're a Roman?" asked Protophanes, catching my accent.

"Yes. The name is Gordianus."

He nodded. "They let me take the oath, you know. I'm going to win the pankration for sure!" Seeing him so close, I realized that Protophanes was a head taller than I, and twice as broad. "But I still don't understand. Why did that fellow with the snake kill the Cynic?"

"Because the man with the snake was an agent of Mithridates," I said. "He didn't come here to enjoy the Games, but to pursue his own agenda. And he believed that Simmius was a Roman spy who might expose him."

"That old windbag?" Protophanes laughed.

"Who better to act a spy than the person least suspected?" said Antipater.

"Maybe," said Protophanes. "But you'd think a spy would keep his head down and not draw attention to himself."

"Or do the very opposite," said Antipater.

"A pity the killer got away. The judges could have got the truth out of him, I'm sure. But what's all this about spying and agents and such? Everyone comes to Olympia in peace. That's the whole point."

"On the contrary, young man, Olympia has always been a hotbed of intrigue," said Antipater. "This is the largest gathering in the Greek world. When so many meet in one place, including some of the richest and most powerful men in the world, there is always more afoot than meets the eye—including espionage. Many a scheme has been hatched in Olympia that has nothing to do with athletics, I assure you."

Protophanes shook his head. Politics did not interest him. "Well, I just wanted to say hello, and thank you for catching that snake. If they had a contest for quick reflexes, you'd be a hard one to beat, Gordianus! When I win the pankration, I won't forget you."

Protophanes walked away. Antipater sighed. "What a pleasant young fellow. I do hope he wins."

"At least he had the manners to thank me," I said.

"Well, then, before the afternoon events, shall we return to our quarters for a bite to eat?"

"What! Surely you don't intend to spend any more time in the pavilion of Exagentus, Teacher."

"And why not?"

"Because the man's a killer! Or as good as."

"Why do you say that, Gordianus?"

"Because of what I overheard last night."

"You say you overheard the blond man insisting that 'the Sidonian' be killed—you thought he meant me, but as you later realized, he actually meant Simmius. But if I understand you correctly, you didn't clearly hear the other speaker—who may or may not have been our host, and who, if anything, seemed to be disagreeing with the killer."

"True enough," I said. "But *someone* in that pavilion is most certainly in league with Mithridates. 'He's liable to expose *us* as agents of Mithridates'—that's what the man with the snake said."

"Even so, what have we to fear from such a person?"

"I exposed the killer! I may have ruined whatever plot they were hatching. What if they mean to take revenge?"

Antipater smiled. "Gordianus, you exposed an assassin. Assassins are expendable. If you fear that you've made yourself a target for retribution by the King of Pontus, I think you're letting your imagination run away with you. Now, let us return to the pavilion. If our host is there, I shall introduce you. Exagentus is quite a nice fellow, I assure you. And he's justly famous for laying a sumptuous table. I don't know about you, but this morning's events have given me quite an appetite."

Of the numerous events we attended over the five days of the Olympiad, my memories are all a blur. There were footraces, chariot races, and horse races, as well as the race of hoplites in armor, a cumbersome, clanking affair that struck me as more comical than fearsome. There was something called the pentathlon, which involved throwing a discus and a javelin as well as jumping and running and wrestling. It made me tired just to watch it. Among the final events were the man-to-man combats of wrestling, boxing, and the brutal pankration. Besides these official events, there were exhibition contests for boys not yet old enough to compete, and in the evenings a great deal of drinking and feasting, including the slaughter of a hundred oxen at the Great Altar of Zeus in front of his temple.

Antipater insisted on attending every event, and enjoyed them all immensely. His delight in the pankration struck me as particularly ironic. Here was a man who had devoted his life to the crafting of beautiful verses, striving to capture in words the most delicate sensibilities and elusive states of mind, reduced to a screaming, stamping, bellowing maniac along with his fellow Greeks at the spectacle of two men grappling in the dirt, pummeling each other's faces with their fists, and gouging each other's most tender parts. The pankration even allowed choking, and during one of Protophanes' early bouts, I thought we were about to see him strangle his opponent to death before our very eyes. The sight of the poor fellow's bright red face, protruding tongue, and bulging eyes caused tears of joy to run down Antipater's cheeks. The loser barely managed to lift his finger to signal submission before he fainted dead away.

Seeing Antipater's behavior at the Olympiad, I realized that, though I had known him most of my life, in some ways my old teacher was still a mystery to me.

When all the punching, poking, bone crunching, arm bending, and general mayhem was finally over, Protophanes emerged victorious in the pankration. His face was bloody, one eye was swollen shut, and his whole body was covered with scrapes and bruises, but his grin was brighter than ever as he accepted his victor's wreath—his second of the Games, for not only did he win the pankration, but the wrestling competition as well, a feat that thrilled Antipater.

"Hercules was the first to win both wrestling and pankration," he gushed, "and in all the hundreds of years since then, only three others have done the same. Now Protophanes is the fourth. His fame shall outlast us all!"

"Even the fame of Antipater of Sidon, Teacher?"

Antipater sighed. "What is the achievement of a mere poet, compared to that of an Olympic victor?"

To his credit, Protophanes was gracious in victory. After the closing ceremonies, and the procession in which the victors were showered with leaves, he sought me out in the crowd.

"Gordianus! What did you think of the Games?"

"Grueling," I said.

"Indeed! But to those of us who win, it's worth all the effort."

"I'm sure. But may I be candid? The so-called spirit of the Games eludes me. Such a fuss is made about the ideals of sportsmanship, discipline, piety, and fair play, yet the contests themselves seem to me sweaty, hectic, brutish, and violent. What's touted as a gathering in honor of sport simmers just beneath the surface with politics and intrigue; we even witnessed a murder! And the unspoken tension between Greek pride and Roman hegemony casts a shadow over everything. It makes me wonder about the times we live in, and the customs men live by—'O tempora! O mores!' as my father says in our native Latin."

Protophanes looked at me blankly. Somewhere along the way I had lost him.

"I suppose you'll be off to the victors' banquet now," said Antipater, sighing at the thought of all the winners gathered in one place.

"Yes, and what a feast it's going to be! But before I go, I wanted to settle a debt."

"A debt?" I said.

"To you, Gordianus. If they'd blamed me for the Cynic's death, I'd never have been allowed to take the oath. You took care of that! The city fathers of Magnesia have promised to be very generous to me—doubly generous, since I'll be taking home not one but two Olympic wreaths." He held forth a leather pouch. "This is all the money I brought with me, but I won't be needing it now—rich men will be fighting each other to provide my lodging and to pay for my dinners all the way home. So I want you to have it."

He pressed the money bag into my hands. It felt quite heavy.

"But I couldn't—"

"Don't be modest, Gordianus. Cynicism gets a man nowhere in this life—and neither does modesty. But if you take my advice, you'll donate whatever portion you can afford to the Temple of Zeus. It's Zeus who makes all things possible. Zeus gave me victory, and I have no doubt it was Zeus who opened your eyes to the truth about the Cynic's death. Now I must be off. Safe journeys to you! If you should ever get to Magnesia, look me up."

"What a fellow!" whispered Antipater, watching him depart. "And what a windfall for you, Gordianus. You should heed his advice, and donate every drachma to Zeus."

I frowned. "A good part of it, perhaps, but not every drachma, surely."

"But what would you spend it on? I've seen you in the market. You care nothing for all the trinkets and souvenirs for sale."

"I did see a couple of desirable items," I said, remembering the blond and brunette who had sauntered by on our first day, as tall as Amazons and wearing chitons no more substantial than a spider's web. I wondered if they were still in Olympia.

V

Interlude in Corinth:
THE WITCH'S CURSE

On our journey to see the Seven Wonders, Antipater and I saw much else along the way. As a poet, and a Greek, Antipater wished to pay homage to his great predecessors, so we stopped at Lesbos to visit the tomb of Sappho, and at Ios to see where Homer was buried. (Had we wished to see where Homer was born, we would have had to stop at almost every island in the Aegean Sea, since so many claimed that honor.)

We saw many remarkable places and things. None could match the Seven Wonders, though some came close. The Parthenon in Athens was certainly a marvel, as was the statue it housed, the chryselephantine Athena by Phidias; but, having seen the Temple of Artemis at Ephesus, and Phidias's statue of Zeus at Olympia, I understood why those were on the list instead.

We stopped at the island of Delos to see the Keratonian Altar, which some claim should be counted among the Wonders. The name of the altar comes from the Greek *kerata,* "horns," because it is made entirely of antlers ingeniously fitted together without any sort of binding by Apollo himself, who used the horns of deer slain by his sister Artemis. To be sure, the altar was an astonishing sight, but the visit was not pleasant.

Under Roman rule, Delos had become one of the largest slave markets in the world, a place of misery and foul odors. Men came to Delos to purchase humans by the thousands, not to marvel at Apollo's altar.

Of the many sites we visited other than the Seven Wonders, one stands out especially in my memory: the ruins of Corinth.

After seeing the Games at Olympia, we hired a driver and a mule-drawn wagon and headed east on the road that crosses the Peloponnesus, that vast peninsula that would be an island were it not for the slender strip of earth that connects it to the mainland. The road was a winding one, skirting mountains and passing through clefts in the rugged landscape. At last, toward the end of a long day of travel, Antipater told me that we were drawing near to the isthmus.

"At its narrowest, the isthmus is less than four miles wide," he said. "A young fellow like you, Gordianus, might easily walk from the Gulf of Corinth on the north to the Gulf of Aegina on the south and back again in a single day, with time for a leisurely lunch beside this road, which at the isthmus links the two parts of Greece."

"The route is certainly popular," I said. Since leaving Olympia, we were constantly being passed by faster vehicles and travelers on horseback.

"Yes," said Antipater, "there's always a great deal of coming and going between the cities of the mainland—Athens, Thebes, and the rest—and the cities of the Peloponnesus, like Sparta and Argos. But the traffic is especially heavy now, and particularly in the easterly direction, since the Games at Olympia have just ended and all the athletes and spectators who poured into the Peloponnesus from the mainland are now heading home again. To do so by land, this is the only route."

The winding road took a turn to the north, skirting a craggy peak to our left that erupted from the earth like a knuckle of sheer rock. As the road crested a hill, I suddenly saw the Gulf of Corinth straight ahead of us, and at the same time, far away to our right, I had my first glimpse of the Gulf of Aegina, a glimmer of silver beyond a long blue ridge.

"With the two gulfs so close on either side, and this road the only route from west to east, I should think this would be an ideal location for a city," I said.

I was rather proud of this astute observation, and expected my old tutor to reward me with a smile. Instead, Antipater scowled. "Gordianus! Do you remember nothing of the geography I've taught you? Do you not realize where we are?"

I was eighteen, and a man, but Antipater had a way of speaking that made me feel I was a boy again.

He shook his head. "Fifty-four years ago, for the glory of Rome, Lucius Mummius utterly destroyed the city of Corinth and its people. And you, a Roman, don't even know where Corinth was! Could you even find it on a map?"

"Of course I could," I protested. "If that's the Gulf of Corinth, to the north . . . and this winding road will eventually take us down to the Isthmus of Corinth, over that way . . . then . . ." I looked up at the craggy peak to our left. "Do you mean to say that's Acrocorinth, the fortified mountain above the ancient city?" I squinted. "Now that I look, I do see the ruins of what might have been a line of walls up there. But that means the city must have been right over there, at the foot of that sheer cliff."

I finally saw what had been in plain sight but invisible to my inattentive gaze—a distant jumble of stones and mounds of earth that were all that remained of the once proud city of Corinth. I felt a stirring of curiosity, but the ruins were a considerable distance from the road, and the late summer day was drawing to a close. The cart and the mules cast long shadows on the tall, dry grass. Antipater leaned forward to speak to the driver.

"Is there a place nearby where we can spend the night?"

The driver turned his head and looked at Antipater as if he were a madman. "Here, so near the ruins? Of course not! The Romans won't allow so much as a vegetable stand to be built within a mile of the ancient walls, much less an inn. Besides, this place is . . ."

"Yes?" said Antipater. "Go on."

"Haunted!" The man lowered his voice to a gruff whisper. "This is as close as I care to come to it. I dread passing by here, every time I make this trip."

"Nevertheless, it's my intention to have a closer look at the ruins," said Antipater.

The driver snapped the reins and urged the mules to go faster. "You'll be doing so without me, then. I tell you what—up ahead there's a road that branches off to the left. That will take us down to the waterfront, to the old port of Lechaeum. There's a Roman garrison there. The soldiers maintain a few of the docks and warehouses, strictly for military use. There's not much of a town, just a few shops and a brothel that caters to the soldiers, but there's a small inn with a tavern. You and the young Roman can spend the night there."

"Where will you sleep?" I said.

"A pile of straw in the stable will be good enough for me," said the driver.

"After a visit to the brothel, no doubt," whispered Antipater.

"And tomorrow morning," the driver went on, "if you're still bent on visiting the ruins, I'll drop you off. You can have a look at the place in broad daylight, and then I'll come back and fetch you before nightfall."

As the road tilted downward we saw the Gulf of Corinth before us, a broad sheet of gold lit by the westering sun. Eventually, the old port appeared as a silhouette of jumbled roofs against the shimmering water. As we drew nearer, the silhouette resolved into ramshackle structures. The inn was the first building we came to. It was a humble-looking place, but after a long day on the wagon I was glad to see it. No people were about. As the wagon came to a halt, a few dogs lying in the dusty street roused themselves and listlessly wagged their tails, looking worn out by the heat of the day but too hungry to miss an opportunity to beg. The driver shooed them away and went inside to make arrangements for us.

I looked around, but there was not much to see. The place had a melancholy, deserted air. All the nearby buildings had fallen into disrepair. Walls had given way. Roofs had fallen in.

"To think, Lechaeum was once one of the busiest ports in all Greece!"

Antipater sighed. "The sister port on the other side of the isthmus is probably just as dilapidated."

"But if the location is so ideal, why do the Romans not rebuild the ports, and reap the profits?"

"Ask the Roman Senate! It's because they're all so jealous of each other, I suspect. None of them is willing to give the authority to rebuild the port to another senator—they can't stand to see a rival become rich off such a lucrative commission. So nothing is done."

"But the driver says there's a Roman garrison."

"Yes, stationed here not to maintain the port but rather to keep anyone from using it! Because it dared to defy Rome, one of the world's most beautiful cities was destroyed, and because the conquerors squabble among themselves, the ports of ancient Corinth are left to rot."

I had never heard Antipater express such vehement disdain for Rome. While I was growing up, he had done his best to teach me Greek and to instill in me an appreciation of Greek culture, but regarding recent history, particularly Rome's conquest of Greece, he had always been circumspect.

The driver returned with bad news: there was no room at the inn.

"What! But this won't do," declared Antipater. "I shall talk to the innkeeper myself." I helped him dismount from the cart and followed him inside.

The innkeeper was not a local, but a discharged Roman centurion named Gnaeus who had served for years at the Roman garrison before retiring to run the little inn and tavern. He explained that another party had arrived ahead of us and taken all four rooms.

"Every room? Who are these people?" said Antipater, speaking Latin in preference to the innkeeper's uncouth Greek.

"A group of Roman travelers, just come from Olympia. They say they want to stay here for a while and have a look at the old ruins up the hill. That's them in the tavern, having some wine and a bite to eat." The innkeeper nodded toward the adjoining room, from which I heard a murmur of conversation and occasional laughter.

Antipater glared. "'A look at the old ruins,' you say? The city had a name, you know: Corinth. Now why don't you go ask your other guests to double-up, and free a room for us?"

The innkeeper scowled and muttered under his breath: "Crazy old Greek!"

"What did you say?" asked Antipater.

"Yes, repeat what you just said," I demanded.

The innkeeper took his first good look at me. His eyes settled on the iron ring on my right hand.

"You're a Roman?" he said.

"Indeed I am."

"Hardly look old enough for that citizen's ring."

"I'm eighteen."

He nodded. "Well, that's different. What are you doing, traveling with this old Greek?"

"Zoticus was my tutor when I was a boy," I said. "Not that it's any of your business."

"Exactly who stays under my roof is very much my business, young man," said the innkeeper, with an edge in his voice that reminded me he had once been a Roman centurion, used to giving orders. "But I like your spirit. I tell you what, I'll do what your Greek friend suggests, and have a word with the other guests. They seem like reasonable men. Maybe I can supply a room for you, after all."

He stepped into the tavern and returned a few moments later, accompanied by a big man with curly red hair and a bristling beard. We exchanged introductions. The Roman's name was Titus Tullius.

"Our host tells me you're looking for a room," he said. "And here I thought we were going to have the inn all to ourselves. I'm surprised anyone else even managed to find this place, it's so out of the way. Just come from Olympia, have you?"

"Yes," I said.

"First time at the Games? Yes, for me, too. Quite a show, wasn't it? Did you see the footraces? That fellow Eudamos made the competition eat dust. And the pankration? Protophanes walloped the competition!"

"Will you give up one of the rooms or not?" said Antipater brusquely.

"Steady on," said Tullius. "It's too early for bed, anyway. Join us in the tavern for a drink."

"I'm an old man, and I'm weary, and I need to lie down," said Antipater.

"Well, why didn't you say so? Yes, by all means, take one of our rooms. We'll manage. We were going to split up three to a room, but we can just as easily fit four to a room, I suppose."

"There are twelve of you?" I said. "Did you all attend the Games together?"

"We certainly did. Now we're seeing a few more sights here in the Peloponnesus before we sail back to Rome. I'm the one who insisted on visiting the ruins of Corinth. The rest thought that would be a bore, but I assured them it will be well worth it."

"That's our intention, as well," I said. I turned toward Antipater, but he was already heading up the stairs. The innkeeper followed after him with a ring of jangling keys in his fist.

Tullius smiled. "It'll be just us Romans in the tavern, then. There's my group, plus a few off-duty soldiers from the garrison. Come, Gordianus, join us."

I did so gladly, thinking a cup or two of wine would do much to soothe my travel-stiff limbs.

Tullius's party consisted entirely of men. I was the youngest in the room, though some of the soldiers were not much older. A single serving woman moved among them. She was neither young nor pretty, and by her gruff manner I judged her to be a freeborn local woman, not a slave.

"Ismene!" called Tullius. "Bring a cup for my young friend."

She gave him a sour look, but fetched a wooden cup and pressed it into my hand, then filled it from her pitcher. "Let's hope this handsome fellow has better manners than the rest of you louts," she said. She gave me a warm smile, then glowered at the others.

"I do believe Ismene is smitten with you, Gordianus!" Tullius laughed.

"Finally, a man to tempt Ismene!" said one of the soldiers, flashing a broad grin. He had a neck like a bull's and the first touches of silver in his brassy blond hair. In every drunken group, there is someone louder than the rest; he fit the role.

"Don't tease her, Marcus," said the soldier next to him, who looked frail in comparison. The frown lines around his mouth betrayed an anxious disposition.

"Why not, Lucius? Are you afraid of Ismene? Or perhaps you're a bit in love with the old battle-axe?" Marcus laughed uproariously.

The conversation settled down, and the chief topic was Olympia. The soldiers envied the travelers for having witnessed the games. Since I had seen some events that others had missed, I found myself joining in the conversation and thoroughly enjoying it. At this point in my journey with Antipater, I was beginning to feel a bit homesick. It felt good to be in a room where everyone was speaking Latin. When the conversation turned from Olympia to Rome—the soldiers were eager for news—I felt quite at home, a Roman among Romans.

"These days, all the talk in Rome is about war," said Tullius. "War looming in the East with King Mithridates, and war looming in Italy between Rome and her unhappy Italian confederates."

"But there's no war yet, in either of those places," said Lucius, looking fretful.

"No—not yet," said Tullius darkly. His companions nodded gravely. "You fellows are well out of it here. Must be pretty quiet duty in a posting like this."

"As quiet as a grave!" said Marcus with a laugh.

Lucius made a sign with his hand to avert the Evil Eye. "You shouldn't talk that way, Marcus. You know this place is lousy with ghosts, and rife with magic."

"Magic?" I said.

"Black magic!" Lucius raised his thick black eyebrows. "Curses and spells, sorcery and witchcraft. It's everywhere you turn in this part of the world."

"It seems to me this part of the world is practically deserted," I said. "Except for a few scattered farms, we saw hardly any signs of life along the road. Where would you even find a witch?"

"You wouldn't have to go far." Lucius looked sidelong at Ismene. She noticed his gaze and glared back at him.

Marcus laughed. "Lucius, what an old woman you are! Afraid of your own shadow."

"Am I? Tell me then, why do soldiers die in their sleep here? You remember Aulus, and then Tiberius—both dead, and with no explanation. And why is everyone afraid to go anywhere near the old ruins, especially at night?" Lucius shivered. "Give me Mithridates or a civil war in Italy any day! At least you know what you're up against when it's another man with a sword that's trying to kill you." He shook his head. "I can't believe you fellows intend to go traipsing around those ruins tomorrow. There's something wicked in that place. If you ask me—"

"Now, really!" Tullius drew back his shoulders and raised his chin. "You're a soldier of Rome, my good man, and I won't have you talking such rubbish. What was Corinth? Just another city conquered by Rome and put to the sword. Was there a massacre? Undoubtedly. Does that mean that no Roman should ever set foot there, for fear of restless spirits seeking retribution? Nonsense! If a Roman should be afraid to go walking in a city defeated by Romans, then we should have to give up all our conquests and go scampering back to Rome! So much for fearing ghosts. As for this magic you speak of, that sort of thing is women's work. Oh, some women are always cursing each other, especially these Greeks—'Hermes of the Underworld, Ambrosia is prettier than me, please make her hair fall out,' or 'Great Artemis, helper in childbirth, all the girls have babies now except me, can't you make their babies get sick and cry all night?' That sort of rubbish. Women squabbling, and asking deities to take sides—as if the gods have nothing better to do. Hardly the sort of thing for a man to worry about, especially a Roman, and especially a Roman soldier."

Lucius shook his head. He drained the rest of his cup, then took his leave without another word.

"Superstitious fellow, that one," said Marcus. "Doesn't like it here. Always brooding. Don't take it personally."

To show that he didn't, Tullius bought everyone another round. Ismene rolled her eyes, but shambled off to refill her pitcher.

An hour or so later I staggered upstairs and crawled into the lumpy bed beside Antipater, having eaten too little and drunk too much. When he roused me at dawn the next morning, my head was full of spiders and my mouth was stuffed with cobwebs.

Down in the tavern, Gnaeus the innkeeper served us millet porridge with a small dollop of honey—the simple sort of breakfast he had learned to cook in his centurion days, no doubt. The other guests were not yet stirring. I envied them the luxury of sleeping late.

The wagon driver seemed as hungover as I was.

"How was your visit to the brothel last night?" asked Antipater cheerfully.

The man only groaned and shook his head. True to his word, he took us to the outskirts of the old ruins, hissing at every bump in the road, then turned back toward Lechaeum with a promise that he would return for us before nightfall.

A defensive wall with gates and towers had once surrounded all of Corinth. Only the foundations remained. Within their boundary, it was possible to discern where streets had run and how blocks had been laid out, but almost nothing remained of the buildings except for scattered stones, fallen columns, broken roof tiles, and bits of charred wood amid the high grass. Here and there I saw evidence of a mosaic that had once been part of a floor, but even these had been broken into pieces and scattered. I saw a few pedestals, but no statues.

The place cast a melancholy spell, especially upon Antipater. He wandered about like a man in a dream. There was a strange look in his eyes, as if somehow he could see the city as it once had appeared.

"Did you ever visit Corinth, before it was destroyed?" I said.

He took a deep breath. "I saw it as a boy. My father was appointed by the elders of Sidon to consult the Oracle at Delphi, and he took me along on the trip. We crossed the isthmus coming and going, and each time we spent a couple of nights here in Corinth. But my memories are a child's memories, vague and dim. It's impossible to know what I actually remember and what I only imagine, and there's nothing here to confirm my recollections. Nothing at all! And yet . . ."

He began to wander again, with a more purposeful look on his face.

"Are you looking for something in particular?" I said.

"I'll know the right spot when I come to it," he muttered.

I followed him for an hour or more, walking up and down the streets of a city that no longer existed. A warm wind began to blow, whistling amid the ruins and causing the dry grass to shiver.

At last he came to a halt. He sighed, closed his eyes, and bowed his head. We were in the midst of what once had been a grand house, to judge by the layout of the many rooms and the traces of a garden with a fountain at the center. Antipater threw back his head. With his eyes still shut, he declaimed in Greek:

"I was Rhodope, the rosy-cheeked, and my mother was Boisca.
We did not die of sickness. Nor did we die by the sword.
Instead, when dreadful Ares brought destruction to the city,
My mother seized a slaughtering knife and a cord.
With a prayer, she slew me like a lamb upon the altar.
Then she slew herself, with a noose around her throat.
Thus died two women of Corinth, untouched and free,
Bravely facing their end, cursing any who gloat."

Utter silence followed his recitation, broken only by the sighing of the wind in the grass. Suddenly I heard someone clapping, then a whole group applauding.

With a start, I spun about. Did I expect to see the ghosts of Corinth? The truth was more prosaic: Titus Tullius and his party had joined us.

"A most excellent recitation!" declared Tullius. He turned to his companions. "Gentlemen, what you've just heard is a fictitious epitaph for a dead mother and daughter of Corinth, composed by the late

Antipater of Sidon. I was planning to recite it for you myself, but good Zoticus here, with his native Greek, has done a far better job than I could have. That was excellent, Zoticus!"

The party responded with another round of applause. None of the traveling Romans had any idea that it was Antipater of Sidon himself who stood before them.

Usually Antipater was delighted to hear his poems praised, but if looks could kill, Tullius would have fallen dead on the spot. Oblivious of Antipater's scowl, Tullius recommenced with what appeared to be an ongoing lecture for the edification of his companions.

"So, gentlemen, is this really the spot where the distraught Boisca slew her daughter Rhodope and then committed suicide? Probably not, since both women are most likely fictional creations. The poet's intent was not to memorialize two actual women, but to remind us of the pathos and terror that must have attended that final day here in Corinth, when the Roman legionnaires under Lucius Mummius pulled down the walls and, under orders from the Senate, proceeded to raze the city to the ground, slaying the men and enslaving the women and children. Any questions?"

"Other Greek cities joined Corinth in the insurgency against Roman rule," said one of the men, "and yet those cities weren't destroyed. Why Corinth?"

"First of all, it was Corinth who started the war by attacking her peaceable neighbors, who were perfectly content under Roman rule, and inciting others to revolt. Also, the Senate never forgot a rather nasty incident that occurred in Corinth before the insurrection, when Roman ambassadors, passing by a private house, had feces and urine dumped on them. Sooner or later, there is a price to be paid for such disrespect! And, finally, it was decided that any future insurrections in Greece could best be forestalled by making a strict example of Corinth. As you will recall, in the very same year, Rome's ancient rival Carthage was utterly destroyed and her people enslaved. As Carthage was annihilated to the west, so Corinth was annihilated to the east. The result: more than fifty years later, the cities of Greece remain firmly under Rome's control—and greatly to their benefit, I might add, since Rome put an end to centuries of bloody squabbling among them. Sometimes, as terrible as the consequences may be, an example must be made."

The men around Tullius nodded thoughtfully and grunted in agreement.

"What utter nonsense!" muttered Antipater.

"Of course," Tullius went on, "when any city meets it end, there are deeper causes at work. Some contend that divine will engineered the destruction of Corinth, but others argue that her own reckless leadership was quite capable of causing the city's downfall without any intervention from the gods. That the Corinthians had grown corrupt and decadent, no one can deny. There is a theory that proximity to the sea, while it may bring commerce and riches to a city, may also bring the vices of luxury and exotic temptations. Men are distracted from the virtues of discipline and bravery and spurred to compete instead in extravagant shows of wealth. The same decay afflicted Carthage, another maritime city, where the love of commerce and foreign goods made the people soft. Corinth was perhaps doubly at risk in this regard, having not one but two ports on either side of the isthmus, only a few miles apart." He nodded thoughtfully. "I am reminded of another of Antipater of Sidon's laments for Corinth, which alludes to the city's special relationship with the sea. In that poem, the beautiful Nereids, daughters of Ocean, bemoan the city's fate."

Tullius paused and cleared his throat. "I shall quote the poem now—that is, if Zoticus here does not object?" He smiled, but this rhetorical flourish was strictly for the amusement of his listeners; he did not even glance in Antipater's direction. "Well, then—

"Where, O Corinth, is your fabled beauty now?
Where the battlements and ramparts—"

"Oh, really, this is too much to bear!" said Antipater, who turned about and stalked off. I followed him. The laughter and the quips of the Romans ("Silly old Greek!") rang in my ears.

"Teacher!" I cried, but rather than halting, Antipater quickened his stride. The way became steeper and steeper as we began to ascend toward Acrocorinth, and still he hurried on. We appeared to be following the course of what had once been a well-maintained road that skirted the steep face of the mountain and circled around to its far side before reaching the top. The road became little more than a poorly kept footpath, switching back and forth as it wound its way up the slope. I began to think Antipater would reach the top without stopping, but eventually he paused for breath. Whether from exertion or anger at the Romans, his face was bright red.

"Do you know the tale of Sisyphus?" he asked me.

"The name is familiar. . . ."

He shook his head, dismayed yet again at my ignorance.

"Sisyphus was the founder of Corinth, the city's first king. Somehow he offended Zeus—the tales vary—and he was given a terrible punishment, forced to roll a boulder up a steep hill only to see it slip away and roll back down again, so that he had to repeat the pointless task over and over again. Some believe this was the very hill where Sisyphus carried out the impossible labor Zeus set for him. That is why this is called the Slope of Sisyphus."

I looked down the rocky incline, then looked upward. We were more than halfway to the top, but the steepest part was yet to come. Antipater resumed the ascent.

We passed the ruined walls of what must have been a fortress, and at length we arrived at the summit and stood atop the sheer cliff that towered above the remains of Corinth. To the north lay the sea. The wharves at Lechaeum were tiny in the distance, with tiny Roman galleys moored alongside them; the walls of the waterfront garrison were manned by Roman soldiers almost too small to be seen. Below us, at the foot of the cliff, I could clearly discern the course of the old walls and the layout of Corinth.

The sun was directly overhead. The harsh light and the lack of shadows made everything look stark and slightly unreal, drained of color and parched by the warm, dry wind. From the ruins below I imagined I could hear a sound like many voices whispering and moaning. The ruins themselves appeared to shimmer, an illusion caused by the rising heat and the undulation of high grass amid the stones. I shivered, and felt dizzy from the heat.

"What really happened here, Antipater?"

He sighed. "According to our friend Tullius, the Corinthians brought about their own destruction. Typical Roman reasoning: blame the victims!

"When the Corinthians and their allies in the Achaean League revolted, they lashed out against the Spartans, who remained loyal to Rome. The Romans used that incident as a pretext to mount a full-scale invasion of the Peloponnesus—they claimed they were merely coming to the defense of an ally. There were several battles. The Achaean League was crushed, and its leaders were either killed or committed suicide. The climax occurred here, at Corinth. The city opened its gates in surrender, but Lucius Mummius had been given orders by the Senate to make an example of Corinth. His soldiers poured into the city and utterly destroyed it.

"Men were rounded up and slaughtered. Women were raped; if they survived, they were sold into slavery. The same thing was done to the children. Houses and temples were looted, then burned. The soldiers were allowed to stuff their pockets with all the jewelry and gold they could carry, but the choicest works of art were claimed by Mummius and sent back to the Senate. Rome was enriched beyond measure. Look inside any temple in Rome; all the best paintings and statues came from Corinth. And half of them are mislabeled, because the ignorant Mummius couldn't tell a statue of Zeus from one of Poseidon!"

Antipater paused for a long moment, lost in thought. "There's a painting by an artist named Aristeides, a stunning work. Hercules is in agony, trying to rip off the poisoned shirt given him by his wife, who thought the magical garment would merely make him faithful to her. Deianira is in the background, horrified by what she's done. The scheming centaur Nessus looks on from his hiding place in the woods, laughing. When I was a boy, my father took me to see that painting here in Corinth. How that image fascinated and terrified me! I never forgot it. Then, a few years ago, I had occasion to enter a temple in Rome, and there in the vestibule, I saw it again—not a copy or imitation, but the very painting by Aristeides! That was when my boyhood memories of Corinth came flooding back. That was when I wrote this poem."

Antipater stepped to the very edge of the precipice. I held my breath, fearful that a gust of wind might push him over, but I didn't dare interrupt him. The words that had sounded pompous and hollow coming from Tullius sounded very different as they poured from Antipater.

"Where, O Corinth, is your fabled beauty now?
Where the battlements and ramparts, temples and towers?
Where the multitudes that lived within your walls?
Where the matrons holding vigil in your sacred bowers?
City of Sisyphus, not a trace is left of you.
War seizes and devours, takes some and then takes more.
Ocean's daughters alone remain to mourn for you.
The salt tears of the Nereids lash the lonely shore."

I stepped beside Antipater. Together we gazed down at vanished Corinth with the moaning of the wind in our ears.

A movement amid the ruins caught my eye. It was the party of Tullius—or so I presumed. The tiny figures were too distant to be clearly discerned, but among them I thought I recognized Tullius by his red hair and bristling beard. They were no longer standing in a group, listening to Tullius, or following him from place to place. They seemed to be poking amid the rubble and moving bits of it about, but toward what purpose I couldn't imagine. I thought of asking Antipater's opinion, but his gaze was elsewhere, and I didn't wish to agitate him by returning his attention to Tullius.

The wind continued to rise. Antipater at last stepped back from the precipice and we headed down the slope.

On the way down, a little off the path I noticed some ruins that had escaped my attention on the way up. Antipater saw them, too, and we left the path to take a closer look.

The largest of the ruins had once been a small temple or sanctuary. Drums from a fallen column lay amid the tumbled stones, and in a much-worn painting on a fragment of a wall Antipater claimed to recognize the image of Persephone, wife of Hades and queen of the underworld.

"Can you not see her regal headband, Gordianus, and the winnowing fan in her hands? Harvesters use such an implement to sift grain. Persephone uses it to winnow the dead as they descend to Hades, revealing some souls to be wheat and others chaff. Ceremonial winnowing fans like that are used in rituals at sacred sites all over Greece."

"What happens at these rituals?"

"No man knows, since the acolytes are all women. Presumably they call upon the powers of the underworld."

"But that's witchcraft, not worship."

Antipater shrugged. "Who's to say where one ends and the other begins?"

The remains of several other small buildings were nearby. Antipater speculated that these might have been used as dining halls and meeting rooms by the women who worshipped at the sanctuary of Persephone. The buildings had all collapsed except one. It was half-buried in rubble but the roof remained intact. It was hardly more than a shack with a door and a window. Antipater pushed open the door and we stepped inside.

It was normal that the air in the room should be cool, but to me it felt unnaturally so. At first glance the dim little chamber appeared to be empty. But as my eyes adjusted, I saw a few objects scattered about the floor—clay lamps, incense burners, and some thin, flattened pieces of black metal. I picked up one of these tablets, surprised at how heavy it was, and at how soft. The metal was easily bent.

"Put that down!" said Antipater.

His tone was so urgent that I did so at once. "What is it?"

"A sheet of lead, for writing on. Don't you realize where we are? We've stumbled into a witch's den!"

I looked about the room. "Are you sure? We're in the middle of nowhere. Why would anyone—"

"The Romans demolished her sanctuary, but this spot is still sacred to Persephone. The women of Corinth must have practiced magic here for centuries. Ever since Jason brought the witch Medea back from Colchis and made her his queen, there have been witches in Corinth."

"But Corinth no longer exists."

"Yet the witches do. These things have been used recently. See the ash in the incense burners? See the dark spots on the ceiling made by the smoke of the lamps? They meet here at night. Someone is casting spells. While chanting incantations to the forces of darkness, they use the point of a blade to scratch curses on lead tablets, which are then placed near the person whom they wish to destroy."

"But all these tablets are blank—except for this one."

I picked up a tablet that was lying apart from the others. The crabbed letters were difficult to read, especially by the dim light, but the Greek was simple. "'I call upon Ananke. I call upon Moira. I call upon Egyptian Ufer of the Mighty Name. Destroy my enemy Eudocia! Destroy her utterly, from the hair on her head to the nails of her toes. Fill her mouth with sawdust. Fill her womb with sand. Fill her veins with black puss and vinegar. Make her—' And then it ends, just like that."

"Put that thing down, Gordianus!"

"But why is it still here?"

"Who knows? Perhaps the curse was interrupted, or the spell went awry, or the person cursing Eudocia changed her mind. Now put it back where you found it, and let's get out of here at once."

I would have stayed longer, curious to see if there was yet more evidence of magic to be found, but Antipater insisted I follow him. Emerging from the chill and darkness, I was dazzled by the harsh sunlight. Stifling waves of heat rose from the rock-strewn hillside.

"When is the driver returning for us?" said Antipater. "I've seen enough of Corinth."

The sun was still high in the sky when we reached the place where we were to await the driver. Antipater found a shady spot under an olive tree and took a nap. I sat against the trunk and listened to the chirring of cicadas in the grass.

At one point, a Roman soldier came by on horseback. His helmet kept me from recognizing him, until he gave me a mock-salute and spoke. "Hot enough for you?"

I realized it was Marcus, the soldier at the tavern who had made fun of his comrade for being so fearful of witches. "What are you doing out here?" I said, keeping my voice low so as not to wake Antipater.

"Just making the rounds." Marcus gave his mount a gentle kick and ambled on. Horse and rider soon disappeared beyond a low hill.

Every now and again I imagined I heard sounds coming from the ruins—men talking, and a clatter like metal implements being struck against stones. Was it possible that Tullius and his party were still nosing about the ruins? If so, what could they be up to? I thought about going to look for them, but decided it would be irresponsible to leave Antipater alone. It also occurred to me that perhaps the sounds I heard were not being made by the Romans at all, but by the ghosts of vanished Corinth. A foolish idea, I had no doubt; but I stayed where I was.

Like Antipater, I had seen enough of that desolate, melancholy place. I was glad when the wagon finally arrived to carry us back to the inn at Lechaeum.

Antipater and I ate an early dinner. Before we headed to bed, we made arrangements to be taken the next morning to the port of Cenchrea on the opposite side of the isthmus, where the wagon driver was sure we could hire a small vessel to take us as far as Piraeus, the port of Athens. Just as I laid my head on the pillow, I heard Tullius's party arrive downstairs, talking loudly and laughing. I feared their carousing would keep me up, but as soon as I shut my eyes I fell asleep.

I woke at dawn. Nightmares clung to me like a shroud. What had I been dreaming about? Witches and curses, no doubt, but my head was such a muddle I couldn't remember. I regretted having consumed so much wine the night before—then remembered that I had drunk only a single cup of watered wine with my dinner. Nearby, Antipater continued to snore.

I rose from the bed, feeling a bit unsteady, and unlatched the simple lock on the door. I made my way down the stairs, wondering if Gnaeus or Ismene would be stirring yet. My mouth was parched and I craved water.

I reached the foot of the stairs, crossed the small vestibule, and stepped into the tavern. What I saw bewildered me at first—my mind could make no sense of it. Then I staggered backward, retching and clutching my stomach.

The room was a scene of utter carnage. Bodies lay in heaps, covered with blood. Among them I saw Titus Tullius. His head was thrown back, his eyes and mouth wide open, his limbs twisted. His throat had been cut. The front of his tunic was so soaked with blood that no trace of its original color remained.

Even as a spectator at gladiator games, I had never seen so much death in one place. Suppressing my nausea, I counted the bodies. There were twelve. The entire party of Romans lay dead on the tavern floor. Every one of them had his throat cut.

I ran upstairs to wake Antipater. He clung to sleep, but finally I was able to rouse him. He seemed confused and unsteady on his feet, as I had been after waking. By the time we went downstairs, the innkeeper was up. He stood in the tavern, gaping at the slaughter and shaking his head.

"It's like a battlefield," he whispered.

"Great Zeus!" cried Antipater. "They've all been murdered. Gordianus, did you hear anything last night?"

"I slept like a stone."

"So did I. But how could the noise have failed to wake us? There must have been a struggle. Surely these men cried out."

I frowned. "And yet, I see no signs of a fight. No benches overturned, nothing broken—and no weapons drawn. It's as if they submitted to what was done to them."

"Or were taken by surprise," said Antipater. "Who was here last night, Gnaeus?"

"Only these men, no one else."

"No soldiers from the garrison?"

The innkeeper shook his head.

"What about your serving woman?"

"Ismene was here, of course."

"Where is she now?" said Antipater.

"I don't know. At night she goes home to a little hut on the outskirts of town. But she's an early riser. She's usually in the tavern before I get up."

"Perhaps something's happened to her," said Antipater.

"Or perhaps she's fled," I said. "You don't think Ismene could have—"

Gnaeus snorted. "If you think Ismene played some part in this, you're mad. Why would she want to harm these men? Why would anyone have done this?"

I thought of the way Tullius had talked about the destruction of Corinth, disparaging its people and blaming them for their own demise. Antipater had been offended by his remarks. Whom else had Tullius offended, here at the tavern or elsewhere? Had the ghosts of Corinth themselves been stirred to retribution by his slanders? Horrified by the inexplicable slaughter, my imagination ran wild.

Antipater thought of a simpler motive. "Perhaps they were robbed."

Gnaeus ran upstairs and returned a few moments later. "Their rooms appear to be untouched. No one's taken their things." He shook his head. "The garrison commander will have to be told. I'll go to him myself."

Not caring to remain in a room full of corpses, Antipater and I waited in the street outside until the innkeeper returned. He was followed by a troop of armed soldiers marching in formation. The dogs yelped and scattered at their approach. Among the men I recognized Marcus and his superstitious friend Lucius. At their head was a silver-haired officer with a weak chin and a patrician bearing.

The officer took a good look at Antipater and me. "You two are witnesses?"

"I found the bodies," I said. "But we didn't witness anything."

"I'll be the judge of that. Quintus Menenius, commander of the garrison here at Lechaeum. And who are you?"

"I'm Gordianus of Rome. This is my old tutor, Zoticus. We've just come from the Games at Olympia. We were going to cross the isthmus this morning and catch a ship over at Cenchrea—"

"Not today, you won't. Show me these bodies, Centurion Gnaeus," he said, paying the innkeeper the courtesy of using his old title. "And you two, come along. I may have more questions for you."

Quintus Menenius had surely witnessed bloodier spectacles in his years of military service, but when he saw the carnage in the tavern he drew a sharp breath and shuddered.

"All these men were your guests here at the inn, Centurion Gnaeus?"

"Yes."

"Were they robbed?"

"Their rooms appear to be untouched. I don't know about their persons."

"Lucius! Marcus! Examine the bodies. See if you find any coin purses."

Moving from corpse to corpse, the two soldiers found small money bags on each, all apparently intact.

The commander furrowed his brow. "No robbery? Then why were they killed? And how was it done, without a struggle?" He shook his head. "Put the coin purses back where you found them, men. These are Roman citizens. There will have to be a scrupulous inventory of each victim's property—for the inquest." He uttered the final word with a tone of dread, and sighed, as if weary already of the mountain of reports he would be obliged to file.

Stuffing a coin purse back where he had found it, Lucius suddenly drew back.

"What do you see, soldier?" said Menenius.

At the same moment, from the corner of my eye, I noticed Marcus; he, too, was returning a coin purse, this one to the body of Titus Tullius—but did I see him remove an object from the little leather bag? I wasn't sure, and no one else seemed to notice. Then I was distracted, for Lucius, having previously drawn back, now cautiously reached for something beneath the body at his feet, then snatched back his hand as if scalded.

"By Hercules, man, what is it?" Stepping over corpses, Menenius stooped down and pulled a thin, flat object from beneath the body. It was a lead tablet such as I had seen in the witch's den.

Menenius heard me gasp. He gave me a sharp look, then returned his attention to the tablet, squinting at the letters scraped into the lead. With a snort, he abruptly crossed the room and shoved the tablet into my hands. "Here, you have young eyes—and you seem to know what this is. Read it aloud."

I scanned the words. Hackles rose on my neck. "I'm not sure I should."

"Read it!"

I took a deep breath. "'Ananke, I call on you. Moira, I call on you. Egyptian Ufer of the Mighty Name, I call on you. Strike down these impious Romans! Rob them of their lives and let them join the dead whom they besmirch. Open their throats and let the blood of life pour out of them—'"

Lucius emitted a stifled shriek and began to shake. He looked as if he might bolt from the room. Only his commander's glowering gaze held him in check.

"Go on!" shouted Menenius.

"'Destroy these Romans, Ananke. Destroy them utterly, Moira. Annihilate the impious defamers of the dead, Egyptian Ufer of the Mighty Name—'"

Lucius began to sway. His eyes rolled up in his head. He crumpled to the floor amid the dead bodies.

"By Hercules, the man's fainted!" said Menenius with disgust. He ordered a couple of his soldiers to tend to Lucius, then snatched the lead tablet from me. "Witchcraft!" he declared. "The local women are mad for it. Was this the work of your serving woman, Centurion Gnaeus?"

The innkeeper looked back at him, speechless.

"It will all come out at the inquest." Menenius sighed. "We'll have to round up the local women and make them talk. Extracting evidence from females suspected of practicing magic—a nasty business, hardly suitable work for Roman soldiers, but there you have it. Garrison life!" He ordered the soldiers to clear the bodies from the room and take an inventory of their belongings, then asked the innkeeper to show him the dead men's rooms. Antipater and I were dismissed, for the time being.

While Antipater stepped outside, saying he needed fresh air, I drew Marcus aside. "Your friend Lucius was terrified when I read that curse."

Marcus grinned. "He'd hide behind his shadow if he thought a witch was in the room."

"So you don't think what happened here was the result of a curse?"

He shrugged. "Who can say? The commander will determine who, or what, killed these men."

"What did you take from Tullius's coin purse?"

The question caught him off guard. He tried to feign innocence. I tried to feign certainty, since I was not at all sure of what I'd seen. I kept my gaze steady, and it was Marcus who gave way. With a crooked smile and a shrug, he produced a finely crafted bronze image of Hercules the size of a man's finger.

"You won't tell anyone, will you?" he said.

"Where do you think Tullius got such a thing?"

"Perhaps he brought it with him, as a lucky charm."

"Then little good it did him," I said. "Do you mind if I keep it?"

For a moment, Marcus maintained his good-natured mask, then abruptly let it drop. "If I say no, I suppose you'll tell the commander, eh?" He glared at me. "Go ahead then, take it. That makes you a thief, too, and no better than me. I suppose we all have a bit of magpie in us, eh? Now, if you don't mind, I have work to do."

Marcus rejoined the others in the gruesome task of moving the dead bodies.

Even though we had told him all we knew, Menenius would not allow Antipater and me to move on until the inquest took place. The driver refused to stay any longer, and headed home to Olympia with his wagon early the next morning.

There could hardly have been a more boring place to get stuck. A full day exploring the ruins of Corinth had been quite enough for me. Lechaeum itself had little to offer beyond the tavern, which I could no longer enter without becoming nauseated. The dusty, sparsely stocked little shops clustered around the garrison offered nothing to tempt me; nor did the brothel on the waterfront, to judge by the haggard women I saw coming and going by the back entrance.

On the bright side, it appeared that the inquest would be held in short order. Things did not look good for Ismene, the serving woman at the tavern. A search of her little hut turned up materials used in witchcraft—the same types of lamps, incense burners, and blank lead tablets that Antipater and I had discovered in the witch's den on the Slope of Sisyphus, along with small lead boxes containing wooden dolls, which according to Antipater could also be used to cast spells. Obviously, Ismene was a witch, and presumably had written the curse tablet discovered in the tavern—but she was nowhere to be found. The soldiers searched every house in the vicinity and questioned all the locals. Ismene had vanished into thin air.

According to Gnaeus, the locals all agreed that witchcraft had killed the Romans. Absent evidence to the contrary, it seemed that the commander was prepared to go along with this idea.

"Do we really believe all those men were killed by a curse?" I asked Antipater. We were sitting under the shade of a fig tree outside the inn, enduring the heat of the day along with the dogs lying in the dust nearby.

"You read the tablet yourself, Gordianus. It called upon the forces of necessity and fate, as well as this Egyptian Ufer, whoever he is, to 'open their throats.' Isn't that exactly what happened—in the middle of the night, with no resistance from the victims, and so quietly that neither you nor I was awakened? That sounds like witchcraft to me." Antipater shuddered. "What's that in your hand?"

Absentmindedly, I had pulled out the little figure of Hercules I had taken from Marcus and was fiddling with it. There was no use trying to hide it, so I explained to Antipater how I came to have it.

"I've been thinking I should give it to the commander, to be restored to Tullius's property, but it's awkward. If I tell him Marcus took it, he'll probably be flogged, or worse. But if I don't tell the commander the truth, he may think I stole it myself. If I say I simply found it, how do I explain that I know it belonged to Tullius?"

"Are you certain it was his?"

"It came from his coin purse."

"Let me have a closer look." Antipater examined the figure under a patch of sunlight. "This is Corinthian. The city's bronze workers were famous for making miniatures like this. Do you see the mottled surface, dark red and green? That's a special patina they developed, which is seen in no other bronze sculpture. And here, this stamp on the bottom—that's the sign of one of the most famous Corinthian workshops."

"Tullius was such a show-off, you'd think he would have shown his Corinthian good luck charm to everyone."

Antipater frowned. "Do you know what I think? Tullius didn't bring this with him from Rome. I think he found it amid the ruins the other day, and filched it."

"I'm not sure 'filch' would be the proper word. After all, if he found it, fair and square—"

"He had no right to take it. By decree of the Roman Senate, nothing can be built within a certain radius of the ruins of Corinth. Nor can anything be taken out. Nothing in, nothing out. There is to be no commerce of any sort, and that includes treasure hunting. Of course, one presumes there's no treasure left, that everything of value was long ago looted or destroyed. But perhaps under all the dirt and rubble, a few precious items might yet remain—like this figurine. That would make this object quite rare—probably worth a legionnaire's salary for a year."

"This little thing? You're joking!"

Antipater looked up and down the street. "Perhaps I exaggerate. Nonetheless, I'd tuck that away, if I were you. And I'd keep my eyes peeled for Marcus. I wouldn't put it past that fellow to knock you over the head and take it back from you."

The day grew warmer still. Antipater fell fast asleep. I found myself looking at the craggy face of Acrocorinth in the distance, and felt a sudden impulse to return there. We had lost the wagon driver, but without Antipater to slow me down, I decided I was perfectly capable of walking there and back. I rose to my feet and headed out, shooing the dogs to keep them from following.

The sunlight was blinding. Waves of heat rose from hillsides covered with dry, brittle grass. I quickly grew thirsty, and realized I should have brought some water with me.

I reached the line of the ruined city walls, and pressed on. I found the spot where we had run into Tullius and his party, and from there, I tried to determine where I had last seen them when I gazed down from the summit of Acrocorinth. Heat and thirst made me lightheaded. The piles of rubble all looked alike. I became disoriented and confused. I began to see phantom movements from the corners of my eyes, and the least sound—the scrambling of a lizard or the call of a bird—startled me. I thought of the mother who had killed her daughter and then herself, and all the countless others who had suffered and died. I felt the ghosts of Corinth watching me, and whispered words to placate the dead, asking forgiveness for my trespass.

At length, I stumbled upon an area that had recently been disturbed. Overturned rocks exposed the worm trails beneath, and clods of earth had been dug up. Some instinct led me to move a particular stone, and behind it I discovered a narrow defile, just large enough for a man to stick his arm inside.

The idea that a snake or a spider or something even more terrible might live in such a crack gave me pause. I took a deep breath, then reached into the dark hole.

My fingers touched something cold and scaly, and I heard a slithering noise. I drew back my hand, then had a glimmer of realization. I reached inside again and felt my hand immersed amid bits of smooth, cold metal. I trapped one of the coins between my forefinger and thumb and pulled it out.

The silver was tarnished almost black, but the images were so finely cast that I could easily make out Bellerophon astride his winged horse, Pegasus. On the reverse was an image of the monstrous Chimera slain by the Corinthian hero. The coin was thick and heavy in my hand.

I became so lost in studying the images that I didn't hear the approach of the horse and rider. When their shadow fell on me, I looked up, startled. The sun formed a blinding halo around the soldier's gleaming helmet.

"Beautiful, isn't it?" said Marcus. "The coin, I mean. It's a funny thing, how some objects are beautiful because they're one of a kind—like that figure of Hercules you took from me. But coins become more beautiful the more of them there are. And there are a great many in that little hiding place you've discovered. It took me months to dig up those coins, along with all the other treasures I've found amid the ruins."

"Treasures?" I said, my mouth dry.

"Vases and such. A lot of the things I find are broken to bits, or melted by the flames, but every so often I find something so perfect I can hardly believe it. Like that little figurine of Hercules that Tullius found yesterday and dared to slip into his coin purse. From what I overheard, he and his friends agreed ahead of time to split anything they found evenly between them, and when they found this particular cache of treasures, they agreed to leave it intact and come back for it later. That was naughty of Tullius, to slip the Hercules into his coin purse while the others weren't watching. What if Menenius had come across it while searching the dead bodies, and realized where it came from?"

I frowned. "Overheard? When did you hear Tullius and the others talking?"

"Yesterday, as they went about their business here in the ruins. They clucked like hens the whole time—and had no idea I was watching and listening. I can thank my training for that. Quintus Menenius may be one of the stupidest men the gods ever made, but he did teach me a thing or two about stealth and surveillance. That sort of thing comes in handy if you want to scavenge treasures from an area that's off-limits, and keep anyone else from doing so." He shook his head. "Titus Tullius and his friends thought they could come here, loot to their hearts' content, and run off with the spoils, and no one would lift a finger to stop them. What fools!"

"Why didn't you simply report them to Menenius? Wouldn't he have arrested them?"

"Menenius would have clicked his tongue, given them a stern lecture, and sent them on their way—then barred all visitors to the ruins, posted guards night and day, and sent a full report to the Senate asking for further instructions. My treasure stores would have been discovered. My little operation would have come to an end. I'd have nothing to show for all my hard work."

"How long have you been doing this?"

"Scavenging the ruins? For months. Almost since the first day I was posted to this gods-forsaken place. I couldn't believe no one else had thought of doing the same thing. The locals are all too superstitious to go nosing about the ruins, and so are most of the Roman soldiers. That silly Lucius keeps the others frightened half to death with his stories about witches and ghosts. I encourage him at every turn, of course. Meanwhile, I come here as often as I safely can, and go treasure hunting. Usually I find nothing. Sometimes I find a ring or a stray coin. And every so often I make a real discovery, like a cameo from a brooch, untouched by the flames and in perfect condition. Or a bag of coins that must have been buried by some wealthy Corinthian, thinking he could come back later and claim it. I hide the things I find. There's no safe way to smuggle them out without someone noticing, and nowhere in this gods-forsaken place to spend the money or sell the precious stones, so my treasures just keep accumulating. How Tullius and his friends were lucky enough to stumble on this particular hiding place, I can't imagine."

"Lucky? Surely it was misfortune that led them here."

Marcus laughed. "Yes, since I observed them doing it. I couldn't report them, because that would ruin my own scheme. And I had no intention of letting them come back here the next day, and the day after that, plundering the treasures I've worked so hard to accumulate. Ugh, this thing is hot!" He took off his helmet and tossed it on a soft patch of ground, then combed his fingers through sweat-soaked tufts of blond hair streaked with gray.

"So you got rid of them," I said. My mouth was so dry I could hardly speak. I was so dizzy I thought I might fall. "Did you kill every one of them, all by yourself?"

"I certainly did. With this." He pulled his short sword from its scabbard. "Had a terrible time cleaning all the blood off afterward."

"But how did you manage it? Why didn't they resist? No, wait—I think I know. You're not alone in this scheme. The innkeeper is in it with you."

"How did you deduce that, Gordianus?"

"The way Zoticus and I slept that night—we were tired from the long day and the heat, but not that tired. It wasn't natural. Some sort of drug was put in our food or wine. Something that made us sleep like dead men. The innkeeper did it."

Marcus gave me a shrewd look.

"And he did the same thing to Titus Tullius and his party," I said. "He put something in their wine that sent them into a deep sleep—so deep that not one of them woke while you killed them at your leisure. Why didn't you kill Zoticus and me, as well?"

"I'm a soldier, Gordianus. I kill from necessity, not for enjoyment. Clearly, your interest in the ruins was historical, or in the case of your old tutor, sentimental. A Roman pup wandering amid the rubble and a doddering Greek declaiming poetry posed no threat to me. I told Gnaeus to drug you so that you'd sleep through the killing; I saw no need to kill you as well. It seems I made a mistake—which I now intend to rectify."

He deftly swung one leg over his horse and dismounted, keeping the drawn sword in his hand. He tightened his grip on the hilt, making ready to use it.

I backed away and tried to stall him with more questions. "The witch's curse—the lead tablet among the bodies—was it a forgery?"

He laughed. "Can you believe the coincidence? Gnaeus and I found it when we searched Tullius's room after the killing. We couldn't believe our luck—a genuine curse tablet, scary enough to make Lucius faint and even old Menenius lose all common sense."

"But who made the tablet?"

"Ismene, I'm sure. Lucius always said she was a witch. I took the lead tablet downstairs and hid it among the bodies. It was perfect, that Lucius should be the one to find it. And the way you read it aloud, with that tremor in your voice—like an actor on a stage! Even I had to shudder. 'Egyptian Ufer of the Mighty Name!'" Marcus laughed so hard he stopped in his tracks. But he was still holding the sword.

"Lucius said something about other soldiers who died, in their sleep," I said. "He blamed witchcraft."

Marcus shrugged. "That was my doing. Aulus figured out what I was up to, and demanded a share. So I poisoned him. A month later, Tiberius did the same. Lucius was sure they died by witchcraft and told everyone so. No suspicion ever fell on me."

"If poison worked before, why didn't you poison Tullius and the rest?" I said, desperate to keep stalling him.

He shook his head. "That would have required a great deal of poison. No, it was quicker and easier and more reliable to give them all a sleeping draft, and then use this." He slashed the air with his sword, so close that a gust of warm air blew against my nose.

While I ran through every question I could think of, I had been looking for something to throw at him. I was surrounded by rubble, yet all the stones and bits of wood were either too big or too small to use as a weapon. Marcus saw my consternation and smiled. He said he killed for necessity, not enjoyment, but the look on his face told another story.

I staggered back, weak from heat and thirst. My heart pounded so hard I thought my chest would burst. Amid the oily spots that swam before my eyes, I glimpsed ghostly faces—the dead of Corinth, making ready to welcome me.

I heard a strange whistling noise.

Marcus abruptly dropped his sword. His jaw went slack and his eyes rolled back in his head. He crumpled to the ground.

I stood dumbfounded, then looked up to see Ismene. She seemed to have materialized from thin air.

"How did you do that?" I whispered. "You killed him without even touching him. You were nowhere near him."

She gave me a withering look. "First of all, he's probably not dead. Feel the pulse at his wrist."

I did so. "You're right, he's only unconscious."

"And not likely to stay that way long. I'd tie him up, if I were you."

"With what?"

She rolled her eyes. "Use the leather reins from his horse."

"Ah, yes, of course. It's the heat—I can't seem to think straight. But I still don't understand how you did that. Was it a spell?"

"Feel the back of his head."

I did so. "There's a big lump. What sort of spell—"

"Really, young man! Did your father never teach you to use a sling?" She held up a bit of cloth. "Witchcraft achieves many things, but as long as there's an egg-sized stone handy, I don't need Ufer of the Mighty Name to bring a man down."

I finished tying Marcus's ankles and wrists. "You're very resourceful," I said. "Are you really a witch?"

"Titus Tullius and his friends are all dead, aren't they?"

"Yes, but that was because—"

"If you don't like my answers, don't ask me questions."

I thought about this, and decided to show her more respect. "The handwriting on the tablet at the inn was the same as the handwriting on the tablet I read in the room on the Slope of Sisyphus. You wrote both curses. That's your witch's den, isn't it?"

"I'm one of the women who use it, yes."

"Who is Eudocia, and why didn't you finish the curse against her?"

Ismene laughed. For a moment her face was transformed. She looked almost pretty. "Of all the questions to ask! Eudocia is someone's mother-in-law. At the last moment, the woman asking for the spell lost her nerve. I still made her pay me. Now, I suggest you drape this soldier over his horse and hurry back to Lechaeum, before you die of thirst."

"What about you? Don't you need the horse?"

"What for?"

"To get away. The commander has the whole garrison looking for you."

"I'm a witch, you silly boy. I don't need a horse to make my escape. Now go about your business and I'll go about mine." She reached into the narrow place, pulled out a handful of coins, then stuffed them into a pouch at her waist. The loose garment she was wearing appeared to have many such pouches sewn into it. Several were already bulging.

"You're taking Marcus's loot?"

"I never intended to do so, but Ananke demands it. Better I should have it than a Roman soldier."

"Titus Tullius impugned sorcery and insulted the dead of Corinth. Now he and his friends are dead. What about Marcus?"

"His own commander will see to his punishment."

"And Gnaeus?"

She spat on the ground. "There's a lead tablet under his bed right now. He'll be dead before nightfall."

Hackles rose on the back of my neck. "And me?"

She smiled. "You've done nothing wrong, young Roman. You and the poet showed only respect for the dead of Corinth, and for the sacred place of Persephone. You do the bidding of Moira in this affair. You are the agent of fate. Do you not realize that?

"Now go!"

By the time I got back to Lechaeum, the sun was low in the sky, casting long shadows. In the dry breeze that moved through the grass I no longer heard the whispers of the dead, only the sound of wind. The ghosts of Corinth were at peace, with me at least.

As I approached the inn, I could see at a distance that Antipater was still asleep under the fig tree. One of the dogs saw me and barked. Antipater shifted in his sleep, but did not wake. I thought I saw a movement at one of the windows upstairs. Had Gnaeus seen me? I hurried on to the garrison.

Lucius was on guard duty. At my approach, he ran to alert the commander. Menenius appeared a moment later. He strode out to meet me, staring at the soldier slung over the horse like a sack of grain. Marcus was just beginning to regain consciousness. He mumbled and tugged fitfully at the leather straps around his wrists and ankles.

"What in Hades is going on?" demanded Menenius.

My throat was so parched I couldn't speak. Menenius ordered water to be brought. It helped a little, but not much. It is not an easy thing, revealing a truth that will lead to another man's death. Marcus was a murderer many times over. He had poisoned two of his comrades and slit the throats of a dozen Roman citizens. If Ismene—or Moira—had not intervened, I would have been the thirteenth. I had a duty to both men and gods to deliver him to justice. Still, I found myself unable to look at Marcus as I told Menenius all I knew, aware that my testimony would lead surely and swiftly to his execution. Once he was fully awake, Marcus might deny my story, at first. But I had no doubt that Menenius would obtain a complete confession from him.

Roman citizens are accorded the dignity of a swift death by beheading, but what did the law decree for a soldier who had murdered his own comrades? Would he be crucified like a slave, or stoned like a deserter by his fellow legionnaires? I tried not to think about it. I had played my part. Now it would fall to Menenius to act as the agent of fate.

The commander dismissed me, saying he would question me again after interrogating Marcus. I walked swiftly to the inn. The first stars had appeared in the sky. The shade beneath the fig tree was now so dark I could hardly see Antipater, but I heard him softly snoring. The lazy dogs did not even look up.

I stepped into the inn. The vestibule was dark, but the doorway to the tavern framed the soft glow of a single lamp. Gnaeus must have lit the lamp. I imagined him standing in the room, alone amid the ghosts of the slain. At any moment, soldiers from the garrison would arrive to arrest him for his complicity in the murders. I had no intention of warning him, but something compelled me to step into the tavern.

Half in light, half in shadow, Gnaeus hung from a rope secured to a beam in the ceiling. His lifeless body still swayed slightly, as if he had committed the act only moments before. Ismene had told me he would be dead before nightfall.

The next day, Menenius allowed us to leave. He even arranged for our transportation across the isthmus. Two soldiers drove us in a wagon, and seemed glad for the excursion.

At Cenchrea, we found a ship to take us to Piraeus, and continued on our journey.

As the Isthmus of Corinth receded in the distance, I wondered if the magic of Ismene had truly motivated all the bloodshed and havoc of the last few days, with no one aware of the full truth except the witch herself. If that were the case, how many times already in my life had I been the unknowing agent of unseen powers, and when would I next fall under the spell of such sorcery?

I shivered at the thought, and hoped never to encounter Ismene again.

VI

THE MONUMENTAL GAUL

(The Colossus of Rhodes)

"Mark my words, Gordianus, that young fellow is destined to become one of the shining intellects of the age, a beacon of wisdom and learning."

This was quite a compliment, coming from Antipater. He was speaking of our host in Rhodes, a man named Posidonius. Considering the flecks of gray at his temples, I wouldn't have called Posidonius a "young fellow," but then, I was only eighteen. To my old tutor, I suppose Posidonius seemed quite youthful. He was certainly energetic, constantly jumping up from his chair to fetch a scroll to elucidate some point, or pacing to and fro across the garden and gesticulating as he recounted some tale about his travels in Gaul, from which he had only recently returned.

Posidonius was not just a scholar and a scientist; he was an intrepid explorer whose quest for knowledge had taken him to many lands. His travels had begun with a stop in Rome several years ago; that was when he first met Antipater, and so impressed the poet that the two exchanged many letters as Posidonius traveled to Africa and Spain, and then to Gaul, where he spent a number of years living among the natives and observing their strange customs. Posidonius had at last returned to Rhodes, just in time for Antipater and me to take advantage of his hospitality.

"Here, this is an example of what I was talking about," said Posidonius, returning to the garden. He carried a long knife, holding it forth on his palms so that we could observe the silver hilt decorated with elaborate whorls and weird animal faces. "This is a ceremonial knife that was actually used by a Gallic Druid in a blood ritual to predict the future. I witnessed the sacrifice with my own eyes. The victim was a captured warrior from another tribe. The poor fellow was made to stand with his hands bound behind his back while two strong men held him fast, then the chief Druid used this very knife to stab him, just above the diaphragm. As the victim convulsed, they released him and carefully observed in what direction he fell, how many times he kicked out his legs, and what sort of pattern his spurting blood made on the ground—and from those observations, the Druids were able to conclude that their chieftain's infant son would be free of the fever afflicting him within three days."

"And did the child recover?" asked Antipater.

"Yes, he did. Of course, most fevers, unless they kill the patient, are over within three days, but the chieftain was nonetheless much comforted by the prediction, and generously rewarded the Druids when it came true."

"Predicting the future from blood spatters—it seems rather far-fetched," I ventured to say.

Posidonius raised an eyebrow. "If a Roman augur may presume to read the will of the gods by watching a chicken peck at some scattered grain, why should a Druid not be able to do so by studying a pattern of blood?" From his blank expression, I couldn't tell whether he was being serious or sardonic.

Since leaving Rome on my travels with Antipater, moving among Greeks in the Greek-speaking part of Rome's empire, I had learned that it was not uncommon for a young Roman to be subjected to subtle ridicule, practical jokes, and even, on occasion, outright displays of hostility. The city of Rhodes and the island of the same name were not yet part of

Rome's empire, having maintained independence even as neighboring islands and much of the mainland of Asia were subjected to Roman rule, and in Rhodes I had not encountered quite as much anti-Roman sentiment as elsewhere. Still, I was not sure what to make of the tone Posidonius often took when addressing me, as if he were making a joke that I was too dull to perceive. Perhaps he simply spoke to me the way he spoke to the students who attended his academy.

It had been ten days since Antipater and I arrived in Rhodes. The ship carrying us had entered the harbor at dusk—and had been one of the last ships to do so, for winter was coming on, and with it the unpredictable gales and storms that put an end to the sailing season.

As we sailed past a long mole that projected into the water, I eagerly looked to see what every newcomer to Rhodes is curious to see: the remains of the fallen bronze Colossus, deemed one of the Seven Wonders of the World despite its ruined state. By the uncertain light I had caught glimpses of the huge and grotesquely disconnected remains that lay scattered on the mole—two feet still firmly connected to a high pedestal, a forearm that lay half-submerged amid the lapping waves, and most disconcerting, because one enormous eye seemed to be staring straight back at me, a gigantic head that lay on its side. Where the other eye should have been there was a gaping hole in the bronze. Perhaps it had been damaged when the giant statue tumbled to the ground, felled by an earthquake 135 years ago.

By the time the ship docked and the harbor officials boarded to inspect our travel documents, it had been too late to take a closer look at the Colossus. Instead, Antipater and I headed directly to the house of Posidonius, which was located in the city's acropolis district, a considerable distance from the harbor.

It was Antipater's plan that we would spend the winter in Rhodes. The large, luxuriously appointed house of Posidonius certainly seemed a comfortable place to do so. Weary of traveling, Antipater seemed content to venture no farther each day than the garden, where he liked to sit and bask whenever a bit of weak sunshine broke through the clouds, or to converse with our host, who joined us whenever a break in his teaching schedule allowed. When Posidonius was absent, Antipater perused our host's large collection of scrolls and travel memorabilia. In the evenings we dined with Posidonius in a charming room that opened onto the garden, usually joined by one or two of his more promising students, or by some person of note in the city. Rhodes was known not just for scholars, but for its athletes, merchants, and artists.

Under normal circumstances, Antipater would no doubt have been asked to address the students at the academy, but Posidonius understood that the poet was traveling incognito. Posidonius told us that he himself had occasionally assumed false identities during his travels, and he accepted Antipater's need for discretion without question. Antipater was always introduced not as a famous poet, but as the humble tutor Zoticus of Zeugma, traveling companion of young Gordianus of Rome.

Antipater had settled happily into this housebound routine, but I was growing restless. From the first morning, I had been eager to return to the harbor and take a closer look at the remains of the Colossus, but Antipater, who had been to Rhodes before and had seen the remains of the statue already, pointed out that there was no hurry, since we would be on the island for months. Whenever I mentioned my curiosity about the Colossus to Posidonius, he responded with a blank expression and told me to be patient. Did he consider me just another empty-headed Roman tourist, determined to check an item off a must-see list?

In fact, Posidonius had a reason to hold off showing me the Colossus, but I did not know that yet.

Just as Antipater and I leaned forward to take a closer look at the ritual Druid blade held forth by our host, a voice boomed out, speaking Greek with one of the strangest accents I had ever heard:

"What are you doing with my knife?"

All three of us gave a start. The knife seemed to jump from Posidonius's hands. He fumbled to keep from dropping it, and cut one of his fingers. The wound was slight, but a few drops of blood fell onto the paving stone at his feet.

The newcomer strode into the garden. His appearance was as

startling as his voice. He was very tall and wore a long, belted robe covered with complex embroidery; the whorls and other patterns reminded me of the decorations on the knife. His sandals, adorned with silver bosses and beaded leather tassels, looked like no shoes I had ever seen before, and left his toes bare. The hood of his robe was pushed back to reveal a great mass of fiery red hair, shot with gray and elaborately plaited. His cheeks were shaven, but the hair on his upper lip had been allowed to grow until it practically concealed his mouth, and hung down in knotted braids all the way to his chest. This was the first time I had ever seen a moustache, and it was a memorable specimen.

"Gatamandix! You gave us all a start," said Posidonius.

I gazed at the newcomer in wonder. By the way he was dressed, by his savage accent, by his assertion that the knife was his, and by the uncouth name Posidonius used to address him, there could be no doubt: the man was a Druid. I had seen surprising things during my travels with Antipater, but this was one of the most unexpected—a Gallic priest hundreds of miles from Gaul, here on the island of Rhodes.

"When did you get back from Lindos?" asked Posidonius.

"Just now."

"And did you have any luck?"

Perhaps the newcomer smiled; with his moustache in the way, it was hard to tell. "We found what we were looking for."

Posidonius's face registered excitement. "Did you bring it back to Rhodes with you? Is it here?"

"We returned by horse, up the coast road, but sent the cargo by ship."

"You found a captain still willing to sail?"

"It took some doing, but Cleobulus thought it would be safer that way. We were told it should arrive tomorrow."

Posidonius raised an eyebrow. "And the price?"

"The amount you sent was adequate, though just barely."

"Splendid! Ah, but let me introduce you to two other guests who'll be spending the winter here—Gordianus, a citizen of Rome, and his tutor, Zoticus. This is Gatamandix, a Druid of a tribe called the Segurovi.

Gatamandix showed great hospitality to me when I was in Gaul. When I returned to Rhodes, he came with me, along with a young fellow of the same tribe. They've just returned from an excursion down the coast to Lindos."

"A expedition to locate some object of value, I gather?" said Antipater.

The Druid seemed reluctant to answer.

Posidonius cleared his throat "We'll speak of the matter later."

Seeing our host wished to change the subject, Antipater turned his attention to the knife in Posidonius's hand. "Do I understand that this magnificent blade belongs to you, Gatamandix?"

The Druid took the knife and gripped the hilt with a light, familiar touch. "I suppose Posidonius told you how he witnessed a 'barbaric' human sacrifice committed with this very knife? I see from your faces that he did. Yes, this is my knife. And yes, I was the Druid who delivered the death blow—like this!" He thrust the knife into empty air.

Antipater and I jumped. The Druid appeared to smile behind his moustache. "Don't worry. The gods demand no sacrifice today."

"Where is Cleobulus?" said Posidonius.

"Your student left us at the door and went on to his parents' house."

"And Vindovix?" said Posidonius.

"He went straight to his room," said Gatamandix. "Tired from riding all day. He's probably asleep."

Posidonius shook his head. "How that young man stays so fit is a mystery; he seems to do nothing but sleep and eat. But it's just as well he didn't come to the garden. Zoticus and Gordianus will be able to—ah, but I'll say no more, or else I'll compromise the experiment."

"An experiment?" said Antipater.

"Yes, in which you and Gordianus will play a central part."

"You never mentioned this before."

"Because the time was not yet right. But now we must make haste."

"Are we leaving the house?" There was a note of complaint in Antipater's voice.

"We are, indeed. The time has come to visit the Colossus."

Posidonius saw the excitement on my face, and smiled. My desire was at last to be realized. But what did Posidonius mean when he spoke of an 'experiment'? He would say no more. I quickly fetched some cloaks, for it was likely to be chilly and windy at the waterfront, then followed our host to the vestibule.

Gatamandix stayed behind in the garden. I glanced over my shoulder and saw the Druid turn the knife this way and that, staring at the blade.

"What do you know about the Colossus?" said Posidonius.

The four of us were strolling past the sporting complex just down the hill from Posidonius's house—four, because we were accompanied by a slave named Zenas who was perhaps ten years older than I and was often at his master's side, ready to take dictation on a wax tablet or to run a quick errand. To our left was the footracing stadium; the long, low wall that supported the viewing stands was decorated with magnificent mosaics of gods and athletes. To our right was one of the long porticos that enclosed the palestra; despite the cool weather, between the columns I caught glimpses of naked youths wrestling on the grass while their tutors looked on and shouted encouragement. I was reminded of something my father had once said: "A Greek will exercise in the nude even if there's snow coming down."

Posidonius's question about the Colossus was directed at me. I cleared my throat. "All I know about the Colossus, I learned from, er, Zoticus," I began, thinking this a rather clever way to deflect any criticism of my erudition, or lack thereof. But Posidonius, an experienced teacher, would have none of it.

"Come, come, young Roman," he said, "either you know something about the Colossus or you do not." Zenas looked amused. He was probably used to watching his master make pupils squirm.

Chagrined, I started over. "As I understand it, the statue was constructed almost two hundred years ago. It was built in the image of the sun god, Helios, whom the Rhodians revere above all others, because it was Helios who at the dawn of time raised this island from the bottom of the sea. The first capital of Rhodes was Lindos, on the east coast, but a new city, also called Rhodes, was designed and built from scratch here on the northern tip of the island a little over three hundred years ago. So the city of Rhodes is relatively young, much newer than Rome or Athens—"

"All very true," said Posidonius, "but you stray from the subject."

"Yes, the Colossus. Well, the story of its creation is this: the city of Rhodes had just survived a long siege by Demetrius, king of Macedon, who in his attempt to take the city built enormous weapons of war and metal-plated siege towers on a scale never seen before. But Demetrius at last admitted defeat and abandoned the island. To celebrate their deliverance, the Rhodians melted down all the bronze from the battering rams, catapults, and towers, and sold whatever else remained of the hated weapons to build a gigantic statue of the sun god, a celebration of life and beauty to match the awesome scale of Demetrius's engines of death and destruction.

"The commission was given to the sculptor Chares, a native Rhodian from Lindos. It took him twelve years to build the Colossus, and no one knows quite how he did it. Some say hoists were used to lift the pieces into place; others say that a succession of spiral ramps were built around the statue as it grew upward, and that each new section was forged, molded, and poured into place atop the previous section. However it was made, when the Colossus was complete, and whatever ramps or scaffolding that surrounded it were cleared away, all who saw the image of Helios were astounded. The statue was by far the tallest ever made—well over a hundred feet, and on its fifty-foot pedestal, it towered even higher. The fame of the statue spread all over the world, from the marshes of Lake Maotis to the Pillars of Hercules, from the upper cataracts of the Nile to . . ." I tried to remember what regions lay to the uttermost north.

"To Gaul," suggested Posidonius.

"I was going to say Ultima Thule."

"Yet I can personally assure you that the Colossus is known in Gaul," said Posidonius. "Even when pairing hyperboles, a speaker should never choose mere rhetorical flourish when a true example is at hand. But go on."

"And so the Colossus stood, astounding all who saw it—until, less than sixty years later, a great earthquake shook the island. Many temples and other buildings were damaged, but the most terrible catastrophe was the fall of the Colossus, which broke at the knees and came tumbling down, breaking into pieces as it struck the ground. And there the Colossus remains to this day, and people from all over the world still come to Rhodes to see the ruins, for no one has yet built a monument to match it."

Posidonius begrudged me a smile. "Very good, Gordianus. Your tutor has taught you well."

We came to an intersection where Posidonius indicated we should turn to the right. Rhodes is a city of wide streets laid out in a grid pattern, and the thoroughfare before us was the broadest and grandest in the whole city, adorned with splashing fountains and lush gardens. Lining the way were literally hundreds of statues depicting gods and famous heroes. Many were dedicated to the generals and city leaders who had defended Rhodes against the siege of Demetrius.

We passed a succession of splendid altars and temples, then came to the city's vast public square, which the Greeks call an agora, and crossed it diagonally. I began to smell the sea and to hear the lapping waves and seagull cries of the waterfront. A few blocks beyond the agora we came to the dual harbors bisected by a broad mole, edged with boulders, that projected far into the water. The harbors were crowded with ships moored for the winter, but with no cargo to unload or vessels setting sail, there were few sailors about, and the waterfront had a strangely deserted feel.

A simple rope barrier barred us from proceeding onto the mole. From a nearby hut emerged a little bald-headed man with a grin on his face and his open palm extended.

"Come to see the famous Colossus, have you?" he asked. "You won't regret it. One of the Wonders of the World, that's for sure. Is it a guided tour you'll be wanting, or—oh, but it's you, master Posidonius. Back again, and bringing more guests? Always good to see you. For such a distinguished citizen as yourself, there's no charge, of course. Here, let me unhitch the rope for you. No Gauls with you this time? My, how those two savages gawked and gaped when they saw our Colossus. Still, your friends are in for quite a treat, especially this young one. You'll never have seen anything like the Colossus, my boy. Now watch your step out there—be mindful of the rocks and the sharp bits of metal as you go wandering among the ruins."

Whether he was charging admission or not, the little man kept his hand out as we passed by, and at a sign from Posidonius I saw Zenas produce a small pouch and drop a few coins onto his open palm.

Under a gray sky and with a brisk wind in our faces, we hiked to the end of the mole. Ahead of us loomed a sight that grew ever stranger as we approached—the fragments of the Colossus, which lay in pieces like the body of a warrior hacked asunder. There were a few other visitors on the mole, wandering amid the ruins, and their presence served to show the scale of the statue. The thing was man-made, but so bizarre, so unearthly, that it evoked a kind of religious wonder. Here was a thumb so huge I could barely wrap my arms around it, and here a finger larger than most full-size statues. Here was an arm, lying athwart the mole like a gigantic serpent, and there a torch the size of a lighthouse that must have been held in one of the statue's hands. Inside some of the fragments I could see the iron bars and hidden bolts that had secured the structure from within; the lower extremities had apparently been filled with stones to act as ballast. In some places the bronze was as thick as my forearm, but in others as thin as a coin.

A thought occurred to me. "With so much of the Colossus intact, why was it not rebuilt after it fell? Could it not have been reassembled?"

"That idea was debated," said Posidonius. "Some wanted to rebuild the Colossus. Others proposed that the broken statue should be melted down and the bronze reused or sold, for the earthquake had caused considerable damage all over Rhodes, and money and materials were needed for rebuilding. To settle the question, a delegation was sent to Delphi."

"What did the oracle of Apollo decree?" I asked.

"That the Colossus should never be rebuilt—but also that the pieces should be left where they lay and never be disturbed. As happens so often with oracles, the answer split the difference and satisfied neither party. Yet the wisdom of Apollo is now manifest, for here lies the Colossus two hundred years after it was made, as famous now as when it stood upright, the pride of Rhodes despite its ruined state."

Rounding a bit of knee, I was suddenly confronted by the statue's genitalia, a scrotum and phallus surmounted by stylized whorls of hair. In their original context, these parts were no doubt reasonably proportioned, but seen on their own they were rather disconcerting. Antipater laughed aloud at the sight, but he also paused to touch the phallus for good luck. Many others had apparently done the same thing, for the bronze at that spot was shinier than elsewhere.

Farther on we came to the huge face I had seen from the ship the evening we arrived, with its staring eye. Radiating from the sculpted hair atop the head was a crown of sunbeams. Some were bent and some had broken off entirely, but a couple were intact and projected like gigantic spearheads sharpened to a point.

The massive stone pedestal, to which the feet were still attached, was itself as tall as any tenement tower in Rome. At its base, on a huge bronze plaque, inscribed in letters so large they could have been read from ships in the harbor, was a dedicatory poem. Antipater saw me mouthing the words—my skill at reading Greek lagged behind my ability to speak it—and he commenced reciting the lines in a booming voice, with as much conviction as if he had composed the poem himself:

"O Helios, this image we raise to thy renown.
The spoils of battle become thy crown.

The reek of war is pierced by thy light.
With thy blessing we end the fight.
The people of Rhodes stand proud and free.
Dominion is ours on land and sea."

Posidonius and I applauded the recitation, and Antipater took a bow.

"Now that you've seen the remains of the Colossus with your own eyes," said Posidonius, "can you imagine what it must have looked like when it stood upright?"

I put my hands on my hips and gazed upward, trying to envision the statue looming above me. "It would appear that Helios was naked, except for a scanty cloak draped over one shoulder—you can see folds of his garment amid the bronze ruins, but they can't have covered much. He stood with one foot a bit forward and the other back, with the knee bent. One arm was lowered, and in that hand he held a torch. The other arm was raised, with the palm open to greet arriving ships."

"Would you say he was handsome?"

"Well, yes, I suppose—but his nose is rather long. Probably the whole face was a bit elongated, to compensate for foreshortening when seen from below, and the features a bit exaggerated, so as to give the face more character when seen from a great distance."

"Very good, Gordianus!" said Antipater. "I don't recall ever teaching you the principles of perspective."

I shrugged. "It only stands to reason. Or perhaps Chares' living model simply had a long nose and strong cheekbones."

Posidonius smiled. "Antipater told me that you're an unusually observant young man, and so you are. You've looked closely at the face, then, and at the rest of the body?"

"I suppose I have."

"Very good. Try to keep the image of that face in your mind when we return to my house."

This request seemed unnecessary; having seen the Colossus at close quarters, who could forget it? But to oblige my host, I stared long and hard at the face of the fallen Colossus.

That evening at dinner, the three of us were joined by Gatamandix. The Druid's manners were as outlandish as his appearance. Instead of reclining, he insisted on sitting upright to eat, perching on the edge of his dining couch as if it were a chair. He explained that he considered it unnatural for a man to swallow lying on his side. He also had a tendency to speak louder than was necessary, and to do so while chewing his food.

We were also joined by a young Rhodian named Cleobulus, who had escorted the Gauls on their trip to Lindos. Cleobulus was a short, snub-nosed little fellow with mouse-brown hair, and his manners were very prim and proper, in marked contrast to those of the Druid. Posidonius introduced Cleobulus as one of his most outstanding pupils, whose special interest was the history of his native island, about which few men could claim to know more.

The first course, an egg custard with figs, was just being served when we were joined by a final guest, the young Gaul who was traveling with Gatamandix. He made no apology for arriving late, and before he sat down on the dining couch next to the Druid he yawned and stretched, as if he had just awakened from a nap.

"Zoticus, Gordianus, this is Vindovix, of the Segurovi." Posidonius looked intently at Antipater and me, as if he wished to study our reaction.

Vindovix was certainly a striking young man. His size was his most impressive feature; he was practically a giant. Also notable was his long hair, which was the color of white gold, and quite coarse; later I would learn that he washed it with a lime solution that not only lightened the color but also gave it the texture of a horse's mane, an affectation much prized by the Gauls. Like Gatamandix, he wore a moustache, though his was not quite as extravagant, reaching only a little past his chin. He had prominent cheekbones, a long nose, and a broad forehead. His eyes

were the palest possible shade of blue, like sunlight on the crest of a
wave.

His brawny arms were left bare by the peculiar garment he wore, a
sort of leather tunic closed by laces in the front; it was so short that
when he yawned and stretched, his midriff was exposed. His bottom
half was covered by a garment called *bracae,* or breeches, made of
supple leather that fitted him like a second skin around his hips and
wrapped separately around each leg, reaching all the way to his ankles, with a sort of pouch where all the seams converged. How a man
could wear something so constraining around his private parts, I
could not imagine.

Like Gatamandix, he wore odd-looking sandals decorated with
tassels and beads. His toes, flecked with golden hair, were uncom-
monly large.

The conversation was about travel—Posidonius's travels in Gaul,
and the Gauls' travels to Greece, with observations about differences
between the two cultures. Antipater occasionally had something to say,
but I was mostly silent, as was Vindovix. Nor did Cleobulus say much.
The young scholar seemed to be in a sour mood, and not overly fond of
the Gauls.

All through the meal, I felt that our host was observing us with a
peculiar and inexplicable intensity. I noticed that his eyes repeatedly
traveled from Antipater and me to Vindovix and back, as if he expected
us to react in some way to the young Gaul's presence. At last, over a
dish of squid in aniseed sauce, Posidonius could contain himself no
longer.

"Zoticus—Gordianus—when you look at Vindovix, what do you
see?"

Antipater tilted his head. "He's a very handsome young man."

Posidonius nodded. "His fellow Gauls would certainly say so. But
would you not agree that his features are a bit—'strong,' shall we say,
by Greek standards?"

Antipater shrugged. "Ideals of beauty differ from place to place.
The young man is certainly fit. And very large."

"Fit? He has the physique of a god!" declared Posidonius. "As for his size, I'll grant that he's bigger than any Greek I know, but he's actually a bit under average for a Gaul. What did Aristotle say? 'Beauty resides in a big body; small men may be graceful and well-proportioned, but not beautiful.' Bad news for us Greeks, eh, Cleobulus?" Posidonius laughed, but his pupil did not. "Yes, Vindovix is a robust specimen, by any standards. But is there nothing else you see when you observe him, Zoticus? No? What about you, Gordianus?"

I wrinkled my brow. "Now that you mention it, he does look a bit familiar, somehow."

"Does he, indeed? And where might you have seen him before?"

"I can't imagine. I've certainly never been to Gaul. And I don't suppose you've ever been to Rome, have you, Vindovix?"

The Gaul smiled, flashing perfectly white teeth. His eyes were half-shut, as if he were still waking up. His accent was thick and his grammar a bit stilted, but then, so was mine when I spoke Greek, though I liked to think I was getting better. "No, Gordianus, never have I been to Rome." With a forefinger and thumb he slowly stroked the tips of his moustache. "If I should come, will you let me sleep with you?"

I laughed. "*Stay* with me, I think you mean. Of course."

Posidonius cleared his throat. "Now think, Gordianus," he said. "Look at Vindovix's face, and tell me if it reminds you of anything— perhaps something you've seen quite recently, here in Rhodes."

"Well . . ." I stared openly at Vindovix, and was a little unnerved at the way he stared back at me, smiling, with his eyes half-shut. "He does look a bit like . . . but it's hard to say, because of the moustache. . . ."

Posidonius raised an eyebrow. "It's as I've told you, Vindovix, you'll have to shave that thing if you want anyone to see the resemblance."

The young Gaul sighed. "Vindovix without his moustache—hard to imagine. So many girls back in Gaul would weep if they should hear of such a thing. But very well—perhaps I shave it off tomorrow. You will help me, Cleobulus?" He looked sidelong at the little Rhodian.

Cleobulus made a face. "I am not a barber," he said. "We have slaves to do that sort of thing."

Vindovix laughed softly. He seemed to enjoy teasing Cleobulus. "Or maybe, if I just cover my mouth with one hand, like this, and lean to one side, and turn my face away a bit . . ."

Vindovix stared at me with one pale blue eye, and suddenly I was seeing the face of the Colossus as I first glimpsed it when I sailed into the harbor, with its one eye staring back at me.

"Uncanny!" I whispered.

Antipater leaned forward, his brow furrowed. "He has the face of the Colossus! How can that be?"

Cleobulus grimaced and shook his head. "Ridiculous," the young Rhodian muttered. "They're not the least bit alike."

But our host was pleased. He clapped his hands and laughed.

"Posidonius, please explain," said Antipater.

"Very well. Now that my little experiment is concluded, I will share the tale. When I was staying with Gatamandix in Gaul, he often asked about the other places I had seen in my travels, and about my home in Rhodes. I was the first Greek who had ever visited the tribe, you see, and none of them had ever traveled beyond Gaul. Imagine my surprise when, as I began to describe to him the landmark for which Rhodes is most famous, it turned out that he knew about the Colossus already. He even knew that it was called the Colossus, and the fact that it represented the sun god. About some things he was mistaken—he didn't know the Colossus had fallen, for example, and he had a rather exaggerated idea of its actual height, thinking it literally bestrode the harbor, with a foot on each side; well, no statue could be that large. But such garbled details invariably occur when a tale travels a great distance. What amazed me was that he knew anything about the Colossus at all."

"How had he heard of it?" said Antipater.

"Perhaps I should allow Gatamandix himself to explain."

The Druid nodded. "As I told Posidonius, the existence of the great

Colossus has been known among the Segurovi for many generations—because it was an ancestor of Vindovix who posed for the statue."

My jaw dropped. I stared at Vindovix, who laughed and slapped his leather-clad knee. "Yes, it was my great-great-great-great-grandfather. He also was named Vindovix."

"But how is such a thing possible?" I said.

"It's *not*," said Cleobulus, clenching his teeth. "At the time the Colossus was made, no Gaul had ever set foot in Rhodes."

"Actually," said Posidonius, "it is *just* possible. The fact is, the Gauls first became known to most Greeks when a Gallic chieftain called Cimbaules made an incursion against the Macedonians, a little over two hundred years ago—at exactly the time when Chares began working on the Colossus."

"I thought the Gauls first invaded Greece some twenty years later than that, when they swept all the way down to Delphi," said Antipater.

"That was the *second* Gallic incursion," said Posidonius. "Everyone's heard of it, because the Gauls caused so much terror and destruction. But there was an earlier invasion—or attempted invasion, I should say, because Cimbaules was soundly repelled by the Macedonians and never reached the Aegean Sea."

"And was this Cimbaules of the same tribe as Gatamandix and Vindovix?" said Antipater.

"As a matter of fact, he was not," said Gatamandix. "But among his warriors it seems there was at least one Segurovi, called Vindovix. And when Cimbaules was defeated, this Vindovix was captured and made a slave—"

"But he didn't die a slave," said Vindovix. "He was still young and strong when he returned to Gaul—young enough to marry and have a son, my great-great-great-grandfather. That Vindovix had many stories to tell of his time among the Greeks, stories that were passed down from generation to generation, until my father told them to me. The most amazing of those stories was about his time on a great island that he called *Rodos*, where a maker of statues used him as the model for the most gigantic statue ever made, which the Greeks called the *Colosso*. For many days he was made to stand naked, with a crown of sunbeams on his head and a torch in one hand, while the sculptor made a small version of the statue, which was then used to make the big one. My ancestor never forgot the day the *Colosso* was dedicated, and he saw his own image tower above the people of *Rodos*. He realized then and there that he was never meant to be a slave, so he jumped in the water, swam to the mainland, and fought his way home to Gaul."

"More likely," said Posidonius quietly, "the sculptor Chares realized it would never do for the fellow to remain on Rhodes. What would people think, if they realized a barbarian slave had been the model for Helios, rather than some famous, freeborn athlete of good Rhodian blood? I suspect Chares gave the slave his freedom and a bit of silver, put him on a ship, and told him never to come back."

"But, even if we grant that this fantastic story could be true," said Antipater, "we have no way of knowing what Vindovix's ancestor looked like."

"Unless he looked exactly like his descendant, who sits before us," said Posidonius. "Certain features, and combinations of features, recur in a given bloodline, generation after generation; like begets like. Can it be a coincidence that Vindovix claims his ancestor was the model for the Colossus, and that both you and Gordianus saw Vindovix's resemblance to the statue?"

"Only after you prompted them," said Cleobulus. "If this was an experiment, Teacher, your methodology was deeply flawed."

"To be sure, the outcome of my little experiment was merely suggestive, not conclusive." Posidonius pressed his fingertips together. "Perhaps we shall learn more when my precious cargo arrives tomorrow."

"Yes, what is this treasure that Gatamandix and Vindovix went seeking down in Lindos?" said Antipater.

"Now that you've seen both the Colossus and Vindovix, and judged the resemblance for yourself, I suppose I can tell you," said Posidonius. "Gatamandix came with me to Rhodes so that he might learn from his travels, but Vindovix came for a more singular purpose—so that he might see the remains of the Colossus with his own eyes. The story of his ancestor's role in its creation has been in his family for two hundred years, and when Fate brought a visitor from Rhodes into his life, it seemed to him that he must be destined to come here.

"And then, my brilliant pupil Cleobulus—whose studies include the history of the Colossus—got word of a life-sized statue made of plaster that closely resembles the Colossus, down in Lindos. Might it be a scale model created by Chares himself? No such model has ever been found before. The thing was said to be housed in a farmer's shed, along with some of Chares' tools. The farmer apparently had no idea what such artifacts would be worth to a scholar like myself, though I daresay I made a fair offer when I sent Cleobulus down to Lindos to ascertain their authenticity and condition. It seemed only fitting that Vindovix should go with him, along with Gatamandix."

"And was the plaster statue authentic?" said Antipater.

Cleobulus cleared his throat. "I have every reason to think so. The statue didn't bear Chares' mark, but then, he wouldn't have bothered to put that on a plaster cast, would he? However, tools stamped with the mark of Chares' workshop were found in the same shed, and also a scroll in a leather case. The document is very faded and brittle, but it clearly shows diagrams and mathematical calculations for enlarging the model to the scale of the Colossus."

"Marvelous!" said Antipater. "What was the statue's condition?"

"Except for a few nicks here and there," said Cleobulus, "and patches of mold and other discolorations on the white plaster, it was in remarkably good shape, considering its age and fragility. It was in a corner of the shed, surrounded by moth-eaten rugs. The old farmer said it had been there since he was a child."

"But did it look like Vindovix?" I asked.

Cleobulus exchanged a look with the two Gauls. His nostrils flared. Gatamandix's face was inscrutable. Vindovix looked amused.

"On that, we had a difference of opinion," said Cleobulus.

"No matter," said Posidonius. "Barring a storm at sea or some other catastrophe, the ship should arrive in the harbor tomorrow. When the statue is brought here and uncrated, we can stand it side by side with Vindovix, and each of us can judge for himself."

"What a splendid occasion that will be!" declared Antipater. "A suitable subject for a poem. . . .

"Thus was the method of Chares revealed,
When upon his model we gazed, eyes peeled—"

Cleobulus glumly shook his head.

After dinner, Posidonius retired to his library. It was his habit to stay up late, reading and writing. Antipater went directly to bed. The two Gauls retired to their guest quarters. Cleobulus, who lived with his parents in a house not far away but was in no hurry to go home, suggested that he and I share some wine and play a few rounds of a Rhodian board game. Away from the Gauls, and after a cup or two of wine, he turned out to be an amiable enough companion, and very good at tossing dice. When I finally won a round, I suspected it was only because he let me.

After conclusively thrashing me in the final round, Cleobulus took his leave and headed home. I visited the latrina at the far corner of the house—Posidonius's plumbing was as modern as any in Rome—and was heading to my bedroom when I encountered a hulking silhouette.

The passage was lit only by pale moonlight, but there was no mistaking the figure before me. Who else was that big, and had such a mane of coarse hair? Though I could see him only dimly, it appeared that Vindovix was no longer dressed in his strange Gallic costume. Indeed, he appeared to be wearing nothing at all. Perhaps that was how Gauls slept, I thought. Presuming he was on his way to the latrina, I stepped aside to let him pass, but he didn't move.

"Can you not sleep, either, my Roman friend?" he said.

"I was just going to bed."

"Alone?"

I shrugged. "Posidonius's house is very large. I have my own room."

"So do I. Perhaps you would like to join me?"

"Oh, no, my room is quite comfortable."

He sighed, sounding exasperated. "At dinner, you said I could sleep with you if I should ever come to Rome."

"Well, that's not exactly—"

"Why wait? We can sleep together tonight."

His meaning at last became clear to me. I looked at the figure before me—more than a head taller than I, and almost twice as broad—and laughed a bit nervously.

"Is it my moustache?" he said. He shook his head. "How you Greeks seem to hate it! I can't understand. In Gaul, a fine moustache is a mark of manhood. It's quite an honor, to be allowed to touch another man's moustache. Here, Gordianus, see for yourself." He took my hand and raised it to his face.

For an instant, my fingertips made contact with the silky hair above his lip, then I snatched my hand away. I mumbled something about heading to my room. He did not yield at all, and I had to squeeze past him. He snorted, sounding quite disgusted.

I hurried down the passage and around a corner—where I ran into our host, vaguely lit from behind by the glow from his library.

"I fear you've offended him, Gordianus," Posidonius whispered.

"Offended him? I don't see how. If anything—"

"The Gauls are not like the Greeks, Gordianus, and certainly not like the Romans. They have their own customs about this sort of thing. He was doing you an honor by inviting you to join him."

"Yes, perhaps, but—"

"And you gave him great offense when you refused. I don't think he's used to that."

"Perhaps not in Gaul, but—"

"Here, step into the library, where we can talk properly." He led the way. Once there, he offered me a cup of wine, and I did not refuse.

"It's a curious thing," he said, taking a sip. "In my opinion, the Gallic women are the most comely of all barbarian females, yet the Gallic men hardly seem to notice them. They're all mad for each other. They even have a form of marriage between men, but that doesn't stop them from being wildly promiscuous. Now among the Greeks, there is a long and venerated tradition of intimate relations between comrades in arms, or between an older man and a younger whom he chooses to mentor. But among the Gauls—well, anything goes! Often they sleep in groups at night, rolling around on fur skins until all hours, the more the merrier. The best-looking young men strut about, flaunting their moustaches and brazenly offering themselves to anyone who might be interested. They have no standards at all."

I frowned, feeling vaguely insulted.

"And if anyone *should* turn him down, a young Gaul takes such rejection as a terrible affront to his dignity. Vindovix is a very proud young fellow. As I say, I don't think he's used to being rebuffed."

I grunted. "How do you know all this about the Gauls?"

Posidonius raised an eyebrow. "A traveler must be open to new experiences, Gordianus, or what is the use of travel? But I was not entirely surprised to find such customs among the Gauls. Aristotle commented on the relations between Gallic men. How he knew, I'm not sure, since Aristotle lived long before the invasion of Cimbaules—"

"Are you saying I should apologize to Vindovix?"

He smiled. "The two of you are set to spend the winter together under my roof. Do try to remember that Vindovix is a very long way from home, and he's not much older than you are."

I shook my head. "I must admit, I don't know much about the world beyond Rome. This journey with Antipater is certainly opening my eyes. As for . . . touching Vindovix's moustache . . . my father taught me that, while the Greeks may take a different view, among Romans carnal relations between males are acceptable only between a master and his slave, and only if the master plays the conqueror, and only if no one ever talks about it. My father frowns on such relations."

"Why is that?"

"He says it's unseemly to subject any slave, male or female, to unwanted advances."

"What if the desire is mutual?"

"I asked him that. Between master and slave, he says, there inevitably exists some element of coercion."

"I think your father is a bit of a philosopher, Gordianus."

"I suppose he is."

"Clearly, you've given some thought to these questions of human behavior. I'm sure things will work out between you and Vindovix, one way or another. Tell me, was your rejection of his advances predicated on your reaction to his primary or secondary substance?"

I recognized this as philosopher talk, but had no idea what he meant.

Posidonius pursed his lips. "Let me put it this way: is it that you find this particular man unattractive, or do you have no attraction to men at all?"

I considered this. "He's awfully big."

"Big? Oh, I see. You find the prospect daunting?"

"Well, yes."

"I don't think you need to worry about that. I believe Vindovix prefers that his partners 'play the conqueror,' as you call it."

"Are you sure about that?" I pictured Vindovix, looming over me in the passage.

Posidonius gave me a knowing look. "Did you not embark on this journey with Antipater to have new experiences? We have a long, gloomy winter ahead of us. A bit of companionship might make the time pass much more pleasantly."

From a small table nearby, a flash of light caught my eye. It was the knife of Gatamandix, its blade reflecting the light of a lamp hung above it. Lying next to it was a parchment with drawings on it.

Posidonius followed my gaze. "How Gatamandix loves that knife of his! It's a sign of his authority, you see. Among the Gauls, the Druids are not just seers, but the guardians of moral conduct; they judge those accused of crimes and mete out punishments, including executions. A Druid's knife is his ultimate tool of enforcement. Gatamandix cursed himself for leaving his knife behind when he went to Lindos; that's why he was so disgruntled to see me holding it when he returned. Even so, I've persuaded him to lend it to me for a few days, so that I can make a thorough study of the decorations on the hilt. The iconography of the Gauls is amazingly complex, quite fascinating, really—"

I tried to suppress a yawn.

"Off to bed with you, then," said Posidonius.

"No, please continue—"

"Off, I said."

Before I knew it, I was back in the darkened passage, and Posidonius had shut the library door behind me. I headed to my room.

The ship from Lindos did not arrive the next morning. Apparently, there had been a windstorm off the coast—exactly the sort of weather that stopped ships from sailing at this time of year, even to make short journeys like that from Lindos to Rhodes. Probably the ship was merely delayed, said Posidonius; but I could see that he was nervous, no doubt imagining the precious plaster model lost forever at the bottom of the sea, or, just as bad, reduced to dust if the crate had come loose from the ropes securing it and been thrown this way and that on a storm-tossed ship. As darkness fell, the ship still had not arrived.

When we all gathered with our host for dinner—the Gauls, Cleobulus, Antipater, and myself—I noticed, with a bit of a start, that Vindovix had shaved his moustache. He looked almost civilized, I thought, and the change definitely heightened his resemblance to the Colossus. I tried not to stare, fearing he would misinterpret my interest, but he seemed to avoid my gaze altogether.

We were still eating when Zenas came rushing in to inform his master that the ship and its cargo had just arrived in the harbor, apparently safe and sound.

"Shall I have the crate unloaded and carted here at once, Master?" said Zenas.

Posidonius's eyes lit up at the prospect, but he shook his head. "No, the hazards of transporting such a fragile object across the city by night are too great. We'll leave that until morning. In the meantime, Zenas, I want you to spend the night on the ship and to keep watch over the crate. I can't trust the crew to do so; after sailing through a storm, they're likely to drink themselves into a stupor. Can you stay awake until dawn?"

"Certainly, Master," said Zenas. "You can rely on me. I'll guard the crate with my very life!"

Posidonius laughed. "And how would you do that—wielding your stylus and wax tablet like a sword and shield? Just see that the crate is securely tied down and that nothing falls on it or bumps into it. At first light, hire some carters to bring it here and make sure they avoid any potholes or sudden jolts."

"The statue will come to no harm while it's in my care, Master. Just let me fetch a heavy cloak to keep myself warm." Zenas took his leave.

Smiling broadly, Posidonius clapped his hands and called for more wine. "Tomorrow, we shall see the face of the Colossus as it was rendered by the hand of Chares himself."

But it was not to be.

Posidonius's guests were all up early the next morning, and Cleobulus, having gone home after dinner, rejoined us shortly after dawn. An hour passed, and then another, and still the crate had not arrived. At last Posidonius sent a boy to check on Zenas's progress.

An hour later the boy ran into the garden. "Master! I looked for Zenas everywhere, but I couldn't find him."

"Is he not on the ship?"

"No. The captain says that Zenas arrived there last night, just as the crew were going to bed. The last time they saw him, he was sitting atop the crate, looking very alert. But when they awoke this morning, Zenas was nowhere to be seen."

"And the crate?"

"It's still there, just as it was, tied down on the deck."

Posidonius frowned. "This is not like Zenas. Not like him at all. I must go to the harbor at once to see what's happened."

"We'll go with you," said Antipater, and we all made ready to set out.

The slave was right: Zenas was nowhere to be seen. But some trace of him did remain. On the deck of the ship, not far from the crate, lay his stylus, and some distance away, amid a coil of rope, lay his wax tablet.

Posidonius shook his head. "Zenas would never mislay or abandon his stylus and wax tablet—not by choice. And why do they lie so far apart? This makes me very uneasy. At least the crate appears to be untouched," he said, walking slowly around it.

"Or perhaps not," I said. "Look there, near the top, along that seam where two planks meet. From the grain of the wood, you can see there was a knothole in one of the boards, but it looks to me as though it's been knocked out and widened by the use of some sharp instrument— you can see the scrapings of a chisel or some other tool on the wood, and here on the deck, directly below, there are traces of shavings and sawdust."

"So there are. You have a keen eye, Gordianus." Posidonius rose onto tiptoes and put his eye to the hole.

"What do you see?" said Antipater.

"It's dark. I can't be sure." Posidonius stepped back. "Captain, did you and your men hear nothing last night?"

The captain was a grizzled seaman with a weathered face and an unkempt beard. He stank of wine. "Most of the men went ashore," he said. "After that storm we sailed through, they wanted to feel solid ground beneath their feet. Those who stayed aboard bunked be-lowdecks, where it's warmer. I slept like a dead man myself."

"Helped by a generous amount of wine, no doubt," said Posidonius.

The captain scowled. "We left it to your man to look after the crate. He seemed sober enough, and eager to do his job."

Posidonius scowled. "Can someone remove the top of this crate?"

"I'll do it myself," said the captain. He fetched a crowbar and a wooden box to stand on.

"Careful!" cried Posidonius, as the man went to work. My teeth were set on edge by the shriek of nails being drawn from the wood.

At last the captain lifted the lid free and handed it down to two of his sailors. He stepped down from the box.

Posidonius quickly took his place. He looked inside. He drew a sharp breath. His shoulders sagged.

"What is it?" said Antipater.

"See for yourself," said Posidonius. With my assistance, Antipater took his place on the box.

Antipater gasped. "By Hercules! What a disaster!"

I helped him down from the box. I stepped aside, deferring to Cleobulus and the Gauls, but all three kept their distance. Cleobulus looked especially anxious, I thought.

I stepped onto the box and peered down into the crate.

No one could fault the manner in which the statue had been packed. The crate was well proportioned, and folds of soft cloth had been tied around the statue to cushion it. These concealed the details of the statue, but its general shape could be perceived, and it was obvious at once that the head was missing—or rather, destroyed, for plaster fragments and bits of dust that had once constituted the head lay scattered amid the packing and on the bottom of the crate.

I stepped down. Reluctantly, or so it seemed to me, the others finally took their turns, starting with Cleobulus, whose face was ashen when he ceded his place to Gatamandix. The Druid merely grunted at the sight of the defaced statue and showed no emotion. Vindovix was so tall he did not need the box to look inside. He stood on tiptoes and peered over the edge. He clenched his jaw. His face turned bright red and his pale blue eyes glittered with tears.

"What am I to make of this?" said Posidonius. "Zenas is gone, and the part of the statue most vital to our inquiry—the head—has been destroyed. Deliberately destroyed, I think we can safely say. The knothole already in the wood was bored and chipped away until a staff of some kind could be pushed through—an iron stave, perhaps—and used to smash the head. Given the deliberate and determined nature of this act, I suspect premeditation. Someone must have known the knothole was there, at a height corresponding exactly to the statue's head. The person who did this must have been present when the crate was constructed; indeed, that person may have seen to it that this particular plank, with its convenient knothole, was placed just so, in order to provide an easy way to commit this act of destruction."

The whole time he spoke, Posidonius stared at Cleobulus, who turned even paler.

"Teacher, surely suspicion should fall first on Zenas," he said. "Why is the slave not here? Why did he abandon his post?"

"If Zenas played some part in this, it was only because someone put him up to it," said Posidonius, continuing to stare at Cleobulus. "But I can't believe Zenas would betray my trust, especially in a matter as serious as this. The fact that he isn't here, and that his writing instruments were left behind, suggests to me that some harm was done to the poor fellow."

Cleobulus swallowed hard. "Then where is he?"

Posidonius at last took his eyes off his pupil. He turned and looked over the ship's side.

"Teacher, if the slave were thrown overboard, his body would have washed against the piers by now," said Cleobulus. "Someone would have seen it—"

"Not if his body was tied to the iron stave that was used to smash the statue's head," said Posidonius, gazing intently at the water below, as if by sheer will he could make the waves give up their secret.

"But this is terrible!" said Antipater. "Is there not some other explanation for what's happened, short of accusing someone of murder and wanton destruction? Perhaps Zenas will turn up yet. Have you never had a slave go missing, Posidonius, and then reappear shamefaced a day later, stinking of wine and the brothel?"

"Not Zenas," Posidonius said. "And what possible motive could he have had to destroy the statue's head? What motive could anyone have to do such a thing?"

To this, no one gave an answer. Cleobulus, still pale but with a

glint of defiance in his eyes, stared back at his teacher for a long moment, then brusquely took his leave and hurried off.

After arranging with the captain to have the damaged statue transported to his house, Posidonius told us he wished to be alone, and
headed off by himself. The Gauls went off on their own, with Gatamandix gripping Vindovix's shoulder, as if to comfort him. I saw them
duck into a seedy-looking tavern on the waterfront. I was left with
Antipater, who expressed his desire to head directly back to the house
of Posidonius.

As we walked away from the harbor, I looked over my shoulder, past
the ship to the distant ruins of the Colossus at the end of the long mole.
The huge fragments of bronze gleamed dully beneath the iron-gray sky.
Beyond the Colossus, dark clouds were gathering over the open sea.

It was a gloomy day in the house of Posidonius.

The Gauls remained absent, as did Cleobulus. Our host at last returned, but shut himself up in his study. Eventually the carters arrived
with the crate. Without enthusiasm, Posidonius emerged from his se-
clusion to oversee the unpacking.

Soon the plaster statue stood in a room off the garden. Even without
its head, the remains presented a fascinating image, showing how the
Colossus must have appeared when it stood intact beside the harbor. If
the living model had been a Greek, this statue surely would have been
larger than life, but its oversized proportions were correct for a hulking
Gaul, and the muscular physique could easily be taken for a reproduc-
tion of Vindovix, or of an ancestor whom he resembled.

"Perhaps the head could be reconstructed," said Antipater hopefully,
but when we sifted through the bits and pieces, the only recognizable
fragments were some broken sunbeams from Helios's crown.

Without a word, Posidonius returned to his library, but emerged a
moment later.

"Have either of you entered my library today?" he asked.

Antipater shook his head, as did I.

"Very odd," said Posidonius. "I'm certain, before we headed for the ship this morning, that Gatamandix's knife was on the small table where I left it. But it isn't there now."

"Perhaps Gatamandix took it with him before we left this morning," suggested Antipater.

"Why would he do that, without telling me?"

A vague apprehension ran through me. "Why do you suppose the Gauls haven't returned yet?" I looked at the dark, churning clouds above. "There's a storm coming."

"They probably drank themselves into oblivion at that waterfront tavern," said Antipater. "Best to leave them to it and let them come home in their own time."

I nodded. "And where do you think Cleobulus went?"

"Back to his father's house, I'm sure," said Posidonius, with a bitter edge to his voice. He returned to his study.

"What a day!" said Antipater. "I'm going to my room to take a nap. And you, Gordianus?"

"I'll look at the statue a while longer," I said, squatting down so as to view it from a low angle, as if I were on a ship sailing into harbor and the model were the full-size Colossus, towering above me. I tried to imagine the head intact, and looking very much like Vindovix, and felt that uncanny shiver of cognition one experiences when a statue suddenly seems no longer inanimate but a living, breathing entity. Was this the ancestor of Vindovix who stood before me, captured by the divinely inspired hand of Chares?

Clearly, as a proud Rhodian scholar, Cleobulus did not like the idea that a Gaul might have served as the model for Helios. But would he have done violence to Zenas, and deliberately deface a statue fashioned by the hand of Chares? Posidonius seemed to think so, but without proof, it was hard to see how he could punish Cleobulus, except by shunning him.

I remembered that the ritual knife was missing, and an unpleasant thought struck me: What if Gatamandix had decided to punish the Rhodian himself? Had he taken the knife for just that purpose? Then

I realized this made no sense, for Posidonius had seen the knife in his study that morning, and Gatamandix had not returned to the house all day, so if the Druid took the knife, it was before we all set out for the ship. He could not have known then that he would want the knife later to punish the defacer of the statue.

Then another thought struck me, more chilling than the first: perhaps Gatamandix *had* taken the knife that morning, intending to use it—but not against Cleobulus.

The idea in my head was mad—or was it? I could have told Posidonius what I was thinking, but his study door was closed, and what if he refuted me? I thought of telling Antipater, but he was likely already asleep, and the old poet would only slow me down—for I suddenly realized that if I wished to act, I must do so at once. I might be too late already.

Without even fetching my cloak, I rushed to the vestibule and into the street, walking quickly at first, then running all the way to the harbor with the cold wind in my face.

After I pressed a few coins in his hand, the tavernkeeper had no trouble remembering the Gauls who had been getting drunk in his establishment all afternoon. "In fact, they left only a short while ago. The young giant was so drunk he could hardly stand. The older one practically had to carry him out."

"Did you see which way they went?"

The tavernkeeper made a face. "I can't see through walls, young fellow."

"Never mind, I think I know," I whispered.

The little hut beside the roped-off entrance to the mole was empty. On such a day, with the sky threatening to open at any moment and black waves lashing the boulder-strewn shoreline of the mole, no tourists were hiking out to have a look at the Colossus. I jumped the rope and ran toward the ruins.

On the way, I saw a thing I never anticipated—the body of Zenas. Whipped by the wind, the roiling water in the harbor must have separated his corpse from whatever had been used to weigh it down, and the waves had thrown it upon the shore. I stopped for just a moment to stare down at his lifeless, bulging eyes and the rope tied around his neck, which had surely been used to strangle him.

Gasping for breath, I ran on.

Why did I think Gatamandix had chosen this place to complete his purpose? It was close, for one thing; and here was the cause of all his grief, the Colossus itself. It was only a hunch on my part, but it proved correct. Deep within the ruins I rounded a corner, and in an open spot amid the huge fragments of bronze, hidden from the waterfront and the harbor but open to the stormy sky, I came upon the two Gauls.

Surrounding us, like the standing stones of the Druids, were strange, gigantic pieces of anatomy—a finger pointing skyward, a bit of a shoulder, the crook of an elbow, and a long, hollow section of thigh to complete the magic circle. In the center, lying across one of Helios's broken sunbeams as if it were a sacrificial altar, was Vindovix, his glassy eyes barely open, insensible from consuming great quantities of wine. Over him stood Gatamandix, holding his ritual knife with both hands raised high above his head, muttering an incantation in his barbarous tongue.

A sudden flash of lightning lit the scene, making it seem garish and unreal. An instant later, a thunderclap shook the ground beneath my feet.

I gave a cry. The Druid saw me and froze. I rushed toward him. He brought down the knife.

I hurtled through the air. The descending blade caught against my tunic and ripped the cloth. It must have grazed my side, for I felt a sudden, searing pain across my ribs. I collided with Gatamandix, and together we tumbled across the uneven ground. I braced myself for a tremendous struggle—but then I heard a loud clanging sound, together with a sickening crack.

Gatamandix went limp. With some difficulty, I extricated myself from the dead weight of his arms, and stood over him. He stared up at me with lifeless eyes. He had struck his head on the giant finger of the Colossus and broken his neck. With his features distorted by a fierce grimace, the Druid's enormous moustache looked more ridiculous than ever.

Spots swam before my eyes. I struggled to fill my lungs, and realized I had not caught a proper breath since I left Posidonius's house. In my dizzy state, surrounded by flashes of lightning, the anatomical ruins around me looked weirder than ever. It seemed to me that I surely must be in a dream.

"Gordianus—you saved my life!"

Vindovix had roused himself enough to sit upright on the sunbeam. For a long moment he looked utterly stunned, then he flashed a lascivious grin. "Gordianus, what a man you are! For this, you deserve a reward—the kind of reward only a true man, a man with a moustache, can give you."

He staggered to his feet and took a few steps toward me, leering at me with half-shut eyes.

"But Vindovix," I said, still gasping for breath, "you no longer have your moustache."

"What?" Perplexed, he reached up to touch his clean-shaven upper lip. Then his eyes rolled up, his knees gave way, and Vindovix the Gaul fell flat on his face.

That night I met with Posidonius in his library. Antipater and Cleobulus were there, as was Vindovix, who sat in a corner, still a bit befuddled by wine and nursing the cuts on his brow and the swollen lip he had suffered when he fell.

I explained what had happened, relying partly on reason and partly on conjecture.

"Gatamandix hated the idea that a Gaul had posed for the Colossus even more than Cleobulus did. According to the story, the ancestor of Vindovix had been a slave—and if a Gallic slave had been used by a Rhodian sculptor to create a monument to a Greek god, that was not a cause for pride, but for shame. To Gatamandix, then, what was the Colossus but a monument to the failure of the Gauls to conquer Greece, and a bitter reminder that a man of the Segurovi had been

enslaved by the Greeks? No doubt he had long been irked by the family of Vindovix and their fantastic story, stubbornly repeated down the
generations. It was Vindovix who really wanted to come to Rhodes, not
Gatamandix. But if Vindovix returned home, not only having seen the
Colossus with his own eyes but bearing some proof that his ancestor
was the model, there would never be an end to the story. Gatamandix—
as Druid, judge, and executioner—decided to take action. That was the
real reason he accompanied you back to Rhodes—not to explore the
world of the Greeks, but to thwart Vindovix's quest to prove the historical reality of his family's legend. Toward that end, he first destroyed
the evidence of the plaster statue; to do that, he didn't hesitate to murder Zenas and throw his body overboard. Then he set out to eliminate
Vindovix, getting him too drunk to resist and preparing to murder him
as a ritual sacrifice. Only he, Gatamandix, would return to the Segurovi, with a story that would refute and forever put an end to the tale of
a Gallic slave who posed for the Colossus of Rhodes."

Posidonius shook his head. "The tale as you reconstruct it makes
perfect sense, Gordianus. How could I have been so blind to Gatamandix's treachery? I was ready to accuse Cleobulus!"

"Of course, we still don't know the truth of the question that set off
this sequence of events," said Antipater. "Was Vindovix's ancestor the
model for the Colossus, or not?"

"You forget that I saw the statue before it was defaced," said Vindo-
vix. "I have no doubt whatsoever. Vindovix, my great-great-great . . ."
He lost track, blinked a few times, and went on. "He *was* the model for
Chares."

"I also saw the statue, and I have no doubt either," said Cleobulus.
"It looked nothing like you, Vindovix. You merely saw what you wanted
to see."

"But surely Gatamandix also thought it looked like Vindovix, or
else he would never have gone to such lengths to destroy it," observed
Antipater.

"That bit of logic counts for something," said Posidonius. "But the
truth remains elusive. We have only legend, hearsay, and subjective

observation to guide us. In this instance, empirical reasoning yields no definitive conclusion. Alas!"

It took Vindovix only a day to recover from his hangover, but I developed a fever from the wound I received from the Druid's knife and was sick for days. With care from my host and Antipater, the fever passed, and I gradually recuperated.

Several days later, during a break in the stormy weather, I sat in the garden. Posidonius and Antipater were nearby, discussing a philosophical question. The slight warmth of the wintry sunshine felt good on my face.

Vindovix strolled across the garden. If anything, the lingering scars from his fall added character to his rugged features. He had begun to grow his moustache, but it would take a long time to regain its former glory

He tugged at the silky hair above his lip, gave me a long, languid look, then walked on.

"Poor Vindovix," said Antipater, "betrayed by a man he trusted. He must be lonely now, the only Gaul on an island of Greeks. I do believe he's rather smitten with you, Gordianus."

"He's certainly persistent," I said.

Posidonius raised an eyebrow. "And winter has only just begun. You'll have to give in to his advances sooner or later."

"What makes you think I haven't done so already?"

Antipater blinked. "*Have* you?"

I smiled and shrugged, feeling quite sophisticated and at home among these worldly Greeks.

STYX AND STONES

(The Walls and the Hanging Gardens of Babylon)

"In Babylon, we shall see not one, but two of the great Wonders of the World," said Antipater. "Or at least, we shall see what remains of them."

We had spent the night at a dusty little inn beside the Euphrates River. Antipater had been quiet and grumpy from the moment he got out of bed that morning—travel is hard on old men—but as we drew closer to Babylon, traveling south on the ancient road that ran alongside the river, his spirits rose and little by little he became more animated.

The innkeeper had told us that the ancient city was not more than a few hours distant, even accounting for the slow progress of the asses we were riding, and all morning a smudge that suggested a city had loomed ahead of us on the low horizon, very gradually growing more pronounced. The land between the Tigris and Euphrates rivers and for miles around is absolutely flat, without even low hills to break the view. On such a vast, featureless plain, you might think that you could see forever, but the ripples of heat that rose from the earth distorted the view, so that objects near and far took on an uncertain, even uncanny appearance. A distant tower turned out to be a palm tree. A pile of strangely motionless—dead?—bodies suddenly resolved into a heap of gravel, apparently put there by whoever maintained the road.

For over an hour I tried to make sense of a party approaching us on the road. The shimmering heat waves by turns appeared to magnify the group, then make them grow smaller, then disappear altogether, then reappear. At first I thought it was a company of armed men, for I thought I saw sunlight glinting on their weapons. Then I decided I was seeing nothing more than a single man on horseback, perhaps wearing a helmet or some other piece of armor that reflected a bluish gleam. Then the person, or persons, or whatever it was that approached us, vanished in the blink of an eye, and I felt a shiver, wondering if we were about to encounter a company of phantoms.

At last we met our fellow travelers on the road. The party turned out to consist of several armed guards and two small carts pulled by asses and piled high with stacks of bricks, but not bricks of any sort I had seen before. These were large and variously shaped, most about a foot square, and covered on the outward-facing sides with a dazzling glaze, some yellow, some blue, some mixed. They were not newly made—uneven edges and bits of adhering mortar indicated they had been chiseled free from some existing structure—but except for a bit of dust, the colored glazes glimmered with a jewel-like brightness.

Antipater grew very excited. "Can it be?" he muttered. "Bricks from the fabled walls of Babylon!"

The old poet awkwardly dismounted and shuffled toward the nearest cart, where he reached out to touch one of the bricks, running his fingertips over the shimmering blue glaze.

The driver at first objected, and called to one of the armed guards, who drew his sword and stepped forward. Then the driver laughed, seeing Antipater's bright-eyed wonder, and waved the guard back. Speaking to Antipater, the driver said something in a language I didn't recognize. Apparently, neither did Antipater, who squinted up at the man and said, "Speakee Greekee?"

This was my first visit to a land where the majority of the population conversed in languages other than Latin and Greek. Antipater had a smattering of Parthian, but I had noticed that he preferred to address the natives in broken Greek, as if somehow this would be more comprehensible to them than the flawless Greek he usually spoke.

"I know Greek, yes, little bit," said the driver, holding his thumb close to his forefinger.

"You come from Babylon, no?" Antipater also tended to raise his voice when speaking to the natives, as if they might be deaf.

"From Babylon, yes."

"How far?" Antipater engaged in an elaborate bit of sign language to clarify his meaning.

"Babylon, from here? Oh, two hour. Maybe three," amended the driver, eyeing our weary-looking mounts.

Antipater looked in the direction of the smudge on the horizon, which had grown decidedly larger but still held no promise of towering walls. He sighed. "I begin to fear, Gordianus, that nothing at all remains of the fabled walls of Babylon. Surely, if they were as large as legend asserts, and if any remnants still stand, we would see something of them by now."

"Bricks come from old walls, yes," said the driver, understanding only some of Antipater's comments and gesturing to his load. "My neighbor finds, buried behind his house. Very rare. Very valuable. He sell to rich merchant in Seleucia. Now my neighbor is rich man."

"Beautiful, aren't they, Gordianus?" Antipater ran his palm over a glazed surface, then lifted the brick to look at the bottom. "By Zeus, this one is actually stamped with the name of Nebuchadnezzar! It must date from his reign." For a moment I thought Antipater was about to break into verse, but his thoughts took a more practical turn. "These bricks would be worth a fortune back in Rome. My patron Quintus Lutatius Catulus owns a few, which he displays as specimens in his garden. I think he paid more for those five or six Babylonian bricks than he did for all the statues in his house put together. Ah well, let's push on."

Antipater gave the driver a coin for his trouble, then remounted, and we resumed our slow, steady progress toward the shimmering smudge on the horizon.

I cleared my throat. "What makes those old bricks so valuable? And why did the Babylonians build their walls from bricks in the first place? I should think any proper city wall would be made of stone."

The look Antipater shot at me made me feel nine years old rather than nineteen. "Look around you, Gordianus. Do you see any stones? There's not a quarry for miles. This part of the world is completely devoid of the kind of stones suitable for constructing temples and other buildings, much less walls that stretch for miles and are so wide that chariots can ride atop them. No, except for a few temples adorned with limestone and bitumen imported at great expense, the city of Nebuchadnezzar was constructed of bricks. They were made from clay mixed with finely chopped straw, then compressed in molds and hardened by fire. Amazingly, such bricks are very nearly as strong as stone, and in the ancient Chaldean language the word for 'brick' and 'stone' is the same. They can't be carved like stone, of course, but they can be decorated with colored glazes that never fade."

"So the famous walls of Babylon were built by—" I hesitated over the difficult name.

"King Nebuchadnezzar." Antipater made a point to enunciate carefully, as he had when speaking to the cart driver. "The city of Babylon itself was founded, at least in legend, by an Assyrian queen named Semiramis, who lived back in the age of Homer. But it was a much later king, of the Chaldean dynasty, who raised Babylon to the height of its glory. His name was Nebuchadnezzar and he reigned five hundred years ago. He rebuilt the whole city on a grid design, with long, straight avenues—quite different from the chaos you're accustomed to in Rome, Gordianus—and he adorned the city with magnificent temples to the Babylonian gods, chief among them Marduk and Ishtar. He constructed a huge temple complex called *Etemenanki*—the Foundation of Heaven and Earth—in the form of a towering, seven-tiered ziggurat; some say the ziggurat rivals the pyramids of Egypt in size and should itself be numbered among the Seven Wonders. For the delight of his

Median queen, who was homesick for the mountain forests and flowery meadows of her distant homeland, Nebuchadnezzar built the Hanging Gardens, a paradise perched like a bird's nest high above the earth. And he encircled the whole city with a wall seventy-five feet high and thirty feet wide—wide enough for two chariots to meet and pass. The walls were fortified with crenellated battlements and towers a hundred feet tall, and the whole length was decorated with patterns and images in blue and yellow, so that from a distance the Babylon of Nebuchadnezzar shimmered like baubles of lapis strung upon a necklace of gold."

He gazed dubiously at the horizon. The smudge continued to grow, but looked more like a daub of mud than a jewel—though it seemed to me that I was beginning to glimpse a massive object that rose above the rest of the smudge and shone with various colors. Was it the ziggurat?

"What happened to Nebuchadnezzar's empire?" I said. "What happened to his walls?"

"Empires rise, empires fall—even the empire of Rome, someday . . ." Even here, far from Rome's influence, he spoke such words under his breath. "Just as the Assyrians had fallen to the Chaldeans, so the Chaldeans fell to the Persians. A hundred years after the death of Nebuchadnezzar, Babylon revolted against Xerxes, the same Persian monarch who foolishly imagined he could conquer Greece. Xerxes had more success with Babylon; he sacked the city and looted the temples. Some say he demolished the great walls, destroying them so completely that hardly a trace remained—only a multitude of glazed bricks, coveted by collectors across the world. A hundred years later, when Alexander advanced on the city, the Babylonians offered no resistance and came out to greet him, so perhaps indeed they no longer had walls adequate to defend them. They say Alexander intended to restore Babylon to its former glory and to make it the capital of the world, but instead he died there at the age of thirty-two. His successor built a new city nearby, on the Tigris, and named it for himself; the new capital of Seleucia claimed whatever wealth and power remained in Babylon, and the ancient city was largely forgotten—except by the scholars and sages who flocked there, attracted by the cheap rents, and by astrologers, who are said to find the ziggurat an ideal platform for stargazing."

"So we're likely to meet astrologers in Babylon?" I said.

"Without a doubt. Astrology originated with the Chaldeans. The science is still a novelty in Rome, I know, but it's been gaining in popularity among the Greeks ever since a Babylonian priest named Berossus set up a school of astrology on the island of Cos, back in the days of Alexander."

We rode along in silence for a while. I became certain that the highest point of the ever-growing smudge must indeed be the multicolored ziggurat, dominating the skyline of Babylon. I could also make out something that appeared to be a wall, but it did not look very high, and in color it was a reddish brown, as if made of plain clay bricks, not of shimmering lapis and gold.

"What about the Hanging Gardens that Nebuchadnezzar built for his wife?" I said. "Do they still exist?"

"Soon enough, we shall see for ourselves," said Antipater.

At last the walls of Babylon loomed before us. I could see that Antipater was profoundly disappointed.

"Ah, well, I was prepared for this," he said with a sigh, as we crossed a dry moat and rode through the gate. Had we encountered it anywhere else, the wall would have been reasonably impressive—it rose perhaps thirty feet and extended as far as I could see along the bank of the Euphrates—but it was made of common reddish brown bricks. This wall was certainly not one of the Wonders of the World.

We passed through a lively marketplace, full of exotic smells and colorful characters. The place exuded a quaint provincial charm, but I didn't feel the unmistakable thrill of being in one of the world's great cities, like Rome or Ephesus.

Then, ahead of us, I saw the Ishtar Gate.

I didn't know what to call it at the time; I only knew that my jaw suddenly dropped and my heartbeat quickened. Bright sunlight glinted off the multicolored tiles, animating the gigantic images of amazing animals—magnificent horned aurochs, roaring lions, and terrifying dragons. Other patterns were more abstract, suggesting jewels and blossoms, but constructed on an enormous scale. Blue predominated, and there were as many shades as one might see on the face of the sea in the course of a day, from the bright azure of noon to midnight indigo. There were also many shades of yellow and gold, and borders made of dazzling green. The parapets that towered above us were crenellated with a pattern that delighted the eye. But the gate was only a fragment, standing in isolation; the wall extended only a short distance to either side, then abruptly ended.

A group of natives, seeing our astonishment, ran toward us and competed to engage us in conversation. At length Antipater nodded to the one who seemed to speak the best Greek.

"What is this?" said Antipater.

"The great wall!" declared the man, who had a scraggly beard and was missing several teeth.

"But this can't be all of it!" protested Antipater.

"All that remains," said the man. "When Xerxes pulled down the walls of Nebuchadnezzar, this gate he left, to show how great was the wall he destroyed. The Ishtar Gate, it is called, to the glory of the goddess." He held out his palm, into which Antipater obligingly pressed a coin.

"Think of it, Gordianus," Antipater whispered. "Alexander himself rode though this very gate when he entered the city in triumph."

"No wonder he wanted to make his capital here," I said, gazing straight up as we passed under the lofty archway. "I've never seen anything like it. It's truly magnificent."

"Imagine many such gates, connected by a wall no less magnificent that extended for miles and miles," said Antipater. He shook his head. "And now, all vanished, except for this."

As we rode on, the man followed after us.

"I show you everything," he offered. "I show you Hanging Gardens, yes?"

Antipater brightened. Was there some chance that the fabled

gardens still existed, so many centuries after the time of Nebuchadnezzar and his Median queen?

"Not far, not far!" the man promised, leading the way. I asked his
name. "Darius," he said, "like the great Persian king." He smiled, showing off his remaining teeth.

We passed through a shabby little square where merchants offered
cheap trinkets—miniature aurochs and lions and dragons—to the
tourists, of whom there were a great many, for we were not the only
travelers who had come to Babylon that day in search of the fabled
Wonders. Beyond a maze of dusty, winding alleys—surely this was not
the grid city laid out by Nebuchadnezzar—we at last came to the foot
of a great pile of ruins. Arguably, this structure reached to the sky, or
once had done so, before time or man demolished it, so in a way it
resembled a mountain, if only a small one.

Darius urged us to dismount and follow him. Before we could go
farther, another fellow insisted that we each pay for the privilege; this
man also promised to look after our asses. Antipater handed the gate-
keeper the requested coinage, and Darius led us to a stairway with
rubble on either side that ascended to a series of small landings. Along
the way, someone had placed numerous potted plants, and on some of
the landings spindly trees and thirsty-looking shrubs were actually
growing from the debris. The dilapidated effect was more sad than spectacular. At last we came to an open area near the summit, where broken
columns and ruptured paving bricks gave evidence of what once had
been a magnificent terrace, now shaded by date palms and scented by
small lemon and orange trees. The leaves of a knotty-limbed olive tree
shimmered silver and green in the breeze.

"Hardly the mountain forest that Nebuchadnezzar built," muttered
Antipater, catching his breath after the steady climb. I felt a bit winded
myself.

"How do they water all these plants?" I said.

"Ah, you are wise, my young friend!" declared our guide. "You perceive the secret of the Hanging Gardens. Come, see!"

Darius led us to a brick-framed doorway nearby, which opened

onto a shaft that ran downward at a sloping angle. Coming up the
dimly lit passage toward us was a man with a yoke across his shoulders, with a bucket of water connected to each end. Huffing and puff-
ing and covered with sweat, the water-bearer nonetheless flashed a
weary grin as he emerged into the light and shambled past us.

"A good thing we're near the river, if men have to carry water up
this shaft all day," I said.

Antipater raised his eyebrows. "Ah, but once upon a time, Gordianus, this shaft must have contained the mechanism that delivered a
continuous flow of water for the gardens." He pointed to various mysterious bits of metal affixed to the surface of the shaft. "Onesicritus,
who saw these gardens in the days of Alexander, speaks of a device like
a gigantic screw that lifted great volumes of water as it turned. It seems
that nothing of that remarkable mechanism remains, but the shaft is
still here, leading down, we may presume, to a cistern fed by the river.
Without the irrigation screw, the industrious citizens of Babylon have
resorted to the labor of their own bodies to keep some semblance of
the garden alive, from civic pride perhaps, and for the benefit of paying visitors like ourselves."

I nodded dubiously. The Hanging Gardens might once have been
magnificent, but the decrepit remains could hardly compare to the
other World Wonders we had seen on our journey.

Then I walked a few steps beyond the opening of the shaft, to a
spot that afforded an unobstructed view of the ziggurat.

The walls of Babylon had been pulled down. The Hanging Gardens
were in ruins. But the great ziggurat remained, rising mountainlike
from the midst of the dun-colored city. Each of the seven stepped-back
tiers had once been a different color. Almost all of the decorative work
had been stripped away (by Xerxes when he sacked the city, and by
subsequent looters), and the brick walls had begun to crumble, but
enough of the original facade remained to indicate how the ziggurat
must once have appeared. The first and largest tier was brick red, but
the next had been dazzling white (faced with imported limestone and
bitumen, I later learned), the next decorated with iridescent blue tiles,

the next a riot of patterns in yellow and green, and so on. In the days
of Nebuchadnezzar, the effect must have been unearthly. Amid the
ziggurat's marred perfection I noticed tiny specks here and there on its
surface. It was only when I saw that these specks moved—that they
were, in fact, men—that I realized the true scale of the ziggurat. The
thing was even larger than I had thought.

The sun was beginning to sink, casting its lowering rays across the
dusty city and bathing the ziggurat in orange light. Etemenanki, the
Babylonians called it, the Foundation of Heaven and Earth. Truly, it
seemed to me that so huge and strange a thing could scarcely have been
created by human hands.

Antipater had similar thoughts. Standing next to me, he broke into
verse:

> "What Cyclops built this mound for Semiramis?
> Or what giants, sons of Gaia, raised it in seven tiers
> To scrape against the seven Pleiades?
> Immovable, unshakable, a mass eternal,
> Like lofty Mount Athos it weighs upon the earth."

Travel-weary and light-headed though I was, I caught Antipater's mistake. "You told me Nebuchadnezzar built the ziggurat, not Semiramis,"
I said.

"Poetic license, Gordianus! Semiramis scans better, and the name is
far more euphonious. Who could compose a poem around a name as
cumbersome as 'Nebuchadnezzar'?"

As darkness fell, Darius helped us find lodgings for the night. The
little inn to which he guided us was near the river, he assured us, and
though we could smell the river while we ate a frugal meal of flatbread and dates in the common room, our room upstairs had no view
of it. Indeed, when I tried to open the shutters, they banged against
an unsightly section of the city wall that stretched along the waterfront.

"Tomorrow you see Etemenanki," insisted Darius, who had shared our meal and followed us to the room. "What time do I meet you?"

"Tomorrow, we rest," said Antipater, collapsing on the narrow bed. "You don't mind sleeping on that mat on the floor, do you, Gordianus?"

"Actually, I was thinking of taking a walk," I said.

Antipater made no reply; he was already snoring. But Darius vigorously shook his head. "Not safe after dark," he said. "You stay inside."

I frowned. "You assured Antipater this was a good neighborhood, with no thieves or pickpockets."

"I tell the truth—no worry about robbers."

"What's the danger, then?"

Darius's expression was grave. "After dark, *she* comes out."

"She? Who are you talking about? Speak clearly!"

"I say too much already. But don't go out until daylight. I meet you then!" Without another word, he disappeared.

I dropped to the floor and reclined on the mat, thinking I would never get to sleep with Antipater snoring so loudly. The next thing I knew, sunlight was streaming in the open window.

By the time we went down to eat breakfast, the sun was already high. There was only one other guest in the common room. His costume was so outlandish, I almost laughed when I saw him. The only astrologers I had ever seen were on the stage, in comedies, and this man might have been one of them. He wore a high yellow hat that rose in tiers, not unlike those of the ziggurat, and a dark blue robe decorated with images of stars and constellations sewn in yellow. His shoes were encrusted with semiprecious stones and ended in spiral loops at the toes. His long black beard had been crimped and plaited and sprinkled with yellow powder so that it radiated from his jaw like solar rays.

Antipater invited the stranger to join us. He introduced himself as Mushezib, an astrologer visiting Babylon from his native city of Ecbatana. He had traveled widely and his Greek was excellent, probably better than mine.

"You've come to see the ziggurat," speculated Antipater.

"Or what remains of it," said Mushezib. "There's also a very fine school for astrologers here, where I hope to find a position as a teacher. And you?"

"We're simply here to see the city," said Antipater. "But not today. I'm too tired and my whole body aches from riding yesterday."

"But we can't just stay in all day," I said. "Perhaps there's something of interest close by."

"I'm told there's a small temple of Ishtar just up the street," said Mushezib. "It's mostly hidden from sight behind a high wall. Apparently it's in ruins; it was desecrated long ago by Xerxes and never reconsecrated or rebuilt. I don't suppose there's much to see—"

"But you can't go there," said the innkeeper, overhearing and joining the conversation. He, too, looked like a type who might have stepped out of a stage comedy. He was a big fellow with a round face and a ready smile. With his massive shoulders and burly arms, he looked quite capable of breaking up a fight and throwing the offenders onto the street, should such a disturbance ever occur in his sleepy tavern.

"Who forbids it?" asked the astrologer.

The innkeeper shrugged. "No one *forbids* it. The deserted temple belongs to no one and everyone—common property, they say. But nobody goes there—because of *her*."

My ears pricked up. "Who are you talking about?"

Finding his Greek inadequate, the innkeeper addressed the astrologer in Parthian.

Mushezib's face grew long. "Our host says the temple is . . . haunted."

"Haunted?" I said.

"I forget the Greek word, but I think the Latin is 'lemur,' yes?"

"Yes," I whispered. "A manifestation of the dead that lingers on earth. A thing that was mortal once, but no longer lives or breathes." Unready or unable to cross the river Styx to the realm of the dead, lemures were said to stalk the earth, usually but not always appearing at night.

"The innkeeper says there is a lemur at this nearby temple," said Mushezib. "A woman dressed in moldering rags, with a hideous face. People fear to go there."

"Is she dangerous?" I said.

Mushezib conversed with the innkeeper. "Not just dangerous, but deadly. Only a few mornings ago, a man who had gone missing the night before was found dead on the temple steps, his neck broken. Now they lock the gate, which before was never locked."

So this was the nocturnal menace Darius had warned me about, fearing even to name the thing aloud.

"But surely in broad daylight—," began Antipater.

"No, no!" protested the innkeeper's wife, who suddenly joined us. She was almost as big as her husband, but had a scowling demeanor— another type suitable for the stage, I thought, the innkeeper's irascible wife. She spoke better Greek than her husband, and her thick Egyptian accent explained the Alexandrian delicacies among the Babylonian breakfast fare.

"Stay away from the old temple!" she cried. "Don't go there! You die if you go there!"

Her husband appeared to find this outburst unseemly. He laughed nervously and shrugged with his palms up, then took her aside, shaking his head and whispering to her. If he was trying to calm her, he failed. After a brief squabble, she threw up her hands and stalked off.

"It must be rather distressing, having a lemur so nearby," muttered Antipater. "Bad for business, I should imagine. Do you think that's why there are so few people here at the inn? I'm surprised our host would even bring up the subject. Well, I'm done with my breakfast, so if you'll excuse me, I intend to return to our room and spend the whole day in bed. Oh, don't look so crestfallen, Gordianus! Go out and explore the city without me."

I felt some trepidation about venturing out in such an exotic city by myself, but I needn't have worried. The moment I stepped into the street I was accosted by our guide from the previous day.

"Where is your grandfather?" said Darius.

I laughed. "He's not my grandfather, just my traveling companion. He's too tired to go out."

"Ah, then I show you the city, eh? Just the two of us."

I frowned. "I'm afraid I haven't much money on me, Darius."

He shrugged. "What is money? It comes, it goes. But if I show you the ziggurat, you remember all your life."

"Actually, I'm rather curious about that temple of Ishtar just up the street."

He went pale. "No, no, no! We don't go there."

"We can at least walk by, can't we? Is it this way?" I said.

Next to the inn was a derelict structure that must once have been a competing tavern, but was now shuttered and boarded up; it looked rather haunted itself. Just beyond this abandoned property, a brick wall with a small wooden gate faced the street. The wall was not much higher than my head; beyond it, I could see what remained of the roof of the temple, which appeared to have collapsed. I pushed on the gate and found that it was locked. I ran my fingers over the wall, where much of the mortar between the bricks had worn away. The fissures would serve as excellent footholds. I stepped back, studying the wall to find the easiest place to scale it.

Darius read my thoughts. He gripped my arm. "No, no, no, young Roman! Are you mad?"

"Come now, Darius. The sun is shining. No lemur would dare to show its face on such a beautiful day. It will take me only a moment to climb over the wall and have a look. You can stay here and wait for me."

But Darius protested so vociferously, gesticulating and yammering in his native tongue, that I gave up my plan to see the temple and agreed to move on.

Darius showed me what he called the Royal District, where Semiramis and Nebuchadnezzar had built their palaces. As far as I could tell, nothing at all remained of the grandeur that had so impressed

Alexander when he sojourned in Babylon. The once-resplendent complex, now stripped of every ornament, appeared to have been subdi-
vided into private dwellings and crowded apartment buildings.

"They say that's the room where Alexander died." Darius pointed
to an open window from which I could hear a couple arguing and a
baby crying. The balcony was festooned with laundry hung out to dry.
The surrounding terraces were strewn with rubbish. The whole district
smelled of stewing fish, cloying spices, and soiled diapers.

If there had ever been an open square around the great ziggurat,
it had long ago been filled in with ramshackle dwellings of brick and
mud, so that we came upon the towering structure all at once as we
rounded a corner. The ziggurat had seemed more mysterious when I
had seen it the previous night, from a distance and by the beguiling
light of sunset. Seen close up and in broad daylight, it looked to be in
hardly better shape than the mound of rubble that had once been the
Hanging Gardens. The surfaces of each tier were quite uneven, causing many of the swarming visitors to trip and stumble. Whole sections
of the ramparts leaned outward at odd angles, looking as if they might
tumble down at any moment.

Darius insisted we walk all the way to the top. To do so, we had to
circle each tier, take a broad flight of steps up to the next tier, circle
around, and do the same thing again. I noticed Darius pausing every so
often to run his fingers over the walls. At first I thought he was simply
admiring the scant remnants of decorative stonework or glazed brick,
but then I realized he was tugging at various bits and pieces, seeing if
anything would come loose. When he saw the expression on my face,
he laughed.

"I look for mementos, young Roman," he explained. "Everyone does
it. Anything of value that could be removed easily and without damage
is already removed, long ago. But, every so often, you find a piece ready
to come loose. So you take it. Everyone does it. Why do you frown at
me like that?"

I was imagining the great temples of Rome being subjected to such
impious treatment. Antipater claimed that the ancient gods of this land

were essentially the same as those of the Greeks and Romans, just with different names and aspects: Marduk was Jupiter, Ishtar was Venus, and so on. To filch bits and pieces from a sacred structure that had been built to the glory of Jupiter was surely wrong, even if the structure was in disrepair. But I was a visitor, and I said nothing.

The way became more and more crowded as we ascended, for each tier was smaller than the last. All around us were travelers in many different types of costumes, chattering in many different languages. From their garb, I took one group to be from India, and judging by their saffron complexions and almond-shaped eyes, another group had come all the way from Serica, the land of silk. There were also a great many astrologers, some of them dressed as I had seen Mushezib that morning, and others in outfits even more outlandish, as if they were trying to outdo one another with absurdly tall hats, elaborately decorated robes, and bizarrely shaped beards.

On the sixth and next-to-last tier, I heard a voice speak my name, and turned to see Mushezib.

The astrologer acknowledged me with a nod. "We meet again."

"It would seem that every visitor in Babylon is here today," I said, jostled by a passing group of men in Egyptian headdresses. "Is that a queue?"

It appeared that one had to stand in line to ascend the final flight of steps to the uppermost tier; only when a certain number of visitors left were more allowed to go up. The queue stretched out of sight around the corner.

Mushezib smiled. "Shall we go up?" he said.

"I'm not sure I care to stand in that line for the next hour. And I'm not sure I have enough money," I added, for I saw that the line keepers were charging admission.

"No need for that." With a dismissive wave to Darius, Mushezib took my arm and escorted me to the front of the line. The line keepers deferred to him at once, bowing their heads and stepping back to let us pass.

"How do you merit such a privilege?" I asked.

"My costume," he explained. "Astrologers do not stand in line with tourists to ascend to the summit of Etemenanki."

A warm, dry wind blew constantly across the uppermost tier. The sun shone down without shadow. The view in every direction was limitless; below me I could see the whole city of Babylon, and from one horizon to the other stretched the sinuous course of the Euphrates. Far to the north I could see the Tigris River, with sparkling cities along its bank, and in the distance loomed a range of snow-capped mountains.

Mushezib gazed at the horizon and spoke in a dreamlike voice. "Legend says that Alexander, when he entered Babylon and found Etemenanki in lamentable condition, gave gold to the astrologers and charged them with restoring the ziggurat to its former glory. 'The work must be done by the time I return from conquering India,' he said, and off he went. When he came back some years later, he saw that nothing had been done, and called the astrologers before him. 'Why is Etemenanki still in disrepair?' he asked. And the astrologers replied: 'Why have you not yet conquered India?' Alexander was furious. He ordered the whole structure to be demolished and the ground leveled, so that he could build a new ziggurat from scratch. But before that could happen, Alexander took ill and died, and Etemenanki remained as it was, like a mountain slowly crumbling to dust."

He gestured to the center of the tier. "This space is vacant now, but in the days of Nebuchadnezzar, upon this summit stood a small temple. Within the temple there was no statue or any other ornament, only a giant couch made of gold with pillows and coverlets of silk—a couch fit for the King of Gods to lie upon. Each night, a young virgin from a good family was selected by the priests to ascend alone to the top of Etemenanki, enter the temple, and climb upon the couch. There the virgin waited for Marduk to come down from the heavens and spend the night with her. When she descended the ziggurat the next day, the priests examined her. If her maidenhead was seen to be broken, then it was known that Marduk had found her worthy."

"And if she was still a virgin?" I asked.

"Then it was seen that Marduk had rejected her, to the eternal shame of the girl and her family." Mushezib smiled. "I see you raise an eyebrow, Gordianus. But is it not the same with your great god Jupiter? Does he not enjoy taking pleasure with mortals?"

"Yes, but in all the stories I've heard, Jupiter picks his own partners, and woos them a bit before the consummation. They're not lined up and delivered to him by priests to be deflowered, one after another. Jupiter's temples are for worship, not sexual assignations."

Mushezib shook his head. "You people of the West have always had different ideas about these things. Alas, for better or worse, Greek ways have triumphed here in Babylon, thanks to the influence of Alexander and his successors. The old customs are no longer practiced as they once were. Virgins no longer ascend the ziggurat to lie with Marduk, and women no longer go to the temples of Ishtar to give themselves to the first man who pays." He saw my reaction and laughed out loud. "You really must learn to exercise more control over your expressions, young man. How easily shocked you Romans are, even more so than Greeks."

"But what is this custom you speak of?"

"In the days of Nebuchadnezzar, it was mandatory that every woman, at least once in her life, should dress in special robes and place a special wreath upon her head, and then go to one of the temples of Ishtar at night and sit in a special chair in the holy enclosure. There she had to remain, until a stranger came and tossed a silver coin in her lap. With that man she was obliged to enter the temple, lie upon a couch, and make love. No man who was able to pay could be turned away. All women did this, rich and poor, beautiful and ugly, for the glory of Ishtar."

"And for the enjoyment of any man with a coin," I muttered. "I should imagine that the young, beautiful women were selected right away. But what if the woman was so ugly that no man would choose her?"

Mushezib nodded. "This was known to happen. There are stories of women who had to stay a very long time in the holy precinct—months, or even years. Of course, such an embarrassment brought shame upon her family. In such a case, sooner or later, by exchange of favors or outright bribery, some fellow was induced to go and offer the woman a coin and lie with her. Or, in the last resort, one of her male relatives was selected to do what had to be done. And at last the woman's duty to Ishtar was discharged."

I shook my head. "You're right, Mushezib—we Romans have a very different way of thinking about such things."

"Don't be so quick to judge the customs of others, my young friend. The so-called wanton nature of the Babylonian people was their salvation when Alexander entered the city. He might have destroyed this place, as he had so many other cities, but when the wives and daughters of Babylon gave themselves freely to Alexander and his men, the conquerors were not merely placated; they decided that Babylon was the finest city on earth."

I sighed. Truly, of all the places I had traveled with Antipater, this land and its people and their ways were the most foreign to me. Standing atop the so-called Foundation of Heaven and Earth, I felt how small I was, and how vast was the world around me.

Mushezib recognized some fellow astrologers and excused himself, leaving me on my own. I lingered for a while atop the ziggurat, then descended the stairway to the lower tier, where Darius awaited me.

As we made our way down, level by level, I repeated to Darius my conversation with Mushezib, and asked him what he knew of the old custom of women offering themselves at the temples of Ishtar.

"Astrologer he may be, but Mushezib does not know everything," said Darius.

"What do you mean?"

"He tells you that sooner or later every woman satisfied a man at the temple and was released from her duty. Not true."

"Surely no woman was kept waiting at the temple forever."

"Some women had no family to rescue them. There they sat, day after day, year after year, until they became toothless old hags, with no chance that any man would ever pay to lie with them."

"What became of such women?"

"What do you think? Finally they died, never leaving the temple grounds, cursed by Ishtar for failing her."

"What a terrible story!" Suddenly, all that I had seen and heard that day connected in my thoughts, and I felt a quiver of apprehension. "The ruined temple of Ishtar near the inn, and the lemur who supposedly haunts it—do you think . . . ?"

Darius nodded gravely. "Now you understand! Imagine how bitter she must be, still to be trapped in the place of her shame and suffering. Is it any wonder that she killed a man who dared to enter the grounds a few nights ago?"

"Let me make sure I understand—"

"No, speak no more of it! To do so can only bring bad fortune. We talk of something else. And when we go back to the inn, we do not walk by the temple again!"

My curiosity about the ruined temple and its supernatural resident was more piqued than ever. Darius read my face.

"Do not go back there, young Roman!" he said, almost shouting. "What do you think would happen, if the old hag sees a virile young fellow like you, barely old enough to grow a beard? The sight of such as you would surely drive her to madness—to murder!"

Darius had become so agitated that I quickly changed the subject.

We spent the rest of the day walking all over Babylon, and I found myself growing more and more dispirited. All the proud structures that had once made the city great were in shambles, or else had vanished altogether. Many of the citizens were in a ruined state as well—I had never seen so many people crippled by lameness or deformity. Apparently these unfortunates flocked to Babylon to take advantage of the charitable institutions maintained by the astrologers and sages, whose academies were the main industry of the city, along with the thriving trade in tourism.

At last, as twilight fell, we wended our way back to the inn, with Darius leading the way. I noticed that our route was slightly different from the one we had taken heading out that morning; Darius deliberately avoided walking by the ruined Temple of Ishtar. To reward him for serving as my guide all day, I could do no less than offer him dinner, but to my surprise Darius declined and hurried off, saying he would return the next morning, when Antipater would surely be rested and ready for his own tour of the city. Could it be that Darius feared to be even this close to the old temple after dark?

As soon as he was out of sight, I turned aside from the entrance to the inn and walked up the street, past the derelict building next door, to the low wall that surrounded the old temple. It was the dim, color-less hour when shadows grow long and merge together, swallowing the last faint light of dusk.

It was not as easy to study the wall as it had been earlier in the day, and the first place I chose to make my climb proved to be unscalable. But on my second attempt, I found a series of toeholds that allowed me to reach the top.

My feet secure in their niches, I rested my elbows on the top of the wall and peered over. The temple was indeed in ruins, with not much left of the roof and gaping holes in the walls. Any decorative tiles or statues appeared to have been removed. The wall of the derelict build-ing next door and the city wall along the river enclosed the courtyard next to the temple, which was entirely in shadow; all I could see were some withered trees and fragments of building blocks and paving tiles. But amid this jumble, as my eyes adjusted to the dimness, I saw a row of waist-high objects that looked like the circular drums of a column—low-backed chairs carved from solid blocks of stone too heavy for looters to carry off.

Seated on one of the ceremonial chairs, almost lost in shadow, I saw an uncertain silhouette. It was impossible to tell whether the figure was facing me or had its back to me—until the figure rose from the chair and began walking very slowly toward me.

My heart raced. All I could hear was the blood pounding in my head. The uncanny silence of the approaching figure unnerved me.

I opened my mouth. For a long moment, nothing came out, and then, my voice ascending an octave, I heard myself say: "Speakee Greekee?"

The figure at last made a sound—a hideous laugh more horrible than the crunching of broken bones. My blood turned cold. The figure reached up with clawlike hands and pushed back the moldering wreath that obscured its face.

Had the thing once been a woman? It was revolting to look at, with hair like worms and eyes that glinted like bits of obsidian. Its pale, rotting flesh was covered with warts. Broken teeth protruded from the black hole of its gaping mouth. The thing drew closer to me, filling my nostrils with the stench of putrefaction. Its low cackle rose to a sudden shriek.

I scrambled back from the wall, desperate to get away. One of my feet slipped from its toehold and I tumbled backward.

The next thing I knew, I was coming to my senses, propped up in a chair in the common room of the inn.

"Gordianus, are you all right?" said Antipater, hovering over me. "What happened to you? Were you set upon by robbers?"

"No, I fell."

"In the middle of the street? That's where Mushezib says he found you. It's a good thing he happened by, or you'd still be lying out there, at the mercy of any cutthroat who came along."

Through bleary eyes, I saw that the astrologer stood nearby. Farther back, a few other guests were gathered around. The innkeeper was in their midst, standing a head taller than anyone else. He frowned and shook his head. Talk of robbers was bad for business.

"No one attacked me, Antipater. I simply . . . fell." I was too chagrined to confess that I had attempted to scale the temple wall.

"The lad must have the falling sickness. Common among Romans," said one of the guests, turning up his nose. This seemed to satisfy the others, who drew back and dispersed.

Antipater wrinkled his brow. "What really happened, Gordianus?"

Mushezib also remained. I saw no reason not to tell them both the truth. "I was curious. I wanted to have a look at the old temple of Ishtar, so I climbed to the top of the wall—"

"I knew it!" said Antipater. He scowled, then raised an eyebrow. "And? What did you see?"

"Ruins—there are only ruins left. And . . ."

"Go on," said Antipater. He and Mushezib both leaned closer.

"I saw the lemur," I whispered. "In the courtyard of the temple. She walked toward me—"

Mushezib made a scoffing sound. "Gordianus, you did not see a lemur."

"How do you know what I saw?"

"A young man with a powerful imagination, alone in the dark in a strange city, looking at a ruined courtyard that he has been told is haunted by a lemur—it's not hard to understand how you came to *think* you saw such a thing."

"I trust the evidence of my own eyes," I said irritably. My head had begun to pound. "Don't you believe that lemures exist?"

"I do not," declared the astrologer. "The mechanisms of the stars, which rule all human action, do not allow the dead to remain among the living. It is scientifically impossible."

"Ah, here we see where Chaldean stargazing comes into conflict with Greek religion, not to mention common sense," said Antipater, ever ready to play pedagogue, even with his young traveling companion still barely conscious after a dangerous fall. "As they rule supreme over the living, so the gods rule over the dead—"

"If one believes in these gods," said Mushezib.

"You astrologers worship stars instead!" Antipater threw up his hands.

"We do not worship the stars," said Mushezib calmly. "We study them. Unlike your so-called gods, the vast interlocking mechanisms of the firmament do not care whether mortals make supplication to them or not. They do not watch over us or concern themselves with our behavior; their action is completely impersonal as they exert their rays of invisible force upon the earth. Just as the heavenly bodies control the tides and seasons, so they control the fates of mankind and of individual men. The gods, if they exist, may be more powerful than men, but they too are controlled by the sympathies and antipathies of the stars in conjunction—"

"What nonsense!" declared Antipater. "And you call this science?"

Mushezib drew a deep breath. "Let us not speak of matters about which our opinions are so divergent. Our concern now must be for your young friend. Are you feeling better, Gordianus?"

"I would be, if the two of you would stop squabbling."

Mushezib smiled. "For your sake, Gordianus, we will change the subject." He glanced at the innkeeper, who was serving some other guests, and lowered his voice. "Whatever you saw or did not see, it was good of you to calm the fears of the other guests—about the presence of robbers in the streets, I mean. Our poor host must hate all this talk of robbers, and of lemures, for that matter. He tells me he's negotiating to buy the empty building next door. By this time next year, he hopes to expand his business to fill both buildings."

Antipater surveyed the handful of guests in the room. "There hardly seems to be custom enough to fill this place, let alone an inn twice the size."

"Our host is an optimist," said Mushezib with a shrug. "One must be an optimist, I think, to live in Babylon."

That night I slept fitfully, disturbed by terrible dreams. At some point I woke to find myself drenched with sweat. It seemed to me that I had heard a distant scream—not a shriek such as the lemur had made, but the sound of a man crying out. I decided the sound must have been part of my nightmare. I closed my eyes and slept soundly until the first glimmer of daylight from the window woke me.

When Antipater and I descended the stairs, we found the common room completely deserted, except for Darius, who was waiting for us to appear. He rushed up to us, his eyes wide with excitement.

"Come see, come see!" he said.

"What's going on?" said Antipater.

"You must see for yourself. Something terrible—at the ruined temple of Ishtar!"

We followed him. A considerable crowd had gathered in the street. The gate in the wall stood wide open. People took turns peering inside, but no one dared to enter the courtyard.

"What on earth are they all looking at?" muttered Antipater. He pressed his way to the front of the crowd. I followed him, but Darius hung back.

"Oh dear!" whispered Antipater, peering through the gateway. He stepped aside so that I could take a look.

The courtyard did not appear as frightening by morning light as it had the night before, but it was still a gloomy place, with weeds amid the broken paving blocks and the ugly reddish brown wall looming behind it. I saw more clearly the stone chairs I had seen the night before—all empty now—and then I saw the body on the temple steps.

The man's face was turned away, with his neck twisted at an odd angle, but he was dressed in a familiar blue robe embroidered with yellow stars, with spiral-toed shoes on his feet. His ziggurat-shaped hat had fallen from his head and lay near him on the top step.

"Is it Mushezib?" I whispered.

"Perhaps it's another astrologer," said Antipater. He turned to the crowd behind us. "Is Mushezib here? Has anyone seen Mushezib this morning?"

People shook their heads and murmured.

I had to know. I strode through the gateway and crossed the courtyard. Behind me I heard gasps and cries from the others, including Darius, who shouted, "No, no, no, young Roman! Come back!"

I ascended the steps. The body lay chest down, with the arms folded beneath it. I looked down and saw in profile the face of Mushezib. His eyes were wide open. His teeth were bared in a grimace. The way his neck was bent, there could be no doubt that it was broken. I knelt and waved my hand to scatter the flies that had gathered on his lips and eyelashes.

A glint of reflected sunlight caught my eye. It came from something inside his fallen hat, which lay nearby. I reached out and found, nestled inside, a piece of glazed tile no bigger than the palm of my hand. Bits of mortar clung to the edges, but otherwise it was in perfect condition; the glaze was a very dark blue, almost black. Mushezib must have taken it from the ziggurat the previous day, breaking it off one of the walls, I thought. What had Darius said? "Everyone does it"—including godless astrologers, apparently, though Mushezib had not been proud of taking the memento if he had seen fit to conceal it inside his hat.

Looking up, I saw an image of Ishtar looming above me. Etched in low relief on a large panel of baked clay built into the front wall of the temple, the image had not been visible to me the night before. Could this really be Venus, as seen through the eyes of the Babylonians? She was completely naked, with voluptuous hips and enormous breasts, but the goddess struck me as more frightening than alluring, with a strange conical cap on her head, huge wings folded behind her, and legs that ended in claws like those of a giant bird of prey. She stood upon two lions, grasping them with her talons, and was flanked by huge, staring owls.

I heard a voice behind me—a woman's voice—issuing what had to be a command, though I could not understand the language. I turned to see that others had entered the courtyard—a group of priests, to judge by their pleated linen robes and exotic headdresses. Leading them was a woman past her first youth but still stunningly beautiful. It was she who spoke. At the sight of her my jaw dropped, for she was the very image of Ishtar, wearing the same conical cap, a golden cape fashioned to look like folded wings, and tall shoes that mimicked the appearance of talons and made her walk with a peculiar gait. At first, blinking in astonishment, I thought that she was as naked as the image of the goddess, but then a bit of sunlight shimmered across the gauzy, almost transparent gown that barely contained her breasts and ended at the top of her thighs. Her arms, crossed over her chest, did more to conceal her breasts than did the gown. In one hand she held a ceremonial ivory goad, and in the other a little whip.

Without pausing, the priestess strode forward. I stepped back to make way for her, concealing the small blue tile inside my tunic as I did so.

She gazed down at the body for a long moment, then briefly looked me up and down. "You are not Babylonian," she said, in perfect Greek.

"I'm from Rome."

She cocked her head. "That explains why you're foolish enough to enter this courtyard, while those who know better stay back. Do you not realize that an uneasy spirit haunts this place?"

"Actually . . ." I hesitated. I was a stranger in Babylon, and it behooved a stranger to keep his mouth shut. Then I looked down at Mushezib. Flies had returned to gather on his face. They skittered over his lips and his open eyes, which seemed to stare up at me. "I saw the thing with my own eyes, last night."

"You saw it?"

"The lemur—that's what we call such a creature in Latin. I climbed to the top of that wall, and I saw the lemur here in the courtyard. She was hideous."

The priestess gave me a reappraising glance. "Did you flee, young man?"

"Not exactly. I fell to the street and hit my head. That was the last I saw of her."

"What do you know about this?" She gestured to the corpse.

"His name is Mushezib, from Ecbatana. He was a fellow guest at the inn up the street."

"Why did he come here?"

"I don't know."

"Was it he who broke the lock we put on the gate?"

I shrugged and shook my head.

She turned and addressed the crowd that peered through the gateway. "This ruined temple is no longer sacred ground. Even so, the priesthood of Ishtar will take responsibility for this man's body, until his relatives can be found." She gestured to the priests. Looking nervous and reluctant, they stooped to lift the corpse and bear it away.

The priestess gave me a curious look. "All my life I've heard about the unquiet spirit that dwells here; the story must be centuries old. Some believe it, some do not. Never have I seen it with my own eyes. And never has violence been done here, until a man was killed a few days ago. That man died the same way, with his neck broken, and he was found on the same spot. Two deaths, in a matter of days! What could have stirred this lemur, as you call it, to commit murder? I must consult the goddess. Some way must be found to placate this restless spirit, before such a thing happens again." She gazed up at the relief of Ishtar, her mirror image, and then back at me. "Let me give you some advice, young Roman. Enjoy your visit to Babylon—but do not return to this place again."

She turned and followed the priests who were carrying away the body of Mushezib. I followed her, watching her wing-shaped cape shimmer in the morning sunlight. The cape was very sheer and supple, capturing the outline of her swaying buttocks. As soon as we were all in the street, the gate was pulled shut and men set to work repairing the broken lock. The priestess and her retinue departed. The murmuring crowd gradually dispersed.

Antipater wanted to see the ziggurat. Darius, eager to get away from the haunted temple, offered to show it to him, and I followed along. The visit took up much of the day. Antipater needed to rest before ascending to each successive tier, and without an astrologer to accompany us, we had to wait in line a long time to reach the uppermost platform.

From time to time, as we walked alongside the massive, crumbling walls, I surreptitiously pulled out the little tile I had taken from Mushezib's hat. I was curious to see from what section of the ziggurat he had taken it. But though there were a number of places where bits of glazed tile remained, I could see no tiles that seemed to match exactly the deep, midnight-blue shade of the specimen I held in the palm of my hand.

An idea began to form in my mind, and other ideas began to revolve around it—rather as the stars revolve around the earth, I thought, and appropriately so, for at the center of these conjectures was Mushezib the astrologer and his fate.

As we toured the city that day, I followed my companions in such a cloud that Antipater asked if I was still dazed by the blow to my head. I told him not to worry, and explained that I was merely thinking.

"Daydreaming about that priestess of Ishtar, I'll wager!" said Darius with a laugh.

"As a matter of a fact, I may need to see her again," I said thoughtfully.

"Indeed!" Darius gave me a leer, then offered to show us the sacred precinct where the priestess resided. I took careful note of the location, so that I could find my way back.

We did not return to the inn until dusk. I wanted to have another look at the ruined temple, despite the priestess's warning, but I feared to go there after nightfall. Besides, I doubted that I could find what I was looking for in darkness.

The next morning, I woke early. While Antipater still snored, I slipped into my clothes and crept quietly down the stairs. I passed the open door to the kitchen next to the common room and saw, with some relief, that the innkeeper and his wife were already at work preparing breakfast.

Without a sound, I left the inn and hurried up the street. The gate was again securely locked, but I found the place where I had scaled the wall before. I climbed to the top, hesitated for just a moment, then scrambled over and dropped to the courtyard.

The dim morning light cast long shadows. I felt a quiver of dread. Every now and then, amid the shadows, I imagined I saw a movement, and gave a start. But I was determined to do what I had come to do. My heart pounding, I walked all over the courtyard, paying special attention to the wall of the vacant tavern and also to the ground along the river wall, looking for any place where the earth might have been disturbed recently. It was not long before I found such a spot.

I knelt amid the uprooted weeds and began to dig.

The sun had risen considerably before I returned to the inn.

"Gordianus! Where in Hades have you been?" cried Antipater. The other guests had all gone out for the day. Only Antipater and Darius were in the common room. "I've been terribly worried about you—"

He fell silent when he saw the company of armed men who entered the inn behind me, followed by the priestess of Ishtar.

Alarmed by the rumble of stamping feet, the innkeeper rushed into the room. His face turned pale. "What's this?" he cried.

Moving quickly, some of the men surrounded the innkeeper and seized his brawny arms. Others stormed the kitchen. A moment later they dragged the innkeeper's wife into the room, shrieking and cursing in Egyptian.

I sighed with relief. Until that moment, I had not been entirely certain of the accusation I had made against the innkeeper and his wife, but the looks on their faces assured me of their guilt.

The rest of the armed company dispersed to search the premises, beginning with the innkeeper's private quarters. Within moments, one of the men returned with a small but ornately decorated wooden box, which he opened for the inspection of the priestess. I peered over the man's shoulder. The box was filled with cosmetics and compounds and unguents, but the colors and textures were not of any common sort; this was the kit of someone who practiced disguise as a profession—an actor or street mime.

The most famous mime troupes, as even a Roman knew, came from Alexandria—as did the innkeeper's wife.

"Take your hands off that, you swine!" she cried, breaking free of the guard who held her and rushing at the man who held the box. He blanched at the sight of her and started back. So did I, for even without the horrifying makeup, the face of the hideous lemur I had seen in the courtyard of the temple was suddenly before me, and I heard again the shriek that had made my blood run cold.

Like a charging aurochs, she rushed headlong at the priestess, who stood her ground. I braced myself for the spectacle of the impact—then watched as the priestess raised her ceremonial goad, backhanded, and swung it with all her might, striking the innkeeper's wife squarely across the face. With a squeal that stabbed at my eardrums, the innkeeper's wife flailed and tumbled to one side, upsetting a great many small tables and chairs.

The guards swarmed over her and, after a considerable struggle, restrained her.

One of the men who had been searching the premises entered the room. He stepped past the commotion to show something to the priestess. In his hand he held a lovely specimen of a glazed tile. Its color was midnight blue.

Gazing at the shambles of the common room, Antipater turned to me and blinked. "Gordianus—please explain!"

Much later that day, in the tavern of another establishment—for the inn where we had been staying was no longer open for business—Antipater, Darius, and I raised three cups brimming with Babylonian beer and drank a toast to the departed Mushezib.

"Explain it all to me again," said Darius. He seemed unable to grasp that the lemur that had haunted the old temple had never been a lemur at all, so strong was his superstitious dread of the place.

I lubricated my throat with another swallow of beer, then proceeded. "At some point—we don't know exactly how or when, but not too long ago—the innkeeper or his wife went digging around the ruined temple grounds. Literally digging, I mean. And what should they discover but a previously unknown cache of ancient glazed bricks, undoubtedly from the long-demolished wall of Nebuchadnezzar that used to run along the riverfront, where a newer, plainer wall now stands. They knew at once that those bricks must be worth a fortune. But their discovery was located in an old temple precinct; the land itself is common property and not for sale, and any artifacts or treasure found there would almost certainly belong to the priesthood of Ishtar.

"The innkeeper clearly had no right to the bricks, but he intended to get his hands on them nonetheless. The best way to do that, he decided, was to purchase the derelict property adjacent to the temple, from which he and his wife could gain access to the courtyard and the buried bricks without being observed. But negotiating to buy that property was taking time, and the innkeeper was fearful that someone else might go nosing about and find those buried bricks. The old tales about the place being haunted gave him a perfect way to frighten others away.

"The innkeeper's wife played the lemur. As we now know, she was part of an Egyptian mime troupe in her younger days. She's an intimidating woman to start with; with the right makeup, and calling on her skills as an actress, she could be truly terrifying, as I experienced for myself. But the lemur didn't frighten everyone away; at least one man must have dared to enter the courtyard a few nights ago, perhaps out of simple curiosity, and he was the first to die."

"Was it the innkeeper's wife who broke the first victim's neck?" asked Antipater.

"She's probably strong enough, and we've seen what she's capable of doing when roused, but her husband confessed to the killing. Those brawny arms of his are strong enough to break any man's neck."

"And Mushezib? What was the astrologer doing in the courtyard in the middle of the night?" said Darius.

"I think it wasn't until after we all went to bed that night that Mushezib's thoughts led him to the same conclusion I reached, a day later. He had no belief in a lemur; what, then, had I actually seen? Perhaps someone pretending to be a lemur—but why? In the middle of the night, Mushezib broke the lock on the gate, slipped inside, and started snooping around. He even did a bit of digging, and found this, which he slipped under his hat." I held up the little tile. "If I'd seen his hands, and the dirt that must have been on his fingers, I might have realized the truth sooner, but his arms were folded beneath him, and the body was carried off by the priests before I could take a closer look."

"You were looking mostly at the priestess of Ishtar, I think," said Darius.

I cleared my throat. "Anyway, the innkeeper must have come upon Mushezib, there in the courtyard. There was a struggle—I heard Mushezib scream, but I thought I was dreaming—and the innkeeper broke his neck. As he had done with his previous victim, he left the body on the temple steps as a warning, and there we found poor Mushezib the next day.

"It wasn't until we went to the ziggurat, and I was unable to find any tiles that matched the one in Mushezib's hat, that I began to think he must have found that tile elsewhere. It occurred to me that he might have found it on the old temple grounds—and the rest of the tale unfolded in my mind. Early this morning I stole into the court-yard and found the spot where the bricks are buried. I also discovered a concealed and crudely made opening in the wall of the vacant build-ing next to the temple.

"I went at once to the priestess of Ishtar to tell her of my suspicions. She gathered some armed men and followed me back to the inn. Along with the tiles the innkeeper had already dug up, the priestess's men also found a secret passage the innkeeper had made between his private quarters and the vacant building next door, which, as I had discovered, had its own concealed access to the temple courtyard, also made by the innkeeper. That was how he and his wife managed to enter the court-yard even when the gate was locked. By passing through the vacant building, the so-called lemur could appear and disappear—and the killer was able to surprise his victims and then vanish, never stepping into the street."

"What will become of that murderous innkeeper and his monster of a wife?" asked Antipater.

"The priestess says they must pay for their crimes with their lives."

"And what will become of all those lovely bricks?" asked Darius, his eyes twinkling at the thought of so much loot.

"The priesthood of Ishtar has claimed them. I imagine they're dig-ging them up even now," I said.

"Too bad you didn't get to claim those bricks." Darius sighed. "You know, I hate to speak of such a thing, but not since the day we met have I been given even a single coin for the many excellent favors I have rendered to my new friends."

I laughed. "Never fear, Darius, you will be paid for your services!"

I patted the heavy coin purse at my waist. That afternoon, after the arrest of the innkeeper and his wife, I had been called back to the sacred precinct of Ishtar for a private interview with the priestess. She warmly praised my perspicacity, and insisted that I accept a very generous reward.

Darius looked at the money bag, then raised an eyebrow. "Was that the only reward she gave you, young Roman?"

Antipater also looked at me intently.

My face turned hot. Was I blushing? "As a matter of fact, it was not," I said, but of whatever else took place between the priestess and me that afternoon, I chose to say no more.

VIII

THE RETURN OF THE MUMMY

(The Great Pyramid of Egypt)

From Babylon, Antipater and I journeyed overland to Egypt, threading our way through rugged mountain passes and traversing sandy deserts. In my imagination I had assumed this corner of the world to be a trackless, unpopulated wilderness, but in truth it was quite the opposite. Our route, so Antipater informed me, had been laid out hundreds if not thousands of years ago by traders carrying goods between Egypt and Persia, some venturing as far as fabled India and Serica. We encountered many caravans going in both directions, transporting cargoes of ivory, incense, spices, precious stones, fabrics, and other commodities.

The accommodations along the way were well organized. At each stop we hired a new beast to carry us to the next—mostly mules and horses, but occasionally I was forced to ride a spiteful creature called a camel. At day's end, there was always an inn waiting for us.

At last, at the ancient port of Gaza, we reached the sea, and reentered that part of the world where one may expect to hear Greek spoken, and even a bit of Latin. It was in Gaza that I first heard the alarming news of what was happening in Rome.

While Antipater and I had been off in Babylon, dreadful omens had been witnessed all over Italy. Mountains crashed together like

Titans wrestling, sending shock waves that ruptured roads and caused buildings to collapse. The earth itself cracked open and spat flames into the sky. Domesticated animals turned feral; dogs behaved like wolves and even sheep turned vicious and attacked their owners. After so many awful omens, no one was surprised when war at last broke out between Rome and the subordinate cities of her restive Italian confederation. Now the entire peninsula was in tumult. Roman magistrates across Italy had been assassinated. In retaliation, and to quell the revolt, Rome's armies had besieged and sacked rebellious cities and put entire regions to the torch.

Worried and homesick, I dispatched a letter to my father back in Rome, asking him to reassure me that he was well and to send his reply to a professional receiver of letters in Alexandria, the city that was to be our destination after we sailed up the Nile to see the Great Pyramid.

Antipater seemed to be far less agitated than I was by the news from Italy. Indeed, whenever a shopkeeper or a fellow traveler imparted the latest gossip about the situation in Rome, I thought I saw a fleeting smile on Antipater's lips. He was a Greek, after all, proud of his heritage and, as I had learned in the course of our journey, suspicious and even disdainful of Roman power. Having now seen with my own eyes so many glorious achievements of Greek civilization, I understood the nostalgia felt by many Greeks for the days before Rome intruded on their world.

From Gaza, we journeyed due west along a flat, featureless stretch of sandy coast, until we came to that region of Egypt called the Delta, where the desert abruptly gives way to a land of lush greenery watered by the mouth of the Nile.

Before the Nile reaches the sea, it spreads out in many channels, like the fingers of a wide-open hand. On maps, this vast, watery region forms a triangular shape not unlike the fourth letter of the Greek alphabet, inverted: Δ. Thus it acquired its name: the Delta.

In the coastal town of Pelusium we booked passage on a boat to take us up the Nile and all the way to Memphis, which lies a few miles south of the apex of the Delta, and from which we would make an excursion to see the fabled pyramids.

The heat was stifling as we sailed upriver on the crowded boat, pass-ing quaint villages and ancient temples. The rank smell of Delta mud filled my nostrils. I spotted crocodiles in the shallows, heard the call of the ibis and the bellow of hippopotami, and felt very far from my father and the war that was raging in Italy.

Long before Romulus founded Rome, even before the heroes of Homer sacked Troy, the civilization of Egypt was already ancient. Some of the monuments we passed on the riverbank were unimaginably old, and they looked it. Weathered granite slabs depicted animal-headed gods in stiff poses alongside images of the Egyptian kings of old, called pharaohs, who wore bizarre headdresses and wielded crooks and flails.

While I gazed at Egypt passing by, Antipater kept his head down and read about it. During our stay with his cousin Bitto in Halicarnas-sus, Antipater had arranged to have several scrolls of *The Histories* of Herodotus copied from her library, including the chapters that de-scribed Egypt and its people.

Along a quiet stretch of the river, we passed a little boy who stood atop the steep bank. I smiled and waved to him. The boy waved back, then hitched up his long, loose garments and relieved himself in the water below. The stream glittered under the bright sunlight and the boy made a game of aiming it this way and that. He grinned and looked quite proud of himself.

Antipater, poring over a scroll, never looked up.

"According to Herodotus," he said, "no one has yet determined the source of the Nile. Those who travel as far as possible upriver, a journey of many months, eventually arrive in a region of vast swamps and im-passable forests where the people are all sorcerers; they are also extremely short and as black as ebony, and speak a language incomprehensible to outsiders. Farther than that, no traveler has ever ventured and come back alive. Nor, according to Herodotus, can anyone adequately explain why the Nile, unlike all other rivers, is at it lowest in the spring, then floods at the time of the summer solstice."

"The solstice is still a few days away," I said. "I suppose that means we're seeing the Nile at its lowest. Will it actually rise high enough to flood the banks on either side?"

Antipater looked up, shading his eyes from the bright sunlight. "Hopefully, Gordianus, we shall witness this famous phenomenon for ourselves. The river is said to rise so dramatically that the banks are flooded for hundreds of miles, irrigating a vast amount of cultivated land and creating the most fertile region on earth. The inundation should begin any day now."

He returned his attention to the scroll in his lap. "Herodotus goes on to say that, just as the Nile is different from all other rivers, so the people who live along its banks follow customs contrary to other people. The women go to market and carry on trade, while the men stay at home and weave. There are no priestesses, only priests, and while holy men in other lands grow beards and wear their hair long, in Egypt they shave their heads—and every other part of their bodies, as well. The Egyptians write from right to left, not left to right. They knead dough with their feet and clay with their hands. They invented the peculiar practice called circumcision. And listen to this: the women make water standing up, while the men do so crouching down!"

I frowned. "I have to wonder if that's completely accurate. If you'd bothered to look up, you'd have seen that little boy—"

"I assure you, Gordianus, no historian was ever more scrupulous than Herodotus. He traveled extensively in Egypt, saw everything, and consulted all the best authorities."

"Yes, but didn't Herodotus write that book over three hundred years ago? The information might be a bit out of date."

"My dear boy, there's a reason Herodotus remains our best authority on all matters pertaining to Egypt. No other writer can match his insight and attention to detail. Now, where was I? Ah, yes—on the subject of worship, Herodotus tells us that the Egyptians are the most religious of all people. They can trace their practices back many thousands of years. Since the Egyptians were the first race of mortals, they built the first temples. It was from Egypt that we Greeks received our first knowledge of the gods, though we know them by other names. Thus the Egyptian god Ammon is our Zeus, their Osiris is our Dionysus, Anubis is the same as Hermes, and so on."

I frowned. "Isn't Anubis the one who has the head of dog? Whereas Hermes—or Mercury, as we Romans call him—is a handsome youth; at least that's how the statues in Greek and Roman temples always show him. How can Anubis and Hermes be the same god?"

"You touch upon a problem that has puzzled even the wisest philosophers. What are we to make of the fact that the Egyptians worship animals, and give animal characteristics to certain gods in their statues and pictures? Some believe their use of such imagery is purely symbolic. Thus, Anubis doesn't really have a dog's head, but is only shown that way because he acts as the loyal guardian of the other gods—their watchdog, so to speak."

"I shouldn't think any god would care to have himself depicted as a dog, no matter what the reasoning."

"Ah, but that's because you think like a Roman, Gordianus. You look for plain facts and practical solutions. And I think like a Greek; I delight in beauty and paradox. But the Egyptians have their own way of thinking, which often seems quite strange to us, even fantastical. Perhaps it's because they care so little for this world, and so much for the next. They are obsessed with death. Their religion prescribes intricate rituals to safely guide their spirit, or *ka,* to the Land of the Dead. To achieve this, they must keep their mortal bodies intact. Whereas we cremate our dead, the Egyptians go to great lengths to preserve the corpses of their loved ones and to make them appear as lifelike as possible. The process is called mummification. Those who can afford to do so keep the mummies of their dead relatives in special rooms where they go to visit them, offer them food, and even dine with them, as if they were still alive."

"You must be joking!" I said.

"Romans may wish to rule this world, Gordianus, but Egyptians are far more concerned with the Land of the Dead. We must keep that in mind when at last we see the largest tomb ever built, the Great Pyramid."

The Great Pyramid! With anticipation we drew near the final destination of our journey. I had seen all six of the other Wonders now, and would be able to judge for myself whether the Great Pyramid was truly the most marvelous of them all, as many asserted. Could it possibly surpass the soaring height of the Mausoleum, or the splendor of the Temple of Artemis, or the ambition of the fallen Colossus? Everyone on earth had heard of the pyramids, even barbarians in the farthest reaches of Gaul and Scythia. Now I was about to see them.

The branch of the river on which we were traveling joined with others, growing wider and wider, until all the many branches converged into their common source, the great Nile itself. Suddenly—ahead of us and to the right, shimmering in the distance—I caught my first glimpse of the Great Pyramid. Beside me, Antipater gasped. He, too, was seeing the monument for the first time.

"Am I seeing double?" I whispered, for it seemed to me that I could see not one but two enormous pyramids.

"I think not," said Antipater. "According to Herodotus, there are three major pyramids on the plateau west of the river. One of them is relatively small, but the other is very nearly as large as the Great Pyramid."

"They must be enormous!" I said.

Some of the passengers on the boat joined us in gaping at the monuments, but others gave them only a glance. The boatmen, for whom the pyramids were an everyday sight, paid them no attention, even as they loomed ever larger to our right.

Then we passed the plateau and sailed on, and the pyramids receded behind us. A little later we arrived at the ancient capital of Egypt, Memphis.

The cities of Greece had been foreign to me, but also familiar, for Romans and Greeks worship the same gods and construct the same types of buildings. Babylon had been more exotic, but it was a city in decline, long past its glory. But Memphis—ah, Memphis! This city was truly like another world.

At first, nothing seemed familiar and I could hardly take in the strangeness of it all—the way the people dressed (I had no names for such garments), the things they ate (I recognized nothing, but the aromas were enticing), the tunes played in the public squares (which sounded like noise to me), the statues of the gods (animal heads, bizarre postures), the colorful picture-writing on the temple walls (beautiful but indecipherable). To be sure, Greek was spoken—by some. The common people spoke another, older language, the likes of which I had never heard before.

We found accommodations at an inn not far from the river, and were given a room on the upper floor. Antipater complained about the steep steps, but when I opened the shutters and raised my eyes above the nearby rooftops, I saw the Great Pyramid looming in the distance

Antipater joined me in gazing at the sight. "Wonderful!" he whispered.

"Shall we set out to see it at once?" I said eagerly.

"No, no!" said Antipater. "The day is far too hot, and the hour too late, and I need my rest."

"Rest? All you did today was lie in the boat and read Herodotus!"

"How lucky you are to be nineteen, Gordianus. Someday you'll understand how an old man can grow tired simply by drawing a day's ration of breath. Leave the shutters open, but draw the curtains. It's time for my nap."

We did not go to see the pyramids that day, or the next, or even the next. Antipater insisted that we acquaint ourselves with the city of Memphis first. To be sure, it was a place of marvels, decorated with shrines, temples, ceremonial gates, colossal stone statues, and towering obelisks the likes of which I had never seen before, all constructed on an enormous scale. The strange architecture of the city exuded an air of mystery and great antiquity. It was easy to believe that mortals had been living and building in this spot since the beginning of time.

Memphis was no longer the capital of Egypt—the heir of Alexander the Great, Ptolemy, had chosen to move the royal administration to

Alexandria—but its monuments were well kept, and the city was bustling and vibrant. I had thought that in Egypt we would arrive at the edge of the world, but Memphis seemed to be its center, the crossroads of all the earth. Among the people I saw every shade of hair color and complexion; I had never known that mortals came in so many hues. The city seemed at once impossibly ancient and incredibly alive.

We dined on tilapia and exotic fruits in the palm grove next to the Temple of Selene (who is also Aphrodite, according to Antipater). We observed the sacred Apis bull dozing in its luxurious enclosure; it seemed quite strange to me that a mere animal should be treated as a god. But the grandest of the temples was that of Serapis, the god most favored by the Ptolemy dynasty. To reach it, we traversed a broad ceremonial walkway lined on both sides by life-sized statues of a creature with the head of a man and the body of a lion. These, Antipater explained, were sphinxes.

"Like the sphinx that guarded the Greek city of Thebes and posed the famous riddle to Oedipus?" I asked. Antipater himself had taught me the story.

"I suppose. But if Oedipus truly met a sphinx, the creature must have come from Egypt. No Greek I know has ever seen a sphinx, but their images are all over Egypt. These statues look as if they've been here forever."

The long walkway was exposed to a strong wind from the west, and drifts of sand, some quite high, had gathered around the bases of the statues. One of the sphinxes was buried up to its chin, so that sand covered the lower portion of its *nemes* headdress and its long, narrow beard. I paused to look at the sphinx's enigmatic face, and recalled the famous riddle: *What creature in the morning goes on four legs, at midday on two, and in the evening on three?* Had Oedipus given the wrong reply, the sphinx would have strangled him, but he deduced the answer: *Man, who first crawls on all fours, then strides on two feet, then walks with a cane.*

At every turn we were accosted by men who offered to serve as guides to the local sites. Antipater eventually picked the one who struck him as the least unscrupulous, a fellow named Kemsa, and charged the man with arranging our transportation to the pyramids. Kemsa, who spoke passable Greek, advised us to wait a while longer, for soon a three-day festival to celebrate the summer solstice would claim the attention of all the locals and tourists in the city; during those three days we might be able to visit the pyramids in peace, without hordes of sightseers around us. The guide also insisted that we buy long white robes and linen headdresses, not unlike those worn by the sphinxes, saying that such garments would protect us from the desert heat.

At last, early on the appointed morning, dressed in our desert apparel, we set out to see the pyramids.

Kemsa supplied a camel for each of us—to my dismay, for I had yet to meet a camel that did not dislike me on sight. This beast was no different. Almost at once, he tried to bite me. The guide chastised the camel by striking him soundly on his enormous nose. After that the creature seemed content to turn his long neck, give me a baleful stare, and spit at me from time to time. Despite his sullen nature, the camel was an obedient mount, and we made steady progress.

First we took a road that followed the west bank of the Nile downriver for a few miles, then we took a sharp turn to the left and ascended to a dry, sandy plateau. We hardly needed the guide to show us the way, for at every moment the Great Pyramid was visible, looming ever larger as we drew closer. By the early light of morning it appeared pale pink in color, and as flat as if it were a drawing cut from a piece of papyrus; but as the sun rose, and the heat increased, the pyramid appeared white and began to shimmer. At times it seemed to levitate above the earth, and at other times it quivered so much that I thought it might miraculously disappear before our eyes, but the guide explained that these uncanny visions were merely illusions caused by the waves of heat rising from the sand.

Larger the pyramid loomed, and then larger still. I glanced at Antipater and saw that he was as astonished as I was. It was one thing to be told that the Great Pyramid is the largest object ever made by men, and another to actually see it. My imagination had been inadequate to prepare me for the awesome scale of what I beheld.

The plateau was crisscrossed with ceremonial roadways and dotted with temples, altars, and shrines, but because of the festival in Memphis there was not a person in sight. The solitude was uncanny. A part of me was glad we had waited for this day, to have the pyramids to ourselves. But I also felt slightly unsettled, that we three should be the only specks of humanity on that vast, sandy plain. My sense of perspective was undone; in vain I looked for some way to judge size and distance.

Only once was the Great Pyramid blocked from view, as we passed close by a very large sand dune that seemed out of place amid the surrounding temples. Once we passed the dune, the Great Pyramid reappeared and filled my whole range of vision, not only from side to side but up and down, for the structure was nearly as tall as it was wide. From a distance, the pyramid had appeared to be made from a single block of stone, so smooth was the surface. Closer up, I could see that it was actually faced with many different stones expertly fitted together, and that these stones were of many different colors and textures—pale violet and glossy blue, sea green and apple gold, some as opaque as marble and others as translucent as sunlight captured in a wave. At a distance all these various stones merged together and appeared scintillating white. I had expected the Great Pyramid to be immense, but I had not expected it to be so beautiful and so finely made, as fascinating to behold close up as it was at a distance.

Around the bottom of the pyramid, great drifts of sand had accumulated. We remained on our camels and began slowly to circle the base. The eastern face of the pyramid was dazzling in the full morning sunlight, the southern face ablaze with slanting rays, and the western face entirely in shadow. Looking up, I watched the sun surmount the tip of the pyramid, where it seemed to hover like a ball of flame on its point.

"Who built such a marvel?" I exclaimed. "And how was it done?"

Kemsa opened his mouth to answer, but Antipater was quicker. "According to Herodotus, the pharaoh Kheops employed a hundred thousand men just to build the roadway to transport the stones from Arabia. That labor alone took ten years; another twenty years were needed to build the pyramid itself. First the structure was built up in tiers, like steps, and then the tiers were fitted from the top down with enormous finishing stones lifted into place by a series of ingenious levers, then the whole surface was polished to a bright luster."

"Is Kheops buried inside?" I asked.

"Herodotus states that Kheops was laid to rest in a chamber deep beneath the pyramid, a sort of subterranean island surrounded by water channeled underground from the Nile."

As I tried to visualize such a bizarre funeral chamber, Kemsa loudly cleared his throat. "Actually," he said, "the stones of the pyramids were not raised into place by cranes or levers, but pulled up huge ramps of earth built especially for the purpose."

"Nonsense!" said Antipater. "Such ramps would have needed to be enormous, larger in volume than the pyramid itself. If such massive earthworks were ever constructed, why do we see no remains of them?" It was true that there were no huge mounds of earth anywhere on the plateau. There were sand dunes here and there, including the large one amid the temples we had passed on our way, but even that mound was minuscule in comparison to the Great Pyramid.

"Those who built up the ramps disposed of them when they were done," said the guide. "The earth was carted to the Nile, which carried it downstream to create the many islands of the Delta. And since you ask if Kheops is buried inside, young Roman, I will tell you that he is not. The Pharaoh so abused his people when he forced them to build this enormous tomb, that when he died they refused to put him in the pyramid and buried him elsewhere. The pyramid is empty."

"How could you possibly know such a thing?" said Antipater.

The guide smiled. "Did I not tell you that I, Kemsa, am the best of all the guides? I know what others do not. Follow me."

Kemsa led us back to the south face of the pyramid, where he gave a sign that brought all three camels to a halt. I would have sat there indefinitely, gaping at the pyramid, had my camel not folded its knees and pitched forward, making clear its desire to be rid of me. As the creature turned its head and prepared to spit, I hurriedly dismounted. Antipater did likewise, though with more dignity.

"Shall we go inside?" said our guide.

"Is it possible to do so?" Antipater's eyes grew wide.

"With Kemsa as your guide, all things are possible. Follow me!"

The face of the pyramid must once have been as smooth as glass—impossible to climb—but time had worn and pitted the stones, making it possible to clamber up by staying low and gaining purchase amid tiny cracks and fissures. I worried that Antipater would find the effort too strenuous, but, as he had done so often before on our journey, my old tutor displayed amazing dexterity and stamina for a man of his years. Antipater would complain of having to climb a few stairs to our room at the inn, but nothing could stop him from scrambling up the pyramid!

Perhaps two-thirds of the way to the top, Kemsa showed us a spot where a flat slab of stone could be lifted on a pivot. The hidden doorway was so expertly fitted that it was practically invisible. Antipater and I would never have found it on our own.

"Astonishing! Herodotus makes no mention of an entrance to the Great Pyramid," said Antipater.

"No?" said Kemsa. "That's because this fellow Herodotus did not have me for a guide. Watch your head!"

Kemsa held the door up while Antipater and I stepped inside. Using his shoulder to keep the door open, Kemsa produced three torches, one for each of us, and used a flint to ignite them. Once the torches were lit, he allowed the door to fall shut.

The narrow, steeply sloping shaft before us plunged into utter darkness. I noted with some relief that there was a rope that could be used to steady one's descent.

"Do you wish to go on?" said Kemsa.

Antipater looked pale in the firelight. He swallowed hard. "I haven't come this far to forego an opportunity that even Herodotus missed." He held his torch in one hand and gripped the rope with the other. "Lead on!"

The guide went first. Antipater and I followed.

"But if there's no tomb at the bottom, what is there to see?" I said. Even though I spoke quietly, my voice echoed up and down the shaft.

"To know that, you must see for yourself," said Kemsa.

I suddenly felt uneasy. What if the pyramid was a tomb after all—
not of kings but of common fools like myself, led to their death and
waylaid by Egyptian bandits posing as guides? Would there be a chamber full of skeletons at the bottom, with my own soon to be added?
What an irony, if the Great Pyramid should turn out to be the resting
place not of Kheops, but of Gordianus of Rome!

I told myself there was nothing to fear; it was only the darkness, the
weird echoes, and the cramped space of the descending shaft that
unnerved me. Clutching our torches and the rope, we continued our
slow, steady descent.

At last the surface became level. After passing through a short hallway we entered a chamber of considerable size. By the flickering torch-
light I discerned a flat roof perhaps twenty feet above our heads. The
walls appeared to be made of solid granite, finely fitted and polished but
without any sort of decoration. The chamber was empty except for a
massive sarcophagus hewn from a solid block of granite. The sarcophagus had no lid. Nor was there any decoration or carving on its surface.

"Can this be the sarcophagus of the great Kheops?" I whispered.
Within such a fabulous monument, I had expected to see a burial chamber of great splendor.

"This is a burial chamber, yes, and that is a sarcophagus," said
Kemsa. "But as I told you, there is no Kheops. Go and see for yourself."

Antipater and I stepped up to the sarcophagus and peered inside.
My old tutor gasped. So did I.

Kemsa, who seemed to know everything about the pyramid, was
wrong about the sarcophagus. It was not empty; there was a body in it.
For a pharaoh, he was very plainly dressed, not in royal garments but in
a long white robe and a simple *nemes* headdress not unlike the clothes I
was wearing. The hands crossed over his chest and his clean-shaven
face were those of a man of middle age, darkened by the sun and
somewhat wrinkled, but for a man who had been dead for hundreds if
not thousands of years, he was remarkably well preserved. I could even
see a bit of stubble across his jaw. Antipater had told me that Egyptian

mummification was a sophisticated process, but this specimen was extraordinary.

Seeing our stunned reaction, Kemsa raised an eyebrow and walked over to join us. When he saw the body in the sarcophagus, he stopped short. By the flickering light I saw his face turn ashen. His eyes grew wide and his jaw hung open. His amazement appeared so extreme, I thought he must be playacting—until he emitted a shriek and tumbled backward in a faint, dropping his torch on the floor.

While Antipater tended to him, I returned my attention to the body in the sarcophagus, and I saw what had made Kemsa shriek.

The mummy had opened its eyes.

The mummy blinked. Then, staring upward into the darkness, the mummy spoke in a hoarse whisper. "Am I still alive? Or am I dead? Where am I? The priest of Isis promised that a savior would come to me!"

My heart pounded in my chest. My head grew light. For a moment I feared that I, too, would faint. But as Antipater had pointed out, I was a Roman. Disconcerted I might be, even discombobulated, but at some level I knew there must be an explanation for what was happening. For one thing, the man in the sarcophagus spoke flawless Greek, with the local accent I had heard in Memphis. He was not Kheops.

Nor was he a mummy, I thought—then felt a quiver of doubt as he reached up and gripped my arm with a hand as cold as ice.

He stared up at me and hissed. "What is this place? And who are you?"

I swallowed hard. "My name is Gordianus. I'm a visitor from Rome. We're inside the Great Pyramid."

He released me, then covered his face and began to sob.

"And who are you?" I said, no longer fearful, for the man in the sarcophagus now appeared more pitiful than frightening. "And what are you doing here? And how long have you been lying in the dark?"

The man ceased to sob and gradually composed himself. He sat upright in the sarcophagus. His movements were stiff. His eyes were dull and his face was drained of all expression. He appeared so lifeless that for a moment, by the uncertain light, I wondered if he might be a mummy after all.

"If you would know the story of Djal, son of Rhutin," he said, "help me out of this accursed stone box. Lead me out of the darkness and back to the sunlight, and I will tell you everything, young visitor from Rome."

When we emerged from the shaft, the glare of the noonday sun was blinding. Kemsa, embarrassed by his fainting spell, cast baleful glances at the stranger, who seemed to be more dazzled by the sunlight than the rest of us. As I was to learn later, the man had been inside the pyramid, in total darkness, for no less than two days.

Kemsa extinguished the torches and made ready to descend, but Antipater held me back. "We find ourselves not far from the summit of the pyramid, Gordianus. Shall we ascend to the very top?"

"But the man from the sarcophagus—"

"What do we care about him?" said Antipater in a low voice. "Yes, he gave us all a fright, but so what? If some local lunatic wishes to spend his time lying in the empty sarcophagus of Kheops, I don't see how that's our concern. We find ourselves at the Great Pyramid at midday, Gordianus, with a chance to stand on the very summit at the hour when the pyramid casts no shadow." He raised his voice and spoke to the guide. "Kemsa, help this fellow down, and give him some water. Gordianus and I will finish the ascent."

Looking displeased, Kemsa nonetheless did as he was told, and the two men began to descend.

"But are you up for this, Teacher?" I said. "You've exerted yourself so much already today, and the sun is so hot—"

Even as I stated my doubts, Antipater started climbing.

Grumbling at Antipater's willful nature, I followed. When I reached the top, panting for breath, my efforts were rewarded beyond my wildest expectations.

The tip of the Great Pyramid must originally have been capped in gold or some other precious metal, to judge by the remnants of pins and clamps that had fixed the metal to the rough-hewn stone beneath. That splendor was no longer to be seen—someone had looted the metal long ago—but the view was spectacular, and like no other on earth. As I slowly turned from north to south, I saw the vast green Delta, the sprawling city of Memphis, the sinuous Nile vanishing into the distance, and the rugged mountains of Arabia beyond. Below us, the various temples and shrines on the plateau looked like models built by an architect; among them I noticed again the large, incongruous sand dune we had passed on our way. To the southeast, I gazed upon the Great Pyramid's rival; its peak was clearly below our level, but it was still enormous. Turning to the west, I beheld the fearful beauty of the Libyan wilderness, a trackless waste of jagged mountains and gorges.

I had thought no view could match those from the Mausoleum in Halicarnassus or the ziggurat in Babylon, but to stand atop the Great Pyramid is truly to look down upon the world as the gods must see it.

The desert wind whistled in my ears and dried the sweat from my brow. For a long time Antipater and I crouched in that timeless spot, taking in the view. Eventually, gazing down at the foot of the pyramid, I saw our guide and the stranger from the sarcophagus, sitting in the shade cast by the camels and sipping water from one of the skins the guide had brought.

"I'm thirsty," I said.

The climb down was trickier than the climb up. We proceeded with caution, taking our time. At any moment, I feared that Antipater might lose his grip and take a tumble—but it was I who made a careless move near the bottom and found myself sliding out of control down the last fifty feet, landing in a pile of sand at the bottom, unharmed but quite embarrassed.

Kemsa allowed me only sips of water, saying it was dangerous to swallow too much, too quickly. To take our midday meal, he suggested we retire to a nearby temple. With the stranger mounted behind Kemsa, we rode our camels to the smallest of the three pyramids. Beyond it, we came upon three much smaller tombs, also pyramidal in shape but built in steps, which I had not noticed before.

"How many pyramids are there in Egypt?" I said.

"There are many, many pyramids," said Kemsa, "hundreds of them, not only here on the plateau, but all along the Nile. Most are very small in comparison to the Great Pyramid."

Before one of these minor pyramids stood a small but beautiful temple dedicated to Isis. Brightly painted columns shaped like stalks of papyrus flanked the entrance. Normally there would have been worshippers in attendance, Kemsa explained, but on this day everyone was at the festival in Memphis. Sitting on the steps of the temple in the shade, we took our meal of flatbread, wild celery, and pomegranates.

Reluctantly, the man from the pyramid accepted a bit of our food.

Antipater paid him little attention, but I was curious. "You say your name is Djal?"

The man nodded.

"How long were you in there?"

Djal frowned. "I have no way of knowing. I entered on the seventh day of the month of Payni—"

"But that's two days ago!" said Kemsa, giving him a dubious look.

"You've been in there all this time?" I said.

"Yes."

"Did you have any light?"

"I had a torch when I entered. But it soon burned out."

"Did you have food or water?"

"None."

"What did you do?"

"I lay in the sarcophagus, as the priest—a priest from this very temple—instructed me to do, and I awaited the coming of the one who would save me. I thought perhaps Anubis would appear with a message from the gods, or one of my ancestors from the Land of the Dead—maybe even the *ka* of my poor father! But no one came. I lay in the darkness, waiting, sometimes awake, sometimes asleep, until finally I could not tell if I woke or slept, or even if I was still alive. And no one came. Oh, what a fool I've been!" He began to weep again—or rather, to go through the motions of weeping, for I think there was not enough moisture in him to produce tears.

"You promised to tell us your story," I said quietly, thinking to calm him.

He nibbled a bit of bread and took a few sips of water. "Very well. I am Djal, son of Rhutin. I have lived in Memphis all my life, as did my ancestors before me, going back many generations, even to the days before the Ptolemies ruled Egypt. The prosperity of my family has varied from generation to generation, but always each son has taken care to see that his father was given the proper rites when he died, and was mummified according to the standards of the first class, never the second or third."

"I'm sorry, I don't understand."

Our guide cleared his throat. "Allow me to explain. There are three categories of mummification. First class is very expensive, second class much less so, and third class is very cheap, only for the poor. When a man dies, the embalmers present the family with a price list of every item required for the funeral, and the family decides what it can afford."

"And this includes mummification?"

"Yes." Kemsa shrugged. "This is something all Egyptians know."

"But I don't. Tell me more."

"A great many skilled artisans are involved in the process. One man examines the body and inscribes marks to indicate where the cuts should be made. Another man uses an obsidian blade to make the incisions. Then the embalmers reach inside and remove all the internal organs. Those that are vital, like the heart and kidneys, they wash in palm wine and spices and place in sealed jars. Those organs that are good for nothing, they dispose of. The brain is the hardest thing to get rid of; the embalmers must insert slender iron hooks and tweezers into the nostrils to pull out all the useless bits of gray matter. The cavities in the body are then filled with myrrh and cinnamon and frankincense and other spices known only to the embalmers, and then the incisions are sewn up and the body is packed in saltpeter. After seventy days, the body is washed and wrapped in long strips of the finest linen, and the mummification is complete. This is the first-class method, which everyone desires, and the result is a body flawlessly preserved, with the hair and eyebrows and even the eyelashes perfectly intact, so that the dead man appears merely to sleep."

"Remarkable!" I said. "And the second method of mummification?"

Kemsa raised an eyebrow. "Those who cannot afford the best must settle for the middle way. No cuts are made and no organs are removed. Instead, the embalmers fill large syringes with cedar oil and inject the fluid through the dead man's anus and mouth and then plug him up, so the fluid cannot run out. The body is packed in saltpeter for the prescribed number of days, then the plugs are removed and the fluid is drained out of him from both ends. The cedar oil dissolves the internal organs, you see, and the saltpeter desiccates the flesh, so that what remains is mostly hide and bones, but such a mummy is protected from corruption and bears some resemblance to the original, living body. Still, such a mummy is not suitable for display, even to family members. Would you care for more pomegranates?"

I shook my head, feeling slightly queasy. "And the third way?"

Kemsa shuddered. "Let us not speak of it. As I said, it is only for the desperately poor who can afford no better, and I do not think you would like me to describe the results."

I nodded. "If a body is mummified in the best way, what then becomes of it?"

"The mummy is returned to the family, and placed inside a wooden case inscribed with the formulas needed to reach the Land of the Dead. Some cases are very ornate, but others are less so, depending on how much the family spends—"

"For our fathers, the sons of my family never purchased less than the very best of mummy cases!" cried Djal suddenly. Then he lowered his face and was silent again.

"So the mummy is put in a case," I said, "and then what becomes of it?"

"After the funeral rites," said Kemsa, "the mummy is taken to the family vault and leaned against the wall, upright in his case, so that when his descendants visit they may gaze upon him face to face. If the family is too poor to purchase a vault in a consecrated area, they may add a room to their house, and keep their ancestors there. Some people actually prefer such a room to a cemetery vault, for it makes it convenient for them to converse with their ancestors every day."

I considered this. "If a man's spirit moves on to the Land of the Dead, of what use is his mummy?"

Kemsa looked at me as if I were a simpleton. Djal wailed and buried his face in his hands.

Kemsa explained. "After death, the *ka* is freed from the body and seeks to find its way through many perils to the Land of the Dead. But for the *ka* to survive, it is essential that the earthly body be preserved from decay and supplied with all the everyday needs of life. The *ka* is not immortal; if the mummy perishes, the *ka*, too, will perish. That is why the mummy must be preserved and protected. That is why a man's descendant must give regular offerings to his mummy—so that his *ka* may continue to thrive in the next world."

"Oh, what have I done!" cried Djal, throwing back his head and beating his fists against his chest. "What have I done?"

"What *has* he done?" I whispered to our guide.

Kemsa drew back his shoulder and looked sidelong at the wretched man. "I think I know. You bartered the mummy of an ancestor, didn't you?"

Djal shuddered and stiffened. "Yes! For a handful of silver, I gave away the mummy of my father!"

"What is he talking about?" I said.

"This man is the lowest of the low," declared Kemsa. "He has used the mummy of his father as collateral."

Antipater's eyebrows shot up. "Herodotus writes of such a practice.

If a man finds himself in dire straits, he may use the mummy of a family member to obtain a loan. So this practice still exists?"

"Only among those who have no respect for the dead," declared Kemsa, who spat on the ground.

"I was desperate," whispered Djal. "The floods came late two years in a row; twice my crops were ruined. All I had left I invested in a caravan to bring incense from Arabia. Then my wife and little daughter both fell ill. I needed money to pay the physicians. And so—"

"You gave up the mummy of your father in return for a loan?" I said.

Djal nodded. "There is a man in Memphis named Mhotep who specializes in such loans. A greedy, wicked man—"

"No man is more wicked than he who abandons the mummy of his father!" declared Kemsa.

Djal raised his chin defiantly. "I had every expectation that I would be able to repay the loan. But then the caravan was lost in a sandstorm, and with it the last of my fortune. All the money Mhotep lent me I had already spent, on physicians. My daughter recovered, but my wife is still ill. The repayment of the loan will fall due at the commencement of the annual inundation, which will happen any day now, and I have nothing to give to Mhotep."

"Sell your house," said Kemsa.

"And put my wife on the street? She would surely die."

"You first duty is to your father. I've heard of this Mhotep. Do you know how he treats the mummies he collects as collateral? As long as there is a chance of repayment, he keeps them in a sealed room, crowded together and starved of offerings but safe from the elements. But if a debtor defaults, the mummy is never seen again. They say Mhotep dumps them in a ravine in the Libyan mountains, where insects and lizards and jackals feast on the remains, and whatever is left is turned to dust by the sun, then scattered by the wind—"

"Stop!" Djal clutched his face and shuddered.

"Tell them what happens to a man who gives up a mummy for a loan and never redeems it," said Kemsa. "You cannot speak? Then I will tell them. If this wretched fellow should die without recovering the mummy of his father, the law forbids that he should be mummified, even by the standards of the third class. Nor can he be given funeral rites. His body will rot. His *ka* will perish forever."

"Oh, what have I done?" cried Djal. "What a fool I am!"

"But you spoke of someone coming to save you," I said. "That was why you were in the pyramid, wasn't it?"

"When I saw the hopelessness of my situation, I went to the priest-hoods of all the temples in Memphis, begging for their help. Only the priests of Isis showed any interest in my plight. They disapprove of men like Mhotep and would drive them from the city if they could. They called upon Mhotep and appealed to him to be merciful. At first he re-fused, but the priests were persistent, and at last Mhotep told them: 'Let this man Djal answer the second riddle of the sphinx, and I will return the mummy to him!' He said it with a smirk, of course, because no one yet has been able to answer the riddle."

"A second riddle of the sphinx?" I said. "Just the other day, seeing the sphinxes outside the Temple of Serapis, Antipater and I recalled the famous riddle that was posed to Oedipus. But I've never heard of a second riddle."

"Nor have I," said Antipater.

"No?" said Kemsa. "Everyone in Memphis knows it. Mothers tease their children with it, for no one can solve it. It goes like this: *I am seen by all who pass, but no one sees me. I posed a riddle that everyone knows, but no one knows me. I look toward the Nile, but I turn my back upon the pyramids.*"

Antipater snorted. "Like most riddles, I suppose there's an obvious solution, but it sounds like nonsense. How could a thing be seen by everyone, yet be invisible?"

"You were unable to solve it?" I said.

"How could I possibly do what no one else has been able to do?" said Djal. "The riddle mentions the pyramids, so finally, in desperation, I came here, to the Temple of Isis that stands in the shadow of the pyra-mids. I prostrated myself in the sanctuary and prayed to the goddess to show me the answer. One of the priests overheard me. I explained my situation. He prayed with me, and told me that Isis had shown him a solution. I was to enter the Great Pyramid, lie in the empty sarcophagus I would find inside, and await the coming of the one who would show me the answer to the riddle. It seemed a mad thing to do, but what choice did I have? As night fell, when no one was watching, the priest showed me the entrance to the pyramid, and lit a torch to light my way. I descended the passage alone. I found the sarcophagus. I lay inside it, like a dead man. When the torch burned out, I was in darkness. But I trusted Isis, and prayed incessantly, and awaited the coming of the one with the answer. But alas, no divine visitor ever came! Only . . . you."

Djal cocked his head and gave me a strange look. I thought nothing of it, until I saw that Antipater and Kemsa were also looking at me in a curious way. And so, I suddenly realized, was a tall, imposing figure who suddenly loomed behind us in the doorway of the temple.

The newcomer was dressed in a long linen gown with splendid embroidery. The garment fitted tightly across his chest but below his midsection it hung in loose pleats to his feet. His head was completely shaved. His staring eyes were outlined with kohl.

"Priest of Isis!" cried Djal, prostrating himself on the steps. "I did as you commanded me, but Isis never came. Nor did Anubis. Nor did any god or messenger, only this young man—a Roman who calls himself Gordianus."

The priest continued to stare at me. "How curious, that Isis should have sent a mortal to do her bidding—and a Roman, at that!"

I cleared my throat. "No one *sent* me. Zoticus and I are travelers. We came to Egypt to see the Great Pyramid, because it's one of the Seven Wonders of the World. It was only by chance that we came on this day, and that we found a guide who knows how to enter the pyramid, and that this poor fellow happened to be inside."

"Only by chance, you say?" The priest pursed his lips. "What sort of man are you, Roman?"

"A man who solves riddles!" declared Antipater, rising to his feet. He gazed at me as if he were seeing me for the first time.

I shrugged, feeling thoroughly disconcerted by the way they all stared at me. "To be sure, on our journey, I have had occasion to use my powers of deduction—"

"On occasion?" said Antipater. "You do so invariably, I would say. Think about it, Gordianus. First in Ephesus, when that girl was shut up in the cave, and then in Halicarnassus, when the widows—"

"There's no need to recite our whole itinerary!" I snapped.

"But don't you see, Gordianus? You *are* a solver of riddles—like your father. I've seen you do it time and again. It would seem that you possess a special ability, a power, that others do not. Such gifts come from the gods. And here we find ourselves at the consummation of our journey, at the first and greatest of the Wonders, and what should appear but a riddle—awaiting *you* to solve it."

"But Teacher, I don't know the answer. I heard the riddle just now, and I have no idea what it means."

"Are you sure? Think, Gordianus!"

I mumbled to myself, reciting the bits I could recall. "Seen by all who pass . . . no one sees me . . . a riddle that everyone knows, but no one knows me . . . I sit among the pyramids . . ." I shook my head. "It means nothing to me."

"But you are the one sent by Isis," said the priest. "Come, let us pray to her, at once!"

We followed the priest inside. The walls of the sanctuary were covered with hieroglyphics recounting the story of Isis, the great Egyptian goddess of magic and fertility, sister-wife of Osiris and mother of Horus. The images dazzled me, though at the time I knew little of her story—how she gathered the scattered remains of Osiris after he was slain by the evil Set and oversaw the miracle of his rebirth.

Dominating the sanctuary was a statue of the goddess. On her head she wore a crown made of two curving horns that held between them a golden solar disk. Between her breasts, suspended from a necklace, was the sacred object called the Isis Knot, shaped like an ankh but with the arms turned down; as I would later learn, it was a symbol of her monthly flow, which in some divine way was connected with the annual inundation of the Nile. One hand was raised to touch one breast; the other held a breast-shaped vessel for the collection of her sacred milk. Her broad face was beautiful and serene, radiating wisdom.

"The goddess will tell me what must be done," declared the priest. "Then you will do as Isis prescribes, and the answer to the riddle will come to you. I am sure of it." He turned to the statue and raised his arms. "O Isis, universal mother, mistress of the elements, primordial child of time, sovereign of all things divine, queen of the living, queen of the dead, queen of the immortals, singular and utmost manifestation of all gods and goddesses, known by many names in many places, we call upon you!"

I shivered and felt slightly faint. What sort of test or labor might Isis demand of me?

I had a feeling I was not going to like the answer.

"Gordianus of Rome, you fool!" I whispered. "How did you ever get yourself into such a predicament?"

There was no one but myself to hear the words. Lit by the last flickering light of my torch, the granite walls surrounding me made no answer.

As the sun had begun to set behind the Libyan mountains, I had climbed once again to the hidden doorway of the Great Pyramid, accompanied only by the priest of Isis. Antipater, Djal, and Kemsa watched from below as the priest lifted the stone panel and lit a torch for me. Then, holding the torch in one hand and clutching the rope in the other, for the second time that day I descended into the heart of the pyramid. Above me, the priest let the panel fall shut.

Alone, I reached the burial chamber.

For as long as the torch burned strongly, I simply stood there, staring at the sarcophagus. Then the torch began to sputter, and I thought to myself: if I am to lie in the empty sarcophagus of Kheops, as Isis prescribed, now is the time to do it. Once the torch went out, I would surely become disoriented and lose all sense of direction. I might also lose my nerve completely, and go scrambling back up the narrow passage, desperate to escape from the bowels of the pyramid.

Isis had directed Djal to seek a solution to his problem by lying in the sarcophagus. According to her priest, she had directed me to do the same thing, promising that an answer to the riddle would come to me. It seemed to me that this Egyptian goddess was singularly lacking in imagination, to prescribe the same ordeal to two suppliants in a row.

When the priest made this announcement, I immediately protested— the very idea was madness—and looked to Antipater to back me up. But my old tutor had done the opposite. He seemed convinced that everything the priest said must be true, and that I was indeed the emissary promised by Isis.

"Everything that's happened since we left Rome has been leading to this moment," he declared. "You must do this, Gordianus. It is your destiny."

Antipater's certainty left me speechless. The priest nodded gravely. Djal fell to his knees and looked up at me imploringly. I looked to Kemsa, hoping he might tell me that Djal deserved his fate, but instead he embraced me, as one might a valiant warrior about to leave on a perilous mission, and wiped tears from his eyes.

"And to think, it was I, humble Kemsa, who led you to your destiny!"

They were all determined that I should do as the goddess desired. In truth, some part of me was flattered by their confidence, and intrigued by the challenge. But once inside the pyramid, that part of me began to dwindle and fade, rather like the flame of the dying torch.

"Madness!" I whispered as I climbed inside the sarcophagus and stretched out full-length. The rough-hewn granite felt cold to the touch. I clutched the stump of the torch and stared at the last dying embers until the orange glow faded to utter blackness. I cast the stump away and folded my hands over my chest.

"Now what?" I said aloud.

No answer came, only silence.

I shut my eyes, then opened them. It made no difference. I was surrounded by infinite blackness. I blinked and suddenly found myself confused: were my eyes open or shut? I had to reach up to touch my eyelids to be sure.

As complete as the darkness was the silence. I found myself making small noises, snapping my fingers or clicking my teeth, simply to reassure myself that I had not gone deaf.

Eventually the utter lack of sight and sound, unnerving at first, began to have a sedative effect. I closed my eyes and lay perfectly still. It had been a long, hot, tiring day. Did I doze, or only imagine that I did so? I seemed to enter a state of consciousness I had never experienced before, neither asleep nor awake.

A succession of images and ideas passed through my mind. As one thought faded, leaving only a dim impression, another took its place. Where was I? What time was it? I reminded myself that it was night, and I was inside the Great Pyramid, but these demarcations lost all meaning. I sensed that I had arrived at a place and a moment that were at the very center of time and space, outside the ordinary realm of mortal experience.

The second riddle of the Sphinx resounded in my thoughts: *I am seen by all who pass, but no one sees me. I posed a riddle that everyone knows, but no one knows me. I look toward the Nile, but I turn my back upon the pyramids.*

I found myself thinking of the rows of sphinxes we had seen on the approach to the Temple of Serapis, some of them nearly buried by windblown sand. As if I were a bird with wings, I seemed to rise in the air and look down upon the young Roman and his old Greek tutor as they talked about Oedipus and the riddle he had solved, and then I flew northward, following the course of the Nile until I came to the plateau and landed atop the Great Pyramid, and looked down on the temples and roadways—and the large, incongruous sand dune among them.

This vision faded and I sat upright in the sarcophagus. There were no longer any walls around me. I was surrounded by a sort of membrane, smooth and featureless and faintly glowing, rather as I imagine the inside of an egg might look to an unborn chick, if an egg could be made of twilight.

Suddenly I sensed I was no longer alone, and turned my head to see a dog-headed figure that stood upright on two legs. Slowly he walked toward me. His face was black on one side, golden on the other. In one hand he carried a herald's wand, and in the other, a green palm branch.

"Anubis?" I whispered.

"You know me better as Mercury." His long snout never moved, yet somehow he spoke.

"You've come!" I said, hardly able to believe it. "The priest said such a thing would happen, and here you are! Will you help me solve the riddle?"

"You do not need my help, Gordianus. You already know the answer."

He was right. I *did* know the answer. "You have no message for me, then?"

"I visit you not as a messenger, but as a herald, to announce her coming."

"Who? Who is coming?"

Anubis fell silent, and then began to fade, as thoughts fade. Traces of his presence lingered on my eyes, even when I shut them. When I opened my eyes again, Isis stood before me.

I knew it was Isis by the crown she wore, with its curving horns and the golden disk between them, and by the Isis Knot between her breasts. Her linen gown was the color of blood. Her skin was golden brown, the color of honey. Her eyes glittered like sparks of sunlight on the Nile. She was unspeakably beautiful.

I had seen many images of gods and goddesses in the nineteen years I had been on earth, but never had I beheld a goddess face-to-face. I felt many things at once. I was fearful yet calm, awestruck yet strangely sure of myself. The unearthly allure of the goddess inspired in me a passion that was equally unearthly, unlike anything I had felt before.

The cold granite sarcophagus melted away. In its place I rested upon an infinite expanse of something soft and warm and pliant, almost like the pelt of a living, breathing animal, if such a pelt could cover the whole earth. Isis removed her crown and hitched it to a star in the twilight sky above her. Her red gown rippled as it fell to her ankles. She reclined beside me.

In Ephesus I had known my first woman; in Rhodes, my first man. In Halicarnassus, Bitto had instructed me in the arts of love, and in Babylon I had coupled with a priestess of Ishtar. But I had never been with a goddess before.

No words could describe the bliss of that union; nor shall I attempt to do so. There is a phrase used by Herodotus when he skirts a sacred matter about which his informants require his silence: I know a thing, but it would not be seemly for me to tell.

I shall say this much and no more: in a place and a moment outside of time and space, Isis and I became one. Perhaps it never happened. Perhaps it is happening still.

Little by little, I returned to this earthly realm, until at last I felt again the hard granite beneath me and felt its coldness around me. I heard the beating of my heart. I blinked and opened my eyes and saw darkness—not the darkness of dreams or the netherworld, but a common, earthly darkness, the mere absence of light, which was nothing to fear.

I sat up. If I had left my body at some point, there was no doubt that I had returned to it. My legs were sore from climbing, my shoulders and neck were stiff from lying on hard stone, and my backside ached from riding a camel.

How much time had passed? An hour, a day, a month? I had no way of knowing. For all I knew, I had died and come back to life.

Blindly, I navigated the chamber, feeling my way along the walls until I found the opening of the shaft. Steadying myself by the rope, proceeding cautiously so as not to bump my head, I slowly made my way up.

When I pushed open the stone panel, I was puzzled, for it seemed to me that the soft light was just the same as when I descended. Had I been inside the pyramid for mere minutes?

But then, from the glow that lit the Libyan mountains, I realized that the hour was dawn, not dusk. Far below I saw the camels sitting with their limbs tucked under them, their heads nodding in sleep. Huddled under blankets, also fast asleep, were Antipater and the others, including the priest of Isis, whose shaved head shone by the first ruddy light of the rising sun.

I made no sound to wake them. Instead I turned around and ascended as quickly as I could to the top of the pyramid. How many men can say they have witnessed a sunrise from the summit of the Great Pyramid? That moment, experienced alone—although in some way I felt that Isis was still with me—I will remember all my life.

But I had another, more practical reason for the climb. I wanted to look down again at the large sand dune among the temples, to be sure that the shape was as I remembered it. It was. I could almost see the thing hidden inside it, as if the breath of a god had blown away the masses of sand. Its back was turned to the pyramids and it faced the Nile, just as the riddle said. It was seen by all who passed—who could fail to notice a sand dune big enough to block one's view of the pyramid? And yet it was unseen—for no one realized what was hidden under the sand. Its riddle was known to all, for everyone knows the riddle of the sphinx. And yet this sphinx was known to no one.

For how many generations had this monument, surely larger than any other sphinx in Egypt, been buried beneath the sand? Long enough that no one living even knew that it existed. The people of Egypt had forgotten that among the temples and shrines on the plateau, set there like a sentinel to guard the pyramids, crouched a giant sphinx, now entirely covered by sand. And yet some memory of this marvel had persisted in the form of a riddle that no one could answer.

Now that I had solved the riddle, the shape of the sphinx within the dune was unmistakable, and surely would be so to anyone gazing down on it from the Great Pyramid. There I could see the outline of the haunches, and there the protruding forepaws, and there, at the highest point, the proud head, which no doubt was covered by a *nemes* headdress. As Antipater had remarked, the solution to a riddle invariably seems obvious once you know the answer.

From far below, I heard a faint cry. I looked down to see that my companions were stirring. Djal had risen to his feet and was staring up at me. Even from such a great distance, I could see the plaintive expression on his face.

I took in the view one final time, then made my way down to give him the good news.

Later that day, while the plateau was still deserted due to the festival in Memphis, the priest of Isis summoned a team of laborers to excavate the highest point of the sand dune concealing the sphinx.

All day they dug. At last their wooden shovels struck something made of stone. They kept digging until very late in the afternoon, by which time the very top of the sphinx's head had been uncovered. The gigantic *nemes* headdress appeared to have once been surmounted by some ceremonial object, long since broken off or worn away by time; to the priest of Isis, the stone remnant suggested a rearing cobra, such as is often seen on the headdresses of sphinxes.

As the sun began to graze the jagged crest of the Libyan mountains, the priest ordered the workers to begin covering what they had uncovered. "Work all night if you must," he told them, "but don't stop until not a trace of your day's labor remains."

"But surely these men should keep digging!" I protested. "Why must they undo their work? Don't you want to see the whole thing? Granted, a full excavation will require many, many days—"

"What the gods have seen fit to conceal, I would not presume to uncover without first consulting my fellow priests and seeking to know the will of Isis in this matter. I allowed just enough digging to be sure that

the second riddle of the sphinx had indeed been solved. All who have
seen must be sworn to secrecy. That includes *you*." He cast a sidelong
glance at our guide. "And you as well, young Roman."

"But surely the will of Isis is already known in this matter," I said.
"Was it not by her guidance that I found the solution? She even—" I
bit my tongue and said no more. They had pressed me for details of my
experience inside the pyramid, and I had revealed all I could put into
words—except any mention of the intimacy I had shared with the
goddess. That experience was too special to share, and beyond words—
and it seemed to me that any mortal who dallies with a deity had best
be discreet.

The priest would not be swayed. He invited us all to spend the night
in comfort at his quarters in the Temple of Isis, and we left the workers
to their labor. For now, the sphinx among the pyramids would remain a
secret.

"Tomorrow I shall go to Memphis," said the priest. "I will convince
Mhotep that the riddle was solved and command him to return the
mummy."

"How will you persuade him?"

"Leave that to me. Your satisfaction in this matter, Gordianus, must
be the role you played in the salvation of Djal."

"I have already received my satisfaction," I said, thinking of my
wondrous experience with the goddess.

"How so?" asked the priest. The others pricked up their ears.

"That must be a riddle to which none of you will ever know the
answer."

"An upstairs room! Why were we given an upstairs room?" wailed
Antipater, clutching the railing and descending one step at a time. For
days after our trip to see the pyramids he had been so stiff and sore he
could hardly move, and had languished in his bed at the inn. On this
day he had at last consented to stir, for we had received a very special
invitation.

As we crossed the city, the exercise seemed to do him good, despite his moaning and groaning. The exotic sights and sounds stimulated us both. Our route took us past the roadway to the Temple of Serapis, and we paused to look at the long rows of sphinxes.

"Teacher," I said, "can you imagine such a sphinx expanded to the enormous scale of the monument that remains hidden on the plateau? If it were uncovered, men would call it the Great Sphinx, and would come from all over the world to marvel at the size of it. And if it were as beautiful as these smaller sphinxes, it would surely deserve a place among the Seven Wonders of the World. Why is it not on the list already?"

"Because, even very long ago, when the list of Seven Wonders was made, no one knew it existed. It must have been covered by that sand since at least the time of Herodotus, who makes no mention of it, and surely would have, had he seen it. But I suspect, Gordianus, that within your lifetime the Great Sphinx, as you call it, will be rediscovered. That priest of Isis will do his best to keep word from getting out, but one of those workers will talk, the news will spread, and sooner or later curiosity will get the better of even the most reactionary priests. Perhaps King Ptolemy himself will order the Great Sphinx to be excavated."

"More likely it will be some ambitious Roman governor, after we've conquered Egypt," I muttered.

"What's that?"

"Never mind."

With the happy thought that someday I might return to Egypt and behold the Great Sphinx, we resumed our journey to the house of Djal.

The dwelling itself was modest, but it had a marvelous location, built on a bit of high ground beside the Nile. A little girl—the daughter of Djal—greeted us at the door and led us to a terraced garden with a view of fishing boats on the river and farmlands on the opposite bank. Djal sat watching the river. When he saw us he jumped up and hugged us both. Antipater groaned at being squeezed so hard.

"What is that wonderful smell?" I said.

"The meal of thanksgiving that my wife has cooked for us."

"Your wife? I thought—"

"She was ill, yes, but now she is much better. We are all better, since the return of the mummy. Come and see!"

He led us to the room where the meal would be served. At the head of the table, leaning upright against a wall, was a tall wooden case with a mummy inside.

"Father, this is Gordianus of Rome, the man who saved you. Gordianus, this is my father."

I had never seen a mummy before. Nor had I ever been formally introduced to a dead man. In the world's oldest land, I was having many new experiences.

I stepped closer to the mummy and made a small bow. As far as I could tell, the old fellow looked none the worse for his time in captivity. His linen wrappings were unsoiled, and his face was remarkably well preserved—so much so that I half-expected him to blink and open his eyes. Anything seemed possible in Egypt.

Djal's daughter came running into the room. "Father! Father! Come and see!"

We followed her back to the garden. The face of the Nile had changed. Where before it had been as still and flat as a mirror, now a series of ripples extended across the whole width. Out on the boats, which bobbed slightly in the tide, fishermen waved their arms and cheered. Across the water, the fields were suddenly filled with farmers hurrying this way and that. Various contraptions with wheels and paddles were set in motion. The irrigation channels that crisscrossed the fields, which before had been dry, now glistened with moisture.

"The inundation has begun," whispered Djal. "And my father is home!" He dropped to his knees, covered his face, and wept with joy.

"Come see!" cried the little girl. She took my hand and led me down a path toward the river. Antipater followed, groaning. On the muddy bank we took off our shoes and stepped into the Nile. Looking down, I

262 THE SEVEN WONDERS

saw the green water turn brown as it steadily rose, covering first my feet and then my ankles.

From all up and down the river I heard cries of thanksgiving. Again and again the name of Isis was invoked. I stared at the sun-dappled water. For just an instant, amid the ripples and sparkles of light, I caught a glimpse of Isis smiling back at me.

IX

THEY DO IT WITH MIRRORS

(The Pharos Lighthouse)

"Why seven?" I said.

"What's that?" muttered Antipater, who was nodding off under the heat of the noonday sun. The crowded passenger boat we had boarded in Memphis had carried us all the way down the Nile, through the Delta, and into the open sea. Now we were sailing west, keeping close to the low coastline. There was not much to look at; the land was almost as flat and featureless as the sea. The broiling sun seemed to leach the color from everything. The pale expanse of water reflected a sky that was the faintest shade of blue, almost white.

"Why is there a list of Seven Wonders?" I said. "Why not six, or eight, or ten?"

Antipater cleared his throat and blinked. "Seven is a sacred number, more perfect than any other. Every educated person knows that. The number seven occurs repeatedly in history and in nature with a significance beyond all other numbers."

"How so?"

"I'm a poet, Gordianus, not a mathematician. But I seem to recall that Aristobulus of Paneas composed a treatise on the significance of the number seven, pointing out that the Hebrew calendar has seven days and that in many instances Hesiod and Homer also attach special importance to the seventh day of a sequence of events. There are seven planets in the heavens—can you name them? In Greek, please."

"Helios, Selene, Hermes, Aphrodite, Ares, Zeus, and Kronos."

Antipater nodded. "The most prominent constellation, the Great Bear, has seven stars. In Greece, we celebrate the Seven Sages of olden days, and your own city, Rome, was founded on the Seven Hills. Seven heroes stood against Thebes—Aeschylus wrote a famous play about them. And in the days of Minos, seven Athenian youths and seven virgins were sent every year to be sacrificed to the Minotaur of Crete. Here in Egypt, the Nile where it forms the Delta splits into seven major branches. I could cite many more examples—but as you see, the list of the Seven Wonders is hardly arbitrary. It exemplifies a law of nature."

I nodded. "But why *those* seven?"

"Now that we've seen all the Wonders, Gordianus, surely you can understand why each was placed on the list."

"Yes, but who made the list in the first place, and when, and why?"

Antipater smiled. He was fully awake now, and doing the thing he enjoyed most, other than reciting his poems—teaching. "The list is certainly very old; it had been around for as long as anyone could remember when I was a child and learned it. But the list as we know it cannot be any older than the youngest item on it. That would be the Colossus of Rhodes, which was built about two hundred years ago. So the list of the Seven Wonders—as it was handed down to me, anyway—is no older than that."

"But who created the list, and why?"

"No one knows for certain, but I have my own theory about that." Antipater looked quite pleased with himself.

"A theory? Why did you never mention it before?"

"Before proposing my idea to you, or to anyone else, I wanted to see all of the Seven Wonders. Having done so, I still need to do a bit of research. That's one reason we're heading to Alexandria. Hopefully, I'll be able to gain access to the famous Library, where I can consult the ancient sources and meet with scholars to determine the feasibility of my theory."

"What theory?"

"Having to do with the origin of the list of the Seven Wonders, of course." He shook his head. "Ah, but look! There! Do you see it?"

Ahead of us and a bit to the left, a bright star appeared to be shining just above the horizon—even though the hour was noon.

"What can it be?" I whispered. I stared at the star that could not be a star, fascinated by the glimmering beam of light.

"Behold the Pharos!" said Antipater.

"Pharos?"

"It takes its name from the rocky island on which it stands, out in the harbor of Alexandria. Alexander founded the city, but it was his successor, King Ptolemy, who made the city great by constructing vast new temples and monuments. The greatest of these—certainly the most conspicuous—was a structure of a sort that had never been seen before, a soaring tower with a beacon at its summit to guide ships safely past the shallows and reefs to Ptolemy's capital. A lighthouse, they called it. In the two hundred years since it was completed, similar towers have been built all over the world, wherever sailors are in need of a high beacon to guide them, but none of these later lighthouses are remotely as tall as the original, the Pharos of Alexandria."

"But we must be a long way from Alexandria. I can't see anything of the city at all."

"The beacon can be seen across the open sea as far as three hundred stadia, they say—in Roman terms, thirty miles or more."

"But how is such a light produced? Surely no flame can burn that brightly."

"By day, the beam is created using mirrors—enormous reflectors made of hammered bronze and silver that can be tilted in various ways so as to reflect the light of the sun. At night, a bonfire is kept burning in the tower, and the mirrors magnify the light to make it many times brighter."

"Remarkable!" I whispered, unable to take my eyes off the scintillating ray of light. Occasionally it appeared to flicker, distorted by waves of rising heat and the haze that hung over the tepid sea, but the light was strong and steady, growing brighter as our ship sailed closer to Alexandria.

At last I began to discern in miniature the features of a coastal city—ships in the harbor, city walls and towers, a vast temple on a hill in the distance—and most prominent of all, the lighthouse called the Pharos at the harbor entrance. At first my eyes deceived me, and I thought the Pharos was much shorter than it was. Then, as we drew nearer and the features of the city resolved themselves in greater depth, I was staggered at the true dimensions of the tower. I had thought it might be as tall as the Mausoleum in Halicarnassus, but it had to be much taller than that, at least twice or perhaps three times as tall.

"It must be as tall as the Great Pyramid!" I said.

I heard a chuckle behind me. "Not quite that tall—at least, not according to those who possess the knowledge and instruments capable of measuring such things."

I tore my gaze from the Pharos to have a look at the smiling passenger who had just spoken, and who now joined us at the railing. His skin was the color of ebony and he had not a hair on his head, which made his white teeth and his necklace of silver and lapis all the more dazzling. I found it hard to judge his age, but he was not young; there were a few white hairs in his eyebrows. His flawless Greek had the elegant (to my ear, rather affected) accent of highly educated Alexandrians.

"My name is Isidorus," he said. "Forgive me for intruding, but I couldn't help but overhear your conversation. Have you truly seen all of the Seven Wonders of the World?"

"We have," said Antipater.

"How remarkable! And I believe you mentioned the Library, and your desire to visit that institution."

"I did," said Antipater.

"I happen to be a scholar at the Library. Perhaps I can assist you in gaining access—unless, of course, you already have the necessary credentials."

"As a matter of fact, any assistance you might give me would be most welcome," said Antipater. "Allow me to introduce myself. I am Zoticus of Zeugma—no famous scholar, alas, merely a humble teacher of the young. And this is my pupil—or former pupil, I should say, for Gordianus is now a man and past the age of schooling."

"A Roman?" said Isidorus.

I nodded. My accent always gave me away.

"You work at the Library?" said Antipater. "I thought the scholars there were seldom permitted to leave Alexandria, except on official business sanctioned by King Ptolemy."

"That is correct. I'm just returning from a journey up the Nile. During the excavations for a new temple, some scrolls were discovered in a buried jar. They appeared to be very ancient. I was sent to retrieve them, so that they may be evaluated, copied, and catalogued in the Library." Slung by a strap over one of his shoulders was a Roman-style capsa, a leather cylinder for carrying scrolls.

"Fascinating," said Antipater. "May I ask what sort of documents these scrolls turned out to be?"

Isidorus laughed. "Don't become too excited, friend Zoticus. The scrolls were in poor condition—the copiers will face quite a challenge, making sense of the faded script and the gaps. And from my cursory examination, they pertain mostly to day-to-day business among petty bureaucrats during the reign of some ancient pharaoh whom no one even remembers. Nothing to do with the Seven Wonders, I'm afraid."

"Speaking of which . . ." I returned my gaze to the Pharos, which loomed even larger before us, so incredibly tall that it defied belief. "How can it be that *this* wonder is not listed among them?"

Isidorus smiled. "Certainly, we Alexandrians take great pride in the Pharos. But I can tell you, for a start, that it is not as tall as the Great Pyramid. Of course, the pyramids—and the Mausoleum, for that matter—are virtually solid constructions, made of stones stacked on stones with very little interior space. Given a large enough base, and enough stones, one could build such a construction to any height and it would remain stable—indeed, immovable, like a mountain. But such an edifice is by definition a monument, not a building of the sort that people can actually make use of, with hallways, rooms, stairwells, and windows. But the Pharos *is* such a building. There are hundreds of rooms inside, on many different levels—storerooms for fuel, workshops for the repair and upkeep constantly required by the complicated lighthouse mechanisms, dining halls for the workers, and barracks and armories for the soldiers who man the Pharos garrison. The Pharos does not merely exist to be gazed upon and marveled at. The Pharos is a working wonder."

As we drew closer, I saw the soldiers and workers of whom Isidorus had spoken, moving purposefully across the island, up the long ramp that led to the lighthouse entrance, and manning the parapets of the tower. The soldiers wore exotic armor that mingled the traditions of Greece and Egypt. The workers wore a sort of uniform that consisted of a tight-fitting green cap and a dark green tunic.

I studied the details of the Pharos. The building was constructed of huge blocks of white stone, with decorations made of red granite; columns of this rose-colored stone framed the massive entrance. The tower rose in three distinct stages. The lowest and largest was square in shape; the four walls gently tapered inward as they rose and ended in an elaborately decorated parapet which featured gigantic Triton statues at each corner, each holding a trident in one hand and blowing a conch in the other. The middle portion was octagonal, and not as tall as the first. The final tower was cylindrical, and the shortest of the three. It was capped by the beacon, which appeared to be housed inside a colonnaded structure not unlike a round temple. Upon the roof of the Pharos stood a gilded statue, so distant that I was not sure which god it represented.

Antipater saw me squinting. "That statue up there is Zeus the Savior, as he is known and worshipped by sailors in many a temple beside the sea. In one hand he holds a thunderbolt, the symbol of his absolute power over land and sea; there is nothing a sailor fears more than a lightning storm. In the other hand he holds a cornucopia, the symbol of his beneficence and the fruits of commerce; all who carry cargoes across the sea seek the blessing of Zeus the Savior."

I squinted again, and was barely able to make out the image Antipater described. "But how can you possibly see all those details?" I demanded, for Antipater's eyesight was not as good as mine.

He laughed. "All I see up there is a glimmer of gold atop the lighthouse. But I know the statue represents Zeus the Savior because of the famous poem by Posidippus—which you should remember as well, young man, for I'm sure I taught it to you. You must know it, Isidorus."

"Indeed I do," said the scholar, who commenced to recite in his elegant accent.

"On the island sacred to Proteus, Sostratus of Cnidos
Built this savior of the Greeks, the Pharos tower.
The coast of Egypt offers no lookouts or mountaintops,
And treacherous rocks rim Alexandria's watery bower.
But Pharos pierces the sky like an upright thorn,
Visible day and night, thanks to the beacon's conflagration.
Even as a ship approaches the Bull's Horn,
Zeus, gazing down, offers salvation."

"The Bull's Horn?" I said. "What's that?"

Isidorus peered ahead and grabbed the railing. "I think you're about to find out, Gordianus. Hold on right!"

Antipater and I followed his example, though I failed to see the need. We were about to sail into the harbor, with plenty of distance between the breakwaters and us. As far as I could see, there were no ships or any other hazards nearby.

Suddenly, from high above our heads, I heard the blaring of a horn. I looked up, and to my amazement realized the noise was issuing from the conch held by the nearest of the four Triton statues that perched at the four corners of the Pharos. The horn blared again.

The ship made a sharp turn to one side. The three of us were showered with sea spray. As I blinked my eyes to quell the stinging, I looked back to see the jagged outcrop of stone around which our captain had deftly maneuvered. The rock did indeed resemble a bull's horn, rising from the foamy waves.

"What just happened?" I said.

"There are watchers posted on the Pharos who observe every ship as it arrives and departs," explained Isidorus. "Our captain has plenty of experience on this route, but in case he had any difficulty in spotting the Bull's Horn, a watcher on the Pharos sounded a specific signal to alert him as our ship approached the hazard."

"But how can a statue be made to blow a horn?"

Isidorus smiled. "That is yet another of the wonders of the Pharos. There's a treatise that describes the Tritons' manufacture and operation in the Library, but I'm afraid King Ptolemy restricts access to such documents; the pneumatic science behind the working of the Tritons is a state secret. But I can tell you that each of the conches held by the four Tritons produces a different note. By sounding two or more horns in unison, or by sounding a sequence of different notes, or by holding notes for various durations, a great many different signals can be given. Experienced captains know the signals that apply to them—such as that simple warning note about the Bull's Horn."

"Amazing!" I said.

"And did you notice the movable mirrors that run along the parapets, between each of the four Tritons?"

I had not. Peering up, I now perceived large sheets of hammered bronze attached to pivots along the parapets, tilted at various angles.

"Those also can be used to send signals, but unlike the horns, their messages can be directed to a specific ship or even to a particular building in the city of Alexandria, by aiming flashes of reflected sunlight."

I gazed up at the Pharos, more in awe of the building than ever.

"Tell me, do you have a place to stay in Alexandria?" asked Isidorus.

"Not yet," said Antipater.

"Then you must stay with me. No, I insist! My quarters are very near the Library. The accommodations are simple, but you'll have your own room. The offer is an act of selfishness on my part, for I greatly desire to hear every detail of your journey to see the Wonders.

And in return, I promise to do what I can to permit your entry to the Library."

"A splendid arrangement!" declared Antipater.

What sort of city could produce a structure as remarkable as the Pharos? As we sailed into the harbor we passed a number of islands with beautiful gardens and buildings; these were the property of the king, extensions of the grand royal palace that lined much of the shore. I had never seen such a handsome waterfront; the buildings stood many stories tall and were appointed with splendid decorations, sweeping balconies, and aerial gardens. The skyline of the city beyond offered glimpses of elegant towers, temple rooftops crowded with statues, and soaring obelisks. Rising above the skyline at a considerable distance, built upon the only hill of any significance, was a temple that appeared to be as grand as any we had encountered in our travels.

In the coming days—and months, as it turned out—I would have ample opportunity to explore every corner of Alexandria. Of all the cities I visited in our journey, it was by far the most impressive. Alexander the Great had chosen the site; an architect named Dinocrates laid out the city in a grid pattern, with wide, palm-lined boulevards and stately intersections decorated with fountains, statues, and obelisks. The temple on the hill was that of Serapis, who combined the attributes of Greek Zeus and Egyptian Osiris; to my Roman eyes, his temple, like so much of Alexandria, was at once familiar and wildly exotic. I had thought that Memphis must be the crossroads of the world, with its heady mixture of tongues and races, but Alexandria was even more cosmopolitan. Any object ever made by man, anywhere on earth, could be found in its teeming markets. In a single shop, I once came across a Roman augur's wand, a terebinth box from vanished Carthage, and a gown made of pure silk from distant Serica.

More important, for Antipater, in Alexandria one might find a copy of every book that had ever existed. The Library of the Ptolemies was said to be the greatest on earth, thanks to its aggressive acquisition policy. Every ship that arrived in the harbor was boarded by customs agents who demanded to be shown any book that happened to be on board. The agents checked each book against a master list and, if it was not already in the Library, they took the volume into custody, sent it to be copied, and only then returned it to its owner.

The Library was only part of a vast royal institution called the Museum, which celebrated all the gifts of the Muses to mankind. Within this sprawling complex were institutes devoted to the study of poetry, music, philosophy, history, astronomy, mathematics, engineering, geography, medicine, and anatomy. Over the centuries, some of the most famous thinkers in history—men like Archimedes and Euclid— had studied and taught there. The Museum contained extraordinary collections of gemstones, dried plants, architectural models, maps, weapons of many nations, and mummified animals. There was even a collection of living animals gathered from all over the world. Sometimes, on a still night, from behind the wall of this zoological compound, I could hear the braying of aurochs from Scythia, the screeching of monkeys from Nubia, or the roar of a tiger from India.

I myself had no way of gaining entry to the Museum or the Library, for while Isidorus was able to finagle a visitor's pass for his newfound friend Zoticus of Zeugma, acquiring another pass for a nineteen-year-old Roman with no official business in Alexandria was beyond his power. And so, on the days when Antipater went off with our host to disappear through the gates of the royal compound, I was left to amuse myself—not such a hard thing to do in a city as vast and fascinating as Alexandria.

My first task each day was to visit the several professional receivers of letters, who were all located close together in a district near the waterfront, in hopes of finding a reply from my father to the letter that I had dispatched from Gaza. Day after day I was disappointed, until at last, one morning, one of the receivers produced a scroll with a tag that read: *To Gordianus of Rome from his father.* The letter had arrived along with payment for its delivery, so I was able to claim it even though my purse was empty.

I quickly walked to the harbor and sat on some steps that led down to the water. With the Pharos looming before me across the harbor, I carefully unrolled the letter. As I read, I saw my father's face and heard his voice:

> *Beloved son,*
>
> *Nothing has so cheered me in recent months as your letter sent from—can there really be a place called Gaza? I must admit, I had never heard of it. And yet, my son has been there—and to Babylon, and Ephesus, and Olympia, and to so many other places. The news of your travels fills me with wonder and joy, and no small amount of envy.*
>
> *I fear the news from Rome is not so cheerful. Italy is riven with war between Rome and her oldest, closest allies. The subject cities of Italy demand a greater share of the benefits of empire. The Senate calls this rebellion. The result is fire, bloodshed, and famine.*
>
> *Do not worry about me. I am perfectly safe as long as I remain in Rome. But the countryside is in chaos, and as a result the city is plagued by shortages and uncertainty, and travel within Italy is difficult. In short, this is no place for you, as long as you are safe and content to remain in Egypt. Toward that end, I have arranged for a bit of money to be deposited with a banker in Alexandria and to be made available to you. It is not much, but if you are frugal it may last you for some months, until it is safe for you to travel back to Rome. Attached to this letter you will find instructions on how to get hold of the money.*
>
> *In your letter, you mention that Antipater is well. What a remarkable old fellow he is! What other man of his years would have dared to attempt such a journey? I hope that you managed to visit the Great Pyramid, and that he climbed all the way to the top, and that he is with you now in Alexandria, still in good health.*
>
> *Write back to me when you receive this letter (and the money) and let me know that all is well.*

I put down the letter, overwhelmed by homesickness. The sight of the Pharos across the water was suddenly strange and unreal, as if I had never seen it before. For a long moment, I felt disoriented and confused. Then other feelings rose in me—a heady sense of freedom and a thrill of excitement. Before, Alexandria had seemed merely a stop on my journey home; now, for the time being, it was to *be* my home. I blinked, and suddenly the Pharos looked familiar to me again, the proud landmark of the city where I was not merely a tourist, but a resident—Alexandria, the greatest metropolis on earth.

That night, as had become customary since our arrival, Antipater and I dined with our host. Isidorus possessed only one slave, who acted as both cook and server. While the woman poured wine and served a tilapia stew, each of us gave an account of his day.

I eagerly delivered my news first, and read aloud the letter from my father. This led to some discussion of the turmoil in Italy. Thanks to his position in the Library, Isidorus was privy to more reliable information than were the rumormongers in the marketplaces, but his sense of the situation was nonetheless quite murky. "No one can yet guess the outcome of such a devastating war," he said. Then, seeing the distress on my face, he assured me that Rome itself would surely be spared from the destruction it had visited on several of its subject cities—a speculation that put images in my head that only added to my anxiety.

Our host quickly changed the subject to the funds my father had sent for me, and explained that my best course was to leave the money in the care of the banker who had received it, withdrawing drachmas only as I needed them. "You should also deposit any documents of importance with the banker, for safekeeping—that letter from your father, for instance."

"Speaking of which," said Antipater, "you must write back to your father at once. Give him my thanks for inquiring after my well-being, and be sure to inform him that I did indeed climb all the way to the top of the Great Pyramid." He took a sip of wine. "And you, Isidorus— how was your day?"

Our host sighed. "Tedious. When you and I went our separate ways after arriving at the Library this morning, I spent several hours piecing together some fragments of the papyri I brought back from my journey up the Nile—only to discover that the document contained nothing more interesting than an inventory of some oxen involved in a bankruptcy litigation. When I asked my superior at the Library if I could be given more interesting work to do, we had quite an argument. Outsiders imagine that the Library and the Museum are a sort of pristine Arcadia, where we scholars lead lives of sublime contemplation, but my colleagues can be quite vicious and petty, I fear. How did Timon the Skeptic describe the Alexandrian scholars of his day? 'Scribblers on papyrus, endlessly squabbling in their birdcage of the Muses!' Alas, friend Zoticus, I hope your day was more productive."

Antipater smiled. "Indeed it was." He pressed his fingertips together and raised his chin. "I believe I may be ready to put forward a theory regarding the origin of the list of the Seven Wonders."

"Truly?" said Isidorus. "Tell us, please."

"Very well. While there remain some gaps in my research, and a few small contradictions that have yet to be resolved, this is what I believe: it was none other than Alexander the Great who decreed that there should be a list of Seven Wonders—and the list itself was devised by the first generation of scholars assembled here in Alexandria by the first King Ptolemy."

"As an Alexandrian, this notion pleases me. But how did you develop this theory?"

"The first inkling came to me just before we left Rome, when I was pondering possible routes for our journey to the Seven Wonders. Studying maps, and noting the site of each Wonder, I was struck first by their far-flung and disparate locations—but then I realized what they had in common: all seven lie within the empire conquered by Alexander. Indeed, if one were to draw a line connecting and encircling them, one would produce a veritable outline of Alexander's empire, comprising Greece, Asia, Persia, and Egypt. This was Alexander's world, composed of many nations, races, and languages—and these were its greatest achievements. It occurred to me that the list of Seven Wonders might have been the brainchild of Alexander himself, who saw it as a unifying principle. 'Never setting foot outside my empire,' I imagined him saying, 'one can see the greatest structures ever devised by mankind—made by different peoples at different times, in honor of different gods, but all brought together by the force of my will, within the unity of my dominion.'"

"Did Alexander himself visit all the Wonders?" I said.

"An excellent question, Gordianus. Most certainly he visited the Temple of Artemis when he liberated Ephesus, and saw the Mausoleum when he captured Halicarnassus; and in Babylon he must have seen the remains of the Hanging Gardens and the Walls, which may have been more substantial in his day than in ours. He refused to compete in the Games at Olympia, but he surely saw the statue in the Temple of Zeus. And after he conquered Egypt, he must have gazed upon its most famous monument, the Great Pyramid. So the list of Seven Wonders could also have served as a sort of memorial of his own journeys."

"But you've left out one of the Wonders," I said.

"Ah, yes, the Colossus of Rhodes—which was not completed until some thirty years after Alexander died. Obviously, Alexander never saw it—but that leads to the next proposition of my theory: Alexander himself did not draw up the final list, but assigned the task to someone else. Perhaps it was his close friend, the historian Aristobulus, or Callisthenes, the nephew of Aristotle, or—this is my guess—his comrade Ptolemy, who was later to become King of Egypt and had his own stake in preserving the mystique of Alexander and the legacy of his world empire. Ptolemy of course had all the resources of the Library and its scholars at his disposal—and it was in the Library, I believe, that the very first compendium of the Seven Wonders was created. I believe this was considerably more than a mere list, but included a detailed history and description of each Wonder. This book may yet be discovered in the archives, with the name of its author or authors appended to it. At the time this compendium was written, the Colossus would have been brand-new, a sensation that everyone was talking about, so it was included alongside the more venerable Wonders to demonstrate that mankind was still progressing and capable of creating new marvels."

"I think the Pharos is a greater achievement than the Colossus," I said. "Why didn't Ptolemy's scholars put it on the list instead?"

"Because the list predated the completion of the Pharos," explained Antipater. "The lighthouse was still being built as the list was drawn up—and even scholars eager to flatter King Ptolemy could not have justified comparing an unfinished building to the Temple of Artemis or the Great Pyramid."

"But now the Pharos has been standing for almost two hundred years," I said, "while the wonders of Babylon are in ruins. Perhaps the Hanging Gardens or the Walls of Babylon should be removed from the list, and the Pharos put in their place."

Isidorus laughed. "What a brash young man you are, Gordianus, to propose such an idea."

"Do you not like it?"

"I love it—but I'm afraid my colleagues at the birdcage of the Muses are so used to scratching out the same old things, not one of them would be bold enough to propose such an innovation. I fear they will resist the theory of Zoticus, as well, unless he can produce the original list. But as yet, this discovery eludes you?"

Antipater nodded. "I've found a number of citations that refer to such a document, but not the document itself. But soon—very soon—I feel sure that I'll lay my hands on it. It's probably moldering away in a stack of uncatalogued papyri, or inadvertently rolled up inside another scroll that has nothing to do with the Seven Wonders."

"Books in the Library can be quite elusive. You may have set yourself a task of many months, Zoticus my friend."

"Then I must pray to Zeus the Savior that I will have that much longer to live," said Antipater.

"I will say a prayer for that, as well," said Isidorus.

"And so will I!" I cried. I had grown so used to Antipater's company that it was unthinkable that anything should happen to him, or that I should be left alone without him in the vast, teeming city founded by Alexander.

That night—thanks to my father's letter, or something disagreeable in the fish stew—I was plagued by terrible dreams. All was a confusion of screaming and bloodshed. My father figured somehow in these night-mares, and Rome itself was swept by fire. The Pharos was transported to the summit of the Capitoline Hill, a finger of stone soaring to an impos-sible height, from which it sent out a beacon not to sailors, but to Rome's enemies, guiding them from all over Italy to the city they longed to destroy.

I tossed and turned and struggled to wake from these nightmares. Like a man submerged in deep water but able to glimpse pale daylight, gradually, fitfully I rose toward consciousness. I opened my eyes to the soft light of dawn. The sheet twisted around me was soaked with sweat.

I heard familiar voices from the room beyond—Antipater and our host chatting amiably as they prepared to head out for the day. Their conversation was muted and the words were indistinct, until one of them opened the front door, and Isidorus, raising his voice a bit, said, "And don't forget to bring your new stylus this morning, Antipater!"

A moment later the door was slammed shut, and silence followed.

I shut my eyes and lay still, exhausted by my nightmares. I was nearly asleep again, when suddenly I bolted upright. Had I heard what I thought I heard, or only dreamed it?

Not "Zoticus," but "Antipater"—Isidorus had called him by his true name.

What did it mean?

As I strolled around Alexandria that day, I should have been in a good mood, for I was no longer a pauper but had some coins on my person, thanks to the funds from my father. With a bit of money, there were endless things to do in Alexandria.

Instead, I found myself walking in circles. That single utterance by Isidorus kept echoing in my head, nagging at me.

There would be a perfectly innocent explanation, I told myself. Antipater had come to trust Isidorus, and so had revealed to him his true identity. That was Antipater's choice, and none of my business. But why, then, had Isidorus continued to address him at dinner as Zoticus?

Because the slave was present, I told myself. Yes, that was it. The woman serving dinner was not to know who Antipater was. But why hadn't Antipater informed me of his decision to reveal himself to our host? Ah, well, he was an old fellow and he simply forgot. But even as this thought came to me, I knew it was a lie. Antipater's mind was as keen as ever, and he never did anything without a purpose. Some sort of relationship existed between him and our host, and I was being kept in the dark about it.

Why?

I found myself in the Rhakotis district, the oldest part of the city. Rhakotis had been a settlement in Homer's time; its narrow, winding streets predated the grid laid down by Alexander's new city. With its shabby tenements, gambling dens, and seedy taverns, Rhakotis reminded me of the Subura in Rome.

Passing through a particularly tawdry part of Rhakotis, I passed a building that was clearly a brothel, to judge by the attitude of the women who stood at the upper-story windows, flaunting their naked breasts and looking bored. A man stepped out of the front door. He looked this way and that, but took no notice of me.

A lightning bolt of recognition struck me, followed by a quiver of doubt. Could the man possibly be who I thought he was?

He was burly and blond, with a neatly trimmed beard, and his clothing was Greek. In a teeming metropolis like Alexandria, there were countless specimens almost exactly like him—and yet, something about the arrogant tilt of his head and the truculent way he held himself as he turned and walked quickly away, clenching his fists, convinced me that he was none other than the murderer from Olympia.

I remembered everything about him in a flash: standing behind me at the Temple of Zeus he had loudly voiced anti-Roman sentiments; later that night I had overheard him speaking to an unknown conspirator—a fellow agent for Mithridates—in the tent of our host; and the next day he had used a snake to poison the Cynic, Simmius of Sidon, and then, in the ensuing confusion, had vanished into thin air, not to be seen again—until now.

They had a saying in Alexandria: "Stay here long enough, and every traveler in the world will cross your path." Apparently it was true.

I quickened my stride to match his. Keeping what I hoped was a safe distance, I followed the murderer.

He apparently had several calls to make, for repeatedly I saw him disappear into a tenement or private dwelling, stay for a short while, and then reappear, always pausing to peer suspiciously up and down the street before proceeding. I had to call upon all the skills my father had taught me to shadow him without being spotted.

His itinerary at last took him to the waterfront, and onto a wharf that appeared to be an embarkation point for workers coming from and going to the Pharos; so I assumed from the uniform—a tight-fitting cap and a tunic of dark green—worn by the passengers who were disembarking from a ferry that had just landed at the wharf. They had the weary look of workers who had just ended a long shift, in contrast to the more energetic demeanor of the similarly dressed passengers who shuffled forward to take their place on the ferry.

There was a guard post at the entrance to the wharf, but the soldier who was supposed to be manning it stood some distance away, his back turned while he talked to a pretty girl passing by. The murderer walked right past him and onto the wharf. I quickly followed him.

He stepped through a narrow doorway and into a long, low structure. After some hesitation, I followed him. The interior was cluttered and dark, lit only by a few high windows. As my eyes adjusted, around me I saw various nautical items—coils of rope, bits of planking, patches for sails, and such. There was also a pile of what appeared to be discarded workers' uniforms; perhaps the garments needed mending.

Suddenly, from nearby, I heard the murderer talking, and the sound of his voice—long unheard but never forgotten—chilled my blood. His voice drew closer. My heart pounded in my chest. I squatted down and hid as best I could behind a stack of coiled ropes. He strode directly in front of me and stopped only a few steps away. Above the ropes, I had a view of his face. Had he bothered to look in my direction, he might have seen me as well, among the shadows.

"Our ranks have grown corrupt and must be purified," he was saying. "Like weeds among the barley, the unfaithful must be pulled up by the root!"

The man who accompanied him was very tall and had a narrow face. He was dressed in the same colors as the lighthouse workers, but his long green gown was elegantly embroidered with images of Tritons holding conches. He wore a high hat shaped like the Pharos and he carried a ceremonial flail to denote his authority.

"Yes, Nikanor, yes," the man was saying, "any and all traitors among us must be eliminated, without mercy. But the reason I asked you to come today was so that you could tell me what progress has been made on the coded message system being devised by our friends at the Library. Their job is to anticipate all possible contingencies, military and otherwise, and my job is to figure out how the mirrors and the clarions can be used to send secret signals between us. But I can't begin to work out the details until you give me the list of secure locations in the city to which such signals are to be directed."

"Is it true, Anubion, that from the Pharos you can aim a beam of light at any house in the city?"

"Provided there is a clear sightline between that house and any of the mirrors located on the Pharos, yes. But the mechanics for doing so are quite complex, and must be worked out and tested in advance. That's why I need the list as soon as possible—"

"Yes, yes, Anubion, you'll get the list," said Nikanor. "But I was wondering—can the mirrors be aimed at the royal palace, as well?"

"Of course they can be, and quite frequently they are; that's how King Ptolemy and his agents send messages back and forth to one another. A message in code is flashed from a mirror in one part of the palace to the Pharos, and then the same message is sent from the Pharos back to a different part of the palace. Thus the king's agents, even though distant from each other in the royal complex, can communicate almost instantaneously, and in secret, as long as the codes they use remain secure."

"Remarkable! No wonder King Ptolemy is always a step ahead of his enemies. But with you in charge of the lighthouse, this system can now be used by Mithridates, as well."

Mithridates! How often had I heard the name of the King of Pontus uttered over the course of our long journey? It appeared that his influence extended even here.

"Lower your voice!" said Anubion. "Most of the workers would have no idea what we were talking about, even if we spoke right in front of them, but if one of them should overhear us, I'd still have to have the fellow put to death. I consider myself completely loyal to King Ptolemy—but Ptolemy is helpless against the Romans, and unless the Romans are stopped, one day they'll devour Egypt along with the rest of the world. Our only hope to stop the Romans is Mithridates. As long as I am in charge of the Pharos, even if I must do so in secret, I'll use its power to—"

"Are you able to see directly into King Ptolemy's private chambers, then?" said Nikanor, interrupting him.

Anubion wrinkled his brow. "What are you talking about?"

"Using the mirrors. They cast light a very great distance, I know. But you can also use them to *see* great distances, can't you?"

Anubion scoffed. "Where did you get such an idea—from our friends in the Library? Yes, I'm aware that some scholars, experts in the properties of optics and light, believe that such a far-seeing device might be created, using mirrors. But no such devices are installed in the Pharos."

"That's not what I've heard. Not only can you see great distances, but from the very top of the tower, using the most powerful mirrors, *you can see into men's minds!*"

Anubion drew back his shoulders. "Now you are no longer talking about science, my friend, but about magic—and nonsense!"

Nikanor gave him a wily look. "Oh, I understand—you can't talk about these things, at least not to me, not yet. But soon enough, you'll see that I'm trustworthy, and you can share all the secret powers of the Pharos with me. And together, you and I will use them to destroy the traitors among us, the ones who claim to be loyal to Mithridates but aren't. They'll die like dogs!"

Anubion cocked an eyebrow and emitted a noncommittal grunt. "When do you meet with your contact at the Library?"

"Today, as soon as I leave you."

"Very well. Tell him I need the list of locations as soon as possible, and after that, a list of the signals and codes he proposes to use. Do you understand?"

"Of course I do. You think I'm stupid, but I'm cleverer than you think."

Anubion pursed his lips. "On second thought, tell our friend at the Library that it's time for him and me to meet face-to-face."

"He won't like that. He says you should stay apart, to avoid suspicion."

"Nevertheless, he should have a firsthand look at the Pharos. He can say that his historical research necessitates a visit, and I was generous enough to offer him a tour. Give him this, to serve as a pass." He produced a ceramic token with a seal on it.

"Shall he come alone?"

"He may bring his new colleague with him, if he likes. Tell them to arrive here at the wharf, an hour after sunrise. Now go."

Nikanor turned to leave, then looked over his shoulder. "Rome is the disease," he whispered.

Apparently this was a kind of watchword, for Anubion replied as if by rote: "And Mithridates is the cure!"

The two parted and headed in opposite directions.

Their final words echoed in my ears. My blood ran cold.

Before I could move, some workers entered the storage house, and I was obliged to remain hidden. As soon as the workers moved on, I stole away, and hurried past the guard post, where the guard was still absent.

I peered up and down the waterfront, but Nikanor was nowhere to be seen.

He had said he would be meeting someone from the Library. I headed in that direction, thinking I might spot him again, but I reached the entrance of the Library without seeing him.

My head spinning, I wandered up the street. What would Antipater think of my story? Would he even believe me, or would he scoff at the idea that I had seen the killer from Olympia so many months later and so many hundreds of miles away? And what of the man's fantastic notions about the Pharos and the magical powers of its mirrors? Anubion had dismissed his ideas—but the keeper of the lighthouse was by his own admission a master of deceit and secrecy. A space between two buildings suddenly afforded me a view of the Pharos—and I felt a shiver, wondering if the unblinking eye of its beacon was watching *me*.

Walking aimlessly, midway between the Library and Isidorus's apartment I passed a tavern. On such a warm day, all the doors and shutters were open. I chanced to look inside, and in a far, shadowy corner I saw Isidorus. He sat facing the street, listening intently to a man who sat with his back to me. So eager was I to talk to someone about what I had seen and heard that I almost stepped into the tavern to join them. Then the man with Isidorus turned his head a bit to one side.

It was Nikanor.

That night at dinner, Antipater asked if I was unwell. I told him I was fine.

"Then stop fidgeting. One would think you were sitting on a needle. And you've eaten hardly a bite of the pomegranate salad. A loss of appetite is most unlike you, Gordianus."

I shrugged.

"Nor have you even tasted the excellent wine to which Isidorus is treating us tonight. Imported all the way from Chios."

I shrugged again. I was intentionally avoiding the wine. I wanted to keep my wits about me.

"Leave the young man in peace, friend Zoticus," said Isidorus. His use of the false name set my teeth on edge. "Less of the Chian for him means more for us."

The two of them shared a laugh and clinked their silver goblets.

I excused myself and headed for my room.

"Sleep well, Gordianus," Antipater called after me. "In the morning, I may have a surprise for you."

As I stepped into my room, I heard Isidorus whisper, "Do you think he's sick?"

"Lovesick, more likely. Some pretty thing must have caught his eye and spoiled his appetite. Ah, to be his age again. I am reminded of a verse—"

Rather than hear him declaim, I shut the door, fell into bed, and covered my head with pillows. Time passed. My mind was a dull, aching void. I threw the pillows aside, returned to the door, and quietly opened it. Antipater and Isidorus were still talking, so quietly I could barely hear them.

"Nikanor has become a liability," said Antipater. "I told you what he did in Olympia, killing that wretched Cynic. I'd known poor Simmius when we were boys together in Sidon, but we hadn't seen each other in fifty years, and he was surely no more an agent of Rome than I am! But Nikanor became convinced that Simmius had recognized me, and would expose me, so on his own initiative Nikanor murdered Simmius— never considering what might happen if he was caught, and his affiliation with Mithridates came out. I might have been exposed along with him, putting an end to my usefulness when I'd hardly begun. Nikanor was always reckless. Now he sees spies and infiltrators everywhere. I think he's gone mad."

Hackles rose on the back of my neck. There could be no doubt: Antipater was an agent of Mithridates. I had no time to think, for Isidorus was talking and I felt compelled to listen.

"You can question Nikanor's judgment, but not his loyalty," he was saying. "No one has made greater sacrifices, traveled greater distances, or taken more risks for the cause than Nikanor—not even you, Antipater."

"You're not listening to me, Isidorus. It's not his judgment I question—it's his sanity. He says things that make no sense. What was it he told you about the Pharos today? Something about using the mirrors to gaze into the royal palace, and to read King Ptolemy's mind?"

"He does have strange notions—"

"He's crazy, Isidorus. He was always a little crazy, but now he's become more so—to a degree that poses a danger to us all."

Isidorus sighed. "Unfortunately, he's my only trustworthy go-between for communicating with Anubion at the Pharos. You said yourself, the very day you arrived, that establishing a system of signals using the Pharos must be our highest priority. Once war breaks out between Rome and Mithridates, what if the Romans invade Egypt? Our ability to communicate in secret will be absolutely vital."

"The Romans will never occupy Alexandria," said Antipater.

"Perhaps not. But even if Egypt stays out of the war, Alexandria will be crawling with spies. The Romans are children when it comes to setting up secret operations. Mithridates is a master at such things, and that may be his greatest advantage. Our ability to use the Pharos to communicate in secret could mean the difference between victory and defeat."

"Let's not get carried away, old friend—you're beginning to sound as grandiose as Nikanor."

Isidorus laughed softly. "All my life, I've been nothing more than a scribbler in the birdcage of the Muses. The idea that I could do something to change the world is a bit intoxicating, I must admit."

"Rather like this fine Chian wine. Shall we finish it?"

"No, I've drunk too much already. I'm off to bed. We have a busy day ahead of us. Are you still determined to take Gordianus along with us?"

"If he finds out that I've been to see the Pharos without him, I shall be at a loss to explain why I didn't take him along. Don't worry, I'll see that he stays out of the way while you confer with Anubion. Gordianus is young and easily distracted."

"You're certain that he suspects nothing of your mission?"

"Not a thing. As Gordianus has demonstrated repeatedly during our travels, he's quite clever in some ways, but terribly naive in others. He's smart, but not yet cynical. He still has a boy's faith in his old tutor; it's rather touching, actually. He's never pressed me about my reasons for traveling incognito, and I'm quite sure he has no idea of my activities in every place we've visited—studying the local sentiments, seeking out and conferring with those who might be useful to our cause, making a list of those who pose a danger to us."

"Even in Babylon?"

"Especially there! The Parthians are suspicious of both Rome and Mithridates, but when the time comes, they must be persuaded to take our side." Antipater sighed. "Ah well, if there's to be no more Chian wine, then I too am off to bed."

As they rose and moved toward their separate rooms, I heard Isidorus whisper: "Rome is the disease."

Antipater whispered back: "And Mithridates is the cure!"

I silently closed the door and returned to my bed.

My head was so filled with painful thoughts that I imagined it might burst. From the very beginning of our journey, Antipater had deceived me. What a fool I had been, never to see through him!

Perhaps I had not wanted to see the truth.

In Olympia, on the night before Simmius the Cynic was murdered, I had overheard two men talking in the tent of our host. One had been Nikanor. The other had spoken in such a low voice that I could not discern what he said, much less recognize his voice. Now I knew that the other man had been Antipater—and both were agents of Mithridates.

Thinking back, I remembered all the times in all the cities when Antipater had supposedly kept to his room while I went out for the day . . . or said he was meeting with fellow scholars to talk about poetry (knowing that nothing was more certain to send me away) . . . or went to some temple without me, since I had already visited the place and did not care to see it again. How many of those times had his actual purpose been a meeting with confederates to plot the rise of Mithridates and the ruin of Rome?

What schemes had he hatched with Eutropius in Ephesus, and with Posidonius in Rhodes, and with all the others he must have met in all the stops we made at Athens, Delos, Lesbos, and elsewhere?

In Halicarnassus, during all those blissful hours I spent with Bitto, I had presumed that Antipater was immersing himself in the volumes of her library—when in fact he must have been carrying on a furious correspondence with his contacts all over the Greek world. I had been oblivious. How had Antipater just described me? "Young and easily distracted."

He and Isidorus were old friends—their conversation made that clear—but for my benefit they had pretended to be strangers on the boat that brought us to Alexandria. How many times had such charades been carried out right in front of me? And now, every day, when the two of them went to the Library, presumably to engage in esoteric research amid the dusty scrolls, they were devising a code that could be used to send secret signals from the Pharos.

A sudden thought chilled me to the bone: what was my father's role in all this? He had certainly abetted Antipater's faked death and his disappearance from Rome. Had he done so knowing of Antipater's mission? Was he, too, an agent of Mithridates, and therefore a traitor to Rome? Had he intentionally kept me in the dark, deceiving me just as Antipater had done?

Almost as disturbing was the only other possibility—that Antipater had duped him as well as me. What did that say about the wisdom of my father, the so-called Finder?

I felt an impulse to rouse Antipater and demand the truth. I rose from my bed, left my room, and went to his door. I stood there for a long time in the darkness, but I could not bring myself to knock. I was not yet ready to confront him. I returned to my bed. To bide my time was the wiser course, I told myself.

Would things have turned out differently, had I followed my first impulse?

I thought I would never sleep, but soon enough Somnus laid his hand on me, and Morpheus filled my head with terrible dreams. All was chaos, noise, and horror. My father and Antipater were in the midst of a bloody riot. Lurking on the outskirts, mad Nikanor suddenly lunged forward and sent a hissing serpent through the air. Then a massive finger of stone erupted from the earth and soared skyward, a white spire amid the fiery darkness. The beacon at the top was impossibly bright. The ray of light seared my eyes and burned into my brain, exposing my deepest fears and stripping me of every secret.

The next morning, at breakfast, I tried to look pleasantly surprised when Antipater made his announcement. I must have looked dazed, instead. I would never make a good spy.

"Gordianus, I do begin to think you're unwell," said Antipater. "Did you not hear me? Isidorus has arranged for both of us to visit the Pharos today. It's quite a rare opportunity. The lighthouse isn't open to just anyone, you know. We shall see it inside and out, and climb all the way to the top, if our legs hold up."

"Wonderful," I managed to say.

Antipater frowned and shook his head at my unaccountable lack of enthusiasm. "Don't just sit there, gaping. Eat your breakfast and get ready to go out."

We made our way to the wharf where the ferryboat carried workers to Pharos. A different, more attentive guard was on duty that morning; he demanded to see our pass, which Isidorus duly presented. We were escorted to the front of the queue and allowed to board the next boat.

Even in my glum, anxious mood, it was impossible not to be invigorated by the trip across the harbor. The air was cool and refreshing. The morning sun glittered on the water. The temples and obelisks of the royal islands to the east were in silhouette, scintillating with fiery outlines, but ahead of us the Pharos was lit from bottom to top with soft yellow light. From a distance it looked too delicate to be made of stone—it seemed to be built of butter or goat's cheese. But as we drew closer, the illusion of softness faded, as if the warming sun itself baked and hardened the massive blocks into sharp-edged stone.

"The Pharos was built of a special kind of masonry," said Isidorus, as if reading my thoughts, "something between a limestone and a marble. They say it actually grows harder as it's exposed to the moist sea air. The Pharos has stood for nearly two hundred years, and the experts say there's no reason it shouldn't remain standing for another thousand."

As we drew near the Pharos, I felt a sense of awe in spite of myself, and a thrill of excitement.

A guard met us as we disembarked. After examining our pass, he led us to a bench shaded by an awning of thatched reeds. Soldiers and green-clad workers were everywhere. The three of us looked rather conspicuous, wearing our ordinary tunics.

After a short wait, we were greeted by an imposing figure in green robes and a high headdress—Anubion, the man to whom I had seen Nikanor talking the previous day.

He looked askance at me, and his greeting to Antipater and Isidorus was stiff and formal; that was for my benefit, of course. I felt absurd, going along with the pretense that the three of them shared no special relationship, and that I knew nothing of their conspiracy.

As he led us up the long ramp to the entrance of the Pharos, Anubion recounted various facts and figures about the lighthouse, as if we were ordinary visitors receiving the privilege of a guided tour. The situation seemed increasingly unreal to me. The Pharos itself was almost too gigantic and magnificent to be comprehended, and the playacting of everyone, myself included, made me feel strangely detached, yet acutely aware of everything that was happening.

We passed through the grand entry of red granite, into a large room with a very high ceiling. I was struck at once by the strong smell of the place, a mingling of odors I had never experienced before. Soon I would be shown the source of these odors, but for the moment I was puzzled.

We were given a choice of ascending by an inner stairwell or by an outer ramp; Antipater preferred the more gradual ascent of the ramp, and so up we went, around and around, passing high windows that admitted bright daylight, sharing the way with workers and beasts of burden hauling wagons full of fuel.

"We use a variety of fuels to feed the fire," Anubion explained. "Egypt is not blessed with forests, but we do have some small trees—the acacia and the tamarisk. Charcoal is also used, as is animal dung, but the brightest flame is produced by liquid called naphtha. Alexander was introduced to naphtha by the Babylonians, in whose lands there are chasms from which this remarkable substance flows like water from a spring. Have you ever heard of such a thing, Gordianus?"

I admitted that I had not.

"Here, let me show you."

We stepped off the ramp and into one of the adjoining storage rooms, which was crowded with large clay vessels. Removing a stopper from one of these, Anubion invited me to take a sniff. I drew back my head at once, recoiling from the foul-smelling fumes.

"The stuff is highly volatile, meaning it will ignite even before a flame touches it, being kindled by the mere radiance of the fire."

"It sounds dangerous," said Antipater.

Anubion shrugged. "Every now and again a worker catches on fire—an example to the other workers to handle the stuff with extreme caution. Water is useless to put out a naphtha fire, so we keep heavy blankets close at hand, which can be used to smother the flames."

We returned to the ramp. Now I understood why the smell of the Pharos was so peculiar and distinctive—the odors of animal dung and naphtha were mingled with the sweat of human toil and the salty smell of the sea.

At length, after ascending many ramps, we arrived at the level of the parapet where the Tritons resided at each of the four corners, with bronze signal mirrors installed between them. The sculptures and the mirrors alike were on a scale I had not imagined. Without warning, one of the Tritons produced a long, blaring note from its horn. I covered my ears, and the noise was still deafening. Whatever mechanism produced the sound was hidden from sight.

The means for adjusting the signal mirrors was more evident. I saw that Antipater and Isidorus took special note of these metal frameworks and fixtures, which could be made to tilt each mirror at various angles, both up and down and side to side.

Below us, the workers and animals ascending the long entrance ramp looked very small. The harbor was ablaze with morning light and crowded with sails. The city looked like a vast, intricate toy built for a god's amusement.

We entered the next stage of the tower, which was set back from the lower portion and octagonal in shape. Stairways led upward along the outer walls, which were pierced by tall windows. The central shaft was occupied by an ingenious lift system by which winches and pulleys raised a platform all the way to the top of the tower; by this means heavy loads of fuel could be transported without men having to carry it. Anubion suggested that we should ride this device all the way to the top.

Antipater stared upward. He turned pale and shook his head.

"But I insist," said Anubion. "You're already out of breath, good Zoticus, and there are many more steps to go. Not only will this device save you a great deal of effort, but you can say that you have ridden the Pharos elevator—a claim few men can make."

Antipater's curiosity got the better of him, and in short order the four of us entered the cagelike contraption and were lifted through the air. The ride was surprisingly smooth, with much less swaying and jerking than I expected. We passed workers who trudged up the stairways around us, and were treated to fleeting glimpses of Alexandria and the sea through the tall windows, which fell below us one by one. At the very end of the ride, the platform gave such a powerful shudder that I gripped the railing and uttered a quick prayer, thinking the cage had broken free of the mechanism and was about to plummet downward. But at last we came to a halt and arrived without mishap.

I was glad for the experience, but relieved to exit the cage. Leaving the others behind for a moment, I hurried past the workers who were going up and down the stairs and stepped outside, onto the open landing with its eight-sided parapet. For a few remarkable moments, I was completely alone. Above me rose the third, cylindrical portion of the tower, shorter than the first two stages, in which the beacon was housed. Peering up at a steep angle, beyond the roofline I could glimpse a bit of the thunderbolt wielded by the enormous statue of Zeus that crowned the Pharos.

Surrounding me on all sides was a truly astounding panorama. Amid a sea of rooftops, the grid pattern of Alexandria was clearly discernible, especially where towering palm trees lined the broad avenues and obelisks marked the major intersections. Even the Temple of Serapis, the city's highest point, was far below me. In the opposite direction, I gazed at an endless expanse of water dotted by ships near and far. To either side stretched hazy coastlines where sand and water met. To the west was only desert, but to the east I could see the green mass of the Nile Delta.

There was a steady breeze, so strong that Anubion—who had just joined me, along with Antipater and Isidorus—grabbed his headdress with both hands, lest it should fly off.

"What do you think, young Roman?" he said.

"You live in a remarkable city—surely the most remarkable I've ever seen."

He nodded, pleased by the comment. "I'm going to show Isidorus the beacon fire, and the circular mirror mechanism housed above it in the very top of the tower. There's not a lot to be seen right now—the flames burn low during the day, and the mirrors are turned outward, so as to reflect sunlight rather than the fire."

"Will I be allowed to see it?"

"Of course—in a little while. But for now, stay here with Zoticus and enjoy the view. I fear your old tutor is not yet rested enough to take the last few flights of stairs."

So this was the ploy by which the lighthouse master and the librarian would be able to speak privately, away from the inquisitive—but easily distracted—young Roman. Anubion and Isidorus disappeared inside the cylindrical tower. I turned to Antipater.

"Our host thinks you're too tired to go up a few more steps," I said, trying to blunt the edge of sarcasm in my voice.

"For the moment. But this bracing sea breeze will soon revive me."

I could remain silent no longer. "Teacher," I began, and was about to say more—*why have you deceived me?*—when from the corner of my eye I saw a figure clad in green step briefly onto the landing, then back into the tower. I caught only a sidelong glimpse of his face, but I knew at once it was Nikanor.

What was he doing in the Pharos? Why was he dressed as one of the workers?

I turned my back on Antipater and hurried inside the tower. Above me, heading up the stairs, I saw Nikanor. I followed him.

With every step, the air grew warmer. As I took the final flight of steps, I felt a blast of hot air, as from an oven. The walls themselves grew hot. I ascended to a circular gallery with a stone railing, and saw below me, in a great bowl of blackened granite, the white-hot flame that was never allowed to go out. I recoiled from the rising heat, hardly able to breathe. If this was the fire at its lowest, what was it like at night, when it burned even hotter and brighter?

The workers handling the fuel and tending the coals were covered with sweat and wore only loincloths; their discarded green tunics were hung on pegs around the gallery. I looked up and saw the circular system of mirrors attached to the domed ceiling. Except for the fallen Colossus, I had never seen pieces of bronze so large. Their reflective surfaces were turned away from me, but the very edges, plated with silver, were almost too bright to look at. I seemed to have entered another world where all was fire, stone, and metal—the fiery workshop of Hephaestus.

Anubion and Isidorus stood across from me, at the far side of the gallery, their images blurred by waves of hot air. Nikanor had just joined them; they started back, surprised by his sudden appearance. As yet, none of them had seen me.

I perceived a way to hide myself. I grabbed the nearest green tunic from its peg, stepped back into the stairwell, and pulled the tunic over my own. A scrap of green cloth came with the tunic; I tied it around my head, wearing it as I had seen the workers do. When I emerged again on the landing, no one took any notice of me. I appeared to be just another of the antlike workers who tended the Pharos.

Anubion was shouting at Nikanor. "What are you doing here? How did you get here?"

I could have told him that: with such lax security at the wharf, and so many discarded uniforms lying about, it hardly required the skills of a master spy for Nikanor to impersonate a worker and board the ferry.

Nikanor ignored the questions and shouted back at him. "I told you there were traitors among us—and now I've seen you consorting with the worst of them, treating the old Sidonian like an honored guest, giving him and his Roman pupil a tour of the lighthouse!"

"Say not another word, Nikanor. Leave the Pharos at once. I'll meet you at the ferry landing and we'll discuss this matter there."

"Who are you to give me orders, Anubion? You, a latecomer to the cause, a filthy half-Egyptian, half-Greek mongrel? As far as I know, you're a traitor as well—a double agent—a spy for the Romans. Last night I looked at the Pharos, and I sensed that you were looking back at me. I couldn't move! The beam transfixed me, as a needle pins a fly! Who knows what terrible powers you wield from the Pharos? You read men's minds, control their thoughts, paralyze their bodies!"

Despite the blasting heat, Anubion grew pale. "He's mad, Isidorus. Completely mad!"

Isidorus stared at Nikanor with wide eyes. His hairless, ebony head was dripping with sweat.

Nikanor drew back. "I see it now—you're all traitors. All against me! You lured me here against my will. You tricked me into coming to the Pharos. You mean for me to die here."

Isidorus swallowed hard. "Nikanor, stop this talk. We'll go outside— breathe some cool air—discuss the matter sensibly—"

But the time for talking was past. Nikanor made his move. He pushed Isidorus aside as if he were made of straw.

A man like Anubion was not used to defending himself against physical attack. The struggle was brief, and horrible to witness.

The stone railing of the gallery came almost to my waist, high enough to prevent anyone from falling accidentally into the open furnace. But the railing proved to be no obstacle to an enraged madman determined to throw another man into the flames. I watched Anubion fly screeching through the air. He caught fire even before he landed, his tall hat and green robes bursting into flame. His screams were terrible. I watched for an instant, unable to look away, then shielded my face as Anubion exploded.

The sudden fireball sent the workers into a panic. When I uncovered my eyes I saw that some had been badly burned. Others, their loincloths ablaze, were scrambling for blankets to smother the flames.

That was the end of Anubion. The master of the lighthouse had become one with the beacon.

I blinked and looked about, then drew back just as Isidorus rushed past me, quickly followed by Nikanor. Neither of them took any notice of me.

I stood for a long moment, stunned, then hurried down the steps after them.

I emerged on the lower landing, coughing and gasping for breath, eagerly drawing the cool sea breeze into my scalded lungs. The panoramic view of Alexandria and the sea, so enthralling before, was now disorienting and bizarre. I staggered from a sudden attack of vertigo, and watched an unearthly scene play out before me.

Antipater was still on the landing. Isidorus had joined him. They stood with their backs against the parapet and the sea, expressions of shock on their faces.

Nikanor was nearby. At his feet lay a blazing torch. In both hands he held what appeared to be a heavy clay vessel. While I watched, he slung the contents toward Antipater and Isidorus, dousing them with a clear liquid. From the overpowering smell, I realized it was the substance called naphtha.

Nikanor threw the vessel aside and picked up the torch.

My heart leaped to my throat. I rushed toward Nikanor, but he saw me, swung his left arm, and struck me across the face. I reeled to one side and fell.

Before I could make another move, Nikanor threw the torch toward the cowering figures of Antipater and Isidorus.

Antipater was closest to me. I sprang to my feet and leaped toward him. If we had tumbled only a little to one side, Isidorus might have been knocked to the ground and saved as well. But we only brushed him as we fell, and as we struck the hard stone floor there was a burst of flame behind me, followed by a bloodcurdling scream.

"Isidorus!" cried Antipater. I rolled away from him and looked up to witness the final act of the gruesome spectacle.

Like a man made of flames, Isidorus rushed toward his assailant. Even Nikanor was appalled by what he had done. He stood transfixed. Before he could retreat, Isidorus embraced him. Was it a vengeful act? I think Isidorus acted purely by reflex, grasping whatever was closest to him.

Joined by the flames, the two of them performed a hideous dance, traipsing and whirling this way and that, until they collided with the parapet. Flailing in desperation, the madman scrambled to climb over it. Isidorus clung to him. Together they went tumbling over the stone wall.

I rushed to the parapet and watched them descend. Down they plummeted, trailing flames like Phaëton when he wrecked the chariot of the sun. They struck a Triton on the lower parapet with a glancing blow that broke them apart and sent them spinning separately into space, away from the Pharos and over the open sea. The dwindling comets ended in two tiny white splashes, followed an instant later by the sound of two minuscule concussions. Then the sparkling green waves closed over the foam, as if nothing had happened.

Behind me I heard a groan. Antipater had risen to his feet. He looked confused and unsteady. I was a bit shaky myself, as I discovered when I stepped toward him. My legs trembled liked reeds in the wind.

"They fell? You saw them?" he said. Had I not been holding his arm, I think he would have fallen. I almost went down with him. His clothing reeked of naphtha.

"Into the sea," I said. "But you, Teacher—are you all right?"

"A bit bruised. Nothing broken. Where's Anubion?"

"Nikanor threw him into the furnace. There's nothing left of him."

Antipater looked aghast, then gave a start. "How do you know that man's name?"

I sighed. "I know a great deal more than that. I saw Nikanor in the street yesterday and recognized him. I followed him. I know what he was up to, in Olympia and here in Alexandria—spying for Mithridates. So was Anubion. So was Isidorus—and you!"

Antipater drew a sharp breath. His eyes darted this way and that.

"Teacher, why did you deceive me?"

He bit his lip. At last he looked me in the eye. "It was for your own good, Gordianus. Had you known, there were times you might have been in great danger."

"Are you saying I wasn't in danger, because I didn't know? That's no answer, Teacher!"

"Do you regret coming on our journey, Gordianus? Do you wish you'd never left Rome, never seen the Wonders?"

"That's not an answer, either. You deceived me. I still don't know what you were up to, in all the places we've been—I can only guess. It's not a question of whether or not you put me in danger. I was tricked. Tricked into aiding and abetting a spy in the service of an enemy of Rome!"

"Rome is not at war with Mithridates—"

"Not yet!" I shook my head, hardly able to look at him. "At the Great Pyramid, do you remember what you called me? 'A solver of riddles, like your father.' You said I had a special ability, a gift from the gods—"

"And so you do, Gordianus."

"Yet all the time, I didn't see the riddle right in front of me! What a fool you must think me. Pouring praise in my ear, but secretly despising me."

"No, Gordianus. That's not true."

"Tell me one thing: how much did my father know?"

"About my mission? Nothing."

"Are you saying you fooled him, as well?"

"I convinced him that I wanted to disappear without a trace, for reasons of my own."

"And he believed you?"

"It's not such a far-fetched idea. Beyond a certain age, many men harbor such a fantasy—including your father, I imagine. You wouldn't understand, Gordianus."

"Because I'm too young?"

"Exactly. The world is not as simple as you think. Did I deceive you? Yes. As for your father, he had his own unspoken reasons for sending you away—he knew that Rome and her Italian allies were on the brink of war and he wanted you well out of it. So he took the opportunity I offered, and didn't question me as closely as he might have. That doesn't make him a fool, only a caring father. As for the choices I've made—I have no regrets. Friendship matters, Gordianus, but there are things in this world that matter more. Rome must be stopped. Mithridates offers the only hope. If you had to be kept in the dark, what of it? In the meantime, you went on a journey such as most men can only dream of. You followed your aspirations, Gordianus, and I followed mine."

I shook my head. I searched for words to rebut him. Suddenly he pushed me away.

"Step back, Gordianus," he whispered. "Get away from me!"

I wondered at this abrupt change, until I heard the sounds of footsteps coming from the tower. At the same time, the Tritons on the lower parapet began to blare discordant notes.

"I'll think of some way to explain my presence here, and some explanation for what happened," he whispered. "But for you, it may not be so easy. Go now! Make your way down the tower and back to the mainland."

"But how can I—"

"They'll think you're a worker. Hurry!"

A group of soldiers poured onto the landing, drawing their swords as they did so. They hardly noticed me. Wearing the green tunic, I appeared to be just another worker, and quite a young one at that. Their attention was drawn to Antipater. Our eyes met a final time, and then he was hidden from sight, encircled by the guards.

One of them began loudly to question him. "What happened here? Who fell? Where is Anubion?"

"It was a terrible thing to witness," cried Antipater, "the ghastly act of some madman!"

I quietly stepped toward the doorway and into the stairwell leading down. As I descended, trying to keep my face a blank, more armed men passed me coming up the stairs. Still more were ascending by means of the mechanical platform in the central shaft. No one challenged me.

I made my way out of the Pharos and down the long ramp. Above me, the Tritons continued to blare. Some of the workers had gathered in groups and were conferring in agitated whispers, but others went about their business, as yet unaware of what had happened. The crowded ferry was just leaving as I arrived. I was the last person to board—just one more figure in a green tunic among so many others.

As we cast off, I suddenly realized that I had no reason to flee the Pharos. I had done nothing wrong. It was Antipater who had insisted that I go. Was it because he wished to spare me the ordeal of an interrogation—or because he feared that I might blurt out the truth to the guards and expose him as the spy of a foreign king? Once again, I had unwittingly allowed him to manipulate me.

I turned and gazed up at the Pharos. At the uppermost parapet, amid the glitter of soldiers' helmets, I saw a shock of white hair. That was my last fleeting glimpse of Antipater.

After landing at the wharf, I discreetly discarded the green tunic and went directly to the dwelling of Isidorus. Soldiers had reached the house ahead of me and were swarming in the street outside. There could have been no better demonstration of the swiftness and efficacy of the Pharos signaling system.

I walked away as quickly as I could without drawing attention to myself. In my mind I enumerated the few possessions I had kept in my room. I would have to do without them.

I slept that night in the open, not a terrible hardship in such a warm, dry climate. The next day, I tried to think through my position. As long as Antipater made no mention of me to the authorities, no one had any reason to connect me to the deaths at the Pharos. Isidorus's slave might have overheard my name, but the woman knew nothing else about me. No one else in Alexandria even knew of my existence, except the professional receiver of letters and the banker who was holding the funds from my father in trust for me. As I saw it, I had no cause to fear the authorities.

Later that day, I decided to pay a visit to the banker—or more precisely, to one of the clerks who met with clients on his behalf. I half-feared that some of King Ptolemy's soldiers would appear from nowhere and seize me, but the man was happy to give me the minuscule disbursement I requested.

"Also, a message was left for you this morning," he said, producing a small scroll of papyrus tied with a ribbon.

I went to a public garden nearby and found a patch of grass next to a palm tree. A mule was tied to the trunk—his young owner was nearby, talking to some other boys—so I chose a spot on the opposite side of the tree, sat with my back against it, and opened the letter.

There was no salutation and no signature—nothing to compromise either of us, should the letter fall into the wrong hands.

I hope you will remember all that was good in our travels. Forget all that was bad. If that means forgetting me, so be it.

I will not ask you to forgive me, for that would imply remorse, and I do not regret the choices I made. I promised to show you the Seven Wonders; I did. I promised your father that

I would see you safely to our final destination; I did. You will say I hid things from you, but every man has secrets, even you.

I am leaving Egypt. You will not see me again, at least not here.

You should stay in Alexandria, if you wish. I had intended to leave a few drachmas for you with the banker, adding them to the funds from your father; but the record of such a deposit might someday be misconstrued as a payment—evidence of an affiliation between you and me that does not exist. I would not want that to happen; nor would you, I think. Eventually you may need to find work, but for a young man as clever as you, that should be no problem.

I am an old man. I may have a few years left, or a few days. But I can die happy now. My lifelong desire was to see the Wonders—that was no deception!—and that wish has been fulfilled, thanks in no small part to you. I could not have asked for a better traveling companion. We may have begun as teacher and pupil, but on this journey I learned as much from you as you ever learned from me. I am proud of you, and I thank you.

Our ways must part now, but if the gods allow, we will meet again.

Burn this letter after you read it, or toss it into the sea.

How could I bear to destroy the letter? For better or worse, it was my last link to Antipater. In a daze, I laid it on the grass beside me. I closed my eyes and tilted my head back, letting the dappled sunlight warm my face. A moment later, I heard a chomping sound, and turned my head just in time to see the last bit of papyrus vanish into the mule's mouth.

X

Epilogue in Alexandria:

THE EIGHTH WONDER

For many days, the fiery deaths at the Pharos were the talk of Alexandria. Various stories were put forth to account for the terrible events, but the one that came to hold sway was this: one of the workers, in a fit of insanity, attacked the master of the lighthouse and cast him into the flames, and this same worker then attacked a visitor whom Anubion had been escorting on a tour, an unfortunate scholar from the Library who had expressed an interest in the history of the Pharos. The killings were put down to the act of a madman; politics and intrigue played no part. A certain Zoticus of Zeugma was occasionally mentioned, but only as a witness. No one seemed to know anything about him—which was hardly surprising, I thought, since no such person existed.

At the age of seventeen, the world had declared me to be a man, old enough to wear a toga. But it was in Alexandria that I truly left my boyhood behind. The transformation happened not in an instant, but over a period of time. It began the moment I realized that Antipater had deceived me.

Before, despite all my travels and riddle solving and amorous adventures, I was still a boy, trusting the world around me—or more precisely, trusting that the world, enormous though it might be, was nonetheless a comprehensible place, susceptible to reason, as were the people in it. People, especially strangers, could be mysterious, but that was not a bad thing; it was a cause for excitement, for mysteries existed to be solved, and solving them gave pleasure. Every mystery had a solution; and by their very proximity, the people closest to us were the least mysterious. Or so I had believed.

"The world is not as simple as you think," Antipater had said to me. It would never be simple again.

My first days and months alone in Alexandria were often languorous, but never boring. I had just enough money to get by, which is all a young man needs. Also, as Antipater had predicted, I began to find work, following in my father's footsteps. The Finder, he called himself—though as often as not, I found myself playing ferret or weasel, digging through other people's garbage. To a young Roman in a vibrant, foreign city, the mysteries I was hired to solve all seemed exotic and alluring—the more sordid and bizarre, the better.

I continued to struggle to come to terms with Antipater's deceit. Thanks to our travels together, I had seen with my own eyes the glories of Greek civilization. Antipater loved that world and desperately wanted to preserve it, at any price. He was a poet who decided to become a man of action, dedicating his final years to the cause of saving the Greek-speaking world from the domination of Rome, which could only be accomplished by Mithridates. Toward that end, Antipater had been willing to sacrifice everything else—including my trust in him. My feelings about this changed from day to day, sometimes from hour to hour.

One evening, as the stars began to come out, I was sitting on the steps of the Temple of Serapis, gazing over the city toward the distant Pharos, when a doubt suddenly occurred to me. It must have been worming its way through my consciousness for months, planted there by Nikanor. He had been certain that Antipater was a traitor to their cause—and had said as much to Anubion before he killed him, railing against "the old Sidonian." Of course, Nikanor had been mad. But madmen are not always mistaken.

What if Nikanor had been right about Antipater?

Was it possible that Antipater was a double agent? Could it be that he only pretended to side with Mithridates, while in fact he was loyal to Rome? If such was the case, might it be that my father knew of the deception and actively took part in it? Indeed, could it be that my father was the author of the scheme? What did I really know about my father's activities and affiliations?

If my father was in fact working for the Roman Senate, and Antipater was a double agent, then the two of them had doubly deceived me—all for my own good, of course. I found this convoluted notion at once disquieting and strangely comforting.

Stop, Gordianus! You're beginning to sound as mad as Nikanor, I told myself. But the worm of doubt would not be put to rest.

How was I ever to know the truth? I prayed that the gods would keep my father safe from all harm, and that I would see him again in Rome. I prayed for them to protect Antipater as well, so that I might speak to him at least once more. But the world is a dangerous place, and prayers are not always answered. What if I was never to know the truth?

Sitting on the temple steps, I stared at the unwavering light of the Pharos—a point of certainty in an uncertain world. I wished for an end to all my doubts, knowing it was not to be. This was manhood, from which there could be no turning back: to know that some mysteries might never be solved, some questions never answered. But a man must persevere nonetheless.

"Why seven?" I had asked Antipater. At the time, it had not occurred to me to ask, "Why make a list at all?"

Now I knew. A list delineates that which is from that which is not. A list can be memorized and mastered. A list gives order to a chaotic universe.

With such thoughts in my head, I took to spending much of my free time on the steps of the Library, listening to teachers and philosophers who freely shared their wisdom with anyone who cared to listen or dared to argue. All schools of thought were represented. I listened to Stoics, Skeptics, Cynics, Epicureans, and Neo-Platonists, along with stargazing Babylonian astrologers and tale-spinning Jewish sages.

At night, I sought pleasures of the flesh. In Alexandria, these were not hard to come by.

It occurred to me that the true wonders a man encounters in the journey of his life are not the mute monuments of stone, but his fellow mortals. Some lead us to wisdom. Some delight us with pleasure. Some make us laugh. Some fill us with terror, or pity, or loathing. You need not travel the world to find these wonders. They are everywhere around you, every day.

But a man who has traveled to the Seven Wonders of the World need never lack for attention. Men and women alike loved to hear the stories I could tell. In the taverns of Rhakotis, my cup was always full. On warm, starlit nights, my bed was seldom empty.

Such was the life into which I settled in Alexandria: hardworking, intellectually stimulating, and dissolute all at once. By the Roman calendar the month of Martius arrived, and with it the birthday of Antipater. Was he blind drunk, suffering his annual "birthday fever," wherever he might be? This was followed by the second anniversary of his false death. Then came my birthday. I was twenty.

I began to feel—dare I say it?—slightly jaded. Perhaps I had traveled too far, seen too much. Pleasures that had amused me began to bore me. Food lost its flavor, inebriation was tedious, and even ecstasies of the flesh seemed repetitious. The philosophers and sages all began to sound alike. Alexandria itself—the most cosmopolitan of cities, center of culture, beacon to mankind—began to seem mundane and ordinary, just another place.

And then . . .

I was near the waterfront one day, passing a market where slaves were sold. It was not one of the better such markets in the city; the goods were usually damaged or in some way second-rate. Some of the slaves were offered so cheaply that even I might have afforded one—had I needed a servant and wished to pay for the upkeep. A cat would have suited me better than a slave, but either would need to be fed.

The item on offer was a toothless old vagrant who had agreed to give up his freedom if anyone would care to purchase him. The crowd hooted and made catcalls. There were no takers. The auctioneer voided the offer, and the disconsolate would-be slave shambled off. The next offering was brought onto the block.

"Not this one again!" cried someone.

"She's back," said another. "Didn't someone buy her just a few days ago?"

"Bought her, took her home—and returned her the next day!" came the answer. "She's a troublemaker, that one. Buyer beware—unless you don't mind having a finger bit off!"

"Looks harmless enough. Not that big—"

"It's the small, wiry ones you have to look out for."

"Nice figure. Could be quite pretty, if someone were to bathe and take a brush to her."

"Pretty counts for nothing, if she's too wild to be tamed."

The auctioneer called for silence. He looked unhappy, like a man with a toothache. "I have for sale one female slave, exact age unknown, though you can see for yourself that she's quite young. I won't pretend that she's fresh—many of you have seen her before. A few of you have even owned her already—and brought her back to be sold again. Her current owner is aware of the problematic nature of this item, and so he is willing to start the bidding at a very low amount." He named a ridiculously low sum, the cost of a few days' worth of bread.

For the first time, I took a good look at the girl on the block. She had kept her head lowered until that moment. Now she looked up, pushed the masses of black hair from her face, and stared defiantly at the crowd. She stood with one foot in front of the other and held her shoulders back. Her posture and demeanor were not that of a slave. Her dark, glimmering eyes met mine.

My heart quickened. Something stirred in me that I had never felt before.

I looked into the little money bag I carried. As low as was the figure the auctioneer had named, I did not have enough.

The auctioneer called out the figure again. The crowd shuffled rest-lessly. No one bid.

"Very well," sighed the auctioneer. "I am authorized to lower the starting bid." He named a figure that was half of what he had named before.

It was exactly the amount I had in my purse. I studied the coins to be sure, then swallowed hard and looked at the girl again. She stared back at me. On her face I seemed to read amusement and disdain. But that was only on the surface, the face she showed to everyone. There was something else in her eyes, something only I could see—an expression at once proud and pleading, demure and demanding.

Never having bid on a slave before, I slowly raised my hand.

"We have a buyer!" cried the auctioneer, looking relieved and slightly astonished. Others in the crowd raised their eyebrows and shook their heads. Some laughed out loud.

Eager to finalize the transaction at once, the auctioneer summoned me onto the block and reached for my purse. As he counted the coins, I asked him what the girl was called.

"A name as peculiar and barbaric as she is. Hebrew, I think: Bethesda."

Looking at her, I spoke the curious word for the first time. "Bethesda," I whispered. "Now I know the name of the Eighth Wonder of the World."

The auctioneer looked at me as if I were crazy. So did Bethesda.

So began the next chapter of my life.

CHRONOLOGY

ca. 2550 BC	**The Great Pyramid** is built in Egypt.
776	The first games are held at Olympia.
ca. 750	**The Temple of Artemis** is constructed at Ephesus; it will subsequently be destroyed more than once (by flood and by fire) and rebuilt.
ca. 600	**The Walls and Hanging Gardens** are built at Babylon by Nebuchadnezzar.
482	Xerxes demolishes the Walls and Hanging Gardens of Babylon.
456	The Temple of Zeus is open for the 90th Olympiad.
ca. 432	Phidias installs the **Statue of Zeus** in the temple at Olympia.
ca. 425	The historian Herodotus dies.
356	13–14 October: Herostratos burns down the Temple of Artemis at Ephesus; Alexander the Great is born the same night. The temple is subsequently rebuilt.
ca. 350	**The Mausoleum** is built at Halicarnassus.
331	The city of Alexandria is founded in Egypt by Alexander the Great.

323 Alexander the Great dies at Babylon.

298 The Celtic warlord Cimbaules makes incursions against the Macedonians and is repelled.

ca. 290 **The Colossus** is completed at Rhodes.

ca. 280 **The Pharos Lighthouse** is built at Alexandria.

281-79 The Celts make a second incursion against Macedonia; Brennus attacks Delphi.

227 The Colossus falls.

ca. 170 Antipater of Sidon is born.

146 The Roman general Mummius sacks Corinth, but spares Olympia; Carthage is destroyed by Rome.

ca. 135 Posidonius is born in Syria.

133 Attalus III of Pergamon bequeaths his kingdom to Rome, which establishes the province of Asia.

ca. 115 Posidonius studies under Panaetius the Stoic in Athens.

110 23 March (Martius): Gordianus is born at Rome.

ca. 106 Bethesda is born at Alexandria.

ca. 90 After travels in Spain, Gaul, Italy, Sicily, Dalmatia, North Africa, and Greece, Posidonius settles in Rhodes.

95 Rome sides with Nicomedes of Bithynia in his war against Mithridates of Pontus.

93 23 March (Martius): Gordianus turns seventeen and puts on his manly toga.

92 Rome aids Nicomedes of Bithynia against Mithridates for the second time.

23 March (Martius): The novel begins in Rome on this day—the birthday of Gordianus and the funeral day of Antipater.

April (Aprilis): Gordianus and Antipater visit Ephesus during the Artemisia festival and see the Temple of Artemis (**"Something to Do with Diana"**).

April (Aprilis) to August (Sextilis): Gordianus and Antipater visit Halicarnassus and see the Mausoleum (**"The Widows of Halicarnassus"**).

Late August (Sextilis) to early September: Gordianus and Antipater attend the 172nd Olympiad and see the Statue of Zeus (**"O Tempora! O Mores! Olympiad!"**).

September: Gordianus and Antipater visit the ruins of Corinth (**"The Witch's Curse"**).

Autumn to winter: Gordianus and Antipater stay with Posidonius in Rhodes and see the remains of the Colossus (**"The Monumental Gaul"**).

91 23 March (Martius): Gordianus is nineteen.

Mithridates invades Bithynia, expels Nicomedes, and sets up Nicomedes' brother Socrates as king; Ariobarzanes, the king of Cappadocia confirmed by the Romans, is usurped and replaced by the son of Mithridates, Ariaranthes Eusebes.

Outbreak of the Social War, as the Italians revolt against Rome.

Spring: Gordianus and Antipater visit Babylon and see the remains of the Walls and the Hanging Gardens (**"Styx and Stones"**).

June: Gordianus and Antipater journey up the Nile to Memphis and visit the Great Pyramid (**"The Return of the Mummy"**).

Gordianus and Antipater travel to Alexandria and visit the Pharos Lighthouse (**"They Do It with Mirrors"**).

90 23 March (Martius): Gordianus is twenty. He solves the case of "The Alexandrian Cat" (included in the collection *The House of the Vestals*).

89 War begins between Rome and Mithridates.

88 Conclusion of the Social War; Rome is triumphant over the rebellious Italians.

80 The dictator Sulla moves the 175th Olympiad to Rome. (The Games are afterward returned to Olympia.) Gordianus is in Rome, and is hired by Cicero, as recounted in the novel *Roman Blood*.

AUTHOR'S NOTE:

IN SEARCH OF THE SEVEN WONDERS

(This note reveals elements of the plot.)

Over the course of ten previously published novels and two collections of short stories, Gordianus the Finder has occasionally made reference to his younger days, and specifically to his journey as a young man to see the Seven Wonders of the World.

For a long time, I have wanted to write the story of that journey. At last the occasion seemed auspicious, and the result is the book you hold in your hands.

Little did I know at the outset that the author's voyage of discovery would be every bit as long and arduous and full of wonders as that of Gordianus. To explore the Seven Wonders, one enters a labyrinth of history and legend, hard facts and half-facts, cutting-edge archaeology and the very latest innovations in virtual reality.

The fascination exerted by the Seven Wonders has long outlasted their physical existence. Only one, the Great Pyramid, remains intact. The others are in fragments or have vanished altogether. To understand the scale and magnificence of these monuments, and the reasons they made such a lasting impact on the world's imagination, we must turn to ancient literary sources—which are sometimes more confusing than enlightening. Images of the Wonders abound, but are often unreliable; over the centuries, methodologies used to visualize the Wonders have ranged from the rigorously scientific to the patently absurd.

I soon discovered that there was no single source I could turn to for answers to all my questions; an authoritative book encompassing all we know about the Seven Wonders has yet to be written. But one book came close, and I didn't even have to search for it; it came to me, arriving by international post at my house one day, a gift from the British editor, anthologist, and author Mike Ashley.

Like Gordianus, Mike visited the Wonders in his own younger days by writing a marvelous book about them, *The Seven Wonders of the World,* published as a paperback original by Fontana in Great Britain in 1980. Learning that I intended to take Gordianus to the Wonders, Mike mailed me one of his archival copies—which proved to be a godsend. Meticulously researched and splendidly written, Mike's book is far and away the best single volume I encountered about the Wonders. Long out of print (and a bit out of date due to subsequent archaeological research), it is a book that cries out for a new edition.

Among my debts to Mike Ashley is the intriguing notion that Alexander the Great may have had a hand in conceiving the list of the Seven Wonders. In the novel, this theory is put forward by Gordianus's traveling companion, Antipater of Sidon, a real historical figure who did in fact write a poem listing the Seven Wonders—probably the very earliest such list that still exists.

The various poems recited by Antipater in this novel are either of my own invention or are freely adapted from the English translations by W. R. Paton in the Loeb Classical Library five-volume edition of *The Greek Anthology,* now in public domain. For insight into the more subtle points of Antipater's work I turned to *Poetic Garlands: Hellenistic Epigrams in Context* by Kathryn J. Gutzwiller (UC Press, 1998); *Dioscorides and Antipater of Sidon: The Poems* edited by Jerry Clack (Bolchazy-Carducci, 2001); and two monumental works by A. S. F. Gow and D. L.

Page, *The Greek Anthology: Hellenistic Epigrams* and *The Greek Anthology: The Garland of Philip* (Cambridge University Press, 1965 and 1968).

The rebus epitaph on Antipater's tombstone also appears in *The Greek Anthology*, attributed to Meleager. The factuality of the poem—and whether it actually appeared on a stone—are matters for conjecture. From Pliny, Valerius Maximus, and a fragment of Cicero we hear about the annual "birthday fever" that supposedly caused or contributed to Antipater's death.

How and when and from whom did the list of Seven Wonders originate? What do we actually know about each Wonder, and how do we know it? What became of the Wonders?

Mike Ashley's book addresses these basic questions; I cannot repeat all that information here. But I can lay down some pointers for the reader curious to know more about the Wonders. Herewith, some notes on sources, following the order of each Wonder's appearance in this book.

About the city of Ephesus and the worship of Artemis, the most useful volume I encountered was Rick Strelan's *Paul, Artemis, and the Jews of Ephesus* (Berlin: De Gruyter, 1996; also published as *Journal of Theological Studies* 49, no. 1, 1998), which contains a long chapter vividly describing the city's devotion to the goddess. Among the ancient sources, Pliny and Vitruvius provide details about the temple, while Strabo and Tacitus tell us about the grove of Ortygia. Very little remains of the Temple of Artemis; a few fragments can be seen at the British Museum in London.

What are we to make of the appendages that hang from archaic statues of Artemis—are they breasts or bovine testicles? See a clear digression on this point in "At Home in the City of Artemis: Religion in Ephesos in the Literary Imagination of the Roman Period" by C. M. Thomas in *Ephesos: Metropolis of Asia,* edited by Helmut Koester (Trinity Press International, 1995). Where was the grove of Ortygia located? I defer to the opinions of Dieter Knibbe and Hilke Thür in their respective papers, also included in Koester's book.

Ephesus appears as a setting in several ancient Greek novels. *Leucippe and Clitophon* by Achilles Tatius describes the procession of Artemis and recounts the story of the virginity test and the Pan pipes in the sacred cave. The novel *Apollonius, King of Tyre*, by an unknown author, was the inspiration for Shakespeare's play *Pericles, Prince of Tyre*, which comes to a giddy climax at the Temple of Artemis and gives us these memorable lines:

Marina
If fires be hot, knives sharp, or waters deep,
Untied I still my virgin knot will keep.
Diana, aid my purpose!

Bawd
What have we to do with Diana?

Gordianus's visit to Ephesus had nothing to do with Dionysus, but everything to do with Diana.

A detailed reconstruction of the Mausoleum can be found in the multivolume *The Maussolleion at Halikarnassos: Reports of the Danish Archaeological Expedition to Bodrum* by Kristian Jeppesen. Volume 5 of the report, published in 2002, analyzes all the architectural, sculptural, and literary evidence (Pliny is our primary source), and includes photographs of a scale model. Fragments of the sculptural remains, including the famous statues thought to represent Mausolus and Artemisia, can be seen at the British Museum.

The grief of the widow Artemisia is described by many ancient authors, perhaps most vividly by Aulus Gellius. Ovid tells the story of Hermaphroditus and his transformation at the spring of Salmacis. Strabo and Vitruvius also mention the spring and its reputed powers. The sexual activity of the widow Bitto is the subject of one of Antipater's poems, but it was my conceit to make her a relative of the poet.

Many books have been published about the ancient Games at Olympia. One of the most accessible is Tony Perrottet's *The Naked Olympics*

(Random House, 2004), which lays out the known facts with all the panache of a modern sportswriter. The *Chronicle* of the ancient author Eusebius lists the Games by date and names some of the winners, including Protophanes of Magnesia, about whom nothing else is known. The viper called a dipsas is mentioned in several ancient sources, including one of Antipater's poems.

Ancient authors were astonished by the magnificence of the statue of Zeus by Phidias. The Roman author Quintilian declared that its "beauty is such that it is said to have added something even to the awe with which the god was already regarded: so perfectly did the majesty of the work give the impression of godhead." Nothing of the statue remains today.

The interlude in Corinth was inspired by Antipater's poems, recited in the novel, and also by a lecture I attended at the University of California at Berkeley in 2011, "Magic and Religion in Ancient Corinth," delivered by Ronald Stroud, Klio Distinguished Professor of Classical Languages and Literature Emeritus. Professor Stroud's vivid account of curses and witchcraft was the genesis of Gordianus's uncanny experiences amid the ruins of a once-great city. For archaeological details I consulted *Ancient Corinth: a Guide to the Excavations* (American School of Classical Studies at Athens, 1960). Was the destruction and depopulation of Corinth as complete as many ancient authors suggest? Elizabeth R. Gerhard and Matthew W. Dickie address this question in their paper "The View From the Isthmus" in *Corinth, the Centenary, 1896–1996*, edited by Charles K. Williams II and Nancy Bookidis (American School of Classical Studies at Athens, 2003).

Sculptor and author Herbert Maryon recounted the history of the Colossus and considered the artistic and engineering challenges of its construction in a long article, "The Colossus of Rhodes," published in 1956 in *The Journal of Hellenic Studies 76*. More recently, Wolfram Hoepfner published his ideas about the monument, with illustrations of a reconstruction, in *Der Koloß von Rhodos und die Bauten des Helios* (Verlag Philipp von Zabern, 2003). Nothing of the Colossus remains, and the exact location it occupied is uncertain. Despite their profound impression on popular imagination, old-fashioned images that show the statue straddling the harbor at Rhodes are works of fantasy, depicting a physical impossibility.

At the time of Gordianus's visit, as recounted in the novel, the polymath Posidonius had recently settled at Rhodes after extensive travels. His writings about the Gauls survive only in fragments; a summary can be found in Philip Freeman's *The Philosopher and the Druids: A Journey Among the Ancient Celts* (Simon & Schuster, 2006). Diodorus Siculus is probably quoting Posidonius when he describes the homosexual behavior of the Gauls: "Although their wives are comely, the men have very little to do with them, but rage with lust for each other. It is their practice to sleep on the ground on the skins of wild beasts and to tumble with a boy on each side. And the most astonishing thing of all is that they feel no concern for their proper dignity, but prostitute themselves without a qualm; nor do they consider this behavior disgraceful, but rather, if they should offer themselves and be rebuffed, they consider such a refusal an act of dishonor."

By the time of Gordianus's visit to Babylon, there was not a great deal left to be seen of either of the two Wonders located there. Numerous reconstructions of the Hanging Gardens have been proposed over the years, drawing on descriptions by Strabo and Diodorus Siculus. Herodotus describes the ziggurat Etemenanki and recounts the Babylonian tradition of temple prostitution. As for the Walls of Babylon, one can gain some idea of their magnificence from the reconstruction of the Ishtar Gate and the Processional Way on view at the Pergamon Museum in Berlin, which was built from material excavated by Robert Koldewey. Parts of the excavation, including images of lions and dragons, can be seen in several other museums around the world. At the site of Babylon itself, archaeological research has been made problematic in recent decades by Saddam Hussein's building projects, by looting during the chaos of the U.S. invasion in 2003, and by subsequent occupation of the site by the U.S. military.

The Great Pyramid at Giza, our only surviving Wonder, has been endlessly explored by books, magazine articles, television programs,

etc. It was equally famous—and mysterious—in the time of Gordianus. Herodotus, Strabo, Diodorus Siculus, Pliny, and Ammianus Mar-
cellinus all wrote about the pyramids.

Herodotus tells us about the use of mummies as security for loans;
Diodorus Siculus repeats this information, and both authors provide
fascinating details about the different forms of mummification.

Neither Herodotus nor the later writers Strabo and Diodorus Siculus (both contemporaries of Gordianus) makes any mention of the
Great Sphinx of Giza, which *is* described by Pliny the Elder, writing a
couple of generations after Gordianus. Pliny notes that Egyptian
sources, too, are silent about the Sphinx. This leads to the hypothesis
that the giant monument was buried by sand for a long period, and
not rediscovered until the time of the last Ptolemaic rulers or even
later. (See the Loeb edition of Pliny, 36.17, and the translator's note by
D. E. Eichholz.)

As readers of the novel will gather, the Pharos Lighthouse was not
among the original Seven Wonders; it was added only later, long after
the list was first devised, usually replacing one of the faded Babylonian
Wonders. (Many other variations occur in the canonical list over the
centuries; the permutations are too numerous and complicated to recount here.) Even after seeing the original Seven Wonders, Gordianus
marvels at the Pharos, the world's first (and for many centuries, only)
skyscraper.

A miracle of engineering, the Pharos survived until the fourteenth
century, when earthquakes sent it tumbling into the harbor of Alexandria. Hermann Thiersch assembled all the literary sources, coin images, and other data about the lighthouse in *Pharos, Antike, Islam und
Occident* (Teubner, 1909); if you can find an original edition of this
classic, feast your eyes on the two enormous foldout illustrations of the
Pharos as rendered by Thiersch. Equally essential to an understanding
of the Pharos's history and appearance is a close reading of the details in
P. M. Fraser's three-volume *Ptolemaic Alexandria* (Clarendon Press,
1972); see vol. I, pp. 17–21, and vol. II, pp. 45–46. Judith McKenzie's
The Architecture of Alexandria and Egypt, c. 300 B.C.–A.D. 700 (Yale

University Press, 2007) also provides useful information about the lighthouse, including the idea that naphtha may have been used as a fuel; see pages 41–48.

Our ideas about the Pharos continue to evolve. In recent decades, underwater archaeology in the harbor of Alexandria by Jacques-Yves Empereur and others has yielded new knowledge and recovered artifacts related to the lighthouse. New techniques of virtual reality and digital reconstruction have also been brought to bear on the mystery of its design and dimensions. During the writing of this novel I was privileged to have access to the work of Anthony Caldwell, research scholar at the Experiential Technologies Center, UCLA. A draft copy of Caldwell's *Reconstruction of the Pharos Lighthouse of Alexandria,* including detailed diagrams of the lighthouse (based on his synthesis of literary, archaeological, and engineering knowledge), fired my imagination.

Everyone could see the Pharos—from a distance of 300 stadia, or over thirty miles, according to Josephus. But could the Pharos gaze back, watching those who watched it? This is from John Webster Spargo's *Virgil the Necromancer* (Harvard University Press, 1934): "The lighthouse at Alexandria threw its beams far and mystified mankind. Its use as a mere lighthouse was eclipsed in the popular mind [in the Middle Ages] and it was regarded as an instrument which could 'see' as far as it threw its beams—a misconception . . . perhaps associated with the knowledge that it had a reflector, a mirror." From the Pharos of Alexandria we may trace a direct line to the many magical mirrors and "all-seeing" towers of fiction in the Middle Ages and Renaissance, all the way to the far-seeing *palantíri,* the Eye of Sauron, and the two towers of Orthanc and Barad-dûr in Tolkien's *The Lord of the Rings.*

A few books that cover all seven Wonders should be mentioned. *Die Sieben Weltwunder der Antike: Wege der Wiedergewinnung aus sechs Jahrhunderten* (Verlag Philipp von Zabern, 2003) by Max Kunze, a catalogue of an exhibition held at the Winckelmann-Museums in Stendal, Germany, contains many useful images. Also lavishly illustrated is *Die Sieben Weltwunder: 5000 Jahre Kultur und Geschichte der Antike* by

Artur Müller and Rolf Ammon (Scherz Verlag, 1966). Kai Brodersen's *Dic Sieben Weltwunder* (Beck, 1996), which includes a comprehensive survey of sources, has gone through numerous editions in Germany, but has not been translated into English. A basic introduction to the Wonders can be found in *The Seven Wonders of the Ancient World*, edited by Peter Clayton and Martin Price (Routledge, 1988); the scholarship of the contributors is sound, but the division of the subject into essays by different authors gives the book a less coherent focus than the previously mentioned *The Seven Wonders of the World* by Mike Ashley.

Looming in the background of the novel are two world-changing events: The so-called Social War in Italy, and the incipient war for hegemony in Asia Minor between Rome and Mithridates. The literature on these events is vast, but I should mention *Intelligence Activities in Ancient Rome: Trust in the Gods, but Verify* by Rose Mary Shelton (Frank Cass, 2005); the chapter entitled "Diplomat, Trader, Messenger, Client, Spy: Rome's Eyes and Ears in the East" was especially pertinent to my purposes. A lecture at UC Berkeley by Adrienne Mayor, author of *The Poison King: The Life and Legend of Mithradates, Rome's Deadliest Enemy* (Princeton, 2010), was particularly rewarding; it is to Mayor that I owe the line, "Rome is the disease, Mithridates is the cure."

Various episodes in this novel were published first as short stories. (Details may be found on the indicia page.) I am grateful to the anthology and magazine editors who first read and commented on those stories: Mike Ashley, Gardner Dozois, George R. R. Martin, Gordon Van Gelder, and Janet Hutchings. I was especially gratified to see Gordianus in the pages of *The Magazine of Fantasy and Science Fiction*, because my first professional sale was to that magazine, many years ago; and I was glad to see Gordianus back in the pages of *Ellery Queen Mystery Magazine*, where the very first Gordianus short story appeared.

I also want to thank my longtime editor at St. Martin's Press, Keith Kahla, my longtime agent, Alan Nevins of Renaissance, and my longtime partner, Rick Solomon, all of whom helped Gordianus and his creator explore the Seven Wonders of the World.

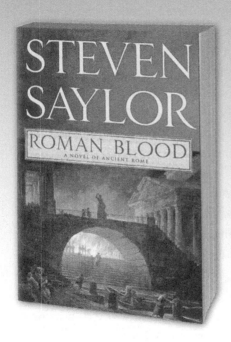
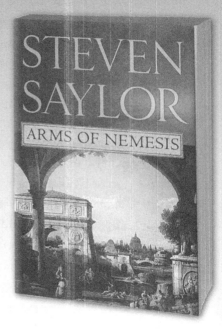

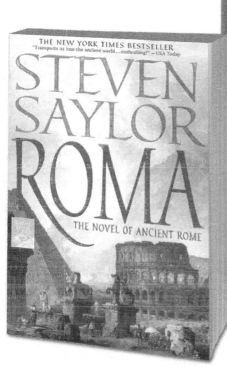
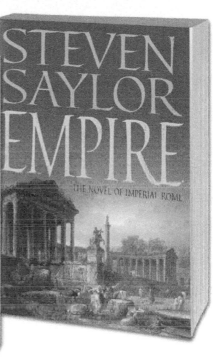

Made in the USA
Coppell, TX
20 April 2021

54186178R00194